STORMY SEAS

What Reviewers Say About Ali Vali's Work

Answering the Call

"[*Answering the Call*] is a brilliant cop-and-killer story. ...The crime story is tight and the love story is fantastic."—*Best Lesbian Erotica*

Beauty and the Boss

"This was a story of love and passion but also of surprises and secrets. I loved it!"—*Kitty Kat's Book Review Blog*

"The story gripped me from the first page, both the relationship between the two main characters, as well as the drama of the issues that threaten to bring down the business. ...Vali's writing style is lovely—it's clean, sharp, no wasted words, and it flows beautifully as a result. Highly recommended!"—*Rainbow Book Reviews*

The Devil's Due

"This is an enthralling, nail biting and ultra fast moving addition to the Devil series. ...*The Devil's Due* is so fast paced you seriously have to concentrate, but once again Ali Vali has produced a brilliant story arc, solid character development, incomparable bad-ass women in traditionally male roles, leading both the goodies, baddies and cross-breeds. This episode closes off some of the loose ends, but sets us up for even more drama in the stories to come. This is a stand-alone, but I would seriously recommend starting this series at the beginning. The overarching story arc is so good, the interrelationships so complex, that while it might make a good read, you will simply be missing too much back history and nuance of personal interplay to get the most from it."
—*Lesbian Reading Room*

"A Night Owl Reviews Top Pick: Cain Casey is the kind of person you aspire to be even though some consider her a criminal. She's loyal, very protective of those she loves, honorable, big on preserving her family legacy and loves her family greatly. *The Devil's Due* is a book I highly recommend and well worth the wait we all suffered through. I cannot wait for the next book in the series to come out."—*Night Owl Reviews*

Beneath the Waves

"The premise of an ancient but much advanced Atlantean race under the sea was brilliantly constructed, with an all female world and an ability to procreate without men. It was skillfully written and the imagination that went into it was fantastic. …The author managed to insert a real fear and menace into the story and had me totally engrossed. The love story between Vivien and Kai was slow burning but beautifully pitched. …I loved this book and it gave so much more than I expected. A wonderful passionate love story with a great mystery."—*Inked Rainbow Reads*

The Romance Vote

"Won by a Landslide!…[A] sweet and mushy romance with some humor and spicy, sexy scenes!"—*Love Bytes*

Balance of Forces: Toujours Ici

"A stunning addition to the vampire legend, *Balance of Forces: Toujours Ici*, is one that stands apart from the rest."—*Bibliophilic Book Blog*

The Devil Be Damned

"Ali Vali excels at creating strong, romantic characters along with her fast paced, sophisticated plots. Her setting, New Orleans, provides just the right blend of immigrants from Mexico, South America and Cuba, along with a city steeped in traditions."—*Just About Write*

Blue Skies

"Author Ali Vali has written a story that is extremely relevant in today's world. *Blue Skies* has plots within plots as the 'old guard' tries to undermine the mission and show that women can't lead. Levine and Sullivan are strong characters who take on the misogynists in government. Vali is skilled at building sexual tension and the sex in this novel flies as high as Berkley's jets. Look for this fast-paced read."—*Just About Write*

Calling the Dead—Lammy Finalist

"So many writers set stories in New Orleans, but Ali Vali's mystery novels have the authenticity that only a real Big Easy resident could bring. Set six months after Hurricane Katrina has devastated the city, a lesbian detective is still battling demons when a body turns up behind one of the city's famous eateries. What follows makes for a classic lesbian murder yarn."—*Curve Magazine*

"The plot is engrossing and satisfying. A fun aspect of the book is the images of food it includes. The descriptions of sex are also delicious."
—*Seattle Gay News*

"In *Calling the Dead*, Vali has given us characters that are engaging and a story that keeps us turning page after page."—*Just About Write*

Deal With the Devil

"Ali Vali has given her fans another thick, rich thriller...*Deal With the Devil* has wonderful love stories, great sex, and an ample supply of humor. It is an exciting, page turning read that leaves her readers eagerly awaiting the next book in the series."—*Just About Write*

Second Season

"Whether Ali Vali is writing about crime figures or lawyers, her characters are well drawn and extremely likeable. Indeed, writing so the reader really cares about the main characters is a trademark of a Vali novel. *Second Season* is no exception to the rule. ...This is a rich, enjoyable read that's not to be missed."—*Just About Write*

"The issues are realistic and center around the universal factors of love, jealousy, betrayal, and doing the right thing and are constantly woven into the fabric of the story. We rated this well written social commentary through the use of fiction our max five hearts."—*Heartland Reviews*

The Devil Unleashed

"Fast-paced action scenes, intriguing character revelations, and a refreshing approach to the romance thriller genre all make for an enjoyable reading experience in the Big Easy. ...The Devil Unleashed is an engrossing reading experience."—*Midwest Book Review*

Carly's Sound

"Vali paints vivid pictures with her words. ...*Carly's Sound* is a great romance, with some wonderfully hot sex."—*Midwest Book Review*

"It's no surprise that passion is indeed possible a second time around."
—*Q Syndicate*

"*Carly's Sound* is a great romance, with some wonderfully hot sex, but it is more than that. It is also the tale of a woman rising from the ashes of grief and finding new love and a new life. Vali has surrounded Julia and Poppy with a cast of great supporting characters, making this an extremely satisfying read."—*Just About Write*

The Devil Inside

"Not only is *The Devil Inside* a ripping mystery, it's also an intimate character study."—*L-Word Literature*

"*The Devil Inside* by Ali Vali is an unusual, unpredictable, and thought-provoking love story that will have the reader questioning the definition of right and wrong long after she finishes the book. ...First time novelist Vali does not leave the reader hanging for too long, but spins a complex plot of love, conspiracy, and loss."—*Just About Write*

"*The Devil Inside* is the first of what promises to be a very exciting series. ...While telling an exciting story that grips the reader, Vali has also fully fleshed out her heroes and villains. *The Devil Inside* is that rarity: a fascinating crime novel which includes a tender love story and leaves the reader with a cliffhanger ending."—*MegaScene*

"...this isn't your typical 'Godfather-esque' novel, oh no. The head of this crime family is not only a lesbian, but a mother to boot. Vali's fluid writing style quickly puts the reader at ease, which makes the story and its characters equally easy to get to know and care about. When you find yourself talking out loud to the characters in a book, you know the work is polished and professional, as well as entertaining. Ever just wanted to grab a crime boss by the lapels, get in their face, and tell them to open their eyes and see what's right in front of their eyes? If not you will once you start turning the pages of *The Devil Inside*."—*Family and Friends Magazine*

Visit us at www.boldstrokesbooks.com

By the Author

Carly's Sound
Second Season
Love Match
The Dragon Tree Legacy
The Romance Vote
Girls With Guns
Beneath the Waves
Beauty and the Boss

Blue Skies
Stormy Seas

Call Series
Calling the Dead
Answering the Call

Forces Series
Balance of Forces: Toujours Ici
Battle of Forces: Sera Toujours
Force of Fire: Toujours a Vous

The Cain Casey Saga
The Devil Inside
The Devil Unleashed
Deal with the Devil
The Devil be Damned
The Devil's Orchard
The Devil's Due
Heart of the Devil

STORMY SEAS

by
Ali Vali

2019

This Trade Paperback Original Is Published By
Bold Strokes Books, Inc.
P.O. Box 249
Valley Falls, NY 12185

First Edition: May 2019

CREDITS
Editor: Shelley Thrasher
Production Design: Susan Ramundo
Cover Design By Sheri (hindsightgraphics@gmail.com)

Acknowledgments

Thank you to Radclyffe for the home you've given me at BSB, and for the awesome family that comes with it. Thank you to Sandy Lowe for all the great advice, and for all you do to keep me on track. My sincere thanks and gratitude to my editor, Shelley Thrasher, for everything you've taught me. All your lessons will always be appreciated. Thank you to my beta readers, Cris Perez-Soria and Kim Rieff. You guys are the best, and your questions and suggestions make every book better. Thank you, Sheri, for the fantastic cover. You hit a bull's-eye with this one.

It's always nice to revisit characters and continue their story. Thank you to all the readers who wrote often about Cletus and Aidan wanting more. That to me is the highest compliment, so as always, every word is written with you in mind.

Thank you to C for all the adventures we've shared, and for all the ones yet to come. *Verdad!*

Dedication

For C

For All Active and Retired Military
Thank You All For Your Service

CHAPTER ONE

W here are you?" Navy Captain Aidan Sullivan asked in a groggy voice. The bedroom in the small French Quarter apartment that overlooked a secluded courtyard had the French doors open, letting in a breeze even though it was July. After eleven in the morning, the air conditioner came on, no matter how romantic the view was.

"I'm making coffee, and you're supposed to still be sleeping," Navy Commander Berkley Levine said from what sounded like the kitchen.

"I'm awake in an empty bed." Aidan rolled over, stared at the ceiling, and combed her blond hair back as she yawned. "You know the rules, Levine."

Berkley appeared in the doorway completely naked, so Aidan focused on her tall, fit body, hoping Berkley wasn't too set on having coffee anytime soon. "Do you plan to get up, or do you need an incentive?" Her straight posture with her hands on her hips looked quintessentially naval aviator—a little cocky and a hell of a lot sexy.

"If you come over here you can incentivize me all you want, baby." She tossed the sheet off and smiled at the thought of how long Berkley would hold out. "You can make up for not being here when I woke up."

"I didn't break any rules—I *was* here when you woke up." Berkley knelt on the bed and fell forward, stopping herself at the last moment before she completely collapsed on her. "And we don't have time for any kind of incentives." Aidan frowned when Berkley kissed her nose and started to get up. "Your parents arrive today, and I don't want to be late picking them up."

She wrapped her legs around Berkley to keep her in place, amazed that Berkley lifted her off the bed and held her while she kissed her on the lips this time. She should be used to the instant arousal by now, but it still stole her reason and had from the beginning.

They'd met in Hawaii nine years prior, and she'd tossed her carefully held caution in all things overboard and gone out with the young, good-looking aviator, only to sleep with her on their first date. That, she still couldn't believe, but Berkley did things to the rational part of her brain, as in turning it off so her primal desires could take over.

"Do you remember our first date?" she asked when Berkley ended their kiss so she could lay her back down.

"I do," Berkley said, lowering her head to suck on her nipple until it puckered steel hard. "That Chinese place you ordered from had fantastic egg rolls."

"You suck," she deadpanned.

"I sure do." Berkley laughed as she made her way down Aidan's body and spread her legs. All she could do was buck up into Berkley's mouth when she sucked her clit in and ran her tongue over it. She'd wanted it to last, but she couldn't possibly curb her need to come.

"Baby, please." She grabbed Berkley's head and tugged her closer. "Put your fingers in," she said before groaning loud enough to feel a reverberation in her chest. Berkley slowed down, which was maddening. "I need you," she said, sounding way out of breath and desperate, but Berkley gave her what she wanted. She slid two fingers in and sucked harder until she came with another loud moan.

"You'd better pray Mr. Comeaux isn't out there watering his lilies," Berkley said as she came up and held her as her heart rate slowed down.

They'd rented the place for a month enjoying the first vacation either of them had taken in years. Granted, they'd met years before, but Aidan had made the worst mistake of her life by choosing the navy over Berkley, leading them to four years apart. Thankfully, Berkley had forgiven her and not only taken her back, but volunteered to join her on the carrier Aidan had been given the helm of.

Their first mission together had almost ended in disaster when Berkley had been shot down over North Korea because of David "Blazer" Morris, a traitorous little shit who was part of her flight team, but she'd miraculously made it out, her backseat, Lieutenant Harvey "Junior" Whittle, in tow with a broken leg. It had been a wake-up call for both of them, so they'd stopped wasting time and admitted what they both wanted in a future together.

"I love you," she said as she threw her leg over Berkley's thighs.

"I love you too, and I was kidding before," Berkley said, holding her tight enough that she moved to lie on her. "Our first date is one of my favorite memories."

"Really?" When Berkley looked at her so adoringly, she felt like she was falling in love all over again.

"Why in the world would you doubt that?" Berkley asked as she wiped her tears, surprising her that she was crying. "You were the most beautiful woman I'd ever laid eyes on, and I didn't figure I had a chance no matter what I tried. You threw me by saying yes."

"You were pretty dashing, stud, so it wasn't a hardship." She leaned down and kissed Berkley until she held her tighter.

"What brought on your question?"

She put her head on Berkley's chest and closed her eyes. "This last year has been completely different from what I thought it'd be, and I'm incredibly lucky you let me back in."

"Now that wasn't a hardship at all, baby." Berkley repeated what she'd said. "Besides, you can't really ever lose what's yours for life."

Hawaii, Nine Years Earlier

"Are you asking me out?" Aidan asked, shielding her eyes from the sun. The sweat from her run was dripping down her back and pooling in the waistband of her shorts. The tall pilot she'd shot down in yesterday's exercise had stopped her, and she almost kept going because of the woman's teasing last night about her height. It was a bad idea, but the fly god was trying extra hard to be charming.

"Are you going to report me if I say yes?"

Aidan definitely remembered the woman's smile from the night before, and she deserved some if not all of that swagger. The woman was truly stunning. "Okay, but it's too late in the day for coffee, so it's either dinner or wait until morning, when I'm ready to drink coffee again."

"Dinner it is."

"Are you going to introduce yourself, or were you raised by wolves?"

"No wolves in my family tree that I know of, and I apologize, but maybe I was trying to wait on the chance you'd turn me in. Berkley Levine." Berkley held her hand out.

"Aidan Sullivan." She took Berkley's hand, not lowering her other one since the sun was still in her eyes. "Do you know where the Beach Grove complex is?"

"No. I don't. I got here yesterday." Berkley moved her around before letting go of her so she'd be standing in her shadow. "Seven sound okay?"

"I get off duty at six, so seven sounds great." The easy smile on Berkley's face made her not only more attractive, but also kind of roguish as she took her hand and wrote her address on her palm with the pen hanging off her ID badge. "I'm in 5B."

"Thank you, ma'am," Berkley said and saluted, which seemed strange until she saw the two officers close by. The salute was sharp, and then Berkley continued her run with a stride that made Aidan think she could keep it up for miles.

"That's trouble all wrapped up in a gorgeous package," she whispered as she kept to the path she was on.

That thought grew exponentially throughout the day until she drove herself nearly insane enough to call Berkley and cancel, only she didn't have her number or any way of contacting her. She was in her underwear, trying not to freak out, when she heard a knock at the door. It was only six thirty, so no way was it Berkley, but she needed to get rid of whoever it was, not wanting company when she ditched her date soon.

"Shit," she whispered when she looked through the peephole, finding an even better-appearing Berkley in a white shirt and jeans. She took a deep breath and pulled her robe tie before opening the door. "Hi. You're way early."

"I wanted to make a good impression, and these are for you." The bouquet of tropical flowers and orchids was beautiful, and that Berkley had thought to bring them made her waver about cutting this short.

"Thank you, and please come in. I got stuck with some last-minute things today and was late getting home." Her one and only vase was in the cabinet over the refrigerator, and Berkley got it down for her when she followed her in there. "Do you mind waiting for me a few minutes?"

"Take your time," Berkley said, watching her deal with the flowers.

"There's wine and beer in the fridge if you want either." She tried to be a good hostess but quickly made it to her bedroom and closed the door before Berkley decided to follow her in there as well.

Since Berkley wasn't in uniform, she put on a pair of shorts and a peasant blouse she'd bought in Mexico, figuring they were going somewhere casual. Berkley was sitting on one of her stools at the kitchen counter when she came back out in her bare feet, but stood and slid her hands into her pockets when she saw her.

"Do you want me to go?" Berkley asked, having lost her smile somewhere between the door and her getting dressed. She just needed to say yes, and the rest of the night would be hers problem free.

"Why do you ask?" Curiosity postponed the smart play.

"You look either nervous or apprehensive," Berkley said softly, "and you're probably not the type to be either. If you are, it's me making you that way, and if I am, I'll go." Anyone who thought to say something like that was someone who deserved her time and attention. "I'm nervous because I've never done this before."

"You've never gone out on a date?" Berkley went from resigned to incredulous in a flash, which made her laugh.

"I'm not that hideous, am I?" She dropped her shoes and sat on the sofa, patting the spot next to her. "I've been on plenty of dates—just not many where I could get court-martialed if anyone found out."

"No one's getting court-martialed." Berkley sat and leaned back, getting comfortable. "It's only dinner, maybe a movie, and maybe… maybe a good-night kiss on the cheek like I'm your sister, if I'm lucky."

"Are you usually lucky?" Berkley Levine was lucky in probably everything she tried, from girls to planes.

"I'm out of practice when it comes to lucky," Berkley said, her smile back. "The military puts you through all kinds of hell before they let you take a really expensive plane out for a spin. I've concentrated on flying for what seems like forever, since Commander Corbin Levine would've been mighty disappointed if I'd failed to make the cut."

"Your father?" Berkley nodded. "I totally understand that."

"I doubt yours is as demanding," Berkley said, making Aidan snort. Her date obviously didn't know who her father was, which was refreshing. "How about some food, we skip the movie and the kiss, and you decide if we do this again?"

"Are you open to negotiation?" She folded her legs under her and smiled, deciding to gamble.

"What are your terms?"

"We order in and watch a movie here." If they stayed in she could enjoy Berkley's undivided attention all night.

"And the good-night kiss?" Berkley leaned toward her but stopped, leaving plenty of room between them to decide the next move without feeling pressured.

"We should get that out of the way." She leaned in as well and knew she'd made the right decision when Berkley kissed her softly at first. Then somehow she ended up straddling Berkley when things got heated. "Are you hungry right this minute?" The question came out of her mouth, and she wondered what the hell was happening to her, but at that moment she had to be naked.

"Famished," Berkley said and carried her into the bedroom.

❖

"You were going to cancel on me?" Berkley picked Aiden up and carried her to the shower. The place they'd rented was small, but it had a surprisingly large bathroom, with a claw-foot tub and a rain shower coming from the ceiling.

"I thought you were a bad idea, and then I saw you." Aidan sat on the counter while Berkley adjusted the water, and the sight of her made Berkley forget about her self-imposed timeline. "You proved my point, but you were so gorgeous I couldn't help myself."

"I'm happy you decided to chance it, and after we make some headway on this crap we've been working on, it's time to retire." She went back for Aidan and kissed her when she wrapped her legs around her waist. "It doesn't matter where we live, but it's time we get a place for our dog and the couple of kids I'm putting in an order for."

"Really?" The way Aidan pulled her hair made her stop before getting under the spray. "You really want that?"

They'd talked vaguely about the future but hadn't made plans other than enjoying their time together and rebuilding their relationship. Aidan might've left her in Hawaii to pursue her career as a naval officer, but Berkley's heart hadn't flinched when she'd completely forgiven her. The only way to heal the heartbreak of Aidan's loss was to believe she was back for good.

"What, the house or the kids?" She turned the water off. "I want both, and I don't want to wait much longer."

"Why?" Aidan asked, squeezing her legs tighter around her.

"Because I want to experience the wonder of seeing you pregnant with our baby, and I want to have a place where I don't have to hide who you are to me." Honesty was best, her father always said, but it was a scary notion if the person you were with didn't want the same things.

"God, yes," Aidan said before kissing her. "We talked about it years ago, but I thought you might've changed your mind."

"Let's make a deal that we'll talk about all this stuff from now on, instead of trying to guess what we want." She headed back to the bedroom and sat on the bed with Aidan on her lap. "No matter our mistakes, going forward, we'll make them together no matter what."

"I'll gladly agree to that deal, and I'm tired of putting my biological clock on snooze."

She laughed and ran her hands up Aidan's back. "Anything else on your mind?"

"We haven't gotten anywhere with our investigation," Aidan said, resting her head on her shoulder and sighing.

"The cockroaches have done a good job of scattering and hiding, for sure, but they'll surface. They have too much invested to back down now."

The initial voyage of the USS *Jefferson*, Aidan's first command, had been a mission to destroy two nuclear sites in North Korea. It had also been the beginning of a mutiny by some supposed patriots, who'd formed a militia group called New Horizons, led by former Vice President Dick Chandler. The men who'd joined Chandler, and were willing to die for his cause, had stolen millions from the defense budget to finance their war to bring down the current government, and they'd recruited both retired and active military to do the job.

New Horizons and its leaders had a problem with the election of the current president, Peter Khalid, and his choice for vice president, Olivia Michaels. The changes they'd instituted, like placing Aidan at the helm of the *Jefferson* and her in command of the flight crew, were in their opinion the death of the America they loved.

"If NSA, the CIA, and the FBI can't find Chandler, how the hell are we going to? We've given enough, honey, and I'm ready to be happy and pregnant." Aidan was hard to argue with, but so was her dedication to duty, and Berkley hated leaving something undone.

"We have a couple of weeks off, with plenty of family time planned, so let's talk about it."

"You promise?"

"I do as long as you promise not to believe everything my sisters say about me."

CHAPTER TWO

Retired US Army General Homer Lapry sat in the fighting chair of the fishing boat he'd hired on the northern coast of South Korea and stared out at the large expanse of water. The contact had been sent to him while he was on vacation, and he'd been thrilled to finally be noticed. His retirement had been shoved down his throat, and he'd been livid from the moment he'd been escorted from his office. President Peter Khalid was on a mission to bring down every military institution and twist it into his perverted view of the future. It was sickening to watch.

"Two boats closing fast, sir," the charter captain said as he brought the engines to idle.

Homer picked up his reel, in case it wasn't who he thought it was, and put his cigar back in his mouth. "You sure you've done this before?"

"Yes, sir, and you have to go with the northern soldiers to get to who you want. That might make you nervous, but it's the only way."

The military boats with multiple weapons in front and back seemed to be overloaded with men, but the one alone at the back was evidently in charge. The man stood ramrod straight and issued orders as the two boats were tied together. "You come."

Homer placed the rod in the holder and moved, the thought of how crazy this was playing in a loop in his head. They'd bombed these people the year before and destroyed their nuclear facilities, and here they were welcoming him into the country. At least, that's what he hoped this was.

"Please sit, General," the man said after shaking his hand.

The trip wasn't as long as he figured, and on shore a helicopter with a sun rising over a mountain was waiting on him. He guessed it was rising and not setting, since the logo was the same as on the initial letter he'd received from what he'd believed was a new Washington lobbying group, New Horizons. The names listed as board members along the side were impressive, but now a number of them were dead or locked away for treason.

Congress had started an investigation almost from the second former Vice President Dick Chandler's home blew up, killing the head of the FBI and four of his agents. The US government was trying to root out those loyal to Chandler and the open rebellion he was waging against what he saw as the downfall of America, being led by Khalid and his bitch Vice President Olivia Michaels.

"Sir, welcome to North Korea," the young man with blond hair and a pristine black uniform with the logo on the pocket said as he saluted. "I'll be your pilot today. If you're ready, we'll take off."

The flight lasted only twelve minutes, but Homer realized why it was necessary as they traveled away from the coast over thick vegetation with no visible roads. "Is this the only way in?"

"There are actually two roads—one that leads to Mongumpó by the coast where you landed, and the other inland toward the capital—but it takes over an hour of rough riding." The pilot circled the large compound and landed on one of the pads close to the forest. "Please follow me, sir."

Over a thousand people, all wearing the same black uniform, were walking around performing different tasks, and they all appeared American. The house at the edge of the main compound was large, beautiful, and strangely out of place. By all accounts this backward country was poor and struggling under crushing sanctions, but this facility made Homer wonder about the truth of that perception.

"Sir." He stood at attention and saluted before taking the hand Dick Chandler held out. "It's a pleasure."

"Thank you for coming, General. Let's sit." Dick led him to a beautiful table outside on the wide porch and sat. "We've got a lot to talk about."

Gromwell Enterprises' private jet came to a halt inside the hangar at the end of their private airstrip. According to the manifest, it was returning from their offices in Montana, so there was no need for customs agents to board. The defense contractor had been one of former President George Butler's biggest supporters, and their loyalty and generosity to the ticket had been well compensated with enough government contracts to last years.

The CEO, Tom Bristol, was waiting for the arrival of his guests, since he was curious as to why all the cloak-and-dagger shit his old friend Dick had insisted on. He'd tried to get some information out of Marine Major Franklin Porche, who'd showed up to wait with him, but asking the man anything was like talking to a corpse.

Rachel Chandler was the first one out, followed by her brother Jeffery and a few other guys Tom didn't recognize. "Rachel, welcome." He held his hand out. "How's your father?"

"He's fine, and thank you for helping us today. Is there someplace where we can talk to Major Porche in private?"

"Sure, but what exactly is going on?"

"I'll fill you in while my sister talks to Franklin," Jeffery said.

He led them all to the offices, and the guy who appeared heavily armed followed them into an empty space while Rachel took the small conference room. Suddenly the small favor for an old friend didn't seem so simple.

"What's all this about, Jeffery? We still have government contracts, so if you're in some kind of trouble, I can't be involved." All the news coverage on Dick's crimes against the government that he'd chalked up to being farfetched had a ring of truth now that it was too late to get out of the mistake he'd made.

"Tom, I need you to sit and be quiet. By helping us get into the country illegally, you're now complicit. That alone will get you some jail time and the loss of all your contracts." Jeffery nodded in the other man's direction, and the guy pushed him into a chair. "Your part is done for today, so hit the road. Think before you don't take any more calls from my father though." Jeffery knocked on the desk with his knuckles, making him look up. "You know him well enough to realize he'll take pleasure in destroying you."

Rachel glanced at the door when Jeffery came in with Kevin Skinner. The trip over had been long with all the refueling stops, and they all appeared exhausted, but they didn't have much time to finalize their plans.

"My father put the big pieces of this together," Rachel said to Franklin Porche, and the man nodded without a hair on his head moving because of the severe marine haircut.

"I swore to Mr. Chandler he'd have my complete cooperation and loyalty, but what's the end game?" Franklin asked, his eyes momentarily going from her to Kevin and the other man with him.

"The old ways of government are too hardwired to completely overthrow what people know, but there's another way to replace it with something that works better."

Franklin ran his hand over the top of his head and laughed. "That's the kind of bull crap the recruiting office tells you, Ms. Chandler. What's the end game?"

"This is our plan for now." She started talking, and Franklin leaned in as if he couldn't believe what he was hearing. "The time for backing out is over, Franklin. You're in this."

"I owe a lot to your father, and I'll spend the rest of my life paying him back. You have no worries on my end."

"Good." Rachel stood but didn't head for the door. "I'll be in touch."

"I guess we'll know in a few minutes how loyal these guys are," Jeffery said and laughed. "If they get on the phone to the FBI we're fucked."

"Do you want to review everything before we go?" she asked, ignoring Jeffery's sarcasm. Their brother Robyn had stayed behind to help their father, so she was stuck with the reluctant one.

"I'm a marine, remember? We're always prepared. Besides, dear ole dad has a spare. I'm sure Robyn will be happy to pitch in if something happens to me."

"It's not too late for me to send someone else."

"Forget it. I'll be fine."

"Remember to stick to the plan, and I'll see you at the safe house once you're done."

"Sure, if we do that, what could go wrong?" He kissed her forehead before leaving for the place outside the beltway.

"Plenty can go wrong, little brother, so hopefully your head's in the game."

❖

"Wait out here, and I'll go in and find them," Aidan said as Berkley drove slowly through the arrival and baggage area of the New Orleans airport.

"Your father's going to think I'm an asshole for not helping with the luggage."

"I'll get a porter, baby, and you can impress him later when you carry it all up the stairs. Or I can tell him you were busy making love to me, so we didn't have time to park." Aidan gave Berkley a quick kiss before hopping out and disappearing into the cool space crowded with passengers ready for the July fourth holiday weekend. "Daddy," she said, putting her arms around retired Admiral Preston "Triton" Sullivan and kissing his cheek.

"Where's Cletus?" he asked gruffly but squeezed her before letting her go. "Your mama packed like we're moving here."

"I made her late, so no giving her a bad time, and I'll get a porter." Her mom joined them a few minutes later when she exited the restroom, and they laughed together as Preston pointed to numerous bags that needed to be loaded. "Come on. Berkley's waiting outside."

Aidan relinquished the front seat to her father and shook her head practically all the way back to the Quarter as her father gave Berkley a hard time about everything he could think of. Berkley's string of "yes, sirs" meant nothing he said would rattle her, but it seemed to be an important part of their relationship.

It took five trips for Berkley to carry all the bags up from the car to the place next to theirs, but her parents were staying considerably longer to scope out the city that might become their permanent home. "Will you promise not to kill my father if I take my mom shopping for a little while?" Aidan asked, putting her arms around Berkley's waist.

"She packed everything she owns. What could she possibly need?" Berkley asked softly as her parents changed in the bedroom into something cooler.

"A few things, but I promise we won't be long."

Berkley slid her hands down to Aidan's ass as she kissed her. They were back to the solid belief that nothing would ever come between them, and that made it impossible to keep their hands off each other.

"Get your hands off my daughter's backside," Preston said loudly, making Berkley lift her hands and take three steps back.

"Behave, or I'll have her put all that stuff back in the car and ship you home," Aidan said, shaking her finger at Preston. "Do I need to separate you two while we go shopping?"

"Shopping? For what? Your mother packed everything she owns. What could she possibly need?" Preston asked, and Berkley laughed until he glared at her.

"That's too scary to think about," Aidan said and kissed her father on the cheek before she kissed Berkley. "Try not to pick up any more bad habits before I get back," Aidan said and pinched her side.

"Can I buy you a beer, sir?" Preston smiled as he placed a cigar in his mouth and offered her one. "I'd like to talk to you about something."

"Lead the way." Preston lit hers before following her out, and she hoped she had time to brush her teeth before Aidan got back. This definitely counted as a bad habit, she was guessing.

They picked a place where they could sit outside to finish their smokes and enjoy the beers they'd ordered. "What's on your mind, Cletus?"

"As you know, we took the assignment the president offered, and after we've put in the time, we were planning to retire. With the change in 'don't ask don't tell,' it's made things easier, but Aidan is still my commanding officer, so I'm not about to advertise our relationship." He nodded and took a large swallow of beer. "To our families, though, I want to declare what Aidan means to me."

"I've got no doubts or fears when it comes to what you feel for my daughter, and I couldn't have asked for better when it comes to her future."

"Thank you, sir, and I hope you mean that. I'd like your blessing to ask her to marry me. The ceremony might need to wait some, but I don't want to postpone making the promises I swear to keep."

Preston put his cigar down and stood, waving her up. "I'm damn proud and happy to give you that," he said, hugging her. "Welcome to our family."

"I have to get her to say yes first." She tapped her glass against his when he sat and raised his.

"I'm sure you're up for the job." He ordered another round before pointing his cigar at her. "Remember to always love her, and that I'll kill you and dump you at sea if you don't."

"I'd never break a promise to the son of Poseidon, sir."

"Smartass."

Dick Chandler watched his troops go through different drills, pleased by how well they were working together since he'd recruited them from different military branches. He'd reluctantly sent Rachel and Jeffery to undertake the next part of his master plan, and it was too late to call them back and send someone else.

"Sir, we received Khalid's most up-to-date calendar a few minutes ago, so we're clear for our mission." Robyn, his son, read from the notebook in his hand, and Dick was long used to Robyn's need for perfection. "Now that Jeffery and Rachel are there, we can start thinking about the next phase."

"What have I told you about rushing?" He saluted a few of the men who were looking his way before turning to face his eldest child. "We have to make sure everything is in place before we move on. If we skip anything, nothing else will fall in line."

"I'm sorry, sir."

"Stop being sorry and learn. Did you speak to your brother before he left?" Robyn had wanted nothing to do with the military, but Jeffery had enlisted in the marines without telling him. It was like his youngest didn't want anything to do with him or his entire family.

"He promised to be good," Robyn said with a smile. "He was looking forward to putting his training to the test."

"All he needs to do is supervise," he said, thinking it'd been a mistake sending Jeffery. Rachel knew how to follow orders as well as give them. "You need to keep talking to him and telling him we're doing all this for the country and our family."

"You know how he is. Jeffery has his own mind." Robyn sat after him and put away all his prepared statements. "I think you're trying to accomplish a good thing, but I had to really think about what I was doing. We had to sacrifice plenty to follow you."

He let out a loud bark of laughter. "You gave up a grunt job at the National Gallery. How exactly is that a sacrifice?"

"It was my chance to do what I loved, but I gave it up for you. The least you can do is respect that choice."

"You and Jeffery are just like your mother." He'd said that from the moment Robyn had learned to walk. The boy was too soft, and he'd never ventured into his personal life only because he was afraid of what he'd find. Jeffery wasn't soft, but his head was too thick to achieve anything in life. "Get back to work and finalize the next part of the plan for review later."

"Yes, sir," Robyn said, and he sounded as if their talk had deflated him. But they didn't have time to worry over a few hurt feelings.

"Are you ready?" he asked into the phone since it was immediately answered.

"I've done jobs harder than this, sir, so it should be easy if your people came through."

"Good to hear, and don't worry about anyone on my end. I've got a few more jobs for you when this one is complete, so I want you back here when you're done, unless I tell you otherwise."

"The price is the same."

"So are the jobs." Dick hung up and glanced over the schedule Robyn had brought in. "You brought this on yourself, Khalid, and when I'm done, people aren't going to believe how easy you made it for me."

❖

The cell walls should've been cool. Cinderblock was, after all, sterile, cold, and something that all institutions had in common. These weren't though. The damn beige blocks were warm to the touch, which made sense—the air in this place was always hot, humid, and fucking uncomfortable. It was far away from the life Erika Gibson had before the bitch she worked for had sent her here. She'd been Captain Aidan Sullivan's second for a few years until Commander Berkley Levine had come along. Then she was working in the mess hall before landing in this pit.

All the months she'd been here were like an endless repetitive misery that reminded her of the movie *Groundhog Day,* only without the comic relief and ice-sculpting lessons. The day after day of this fucking heat was like an enveloping wool coat meant to drive you insane because you could never take it off.

"Hey, I demand a shower," she'd screamed, followed by a yell to try to bleed out the insanity that clawed the inside of her skull like a badger in a field burrowing a den. The only out was tying her bed sheet to the bars and hanging herself, but she was constantly monitored, and her jailers would probably end up tying her to the bed.

"You need something, Ms. Gibson?" Walby Edwards, head CIA interrogator, asked, standing outside and appearing like he was ready for eighteen holes of golf.

"I want a shower." She'd have no problem wrapping her hands around this guy's neck and would gladly watch the life drain out of him.

"Come with me," Edwards said when a guard joined him and waited for the door to unlock. This wasn't something she fought anymore since the guards didn't tolerate noncompliance at all.

They walked to a new section of the facility, and she looked up and down the hall to get a hint of where she was going. Hopefully it was outside, and along with the sun, a firing squad would be there to put an end to the heat and the long stretch of identical days she knew would drive her over the edge.

"What's this about?" she asked, her pesky desire to live kicking in.

Walby opened the door at the end of the hall, and she held back a sob as the cold air brushed over her skin better than any lover she'd ever had. "Sit." Walby stood behind her chair, holding a glass with ice in it.

Funny how the very small things in life stood out when they were gone. She often thought of ice water and chips. "Are you going to answer my question? What's this about?"

"It's been a year, Erika. A year of heat, of bad food, of listening to the other prisoners, and most importantly, a year without your family."

The clink of the ice against her glass made her think of the mundane days she'd wasted in her life and wished God would give them back. "Don't you think it's time to start answering questions?"

"What do you think I can tell you?" He refilled her glass after she drained the first one. "I'm innocent, yet you've kept me here without charging me or letting me talk to anyone who can legally help me."

"Drink up then, Ms. Gibson. If that's how you want to play it, we won't play at all."

She savored the cold water but didn't smile, but oh she wanted to. "Good."

"Since you want progress, we'll accommodate you."

"Good," she repeated, finishing her second glass, but Walby didn't refill it again. "You have all misjudged me."

"You decided to play for the wrong team, and the military is ready to press charges. That's what I meant." He took the glass before she was able to slide a piece of ice into her mouth and dumped it into the trash. "Trust me. You're not getting out of this, and more importantly, you're never leaving here."

"I simply talked to that bastard Blazer. I talked to him and Skinner," she said of Hattie Skinner, another crewmember on the *Jefferson*'s first mission. "Aidan totally misunderstood."

"*Captain Sullivan*, Ms. Gibson," he said, enunciating Aidan's title, "caught you and Ms. Skinner in an act of treason. That's what she'll testify to, and continuing to downplay your part will not show the court you have an ounce of remorse." Walby poured himself a Coke and seemed to enjoy the fizz when it hit the ice in his own glass.

"Why don't you believe me? It's the truth."

"You aren't acquainted with the truth, but your small apartment and bunk area tell a different story. Electronic trails leave enough rope to hang you with."

She stared at him and truly detested him. "You can fuck off, and you can tell Aidan the same thing. That big bitch she's creaming her pants for isn't going to save her forever."

That was it then. Her outburst would seal her fate, so all she had left to do was wait and trust she'd be rewarded with freedom for her part of General Chandler's plan. With any luck, Chandler would leave her here, only she'd be in Walby's chair watching him slowly lose his mind.

"So clichéd, Ms. Gibson."

"Not if it's a promise. You and the rest have no idea what's coming. Enjoy the cold drink. It's only a matter of time before you'll be standing in hell."

"You've already beaten me there," Walby said and laughed. Something in her finally fractured, and she stood and ran for him, but he only laughed harder when he put her in a hold she couldn't escape.

The guard took over, and the wall of heat hit her like an open oven on broil. Walby was right. "Oh, God."

She *was* in hell.

CHAPTER THREE

Aidan and Mary Beth arrived a half an hour after Berkley and Preston, and they separated with plans for dinner in an hour. Berkley and Aidan shared a shower, and Berkley dressed while Aidan put on makeup, then got thrown out of the bedroom so Aidan could get ready. "I want to surprise you, so lose the pout, fly girl."

The time alone in the front room gave Berkley a chance to make sure she was ready, and she was both nervous and anxious to get going. There was no way to make up for the years they'd lost after they broke up, but tonight was the first step in assuring it would never happen again.

It took another twenty minutes before Aidan opened the door and stepped out in a midnight-blue dress that left Berkley speechless. "My god—you're so beautiful," she finally got out, holding Aidan's hands and not able to stop looking Aidan up and down. "Truly stunning."

"Thank you, and you should remember this the next time you complain about shopping." Aidan pulled her down by her jacket lapels and kissed her. "I love you."

"I love you too, and I'm going to have a hard time not rushing through dinner."

"My mother has been reading about this place for months after your mom mentioned it, so you might be out of luck when it comes to quick, baby. Later on, though, I hope to have the same problem when I get you all to myself." Aidan kissed her again before smoothing her jacket back in place. "You're too sexy for words in this suit, and I'm planning to take my time peeling it off you later."

"You're a cruel woman, my love, but damn if I don't love your torture techniques."

Preston didn't mind sitting in the back this time, and she gladly held Aidan's hand all the way to Blanchard's in the Garden District. The hostess greeted Berkley with a hug before leading them to the upstairs dining room, since she'd been here often with her parents. Someone from the kitchen staff came up before they ordered drinks and asked if she and Aidan minded coming down to talk to their head chef for a few minutes.

"You two go ahead," Preston said, taking Mary Beth's hand. "I love your company but wouldn't mind getting my girl alone for a few minutes."

She held Aidan's hand as they descended the back stairs that led to the kitchen, and they did spend some time talking to Keegan Blanchard, who seemed happy to help with what Berkley had called about earlier. "Thank you both for your service, guys, but there's one more spot you need to see before I get to feed you. Berkley, you know the way, right?" Keegan asked.

"Thanks, and yes, I do." She led Aidan outside from the kitchen door and to the garden by the outdoor seating space.

"This is a beautiful spot," Aidan said, sitting on the bench under the big oak. "It's like a secret garden."

She sat next to her and nodded. "This is a special spot." She had to stop and take a few breaths to calm down. The box in her pocket had been in her travel kit for three months, but she'd waited until they were in this place, on this bench. "The Blanchards are old friends of my mom and her family, and have been since Della Blanchard, the current owner, went to school with my grandmother."

"Really? It's nice they still keep in touch. You must've come here often."

"I have, and I'm glad your parents accepted my invitation. Tonight I wanted to share an old family tradition with you."

"If it's making out under this great tree, my father will eventually hunt you down and drag you back inside." The teasing made Berkley smile, and Aidan kissed her.

"Maybe later, when I'm not under Triton's gun," she said, taking Aidan's hand. "And that's not the tradition I'm talking about."

"If it involves you putting your hands under this dress, you can forget it." Aidan tapped her on the nose and laughed.

"Such heathens you think the Levines to be." She kissed Aidan again and couldn't wait any longer to ask. "My father proposed to my mother here," she said softly, and Aidan's fingers tightened around hers. "That proposal was one of many, and I thought all those yeses would bring me luck."

"Bring you luck?" Aidan asked, sounding out of breath.

She moved down to one knee and took the box out of her pocket. "You are the love of my life, and I think that's been true from the moment I showed up at your door with flowers. You're beautiful, but so much more than that." She opened the box, took out the ring her mom and sisters had helped her shop for, and held it up. "We may not know where life will take us, what our futures hold, or what we'll face, but I never want to do it without you by my side. Will you marry me?"

Aidan had pressed her hands to her mouth and had been nodding as she spoke, but then she stopped and simply said, "Yes." They kissed, and she'd never experienced this level of happiness. "I love you."

"This means you're stuck with me," she joked as she placed the ring on Aidan's finger.

"There's no place I'd rather be, my love, and wow." Aidan held up her hand and studied her finger. "Thank you for sharing your family's traditions with me and for this. It's beautiful."

"I understand that, until we're out of the service, you won't get to wear it every day." She reached into her coat pocket and took out a platinum chain. "But knowing you might want to keep it close, I got you this. Thank you for saying yes."

"God, baby, I'm so ready for the picket fence you promised me," Aidan said and kissed her again.

"I know exactly what you mean. Let's go celebrate, and you can tell Triton I didn't screw it up."

"You realize he's going to be as happy as I am, don't you?"

"He seemed pretty happy when I talked to him today. I think he just doubts my romantic abilities."

"If he only knew…he'd kill you slowly and with a lot of pain…but it would put that fear to rest."

Berkley gave Keegan a thumbs-up when they went back in, and she promised to send something up to toast the occasion. The celebration and hugs started when Aidan lifted her hand and Mary Beth slapped hers together.

"Remember everything I said," Preston said when he hugged Berkley tightly.

"I will. You have my word, sir."

"I've got no worries, and congratulations. I'm damn proud to call you family." Preston released her and swiped at his eyes. For all his gruffness, he was a softy at heart.

"Thank you, sir."

"No, thank you for loving our little girl, Berkley. I'm always going to worry about her, but it'll be nice to share the load with you."

"She's in good hands, ma'am, but then so am I," Berkley said, and Aidan caressed her thigh. "Now we have to work on you guys moving down here, and we can enjoy retirement together."

"You're really thinking of retiring?" Preston asked.

"We can't just yet, but hopefully soon, Daddy. Tonight, though, isn't for talking about that."

"No. Tonight is for eating fast so I can get this beautiful woman home," Berkley said, and Aidan slapped her arm. Preston simply laughed, making her think it was okay to order. "Waiter."

❖

President Peter Khalid stopped talking until the White House staff finished serving dinner. He'd gone to the residence to see his family for a bit, but these dinner meetings with Vice President Olivia Michaels, Defense Secretary Drew Orr, NSA Director Calvin Vaughn, CIA Director Marcus Newton, new FBI Director Jonas Chapman, and head of security for the Pentagon, Commander Mark "Rooster" Palmer, happened once a week. He'd been in office just over a year, and so far, he'd spent a lot of his presidency trying to weed out traitors who'd been sprinkled throughout government by the previous vice president.

"Any new leads?" Peter asked, glancing at Calvin.

"Chandler has effectively disappeared and left no trail of where he could be. We have every one of our allies working on this search as well, which leads us to conclude he's fled to a rogue state." Calvin shook his head in apparent disgust, and Peter shared the sentiment. "This man was a heartbeat away from the highest office, and this is what he was doing. It's the most treasonous act in our history, sir."

"No ideas or guesses?" Peter asked, wondering what a rogue nation would gain from harboring Chandler.

"Sir, we have too much at stake to guess," Drew said. "We've started a complete investigation of every branch of the military, searching for any connection to New Horizons and anyone serving, no matter their rank. The number of folks in custody is growing, but we'll keep at it until we reach everyone."

"Anyone talk so far?" Olivia asked, beating Peter to it.

"The only cooperating person so far is Jerry Teague's assistant, who swears on a stack he didn't know what he was getting into," Rooster said and snorted. "He's full of it, but the heat down at Gitmo is starting to twist his brain. Walby Edwards has been interrogating the others, but so far all they're doing is screaming their name, rank, and serial number as well as how unfair we're treating them. Erika Gibson and the other woman, Skinner, are complaining about the heat."

"This is a war of their own making, and if they hadn't joined, they wouldn't be hot. It's pretty simple," Peter said, taking a sip of his beer. "We need some breakthroughs on this, but I appreciate your hard work."

"You all have done great work, but are we ready for our next phase?" Olivia asked.

"The excuse they've used up to now for their actions has been Captain Sullivan and Commander Levine, and they're on board with what we've asked of them so far. We don't foresee any problems," Marcus said. "From my understanding, they're ready to return to sea, even if that means becoming a target for these fools. They're also okay with having some of my guys on board once the *Jefferson* sets sail."

"Is that totally necessary?" Jonas asked.

"It's important for me to know what's happening on that ship," Marcus said staring at Jonas like he was some irritating fly trying to land on him. "Sullivan will answer to Command and might not have time for us, and I for one don't want to be out of the loop."

"Just as long as they don't get in Aidan's way," Olivia said.

"Give me more credit than that." Marcus tried to bleed the sarcasm from his tone, but from Olivia's expression, he'd failed miserably.

"Thank you all, and I expect you all tomorrow with your guests, but if you'll excuse me, I'll leave you with Olivia to finish this." Everyone stood with him, and he walked with his Secret-Service agent back to the Oval Office. "How's the family?" he asked Agent Lainey Willcott.

"My son has a summer cold, but aside from that, all's well, sir." Lainey filled in some nights when the lead of the president's security detail, Shimmy Laurel, needed her. "I'll be waiting outside the door if you need anything, sir."

"How about some good luck?"

"Luck then, Mr. President," Lainey said, opening the door to his office, prompting his secretary Judy Harper to excuse herself.

The man waiting on him appeared comfortable, but then the space had been his office for the eight years before Peter arrived. President George Butler had been in office only nine months when the terrorists had attacked on American soil, and he'd become a wartime president for the rest of his term. It was a quagmire Peter was still trying to navigate a way out of, but it was time to bring George in on their investigation.

"George, thank you for coming." He walked in and shook hands with the former president before George embraced him. They might've disagreed on almost everything politically, except for keeping the American people safe, but he couldn't help but like George and his good-ole-boy demeanor. "How are your parents and family?"

"Dad is as ornery as ever, but my mama is too, so it balances out. Victoria and the girls are great after leaving the glare of this fishbowl, and I can't disagree on that sentiment." George nodded when he pointed to the coffee service Peter had brought in, since his predecessor didn't drink any alcohol. "And I was glad to come," George said, then laughed. "Hopefully it's not for you to beat me with a hose over this Chandler business."

"There's no way in hell you had anything to do with this, so you've got no hoses in your future." They sat across from each other and chuckled. "I am, though, going to ask you for your help."

"Mr. President, how can you be so sure? That I'm not involved, I mean."

"You and your father served our nation when called to do so, and I, as well as every American, thank you for your service. No man or woman who enlisted during wartime would try to destroy what they fought to defend. Granted, I have plenty of enlisted men and women in custody right now, but I in no way think of you betraying something you love."

"You're damn right," George said with conviction.

"Then stop with the Mr. President and help me solve this."

"I'll be happy to, Peter. Dick Chandler was my mistake, and I'd like to be a part of bringing his ass in to answer for his crimes. You give me a job, and I'll do my best to find him and serve him up to whatever court you want him to face."

"It would send a strong message if you'd join the team we have working on this. You're the only one I can think of, aside from Chandler's family, who knows him better."

George stared at him as if he'd lost his sanity by asking him that. "Dick was a con man who blinded me with his line about his connections in the oil and gas industry. It's the world I come from. My goal was to bring us to oil independency, and he said he was the best man for that job." The sudden honesty was a clue George regretted his first and most important decision. "Once we were elected under a cloud of doubt because we lost the popular vote, he showed his hand. He wanted the power I could wield but knew he could never win on his own."

"Thank you for sharing that." He reached over and placed his hand on George's knee. "I understand now more than ever what you said about legacy. I really don't want another civil war on my watch."

"Believe me, they'll blame us both. You tell me what you want, and I'll give you all I've got." George spoke with such passion, Peter thought he'd won an important battle that'd be crucial in flushing more of Chandler's minions out of government.

"Let's get to work."

CHAPTER FOUR

A idan woke before the sun and listened to the rain lashing the windows. The last year had been everything she'd fantasized, but last night had been a total shock. They'd talked about a future together, and she'd mentioned not being able to have that big day many of her friends had enjoyed. Leave it to Berkley to prove her wrong.

"Are you okay?" Berkley's deep voice made her shiver, so she pressed closer to her.

"I'm too happy to sleep." The ring on her finger still didn't feel real, which made her run her thumb over the band again. "You're everything I've ever wanted from the moment you first touched me."

"With everything that's been happening since we've been back together, I've learned a valuable lesson," Berkley said, moving so they faced each other. "I never want to put anything off, especially if it comes to showing you how I feel about you."

"You seldom have." She leaned forward and kissed Berkley softly. "I'm the screwup in this relationship, remember?"

"You're the woman I love and am planning to spend the rest of my life with, and I happen to have great taste, so stop knocking yourself. I'm thankful we both got our mistakes out of the way early on and not after we make the kind of commitment I want." Berkley moved until she was on top of her and kissed her. "The way I see it, we're old enough to know what we want now, so we're home free."

"Thank you for loving me."

There was a loud knock on the door before they could kiss again, and Berkley dropped her head to Aidan's shoulder when she heard Preston in the hallway. "Cletus, get your hands off my daughter and open the door."

"What in the world?" Aidan asked, laughing. "The sun just came up," she said, glancing over Berkley's shoulder.

"We're going out to breakfast, and then we volunteered to pick up the tremendous amount of meat my father ordered. I didn't think we were starting this early, though." Berkley gave Aidan another quick kiss before she jumped up and searched for her sleep pants and T-shirt. "Good morning, sir."

"You're not dressed?" Preston asked, coming in and appearing as if he'd been up for hours.

"My mistake. I thought we said eight," Berkley said, realizing Preston's clock ran earlier than hers. "If you give me a minute, I'll be ready."

Aidan came in and started making coffee. Berkley stopped and watched for a moment, knowing her life with Aidan would be way different from the military existence she'd had for so long, but she'd never be bored. The fact that Preston and Mary Beth came along as part of the package would make it much more interesting.

Their errands and breakfast took over an hour, and Berkley enjoyed Preston's company as he shared some of the stories from his days of active duty. He and Mary Beth had met her parents, but today they'd be introduced to the rest of her family as they enjoyed the holiday.

"Are you sure we're not too early?" Mary Beth asked as they drove to the north shore of Lake Pontchartrain to Berkley's mother's family compound that faced the water. Her grandparents had built it and owned it for years as a weekend retreat large enough for their family.

"Believe me, ma'am, my dad's been up as long as Mr. Sullivan has," she said, and Aidan squeezed her fingers.

"Cletus, if we're going to be family you can't keep calling me Mr. Sullivan," Preston said, making it sound like an order. "Let's start with Preston and Mary Beth, and see where that leads us."

"Where that leads us? Isn't that your names?" Berkley asked, confused. "What other possibilities are there?"

"Grandpa and Nana, but you've got plenty of time for that. We just wanted a jump on those names before Corbin and Maggie decide to get cute," Preston said, making everyone laugh.

The day had gotten Louisiana hot by the time they arrived, and Berkley wasn't surprised that the rest of her family was already there. Her grandfather had founded a successful air-freight company, but he'd been a marine before that and was a stickler for promptness. They were forty-five minutes early, but they were already late.

Her grandfather stood at the center of the wide wraparound porch of the Acadian-style home and tapped his watch. "Papa, the sun's barely up so smile, and you've got people to meet so lose the glare," Berkley said, hugging the much-shorter man with the straight posture that had been perfected in boot camp. "Where's Bubbe?"

"Inside cooking for about a thousand people, and not a damn bit of it has a lick of salt. Damn heart doctor."

Berkley's grandmother came out and flicked her husband with a kitchen towel to stop the health-food tirade before it really got started.

"Bubbe, Papa," Berkley said after she was kissed a dozen times by her grandmother, "this is Admiral Preston Sullivan and his wife Mary Beth. Guys, these are my grandparents."

"It's an honor to meet you both, sir," Preston said, shaking her grandfather's hand. "Ma'am, it's a pleasure."

"Around here we're Papa and Bubbe. Welcome," her grandfather said, opening his arms to Aidan. "Come here, beautiful girl. Still giving our Cletus hell?"

"I'd say yes, but she might take this back." Aidan held up her hand, and all the Levine sisters surrounded her.

"You did it by the big tree?" her grandfather asked once he'd gotten his hug.

"Things that sound dirty but aren't," Berkley said and got a hard flick from Bubbe's towel. "Yes, sir, I did, and she said yes, even if you all come as part of the package."

"Get inside, troublemaker, and help your father with the grill," Bubbe said.

Corbin helped Berkley with the cooler of meat from the butcher her grandparents used and set it next to the grill that was roaring with the logs Corbin had put in to burn down. They sat close by, drinking some beers with her grandfather and Preston, while her sisters, mom, and grandmother joined Mary Beth and Aidan inside. They'd visited here a few times, and she was glad Aidan loved her family as much as she did.

"You're growing up, Cletus," her grandfather said, and she smiled. She was over thirty and a navy pilot, but to him, she'd just climbed down from her highchair. "And come home with the prettiest girl I've seen since your Bubbe."

"Thanks, Papa, and she said yes to moving back with me too. We've got a couple of weeks to convince these guys to join us." She pointed to Preston.

"Don't worry. He won't be a problem," Papa said, handing Preston a Cuban cigar. "Once the babies come, you won't be able to keep him out of your house."

"The babies might have to wait, Papa."

"We see how Aidan looks at you and vice versa," Preston said, touching his cigar to the match Papa had struck. "She might be pregnant already."

She blushed as the three men laughed. "See, he won't be a problem," Papa said.

"There's no way this was a good idea," she said, and the men only laughed harder.

❖

"Way to go," Berkley's sister Ann said as she held up Aidan's hand. "Every single woman in New Orleans will be crying over this for months to come."

All three of Berkley's sisters—Ann, Willow, and Suzette—were married, with two girls each. Berkley was the oldest, but all the women in her life, from Bubbe down to each niece, babied and doted on her with the kind of love found only in close families. That they had accepted her was a blessing. "I don't know about that, but I'm not letting her out of my sight on the off chance that's true," she joked, sitting at Bubbe's large kitchen table. "Where are my babies?"

"We sent them to get fireworks with our immature spouses," Willow said. "I swear if my husband had said the words bottle rocket one more time, I was going to smash him over the head with one."

The sudden noise of slamming doors made Aidan smile, and she opened her arms to the six little girls who ran in and jumped on her. No matter their partners in life, all the Levine sisters were redheads like Maggie, Berkley's mom, and they'd given birth to six little clones with the same coloring.

They all enjoyed getting to know the Sullivans and celebrating Berkley and Aidan's good news as Corbin and Berkley grilled everything that'd been packed in the cooler. By the afternoon, Berkley had tired out her nieces enough in the big pool that none of them complained when they'd been led inside to be changed into dry clothes. The family sat around and talked while Berkley joined her in-laws and father on the levee to shoot off the ton of fireworks they'd purchased.

Aidan sat with her parents holding River, the newest addition to the family, as she sucked on her evening bottle. "You look beautiful doing that," Maggie said as she joined them.

"You have beautiful grandchildren," Mary Beth said.

"They're a wonder, for sure, but I'm still waiting on my Berkley and Corbin lookalike," Maggie said. "Those two are still the only two brunettes in the bunch."

"I'll see what I can do, but I've got to get her to retire first," Aidan said, lifting the baby to her shoulder.

"Don't worry. We'll work on her," Ann said, "but right now I'm happy for both of you. We're proud of her for so many reasons, but getting the girl to say yes has surpassed all of them."

"I'm looking forward to retirement, but hell if I won't miss her in that uniform," she said, and they all laughed.

"I totally understand that." Maggie kissed her cheek. "Let's see if the pyromaniacs will take a break for chocolate cake."

"They still have those big boxes, so I don't know," Mary Beth said as Preston and Papa headed out with a large box of matches.

"This has been a great day," Aidan said, hoping this would be as exciting as life got for a while. Until they were out of the service, she doubted that would stay true. "But here's hoping," she said as she watched Berkley have fun with her family.

"Thank you all for coming," Peter Khalid said as everyone sat on the lawn enjoying the meal the staff had prepared. The press conference that morning with former President Butler was still the topic of discussion on the news channels, according to his staff, and he planned to keep it in the headlines.

The only way to make the rats feel cornered was to remove as much support for their cause as he could, and George was still a favorite in conservative circles. If he thought a man he'd entrusted with the second-highest office in the land was a traitor, those right-leaning circles were more apt to believe it.

"Sir, would you like to move to the balcony?" Shimmy Laurel asked, standing next to Peter in jeans and a golf shirt. He'd ordered his Secret Service detail to dress casual and fit in, and was glad to see every agent out there was dressed the same.

"I'm okay down here until everyone's finished. There are too many guests to be comfortable up there," Peter said, and Shimmy appeared not to like his answer. "Don't worry so much. Looks like everyone's enjoying being an American and has taken the day off from the revolution."

Shimmy smiled but shook his head. "I'm never going to let my guard down, sir, no matter what day it is."

"I told them to save you a plate. Make sure you eat once I'm inside and you can take a breath." Peter patted him on the back and joined his wife Eva at their table. He leaned in and kissed her cheek, glancing at his kids playing close by. "You know," he said softly to Eva. "Sometimes I feel like I'm going to wake up and be back in that crappy apartment in Detroit, and you and all this won't have been real."

"Oh no, my love," Eva said and kissed him on the lips. "You outgrew that kid a long time ago, and you're the guy who's going to continue making history. I love you and that kid though, and I'm really proud of you."

He smiled at her sweet words, and then there was only darkness. The world had gone mad.

❖

"We interrupt—" the radio announcer said in a shrill, panicky voice.

"Berkley," Aidan said, holding up her phone and walking to a quiet spot. "Yes, sir, we'll be there by tonight."

"What?" Berkley asked as her family became visibly upset. "What's going on?"

"Someone shot President Khalid—he's dead," Aidan said, falling against her. "Oh my god, Berk, he's dead. Those bastards killed him."

"It's okay." Berkley held her, but being okay was the last thing on Berkley's mind. Peter Khalid was a good and decent man whom she was proud to serve, and now he was gone. That Chandler's group would go this far was shocking, and in her gut, she was certain that's who was responsible. "Did they order us back?"

"Olivia Michaels will be sworn in shortly, and Drew wants us there."

"Come on then." Berkley walked back to her family, where her father was finishing a call himself. Like Preston, Corbin was retired, but he still had connections, and it sounded like he was using them. "We've got to go back," Berkley said as Mary Beth embraced Aidan.

"Sit tight," Corbin said. "I've got a lift coming for you and a plane ready in Belle Chase. Some of the boys will follow you and fly it back." Corbin walked to her and gave her a bear hug. "Be careful, and call once you get your orders. I know Olivia, and she'll persist until she finds a way to punish whoever's responsible. My gut says you and Aidan will be in the middle of whatever her plans are."

"I will, I promise. Spend that time trying to convince the Sullivans to stay. We're not officially family yet, but I think it'll be easier for them with you guys close by."

"Your mother's the woman for that job," Corbin said and squeezed her one more time, giving Maggie a chance to take his place.

"Don't forget you own a phone and have a mother," Maggie said, holding onto her as if it'd be a while before she did it again. "This is so unfair, but you go get those bastards. Keep yourself in one piece though, and take care of Aidan. We're happy for you both, and so proud to welcome her to the family."

"Thanks, and I'll be in touch. I was telling Dad about the Sullivans," Berkley said, watching Aidan with her own parents.

"Don't worry about that. Mary Beth and I'll spend our time shopping for real estate—they're not going anywhere." Maggie kissed her cheek and whispered how much she loved her in her ear, then pointed her toward the Sullivans. "Go make all the promises you intend to keep not only to their daughter's happiness, but also in keeping you both safe."

"Cletus," Preston said as Mary Beth stood next to him. "You take care, and watch over my little girl."

"You have my word, sir, and don't make me worry about you two while we're away. Stay put, and we'll be in touch when we get a chance." She took his hand and pulled him toward her. "I love you both, and I promise to take care of Aidan." Mary Beth nodded and hugged her as well.

"Here," Preston handed over the compass that resembled a pocket watch with Aidan's picture in it. "You might need it to remind you of what's waiting for you."

"Thanks, and I'm planning to avoid any long hikes if I can help it." She'd told him about what had happened in North Korea and how she and her partner Harvey Whittle had escaped. The compass had been a godsend as they slowly made their way along the countryside after they'd been shot down.

"My wife and daughter are expecting a wedding, so no sightseeing no matter what," Preston said. "You'll both be in our prayers."

"Thank you, sir, and I'll be waiting at the altar."

"Are you ready?" Aidan asked as they spotted the helicopter in the distance.

"With you—always."

CHAPTER FIVE

FBI Director Jonas Chapman watched in horror as the Secret Service cleared the lawn, the agents closest to the president covered in blood and gore. A sniper had gotten a shot off, and it'd blown one side of Peter's head off. They'd had to carry Eva Khalid away since she hadn't wanted to leave her husband's side. Even in his shock, Jonas had the presence of mind to film those closest to the action to record their reactions.

"Jonas," CIA Director Marcus Newton yelled as more Secret Service surrounded him. "Come on, get inside."

He couldn't move though, and he swept his phone around slowly a few more times. When his former boss had died in the explosion at Dick Chandler's home, he'd had a hard time believing the former vice president was the head of some revolution against the government, but Peter had convinced him. From that day, he'd not only agreed to head the bureau but also to avenge his boss's murder. He and the four agents standing with him had been good friends and dedicated public servants, but had been murdered like unsuspecting livestock being led to slaughter.

"Sir, you really need to take cover," his second, Special Agent Erin Mosley, said, tugging on his sleeve. "They haven't located the shooter, so you don't want to stand out here and make an enticing target."

He followed Erin into the White House, noticing that while she was in control of the situation, she was crying. Peter Khalid had been elected on a wave of hope the world could be a better place, and the crowds had loved him on the campaign trail from the first day. Jonas hadn't voted for him, but after meeting him, he'd jumped at the chance to work for him. The sons of bitches who'd killed him in front of his children would suffer, even if it took the rest of his life to get it done.

"We need to get to the Situation Room," he said as he navigated the crowd.

"First they need you in the Oval Office," Defense Secretary Drew Orr said. "This is a cluster fuck no one saw coming."

"We need to nail these bastards," he said, and Drew nodded.

They were escorted to the Oval Office, and the people gathered there appeared somber and shell-shocked. Jonas was no elite marksman, but a shot like that in the dark took skill not many had. That would be one of the first lists they would investigate, and with luck, it'd lead to another nest of these assholes.

"We need to get moving on this, Jonas," Marcus said as he stood to his right. "The American people will expect us to retaliate against someone. Our agencies need to be in lockstep until we find that target, and we need to make sure it's the right one. The public won't accept thin evidence again if any action we take has consequences beyond our borders. Once you start your investigation, don't think of keeping anything from me."

"None of your people heard any chatter about this?" Marcus was like every CIA man he'd met in his career in that he wanted everything but didn't like to share much. "Something like this took planning and wasn't spontaneous. No one kills the leader of the free world on the one day a year we celebrate that freedom without wanting to send a message."

"Chandler had eight years of undetected access to the entire government to build his little army," Marcus said. "He'd ask for regular updates on a number of things, so it's hard to pinpoint what he was really after, and he was the vice president, for fuck's sake. We couldn't decline his requests for classified information. If you're looking to blame someone, don't put the focus on me or my people."

"He wanted to seize control of everything, which sounds ludicrous, but then so is the assassination of the president on the grounds of his home. It's time to take the gloves off and find something. Tonight can't go unpunished."

Drew Orr and Rooster, head of Pentagon security, joined them, obviously hearing his last statement. "Save it for the briefing, but first we have to take a moment to respect President Khalid and our new leader."

"That's our problem," Marcus said. "We shouldn't wait for anything or anyone."

"Put your macho persona on ice for now and pay attention," Jonas said, not believing Marcus's callousness in this situation.

Olivia Michaels entered with Eva Khalid and her daughters. The first lady's shirt was still stained with Peter's blood, and their girls appeared lost and sad. Behind them were Olivia's husband Gabriel and their teenage son. Eva clung to Olivia's hand as she stared at the desk Peter loved to work behind.

"Ma'am," the chief justice said as Gabriel moved closer with their family bible, and a few trusted media outlets that were allowed in. "If you're ready."

Eva helped Gabriel hold the bible as Olivia placed her hand on it and took the oath of office. "I do solemnly swear that I will faithfully execute the Office of President of the United States, and will to the best of my ability, preserve, protect, and defend the Constitution of the United States."

"Congratulations, ma'am," the justice said, shaking Olivia's hand.

"Ma'am," Jonas said, holding his hand out to Olivia. "You have my and every agent in the bureau's commitment to work until we achieve justice for President Khalid." He took Eva's hand next. "My sincerest condolences on your loss, ma'am. Your husband was a fine man, a great leader, and an even better friend. He'll be missed."

Jonas moved back and observed the rest of the group who followed his lead. He didn't want to think anyone around him was capable of such savagery, but it was no time to give anyone a pass simply because they'd been invited in."

"I'd like to sit with you when you review the footage you took," Rooster said quietly.

"Did you see something?"

"No, but we can't take any chances. If we find something, Walby Edwards will be busy for months to come," Rooster said of the CIA interrogator he'd sent in to talk to the first men they'd caught. A few minutes with Walby had led Jerry Teague and Adam Morris to kill themselves, but the others had hung tough. "I don't believe in hard interrogations, but this might constitute an exception."

"We need to do whatever's necessary to make sure this doesn't happen again."

"That we will, so keep your eyes open, Jonas, and remember that Chandler went after the former FBI director first."

"That I haven't forgotten." He glanced at Rooster before turning his attention to Olivia's secret-service lead agent. He'd met him numerous times at their weekly meetings at the White House, and tonight something was off about him.

"Anything wrong?" Rooster said loud enough for Drew to turn around.

"We need to review what I got before anyone leaves this room," he said, trying not to raise an alarm.

"What?" Drew asked, but Jonas looked to his second, Erin Mosley, who'd joined them. Erin was one of the only people present not dressed for a cookout.

Before he could answer, Olivia's lead secret serviceman moved to reach for his weapon, and Jonas yelled, "Gun."

Erin was quick on the draw, and Agent Lainey Willcott tackled Olivia and Eva to the ground, covering both women as best she could. When the excitement died down, the lead agent was screaming in pain as he held what was left of his right hand between his legs. Erin had stopped him before he assassinated the new president a few minutes after she was sworn in, but she chose not to kill him. Dead men couldn't answer questions.

"What kind of hell is this?" Jonas asked.

"You okay back there?" Berkley asked after she and Aidan had flown for an hour in silence.

"Yes. I'm enjoying the ride. Will you still take me flying when you're working for your grandfather?" Aidan's voice sounded mellow, but Berkley didn't blame her for relaxing before they entered the storm of crap they were headed toward.

"Papa doesn't own anything this fast, but slow is good too." Aidan laughed at that, and she smiled at how the words could be interpreted.

"Yes, slow is nice, but hopefully you won't get bored with that."

"Don't worry about that, Captain, and prepare for landing. They're limiting air travel into the capital, so we might have to drive a bit."

"I'd offer to help, but you told me not to touch anything."

"I just didn't want you to eject yourself for a more dramatic landing than I had planned." She laughed before radioing the tower. "We'll talk later, so don't forget about me."

"That would take a severe blow to the head to accomplish, and even then it'd be impossible."

They landed, and an escort took them to the helicopter starting up close by. "Ma'am, Defense Secretary Orr said you're expected, so you've been cleared to land at the White House."

"Some more crap must've gone down," Aidan said, plucking at her flight suit.

Berkley smiled and nodded. "I'm sure Drew will take care of bringing us up to speed, and I'm guessing that's the only person we're meeting with. Don't worry. You look fine."

"If we're only meeting with Drew, we'd be going to the Pentagon." "He and everyone are probably locked in the Situation Room. With that mind trust, I doubt we'll have that big a part to play." They strapped in and stared at the crowds on the streets of the capital. Most of the people were holding candles, most likely for the magnitude of what had happened. "My God."

"Indeed, Commander Levine," the pilot said. "I think the number of people has doubled in size since our trip up here."

They put down on the lawn where Marine One usually landed with the president, and a group of Secret-Service agents surrounded them and walked them inside. Rooster was waiting at the door and pointed to an empty office once they'd made it through security. He had a garment bag for each of them, but he sat before handing them over.

"Drew asked me to come down and talk to you before you get sucked into all this."

Berkley nodded and sat. "How in the hell did this happen?"

"President Khalid's assassination is horrible, but right after President Michaels was sworn in, the head of her detail tried to kill her. For all the checks and precautions we've put in place, we obviously left a big hole right at the top."

"Jesus," Aidan said softly. "Why did you need us back?"

"I know we had something in place for you two once your leave was over, but Drew and the president have something else in mind, and he wanted me to soften you up a little." Rooster placed his hands flat on the table and appeared fatigued. "Drew had been Peter's roommate in college, and he believed in him. I'll leave it up to him to tell you what he wants, but think before you turn him and the president down. At times like this we need every true patriot the country has." He stood and handed over the bags. "I checked and had these put together from the information in your files."

"Thank you, Commander," Berkley said to Rooster, saluting him before he stepped away.

"I'll be outside when you're ready."

Their dress whites had the correct rank and all their commendations, and they put them on silently. Once Berkley had her shoes on, she held her hand out to Aidan. "No matter what, we do this together."

"You know it. I love you."

Rooster and a few agents escorted them upstairs, which meant they weren't going to the Situation Room they were familiar with. Aidan briefly glanced her way and hiked her eyebrows but didn't say anything. They made it down a hallway bustling with people and were asked to wait.

"Captain Sullivan and Commander Levine, if you'll follow me. The president will see you now," an older woman said, leading them to the door, with Rooster right behind them.

The Oval Office was crowded, but Berkley's eyes fell on Eva Khalid and her children. The act had been beyond cruel and had to have been burned into their memories forever. "Ma'am." Berkley bent down and offered the first lady her hand. "My sincerest condolences on your loss. Your husband was one of the greatest men I've ever had the pleasure of meeting, and it was an honor to serve under his leadership."

"Are you Commander Levine?" Eva asked, and her youngest daughter placed her hand over theirs.

"Yes, ma'am. Captain Sullivan and I were on the *Jefferson*'s maiden voyage, and I appreciated his confidence in us." As the room went quiet, Berkley heard the click of cameras, but this wasn't about a photo op or publicity. "He'll truly be missed, but he opened plenty of doors for the women who'll come behind us. I think he always had his girls in mind and wanted to throw open any previously forbidden places for them."

"Thank you both for your service, and thank you for what you just said. Peter spoke about you both and what you did to carry out your mission. He was so proud."

"Thank you, ma'am," Aidan said, and Eva stood once they were done.

"I'll leave you to it, and remember your faith in him when you're called to duty again. My husband deserves justice," Eva said, but her eyes were on Olivia.

The photographers got a few more pictures, and the room was cleared after Eva and Olivia embraced. It was getting late, but everyone left appearing wired. "Aidan," Olivia said waving to the sofa, "and Berkley. We have got plenty of meetings still to come, but if I could have a few minutes."

Drew and Rooster sat opposite them but didn't say anything. "Whatever you need, ma'am, we'll gladly do," Berkley said.

"Peter was killed tonight, and the head of my security detail tried to murder me right after I took the oath of office. This has gotten way out of control, and it's time to go on the offense," Olivia said, pressing her hands together.

"We need to flush out Chandler and as many of his followers as possible and eliminate the threat," Drew said. "We think, with some incentive, we can do that."

"What incentive?" Aidan asked.

"I'd think that would require bait, Captain," Berkley said.

"You'll be on a heavily armed ship with plenty of soldiers on board, Commander," Olivia said and finally smiled.

"If we're talking the *Jefferson* we're ready to go, ma'am," Aidan said.

"I am asking you to return to sea and participate in some military exercises with Great Britain and South Korea. No one can effectively disappear as well as Chandler has unless he's somewhere we can't readily see with repositioning satellites, and even then, it's not guaranteed." Olivia's smile widened, as if Berkley figured the president didn't sense this would be a hard sell to get them to go back to sea. "New Horizons seems to have a certain set of rules when it comes to where and when women should serve, so he might want to come out and play if you two go back to your regular posts."

"We'll gladly go where you send us, ma'am," Aidan said.

"Thank you, and I'm sorry Peter isn't here to give you his gift, Commander," Olivia said and walked to her desk. "It's my honor, though, to have this be my first official act as president. For your outstanding heroism in the face of getting shot down behind enemy lines and carrying your partner out, I award you the Navy Cross," Olivia said as she opened the box and pinned the medal on Berkley's chest.

"Thank you, ma'am," Berkley said, coming to attention and saluting. "I appreciate the honor and wish I could share it with my team."

"Don't worry about that. I'll take care of it, and I won't forget Lieutenant Whittle, but I've got one more thing." She opened another smaller box and held it up to Berkley. "Let me be the first to congratulate you, Captain Levine. This is so very well deserved."

Berkley saluted again and smiled. She hadn't been looking for a promotion, but this would make her relationship with Aidan so much easier unless Olivia produced another box with a promotion for Aidan. "Thank you, ma'am."

"Gentlemen," Olivia said to Drew and Rooster, "will you excuse us a minute? I'd like to speak to Berkley and Aidan privately." Olivia invited them to sit again and released a long breath. "It may seem I'm putting you out there for one or more of these fools following Chandler to take another shot at you."

"Ma'am, Berkley and I will gladly go back to sea and carry out any orders you have. It was our privilege to serve President Khalid, and we are forever grateful for his belief in us." Aidan spoke with the heart of someone who believed in what she was saying. "Serving you, though, will be the greatest honor of my life. I know plenty of little girls and women out there have waited for someone like you to ascend to the presidency, and our time has come."

"What she said, Madam President," Berkley said, and Olivia laughed. "Congratulations again, and we've got your back."

"You're my recruiting poster for strong, capable women in uniform, and Corbin is a great friend of Gabriel," Olivia said of Berkley's father and her husband. "I don't know how often they speak, but he reached out to Gabriel when you were reported MIA."

"I know they were in school together for a couple of years, but he never mentioned it."

"That's probably because Corbin never asked anything of Gabriel since he had faith in you. As long as you were breathing, he knew you'd make it out."

"Thank you for sharing that, ma'am," Berkley said.

"I'll deny this next part, so it'll never leave this room," Olivia said with a warm smile. "Congratulations on what most probably means more to you both than the medals and promotions. If I have to sail you into danger, it's good to know you have each other."

"We appreciate that, ma'am, but how did you know?" Aidan asked, and Berkley almost choked.

"That's a beautiful ring, Captain. Triton will hopefully be joining my group of advisors, and he's a proud dad who couldn't keep this secret. He also knew, as a parent myself, I'd be happy for you both. I'll also be happy to dance at your wedding since I'll take up Peter's baton to change our more-than-archaic military rules. For now, though, know I'm thrilled for you, even if I won't declare it publicly." Olivia stood and slapped her hands together. "Aidan, do you think you can change out Berkley's rank insignias? I'd like you both to stand with me at the press conference."

"I'll be happy to." Aidan took the box from her, and the secretary led them to another empty office for some privacy. "Congratulations, my love," Aidan said putting her arms around Berkley. "I'm so proud of you."

"I love you so much, and I'm glad you were here for this. We might have the sweetest role in the upcoming days, getting away from all this palace intrigue." Berkley kissed Aidan before sitting so Aidan could reach her shoulders. "You ready to take me sailing, Captain?"

"Past ready."

❖

Speaker of the House Chase Bonner flipped through the various news channels, but so far not one talking head could confirm anything besides that the grounds of the White House had been cleared, and there might've been an attempt on the president's life. Homer Lapry had joined his family for their fourth festivities, and the retired general had plenty to report from his recent meeting with Dick Chandler.

"He said to be ready for something big, but I wasn't expecting this. You think they could've really taken that piece of shit down?" Homer asked, holding his glass like he needed the comfort of the whiskey inside it.

"It hasn't been safe for me to contact him, so tell me again what he said verbatim." Chase was holding on to the speaker's position by a thin margin, and things were starting to swing back Khalid's way, especially after Chandler's open revolt. Nothing scared voters more than violence in their streets.

"He wanted an update on what was really going on here as far as recruitment goes, and if anyone suspected where he was. I told him everything you told me to, and he finished with the something big." Homer took a large gulp of his drink, and Chase was disgusted at how he was slurring his words.

"We'll have to wait and see then," Chase said, glancing at his watch. It'd been three hours since they'd reported an occurrence at the White House, and his phone hadn't rung. "Excuse me a moment."

"I'll holler if anything new comes on." Homer got up to pour himself more whiskey.

"Anything?" Chase asked his assistant, Ron Bollinger, when he answered.

"The press was allowed in, but Director Chapman has them locked down, from what I heard. Whatever happened has been contained until a statement is issued. Do you want me to call and give them a quote about how the people need to know?"

"Give it another thirty minutes, and I'll give you something. Get over here and bring the guys with you. I might need help getting this asshole Homer Lapry back into his car if he drinks any more of my liquor."

"Yes, sir, and I'd like to be the first to congratulate you, even if it is premature."

"Save the champagne for later."

"Ma'am, are you ready?" Peter Khalid's secretary, Judy Harper, asked as Olivia stood at the door of the spot where Peter had liked to give press conferences.

Aidan and Berkley stood with the rest of the group that had been present in the Situation Room while every relevant security person recapped what they knew so far. Thanks to Secret Service Agent Lainey Willcott, their best viable witness was in surgery to repair his hand and be checked for devices some of the New Horizon guys had used to take their own lives if caught.

"I'm ready," Olivia said, having changed into a business suit for the first time she addressed the nation as president.

"We're with you, Madam President," Drew said, and Olivia nodded.

"Good evening, ladies, gentleman, and my fellow Americans," Olivia said, and the cameras started in earnest. "It is with deep regret and sorrow that I report to you that at seven forty-six this evening, President Peter Khalid was assassinated in front of his family, friends, and colleagues. The Secret Service did an excellent job keeping Eva Khalid and her daughters safe, as well as everyone else."

Olivia placed her hands on the podium and stared right into the cameras. "An hour later Chief Justice Morgan swore me into office, and immediately following that, the head of my secret-service detail tried to assassinate me in the Oval Office."

Berkley was sure the press, along with everyone at home, was shocked into silence. The events of the day would most probably go down as the most bizarre in their history, but right now all she could think of was the months to come. She and Aidan deserved a life, and this situation could take years to resolve. They needed to have a long conversation later.

"The rogue militia group calling itself New Horizons has made its intentions clear. They have declared war on our way of life, our beliefs, and our independence. I vow to continue Peter's work and also to root out everyone responsible for today. This atrocity will not be allowed to stand." Olivia spoke those words firmly, emphasizing them by bringing her fist down on the podium. "I ask you all to pray for Eva Khalid and her daughters, so they may heal from this horrible event, and pray for our nation to come together. Thank you, and I'll take questions."

"Madam President." A political correspondent from NBC started first. "Can you confirm the rumor that Dick Chandler is spearheading New Horizons?"

"Mr. Chandler's home, as you know, exploded a year ago, killing the former FBI Director and four of his men. From that day Chandler, his wife, and his three children have not been seen, and we can confirm that they were not in the house at the time of the explosion." Olivia answered each question, taking over an hour with the media. It was as if she wanted to show she had nothing to hide, and Berkley thought it was a good move. She hadn't come right out and accused Chandler, but she hadn't provided him or anyone working for him any cover. "Thank you, everyone, and I give the American people my word I'll work hard on their behalf to find every single person responsible for this tragedy."

"Get some sleep, people, and be ready to go in the morning," Olivia said as her husband and son joined her. "We'll be returning to our residence until Eva's ready to move. Make sure everyone knows she's not to be rushed."

"Yes, ma'am," Judy Harper said. "Like I said, I'll stay on until your staff is up to speed, but if you want your own team, I'll understand."

"Judy, you're not going anywhere," Olivia said before returning to the Oval Office.

Everyone was probably thinking the same thing, since a new administration always meant new staff, but it was too late to worry about anything that night. Berkley and Aidan accepted a ride to Aidan's apartment from one of the FBI agents since they were both mentally and physically exhausted. The closing of the door was the best sound Berkley had experienced since they'd left her family behind.

"I'm so proud of you, baby," Aidan said, touching the Navy Cross. "You deserve this, and I guess I can't order you around anymore."

"You can order me around whenever you like, especially if you order me to strip and lie down."

CHAPTER SIX

Berkley and Aidan attended meetings in DC for the next four days as the *Jefferson* made its way back to Annapolis under Commander Devin Clark's command. The man who'd helped Aidan take their known saboteurs into custody when Berkley was trying to make her way out of North Korea had spoken to Aidan numerous times that week, and was ready to turn over command to her and return to his post as the ship's head security officer.

"Where are you headed off to in this crisp uniform?" Aidan asked Berkley when she joined her in the kitchen in a robe. Berkley had dressed while Aidan showered and was on her second cup of coffee. "You're too good-looking for words, Captain."

"You can salute me later," Berkley said, handing her cup over. They hadn't gotten back to Aidan's apartment until two that morning, so they'd slept longer than usual. "But I'm off to do a favor for Drew and the Defense Department this morning."

"Where are you going?"

"CIA Director Newton and his spooks have hit a dead end with Captain Umeko, and they wanted me to visit her this morning. Director Newton was pretty insistent that I try to get her talking."

The beautiful Jin Umeko was the pilot who'd shot Berkley and Harvey out of the sky after they'd destroyed the nuclear site that had been their target. Jin had never, according to the CIA and FBI reports, given them any information aside from her name and rank but surprisingly had added one name. For some reason it seemed important to her that they know Minseo Umeko had been her mother.

The crew of the *Jefferson* had captured Jin, along with Kim Jong Il's main enforcer, Lowe Nam Chil. Jin had never revealed why Lowe had been in the plane when Jin tried to stop Berkley's second escape, but she had told Berkley who the short, fat man was. Since those first cordial conversations, Berkley hadn't seen Jin but knew she was placed in a safe house in Arlington, Virginia under guard.

"What do they expect out of you?" Aidan said, putting the cup down slowly and suddenly not appearing happy.

"They want to see if she'll open up to someone familiar and thought it was worth a try before I sail away with you, cute stuff." She tugged Aidan forward by the tie of her robe and put her arms around her. "I'm sure it'll be like our too-short talks where she was nice but didn't give up anything."

"My parents are due back tonight," Aidan said and kissed her in the vee her shirt made. "Daddy accepted the president's offer of an advisory position, which means they'll be in DC for the foreseeable future. If you're not too late, maybe we can take them to dinner and celebrate your promotion and shiny new medal."

"Sweetheart, it's nine thirty." She tapped her watch. "I'm sure I'll be back way before dinner."

"Don't discount your charm, baby." Aidan lifted her head, and Berkley took the move as an invitation to kiss her, so she did. "But hopefully Captain Umeko found some happiness. She seemed so sad when we took her on board, and I don't think it was because of being shot down."

"In my opinion, she gave up instead of being shot down. She's a good pilot, from what little I saw, which means she bailed deliberately." Berkley kissed Aidan one more time before picking up her cup and keys.

"Try to figure that out, but hurry back. We've got two days off coming up, and I have plans for you."

Berkley saluted and waited until she heard Aidan lock the door behind her. She was making the trip for official reasons, but she really was curious as to why Jin Umeko had dropped into their lives. She sensed a story there that seemed more important than national security and wanted to hear it.

The safe house was located in the type of neighborhood that had plenty of space between the grand homes, and security details weren't an uncommon sight. It was a beautiful hilly area with plenty of mature trees that hid the houses from view. She hoped Jin had been here for the fall foliage and that it'd brought some joy into what her life had become, because Aidan had been right. Jin was overwhelmingly sad and appeared like someone who'd given up on almost everything.

Berkley stopped at the guard shack and handed over her ID. "Captain Levine. I should be on the list. Director Newton cleared me."

"Please come in and park to the right, Captain. We'll take you up to the main house," the MP said as the massive gate swung open. Another security guy drove her in a golf cart to the house and escorted her out through the back to the pool area.

It was hard to fathom who exactly the CIA put here, but from the beautiful surroundings, the only incentive to talk and spill state secrets would be the threat of being sent somewhere else. Jin was sitting on a towel with her legs crossed and her eyes closed. She appeared to be meditating, so Berkley sat close by and waited for her to finish.

Jin stood almost as soon as Berkley sat down and studied the back of the house. "Good morning, Commander," Jin said, her English sounding much better. She might not be sharing secrets, but she must've been practicing by talking about something.

"Good morning, Captain, and it's a rank we now share. I feel like I should thank you since you might've had something to do with my promotion." Berkley stood and bowed slightly.

"You were shot from the sky because your man made a mistake. If not, I don't think you make an easy target, and congratulations." Someone came out with a tray and placed it on the table. Without asking, Jin started to prepare two cups of tea. "Have they sent you to loosen my tongue?"

If they'd met under any other circumstances, she and Jin might've become good friends, she thought as she accepted the cup. "I'm not sure what they have planned for you, but it'd make your life easier if you answered their questions. The way you went down makes me think you weren't that loyal to your supreme leader, and I went down because the man on my wing betrayed me and his country."

"No one has ever said that to me—the part about me going down." Jin sat with her legs folded under her holding her cup in both hands.

"No one here has ever seen you fly, and they're perhaps not interested in why you were there with Lowe Nam Chil, aside from your job as a pilot. I'd bet that story is the more interesting, since I doubt you know enough to bring down the Kim regime. He, on the other hand, probably does."

"Chil ejected us, but you are what I believe you Americans call a breed different."

"The expression is a breed apart, but very good. Being like everyone else in all things is boring, and the answers are found where no one else is looking. Will you tell me the story?"

"And what will knowing that get you, Captain?" Jin asked, but with a smile.

"I have everything I need to be happy, and you can believe me or not, but I'd like the same for you. Obviously, you won't get that in North Korea, but why not give yourself the chance to start over?"

"All right," Jin said and inhaled deeply before taking a sip of tea. "My father was a security commander and general in Kim's army. Because of what happened I would think he was fed to Kim's dogs, but we all sometimes get what we deserve. He and I were not close, since he abandoned me and my mother for glory in Kim's world." Jin sounded distant, as if she were talking about someone other than herself.

"Did he force you into the military?"

"I had no other options once I was old enough, and I went at my mother's urging. My father was a powerful man, and because he held no love for me, he could make our lives bad if I had refused." Jin took a sip of tea and shivered even though it was warm outside. "He pushed me until I became a pilot but reminded me constantly that I would never rise to his expectations. I tried for years in honor of my mother, but she became ill and died when you came into my life."

"I'm sorry, Captain." Berkley put her cup down and pressed her hands together. "I had no idea, and I am sorry for your loss. It sounds like you were close and that you loved her very much."

"I did, and you and your team hitting the targets maybe cost me my grandparents. The day I was shot down was the day I gave up. I was ready to join them in peace."

"I'm sure saying that I was only carrying out orders won't get me your forgiveness."

Jin smiled again and shook her head. "I only meant you arrived a day too early. I planned to return to be with my mother in her final moments and then try to flee with my grandparents. The bombing of the facility I had been charged with trying to protect gave me no choice but to take to the air and fight back."

"I wish things had turned out differently for you, but I'm sure you'll never forget them. Maybe with time you'll find something or someone to live for. To live a good and happy life will honor your family more than giving in to despair, especially now that you have a chance. From what I understand, Chil is not a good man, but we all owe him for saving you both."

"Like you say, though, your people want something from me. All these pretty things will not last."

"I'm not here to force you to talk if you don't want to, but why remain so loyal to people who took so much from you?"

Jin stared at her, and Berkley could almost see her mentally struggling to decide how much to share. "I think my silence will grant someone I love a few more months of life. Maybe not a life she wants or had with me, but another day to see the sun and breathe."

"What's her name?" Berkley asked, smiling.

"You are not disgusted?"

"Love is what's important, Captain, not the packaging it comes wrapped in," she said, and Jin finally smiled.

"Yong Nam is who I flew with and who I shared my life with. I cared about her, but not enough, and my attention to her cost her too much."

"Thank you for telling me, and Yong probably doesn't see it that way." Jin hesitated, then nodded. "I wanted to come tell you I might not see you for a while. I'm going back out to sea."

"Will you go back to Korea?"

"I don't know, but I'll be gone pretty soon, and I didn't want you to think I'd forgotten about you. Know that I wish you well."

Jin lowered her feet to the ground and put her teacup down as well. "Has Lowe Nam Chil broken?"

"He's not anywhere this nice, but I don't believe so. I'm not far enough up the chain to know all the secrets."

"Your people need to place him under the fear and pain he inflicted on so many. He is an animal but a cowardly one. He is the one with a head full of secrets, and the ones he is going to say he has forgotten are in his home. Supreme Leader Kim trusted him with everything."

Berkley thought whoever was listening in must've been enjoying this more than the weather Jin usually talked about. "I'll let them know. Thank you."

"Tell them I cannot share unless I know why they are asking. I do not know as much, but if I know the problem, I can maybe help."

"I'll tell them that too." Berkley stood and bowed again. "Take care, and I'll see you when I come back. Remember, the best way to honor your mother is to find happiness."

"Be well, Captain, and good flying. I miss the cockpit and my family the most. I loved to fly."

"Thank you, and I look forward to speaking with you again."

"May I ask a favor?" Jin stood with her hands pressed together.

"Sure—yes."

"If your government sends you back to Korea, come back before you go. Bring your important people to talk as well."

"Thank you, and I will."

"I will not forget what you said about my family, and instead of love I might live for vengeance. I have known loss, and many must feel the same."

She nodded and held her hand out. "There's no rule you can't have both."

Jin took her hand and cocked her head to the side. "What do you mean?"

"The best vengeance is to be happy. When you are, you break your chains, so don't be afraid to fly again."

"Thank you for the chance, ma'am," Lieutenant Nova Brown said as she walked the *Jefferson*'s deck with Aidan.

The ship had been moored the night before, and Devin had called her that morning. He'd joked that he was ecstatic to be turning over the proverbial keys to her again. Nova had graduated from the Academy the year before and had passed every security screening both she and Berkley had thought of. The young woman was eager to serve, and after a couple of hours of walking the ship, Aidan liked her.

She needed a second but was gun-shy after Erika Gibson's betrayal. Erika had been with her for a few years, and it wasn't until Berkley had come aboard and back into her life that Erika showed her true self. That Erika had helped the people on board who were trying to sabotage her and the mission, and kill Berkley, had made her not care what happened to the woman.

"I'm glad you accepted, and we'll be busy making sure we have everything in working order before we ship out. Did every team leader give you a list?" Having the *Jefferson*'s metal under her feet made her feel great. Deployment would cut into her nights with Berkley, but Berkley was inventive when motivated, so she didn't expect to spend many lonely nights.

"Yes, ma'am. All our repairs will begin today, and the flight team will be here tomorrow with Commander Levine." Nova seemed to be reading a list from the folio in her hand, but Aidan didn't mind thoroughness. "I hope you don't mind that I set the meeting up without asking."

"It's Captain Levine now, and I'm sure she'll appreciate it." They stopped at one of the open doors that raised the jets to the deck for takeoff. A team seemed to be doing maintenance on all the jets, and she blinked a few times from the sudden jab of fear that someone not loyal to her or Berkley would do something to knock Berkley from the sky.

"Your quarters are ready if you'd like to inspect them." That seemed to be the next item on Nova's list, and Aidan was coming to like her efficiency. This time around she didn't plan to let her guard down like she had with Erika.

Wherever they'd shipped her old assistant, she took a moment to hope it was unpleasant. That Erika would contemplate hurting Berkley as a way to Aidan's heart still made the rage rise faster than she could control it.

"Are you okay, ma'am?"

"Sorry. Bad memories from the last time I was aboard. Let's go." They started for the closest door and heard the shouting when they were twenty feet from it.

Her security officer Devin was running toward them, and from his expression, this was no exercise. The intercom came on, and someone on the bridge was ordering people to stop or they would be fired upon. A hail of gunfire broke the calmness of the morning, hitting various spots on the deck as Aidan thought about going up the outer stairs to the bridge.

"Follow me, ma'am," Nova said, and Devin followed them with a gun at the ready. It was official—the world had lost its mind. That a US naval carrier would be fired upon in the middle of the naval academy meant Chandler had taken the shackles off his followers. Another round of bullets hit things around them, and Nova went down as if she'd tripped.

"Come on." She reached down to help Nova up, but the young woman wasn't moving. "Jesus Christ," she said, but Nova was gone, her eyes still open but unfocused.

"You need to get inside," Devin said, grabbing Nova's collar and dragging her with them as more bullets hit around them. "Three small crew boats coming this way with what appears to be cadets onboard, and they're using live rounds." Devin stopped to listen to something from his earpiece. "They're readying SMAWS, ma'am. I think they intend to fire on us."

If they had enough shoulder-launched assault weapons and aimed for a specific spot, they'd breach the hull, and Aidan wouldn't allow that. She grabbed Devin's radio. "This is Captain Sullivan. If they don't turn away, fire at will. Try not to kill everyone, but do not let them fire upon us."

"Yes, ma'am," the bridge answered, and almost instantly their surface weapons came to life. Aidan placed her hand on Nova's forehead momentarily, then pushed Devin out of the way and ran through the ship, headed for the bridge. "Report," she yelled back to him.

"Two sunk and the third has turned back."

"Get coast guard out there and put boats in the water. I want these bastards," she said as she took the stairs two at a time. Her people were already in the water, but at first glance the bodies floating were all dead.

"Please stay here, ma'am," Devin said, saluting. "I'll report once I get down there."

"They weren't naval craft, ma'am, but the men on board appeared to be naval cadets from the academy," the senior officer who'd been in charge said. "We fired when they didn't heed our order to stop. They got one SMAW off, but it hit the dock."

"You did everything by the book, Lieutenant. Start a watch as of now, and tell everyone on the ship if anyone else is about to launch any other SMAW, I'm holding them personally responsible for any damage. Do not let anyone fire on us." Her phone rang, so the officer went to carry out her orders. "Hey," she said, moving outside for more privacy.

"Want me to swing by and pick you up?" Berkley asked, and the sound of her voice calmed her.

"I'll probably be a while. Someone fired on us just now and killed my new second. She was a sweet kid and was hit as we ran for cover."

"What? Wait there. I'm coming." She knew Berkley didn't think she needed saving, but backup didn't hurt, and she was glad Berkley was on her way. "What the hell?" Berkley asked, but it sounded as if she was reacting to something on her end.

"What?" she asked, then heard gunfire, and it sounded like Berkley sped up. A crash followed, then nothing. After seeing Nova die in front of her, she didn't need any more bad news. "Berkley? Berkley, answer me." She heard nothing from the other end, and that's what her life would be filled with if something happened to Berkley.

Nothing.

CHAPTER SEVEN

Berkley figured she had time to pick up Aidan, as well as check in with her crew if any of the guys were still on board. They had dinner reservations with the Sullivans that night, but that was hours off. She was four miles from the interstate and was enjoying the wooded area as she called Aidan.

Aidan sounded out of breath when she answered, and the reality that someone would dare attack one of their ships on American soil was game-changing. But this was the second time Chandler had tried to take the *Jefferson* down. His first attempt had ended with the downing of all the jets that'd attacked them off the West Coast after their North Korean mission, the squad leader being David Morris's little brother, Travis.

Morris was in custody for his part in getting her shot down in North Korea, and their father Adam had killed himself after Drew had taken him in. The whole Morris family had bought into Chandler's delusions of a new United States, with him as supreme leader for life, which made her wonder if any other Morris sons were lying in wait.

Two black vehicles pulled out and blocked the road, making the top of her head tingle in anticipation, so she stayed in the car and waited. "What the hell?" The words left her mouth when the back doors opened, and the men started shooting.

Berkley put the car in reverse and floored it, slamming the brakes to spin it around, but the third vehicle she hadn't seen slammed into her, pushing her car into a tree. She'd dropped her phone, and the airbag deploying had slammed her head back and to the side. The blow had caused instant pain, but it only lasted a second.

People were shouting, but they seemed so far away as Berkley tried to swim to the surface of the blackness she'd fallen into. With Herculean effort she opened her eyes and saw a familiar face, but she couldn't place it. The woman smiled at her before hitting the side of her head with the butt of her gun.

"Get her out of there, and make it fast," Rachel Chandler said to the two men standing closest to her. "I don't want to mess with the rent-a-cops this area is so fond of."

"Yes, ma'am," the man said, already lifting Berkley out and dragging her to the road.

"Burn the car, and the one we wrecked. Don't leave anything behind."

Rachel could hear the sirens in the distance, which meant the gunfire had been reported. Berkley Levine wasn't so hard to bring in with the right strategy. If her brother Jeffery had completed his assignment, then Michaels's plan to outsmart her father would fail as quickly as her presidency.

She heard the slam of the hatch on one of the vehicles, so she signaled everyone to move out. Her phone was still silent, and she was anxious to know about Jeffery. He was the only one in the family who'd needed considerable persuasion to join their cause, but that had stemmed from his reluctance to leave his marine brothers behind. "Make sure that Korean bitch doesn't talk to anyone," she said into the phone once their contact in the White House answered. "I doubt she knows anything useful, but it's no time to take any chances."

"I know what my job is," the deep voice said in a whisper. "Worry about your end of this."

"Nothing from my brother?" Rachel asked her assistant Vander Lever after disconnecting the call.

"No, ma'am." Vander combed his blond hair back and retrieved his phone. "I'll call our lookout and ask for an update."

The call was short, and her hands curled to fists when Vander exhaled. "What?"

"All three of our vessels were hit, and Sullivan's got boats in the water."

She cursed softly. "Survivors?"

"According to our contact, more than half. The countermeasures weren't deployed."

She touched the device in her forearm that would guarantee none of them would divulge anything if captured. Above all else the fight had to continue, her father had repeated over and over. Adam Morris and Jerry Teague had taken that lesson to heart and willingly carried all their secrets to the grave.

"We need to know where they're being held." The need to hit something was making Rachel twitch obviously enough for Vander to slightly tilt away from her. "Can I trust you to deal with Levine?"

"The plane's ready, and we've been cleared. All I need to do is get there."

"Take off—"

"Excuse me, ma'am," Vander said, putting his hand up tentatively as if he feared the interruption. "That's the only plane we have available at the moment to get you out of here. Whatever you need, ask, and I'll do it so you can deliver Commander Levine."

"Your job is to follow orders." She slapped him hard enough to make her hand sting, but he sat still as if he'd put up with fifty more. "I'm sure I can figure out how not to get caught and find my way back."

"Yes, ma'am."

She'd learned how to lead from her father, but it irritated her that men like Vander still saw only a woman who needed taking care of when they looked at her. "Try to concentrate on what you have to do, and stop worrying about me."

"It's my job to worry about you, ma'am."

She ignored him, knowing why her father had placed Vander with her, and why Vander was so eager to be by her side. Vander wanted the power that would come from an advantageous marriage, and if that was what he was waiting for, death would come first.

She didn't want to do it, but she called Jeffery. The call went to voice mail, and sweat broke out along her forehead. She'd told her brother to be in the boat that struck last. Their first two were dispensable, but they should've gotten off some shots. Once the *Jefferson* was crippled, Jeffery could take the credit for the killing blow.

"I gave you an order," she said to Vander. "Stop the car."

She got out and climbed into the car behind them. "Where to?" the driver asked.

"Get me as close as you can." She checked her phone again for breaking news. "If we can get him out of there, we will."

Aidan tried calling Berkley again for the fifth time, and again it went straight to voice mail. The gunshots weren't her imagination, and she was about to peel her skin off if she didn't hear Berkley's voice. Devin didn't let her stew too long and touched her forearm.

"What's wrong?" he asked, walking her away from the others.

"Berkley called, but it sounded like someone was shooting at her. Now she's not answering." Saying it out loud brought very real and acute pain to her chest. "My god, do you think this was a coordinated attack? She was out there alone."

"Where was she when she called?" Devin asked.

"She went to a safe house in Arlington and was on her way back." Aidan tried the number again and brought her hand up to her chest. Berkley's ring was on the chain Berkley had given her, and taking it off had been difficult, but Berkley had kissed her ring finger and placed the chain around her neck. "If whoever these bastards are knew that, she could be dead."

Devin tightened his hold on her and shook his head. "Don't think that."

Aidan called Drew's office and requested the guards at the safe house go out and check. One of Drew's assistants placed her on hold, and Drew came on a few minutes later. "Aidan, we're on top of this, but Berkley was ambushed leaving the safe house. They found her car and another vehicle burning, but no bodies. It's my strong opinion that she's still alive, so don't think otherwise."

"How did this happen? Between here and where she was, explain to me how. It was a coordinated hit meant to take us both out."

"I understand that and have NCIS on the interstate looking in every direction. We also shut down every small airport within a two-hundred-mile radius." Drew sighed, and she hoped it wasn't a sign of defeat. "The gunshots were close enough for quick action, and that narrows where they can go."

"Find her, because Corbin Levine will not understand if you don't, and neither will I."

"Concentrate on the *Jefferson*, and let me worry about Berkley."

"Devin, make sure all the prisoners are searched before they're brought on board, and separate them once they are. Let's see who they are before the government alphabet gets ahold of them. I'm going to assess the damage, but notify me once you have them rounded up."

"I'll have someone take care of that, and you go inside." Devin put his hand up before she could protest. "Remember, there's a sniper out there who's already brought down a high-value target. Let's not give them another chance."

"I'll be on the bridge. Don't keep me waiting long." *That goes for you too, Berkley. Don't you dare keep me waiting.*

❖

Berkley came to in a moving vehicle with her face pressed against the carpet of what she guessed was the cargo area. The lessons she'd learned early on of never getting in the car made her want to laugh now, since the police officer they'd sent to her high school was probably right. Whatever happened next would make her wish she'd been shot.

"Slow down before you get us pulled over." The man who'd said that didn't sound familiar, and she didn't want to invite any other gun butts to the face by raising her head to see if she recognized him. It was more important to get out of here than to start asking questions.

"It's the interstate, Vander," another man said, sounding annoyed. "I'll get pulled over if I slow down, so take your pissy mood out on someone else. You should be used to Rachel trying to ditch you."

"Shut the fuck up and drive."

Vander and his buddies had zip-tied her hands and feet, so that was the first thing to undo. If they were on the interstate, she still had a chance to get away in a crowd of cars. Berkley rolled to her back and lifted her hips to bring her hands forward. Once they were in position, she brought her hands over her head and down fast and hard away from each other, breaking the tie. That training had come much later, and she was thrilled it worked.

After she used the small pocketknife in her pocket, her feet were free. For kidnappers, these guys weren't professionals. Unless Vander was sitting next to someone short enough not to be seen over the seat, he was alone in the second row, and after a deep breath she moved. She grabbed him by the head and twisted until she felt a snap before sliding over the seat and grabbing the driver.

The guy in the passenger side turned and tried to get her hands off the driver, but letting go wasn't an option, so she continued to pull no matter how many times the guy punched her. Everything stopped when they hit two cars before crashing into the concrete highway divider. The passenger-side guy flew out the windshield since he'd unbuckled himself to attack her, and the driver seemed dazed from the airbag deployment.

He was pawing at his side, so Berkley twisted harder before she got shot, and finally the same snapping sensation happened, and the guy went limp. "Shit." She reached down and tugged the driver's weapon free in case there was more than one vehicle. This time it wouldn't be so easy.

She checked all sides before opening the door and asking one of the motorists who'd stopped to call the police. Her phone was gone, but the woman who said she was a nurse handed hers over and went to get her first-aid kit for the cuts to her face. In all the excitement and remembering how her call to Aidan had ended, she wanted to call her back.

"It's a long story, but I'm okay now." The gunfire started again as soon as she'd spoken, from the SUV that'd stopped in the middle lane. The woman who'd helped her lay dead ten feet away, which made Berkley angry. It was the kind of anger that made her want to break some more necks, but all she could do for now was take cover and fire back.

The sirens must've spooked the second vehicle's occupants, since the windows went up and they sped off. "Aidan, sorry to scare you, but it's been a hell of a day. We need our people down here to investigate this."

"NCIS should be on scene shortly, and I want you here as soon as they release you. I mean it, Berkley. Don't hang around trying to get information."

"Yes, ma'am." She placed the phone with the woman who'd lent it to her, furious that the poor stranger had been killed for stopping to help someone in need. The police arrived first and secured the scene for the naval investigators, who arrived fifteen minutes later.

"If you want, we can take your statement at the *Jefferson*, Captain. We received a message from Captain Sullivan not to keep you out in the open too long," the woman agent said as her team searched the SUV.

"Thank you," she said, tucking the pistol she'd taken from one of her kidnappers into her pants.

"You can leave it," the woman said.

"I tell you what." Berkley put her hand on the weapon. "As soon as I'm aboard the carrier, you're welcome to it. Until then, I'm in no mood to go through that again." She pointed to the wreck.

The agent seemed hesitant but finally walked to the car and told her to get in, after informing her team where she was going. "Are you usually this distrustful?" the agent asked after weaving around enough cars to get going.

"If you knew what's happened to me in the last year, believe me, you wouldn't lead with that question. People in every branch of government are buying the bullshit Chandler is shoveling, and each one of them thinks killing me will merit a badge of honor."

"Maybe they believe he's right," the woman said. "Not about the killing-you part, but the rest of it."

"*Maybe*, but what he wants goes against everything I hold dear. That includes not being sidelined because of my gender. Think about that before you reach the point of no return if you're thinking about a new world order. Think fast, though, because if you make one wrong turn, I'm going to mess up the upholstery with your brains when I pull the trigger."

"You could die in the fiery crash that might cause."

"I survived one today, and I'm willing to gamble again." The answer made the woman smile, but Berkley didn't let her guard down.

"You've got nothing to fear from me. I've been up against that argument enough times in my career, and it's usually with some clueless guy who thinks I should be getting him coffee."

They arrived at the Academy, and Berkley directed her ride to the pier where the *Jefferson* was moored. The area was full of military police, but the woman's badge got them through the crowd. Berkley glanced up at the bridge, and Aidan appeared a few seconds later.

"I'll be happy to give you a statement, but I need like twenty minutes," Berkley said, and flagged down one of the ship's crew. "Escort this agent to the mess hall."

"Aye, Captain."

"I'll meet you there once I get cleaned up."

Berkley headed for her quarters, figuring Aidan wouldn't be far behind, and was glad when Aidan pressed up against her while she was washing the blood off her face. It was only now that the pain in her head from the blow, plus the pain in her entire body from the car accident, threatened to bring her to her knees.

"Cletus, you have to stop scaring the hell out of me," Aidan said.

"We should've stayed in bed today." She pressed a towel to her face before turning and putting her arms around Aidan.

"Do you think Jin Umeko had anything to do with this?" Aidan placed her hands on her chest and gazed up at her with a somber expression. "Could her and that Chil guy's capture have all been a setup?"

"Chil is in a cell at Gitmo, and Jin comes across as sincere." She kissed Aidan's forehead and took a deep breath to try to dispel her fear. That they could so easily be separated from each other scared her more than anything. "You doing okay?"

"We've got a few guys in the brig, and a lot more in the morgue. I'm not sure what they were trying to accomplish, but firing on a carrier wasn't the brightest move." Aidan caressed her cheek and Berkley kissed her. "Who's your friend?" Aidan asked of the woman who'd driven her back to the ship.

They went to the mess hall together, but Aidan was called away to deal with what had happened on the ship. Berkley gave her statement, and the agent provided her with a contact number and a promise she'd keep her informed of their progress. She sat back and closed her eyes for a minute to try to dull the pain in her head, and the thought of being at sea suddenly appealed to her. If anything, the carrier might be huge, but it narrowed the pool of people trying to kill them.

"Head down to sickbay and have the doc take a look at you," Aidan said softly. "I have to stay, and I'll feel better if he clears you. If he does, go take a nap."

"Yes, ma'am, but sound the alarm if you need to."

"Anyone else who fires on my ship will be in for a very bad surprise. Have the doctor call me if he finds anything."

"Okay, but have Devin put divers in the water. The ill-fated attack might be cover for someone trying to attach something to us."

"Tell him to rule out concussion, since your brain seems to be working fine. I've already ordered that measure, but it's nice that you're firing on all pins," Aidan said and smiled. "And remind me to kiss you later."

"That's the kind of orders I don't mind following."

Olivia took a moment before sitting down at her desk in the Oval Office. She'd agreed to be Peter's running mate after losing the historic primary election that would've placed either a woman or an African-American in the White House for the first time. It was a hard truth to accept, but after that initial meeting to join forces instead of fight each other, she had to admit she liked Peter a lot.

They shared the same values, beliefs, and ambition, and all those factors had laid the groundwork for a great working relationship. They'd planned to stay for eight years, followed by another eight with her in the White House and Peter at her side on the campaign trail, and beyond that in an advisory position. This outcome had never crossed their minds since they knew they faced opposition, every administration did, but not enough to kill over.

Peter's former assistant Judy, along with Olivia's assistant Maggie Junip, stood in front of the desk waiting, it seemed, to get started. "Don't forget to watch over us, Peter," Olivia said softly, and Judy nodded.

"Ma'am, I'll bring Maggie up to speed on everything, but my offer to leave stands," Judy said, her eyes appearing red and swollen from crying.

"I realize you've been with Peter since he got out of law school, and it might be tough working for someone new, but I do want you to stay." Olivia came around and took Judy's hand. "What happened will haunt all of us forever, and the coming months will be split between what is basically a civil war and running the country. I need your experience, but more importantly, I think you'd want to be here when we get these animals."

"Thank you, Madam President, and I'll be happy to stay."

"Good. Let's get started." Olivia took a deep breath and finally sat.

"The appointment you requested is waiting, and the Speaker phoned and asked if you had a moment," Judy said.

"Thank you, but not now when it comes to Bonner." Judy placed a folder in front of her and nodded. The sheet at the top that summarized the content came close to making her whistle. This many confirmed kills made the sniper almost mythical, but if she had learned one thing in politics, it was that military types never fudged when it came to stuff like this.

"Before you get started, Director Chapman also asked for a few minutes," Maggie said. "He wanted to brief you on a few things."

"If he goes over fifteen minutes, come back so I don't keep my guest waiting too long."

"Yes, ma'am," Maggie said, ushering Jonas in.

"Thank you for seeing me, ma'am. I wanted to come let you know before you hear it on the news, but your lead agent turned traitor killed himself in the hospital. Marcus Bonner went to interview him, and somehow he'd managed to inject a syringe full of air into his IV."

"Did he say anything to anyone before he died?" The thought of someone she'd known and spent so much time with and trusted with her safety being dead should've affected her more, but the man had tried to kill her. He'd been hired to protect her, and instead he'd tried to shoot her on the order of someone who was trying to tear the country apart.

"Not a word, and that's damned aggravating. According to Marcus he was dead when he went in, but the agent on the door said no one had gone in or out after he'd accompanied the nurse in fifteen minutes before. We need to know how someone got to him. If anything, it'll help us from letting it happen again."

"Thank you, and if you don't mind sticking around, I'll meet with you after I'm done with my next appointment."

"I'll be here, ma'am, and I'll let them know you're ready."

"General Carl Greenwald, ma'am," Judy said, ushering in a tall, handsome man with a thick head of white hair a few minutes later. With his tan it made him even more attractive.

"Madam President," Carl said with a warm smile and a deep voice. "My granddaughter is one jealous little girl today. Congratulations, ma'am."

Carl had been checked extensively by both the FBI and Secret Service before she was allowed to meet with him in private, but it was the first step in keeping her promises to Eva Khalid. "Thank you, General, and thank you for getting here so quickly. My apologies for keeping you waiting."

He waved the apology off and shook her hand. "I was waiting on your call, ma'am, after what happened. If someone we trained is responsible for this, I'll be deeply ashamed. It'll be a black eye to the program, but we'll do whatever it takes to eliminate the threat."

"How many people could have made that shot?" The branches of the military all had a Carl Greenwald, but Carl's special operations unit was the best by far. His recruits were the ones they sent in when a problem had to be eliminated without leaving a trace.

"Have they narrowed the position where the shot was taken from?" Carl crossed his legs and placed a binder he'd carried in on his knee.

"The FBI's working on it, but the preliminary report said it was quite a distance."

"Factoring in the time of day and distance, I narrowed it down to eight, but my top pick is a nonstarter." He stood and handed over the folder. The name at the top of his list matched the report Jonas had sent.

Major Wiley Gremillion, code-name Black Dragon, had more confirmed kills than anyone else on the list and had retired a few years before to her hometown of New Orleans. She lived with Aubrey Tarver and her daughter Tanith, and was now a professional artist. It was an interesting career choice for someone who'd spent years in a sniper's nest, but from every report, Wiley was successful at it.

"Why a nonstarter?" she asked.

"Wiley's father is career military, as was Aubrey's father, so they all believe in the code and honor of why we serve. Besides, it's hard to be two places at one time. Major Gremillion was in New Orleans with her family." Carl tugged his jacket down and lost his smile. "She's no more a traitor to her country than I am."

"Do you think she'd meet with me?" Olivia moved to the next name and their statistics.

"I'll contact her if you like. Would you like my team to recon the area and find the nest?"

"General, please don't be insulted by what I'm going to say, but I can't put my complete trust in too many people at the moment. From what's happened, we can assume Chandler has more than enough people in the military to continue to cause us problems." She looked him in the eye as she spoke and was glad when he nodded. "If you trust Major Gremillion, I'd like to talk to her and pick her brain."

"Good choice, ma'am."

"Thank you, General, and thank you for your loyal service. I need as many good guys as I can muster."

"Whatever you need, ma'am." Carl stood when she did and offered his hand. "I never thought I'd see a woman commander in chief in my lifetime, but I'm glad I have."

"Do you have your phone?" she asked and almost laughed when the older man shyly nodded. "Let's take a selfie, and you can send it to your granddaughter with an invitation to visit whenever she likes."

"That'll definitely up my cool-grandpa status."

"Ma'am, I hate to bother you, but we've got a situation," Maggie said, entering the office.

"Tell me," Olivia said, leaning against the desk when Maggie told her about the *Jefferson* and what had happened to Berkley. "It's like a waking nightmare."

"Yes, ma'am, and it's time we ended it," Carl said.

CHAPTER EIGHT

Y ou and Captain Levine made a good call," Commander Mike Dyer, Aidan's deck leader said a few hours later. "We found two devices that most probably wouldn't have sunk us, but they would've crippled us for at least a month."

"Has anyone spoken up?" Aidan asked as she squeezed the back of her neck. They were meeting in the conference room between her quarters and Berkley's, and considering the reports of her senior officers, it was amazing the *Jefferson* was still all in one piece. The realization of how close they'd come to real damage was giving her a headache.

"No, ma'am," Devin said. "The most vocal guy claims they're prisoners of war, and if we don't let them go—"

"It'll spell our doom," Berkley said, wiggling her fingers when she came in. Both her eyes were black, and a line of stitches went from her temple into her hairline, but she hadn't lost her sense of humor. "One of your guys down there told me he thinks he might recognize one of the prisoners, Devin."

"Who is it?" Aidan asked, thinking she'd have to call her parents, so they wouldn't worry and cancel their plans.

"Jeffery Chandler," Berkley said, and Aidan shook her head. "If he's right, we've got one of Dicky's kids in custody."

"Excuse me, everyone," Aidan said and stood. "I've got to make some phone calls if that's even possibly true." She stepped into her office and asked for a secure line to Drew. It took a few minutes to find him in the White House.

"Aidan, is everything under control?" Drew asked, and she could hear voices in the background. "I'm going to put you on speaker with the president and the Security Council."

"We've removed two explosive devices from our hull, recovered twenty-two bodies, and have another eighteen locked below deck. One of our crew believes one of the men captured is Jeffery Chandler, Dick Chandler's youngest child."

"Calvin." Olivia's voice came on next. She was addressing her national security advisor. "We need to know for sure, and if it is Jeffery, we need to drop him in a hole. If Chandler has any other loyalists at the Academy, they'll do whatever it takes to get him back."

"Between our people and Jonas's guys, we'll take care of it, ma'am," NSA Director Calvin Vaughn said.

"Naval Command and the coast guard are also setting up patrols to help secure the *Jefferson*," Drew said.

"Captain, you did an excellent job today, and you're free to fire at will if fired upon. It pains me to end American lives, but not at the expense of anyone on that ship," Olivia said.

"Yes, ma'am, thank you. I'd appreciate a heads-up if you plan to move any or all the prisoners, but I'd like them off my ship. They're responsible for one dead and a few injuries today."

"Trust me, they won't be there long. I want you to concentrate on what you have to do, and we'll take care of the rest," Olivia said. "How is Captain Levine?"

"She looks like she was kicked in the face by a mule, but she's okay. It's been a strange day for sure."

"Unfortunately, it most probably won't be the last one," Drew said. "I'll call as soon as we make arrangements."

"Thank you, and if possible, Captain Levine would like an update on what happened today. She'd also like to know if Captain Umeko is okay." Berkley actually hadn't asked for either thing, but she'd most probably want to know.

Aidan stepped back into the conference room and briefly glanced at Berkley. "Are they coming for these guys?" Devin asked.

"Eventually, so make sure our watches are up for the remainder of the day, and they'll continue until I say otherwise," Aidan said. "If anyone approaches you without radioing first, blow them from the water—don't take any chances."

"Yes, ma'am," everyone said and left, leaving her alone with Berkley.

"NSA and the FBI will coordinate getting these assholes off my boat, and I asked Drew to update us about the idiot who tried to take you, and about Jin Umeko."

"If she's a plant sent here to kill or undermine us, my instincts are way off," Berkley said, rubbing her temples. "What's this going to do to our schedule?"

"It might delay us for a few days, but I'm planning to sail as soon as we get the go-ahead. Not everyone on board might be loyal to us, but it at least narrows the field of misguided assholes." Aidan locked the door and put her arms around Berkley. She pressed her ear to Berkley's chest and listened to the steady and comforting beat of Berkley's heart. "Let's go save the world, Captain, and then we might be able to go home and live happily ever after if we're lucky and do a good job."

"Ma'am," a man's voice came over the intercom.

"Yes," she said, not moving away from Berkley.

"There's a call for Captain Levine, ma'am. Someone named Captain Umeko."

"Patch it through." She held the phone out to Berkley and wondered again if Berkley perhaps had placed too much faith in someone who was literally a stranger.

"You can lose your frown, sweat pea. I'm not that naive."

"Naïveté has nothing to do with it, baby. It's your heart I worry about."

Berkley smiled and kissed her forehead. "I'm not worried. My heart's in good hands."

"God, you're sappy." The tease broke the tension, and she exhaled deeply. "Let's see what fresh hell awaits us."

Dick Chandler gripped the satellite phone so tight a muscle in his upper arm started to cramp. His New Horizons soldiers were some of the most elite the United States had trained, but he'd chosen some because of their fervor for the cause. The fanatics were sometimes necessary because they were so willing to die to advance their fight.

He was willing to sacrifice as many of them as necessary, but that did not include his children, especially his sons. "Do whatever you have to, but get me some information. How in the hell did this happen?" His screaming brought his wife Ruby into his study with her hands up as if in question of what was going on.

"Do you want to risk the few people we have inside?" Rachel asked, her voice devoid of emotion. Of his three children, Rachel was the most like him, and he'd never been able to instill the same ruthlessness in his boys.

"Did you order him to be in the first boat?" This was supposed to have been an easy exercise with minimal casualties.

"We reviewed the plans incessantly, so there shouldn't have been any confusion about what his position should've been." The way Rachel sighed made him think she was losing patience with him. "We also didn't think that bitch would open fire, since cadets were on board those vessels, but from Kelly's report, we lost a majority of our men."

"Call our contacts and find out about Jeffery. Don't disappoint me." He severed the call and swallowed the urge to scream.

"What about Jeffery?" Ruby asked.

"Our plan didn't go off like we wanted so he's either injured or in that bitch's brig." He had to believe his beautiful boy was only hurt, since the alternative would rip him to pieces.

"You had to send him, didn't you?" Ruby's voice was, as always, like ice. She wasn't taking the heat and isolation well and blamed him daily for taking away their nice life. "You had to use my son to prove what a big, brave man you are. Where were you in the fight when it was your turn?"

"They're as passionate about our struggle as I am," he said softly, trying to shut her up. "I'm doing all this for them. After we win a Chandler will be in charge of the country forever."

"You did this because of your ego, Dick, and nothing more. Let's not delude ourselves now, and your big master plan has made us outcasts." Ruby wiped her forehead to clear away the sweat, and her hand came down in a fist. "You and your friends just want to go back to a world that doesn't exist. We've evolved from the forties and fifties, darling, and there's no going back no matter how hard we try."

"You don't want to understand out of stubbornness, but what's wrong with what I'm fighting for? People like Khalid are leading us to a place where the entire world will crush us for our weakness."

Ruby laughed at him like she always did when he preached, as she loved to say. "We evolved because we all weren't born white men." Her constant mocking had slowly fired his temper. "All you've managed to do was exile us in this fucking country run by a guy who likes to feed his family and enemies to his dogs. What you don't understand, or refuse to, is eventually it'll happen to us when he realizes you can't and won't win."

"That simple asshole knows better than to try anything here."

"Remember this conversation then, and I'm leaving the first chance I get. Sitting in a cell is better than this, so don't talk to me unless it's about the children or how I can get the hell out of here."

"No one's leaving until I command it."

"Find my son," Ruby said and left him in peace.

His time in the vice presidency had been filled with changing the world around him as much as he could get away with, but it hadn't been enough. After people lost their patriotism and belief in the war in the Middle East, his vision had changed. He'd spent the last two years funneling money out of the defense budget and recruiting those who would be loyal to him.

Followers had been hard to find at first, but the biggest motivating factor had been Khalid's election. Once he took office and promoted women like Aidan Sullivan over much more deserving men, the offers to join had been hard to keep up with. Sullivan's father was a legend and a hero, but his daughter should've known her place, and that was nowhere on a US carrier unless it was in the mess hall or the secretarial pool.

His pilot entered and saluted sharply. "Sir, this just came in from the Pentagon," he said, handing over a piece of paper.

The message contained only a website, a username, and a password. When he opened it he smiled at the sight of the mission the military was pursuing to capture him. The idiots weren't even looking in the right hemisphere.

"Man the phone and come get me if you hear from Rachel."

"Yes, sir. Where will you be?"

"In my quarters teaching my wife some manners."

Army Major Wiley Gremillion led her partner Aubrey and their daughter Tanith through a martial-arts warm-up exercise, enjoying the early morning. Her two loves had finally come back to her, even though she was to blame for walking away to keep Aubrey safe. Letting Aubrey go had ripped holes in her soul, but the girl she'd met very early in her life had never given up hope for them. Aubrey's faith and love had brought them back together, and as a bonus had included Tanith in her life.

"Mama, rotate your hips more," Tanith said.

"My hip rotation's fine. I haven't had any complaints in that department, thank you," Aubrey said and winked at Wiley. "You two experts finish, and I'll start lunch."

"None for me," Tanith said, bowing to Wiley. "I'm going to the movies with Tiffany, remember? Her mom's taking us for pizza first."

"Go shower then, and don't forget about tonight. Your grandparents are coming for dinner, so don't be late." Aubrey opened her arms to

Tanith before the kid turned and embraced Wiley. "How hungry are you?" Aubrey asked her, stepping into Wiley's arms once they were alone.

"I'm starving, and I think your hip rotation is exquisite, if you're wondering."

"See, and you think you're not romantic." Aubrey laughed. "You want a sandwich or something hot?"

"Something hot, but I can't have it until the kid leaves for pizza and a movie." She kissed Aubrey, and even though they had been back together for more than a year, the feel of Aubrey's lips still made her pulse race.

"Come on, and I'll make you some coffee while we wait."

The old warehouse Wiley had converted into a three-story home was something she'd been willing to part with, but Aubrey and Tanith loved the large space and location, so they'd stayed. Being an instant parent to a now nine-year-old had been tricky at first, considering she didn't know what the hell she was doing, but she spent so much time with the kid she wished she'd been there from the beginning. In her absence, Aubrey had chosen a donor with a lot of Wiley's attributes, so the kid looked a lot like her from the first day, and she often wondered what it would have been like standing next to Aubrey the day Tanith was born.

"Mom and Dad want to treat us to dinner tonight. Is that okay with you?" Aubrey moved around the now-stocked kitchen and smiled. That initial trip to Williams Sonoma for pots, pans, utensils, and a variety of gadgets had surprised her, but she'd dutifully carried everything to the car. She still didn't understand why they needed so many pots, but she wasn't complaining.

"Sounds good to me, and it's our turn to treat."

"You and Daddy can fight over the bill later." They both glanced at the stairs as Tanith charged down like she was an Olympic alpine skier, the buzzing intercom stopping any reprimand they had.

"Here." Wiley took three twenties from her wallet and handed them to Tanith. "Be careful and good."

"I will, and thanks. Love you, Mom."

Wiley never tired of hearing that phrase, and she cherished her new title. "Love you too. Come on. I'll walk you down." Tiffany's mom gave her their itinerary and promised to have Tanith back by four that afternoon.

The domesticity of all this made her laugh since her life was the complete opposite of when she was simply the Black Dragon. It had been her code name in the army before she retired as the most successful sniper to date. She still did the occasional job for the military and for herself, which quelled her sense of justice, but for the most part, she was an artist who enjoyed the peace of creating canvases.

"If you don't hurry, I'm starting without you," Aubrey said as she stripped off her T-shirt.

Wiley took the steps two at a time and scooped Aubrey into her arms. "Don't make me get rough with you." She kissed Aubrey softly and carried her into their bedroom.

"You don't scare me." Aubrey kissed her neck. "You're nothing but a teddy bear." The room was bright, and Wiley loved being with Aubrey when it was freeing to show Aubrey every bit of herself and how she felt.

"You definitely softened me up." She bent and put Aubrey down to strip her clothes off.

"You're kidding, right?" Aubrey poked her in the abdomen with her toes. "Finish getting undressed and get in here—"

The phone rang before Aubrey could continue her teasing, and they both stared at it. Wiley didn't get a lot of calls on that line, and she wanted to ignore it. "They can wait," she said, dropping her shorts.

"If it's Don, he'll just keep calling until he wears my sanity down to nothing, so answer it. Maybe they'll eventually leave you alone."

Wiley sat and exhaled when Aubrey pressed up against her back. "Gremillion," she said impatiently into the phone.

"Wiley, it's Don." Colonel Don Smith was her handler and connection to the military. No one became as successful as Wiley without some strings being attached to their retirement. Don was one of the concessions she'd made to try to reclaim her life and her freedom. "It's been a while, but I need to talk to you."

Her last official assignment had been over a year ago, and then her phone had gone silent. "What's going on?" She didn't mean to sound harsh since Don had been her only friend once upon a time.

"I'd come to you, but the president requested a meeting. How fast can you get here?"

"Why would the president need to see me?"

Aubrey's head came off her shoulder at that question.

"We can't discuss that topic over an unsecured line, but you need to get here, Wiley. The shit that's going on here is mind-boggling."

Wiley exhaled and shook her head. If she hadn't gone into special forces, she probably would've ended up in Washington keeping a desk company for all those years. Her father was a master at that life, but she wasn't known for her diplomacy. "If that's an order, I won't turn it down, but our life is here. We're not uprooting our kid for anything or anyone."

The firm statement of fact made Aubrey kiss her neck. "This isn't a permanent post, but I'm sure they'd love to have you if you decided to stay."

"That won't be happening, but I'll make arrangements and let you know." Wiley hung up and slammed the phone down. "Shit. I don't want anything to do with whatever this is."

"Let's get packed. There's no way you're going alone."

She caught Aubrey before she got up and rolled on top of her. "We've got something better to do than pack."

"So true, lover, so true."

CHAPTER NINE

"Raise anchor and set the short course for Naval Station Norfolk," Aidan said from her chair on the bridge. "If we get attacked, we'll have plenty of backup."

"Aye, Captain," her navigator said.

"I want everyone on board hypervigilant." She stood and stepped out to overlook the area. They wouldn't have any problem firing on anyone else trying to get near them. Three fighter jets were brought up as the crew prepared to sail, and Berkley was down there in her flight suit. Her phone rang, and she smiled when she saw Berkley with her cell pressed to her ear.

"Do you know one of my favorite things about you?" Berkley asked, momentarily glancing up.

"What?" She leaned over the rail and tried to calm her need to go down and have Berkley close by.

"That cute ass of yours." Berkley walked away from any potential eavesdroppers.

"Okay." She laughed at the declaration, wondering why Berkley had chosen now to tell her that, other than when they still had cell service and she could.

"So do me a favor and go inside and don't make such a beautiful target. Later on, I'll need that beautiful ass in one piece."

"Aye, Captain," she said and lifted her hand in salute before going back inside. The trip would take a couple of hours, and because of what had happened, every branch of the armed forces was on high alert.

"Ma'am," one of the bridge officers said. "You have a call from the Pentagon."

"Sullivan," she said, grabbing the nearest phone.

"Captain, this is the undersecretary. My apologies for bothering you, but I need you and Captain Levine to report to Secretary Orr's office as soon as possible."

The undersecretary had been out of the country when all this had begun, and Jerry Teague had used his absence to advance his cause while he still had time. "I'm under orders to reposition our ship at the moment, sir. Can this wait until tomorrow?"

"This morning, Captain Levine visited Jin Umeko. As Captain Levine was ambushed, so was a compound where Umeko was being held. By the time backup arrived, most of our personnel was dead, but Umeko survived."

"Is she hurt?" Aidan massaged her temple and exhaled a long breath.

"Thankfully her training kicked in, and she was able to disappear into the woods behind the house. She waited until the contact we gave her showed up and moved her here."

"Can we land close by? We're underway now."

"That'll be fine. I'll have someone waiting when you land, and I'm looking forward to working with you and Captain Levine. We all owe you a debt for what you've been able to do, but from the looks of it, we still have plenty on our plate."

"Thank you, sir, and I'll be there soon."

"What now?" Devin asked as he entered. "I'm getting tired of all these cryptic messages."

"You have the conn, Devin. I have a hot date I need to get to." He shook his head and took her seat. "Captain Levine," she said into her cell. "Prepare to take off. We have to report to Secretary Orr's office."

"Yes, ma'am."

The plane was ready, but she met Berkley in her room as she packed a bag for when they landed. "Harvey's going to drive your car back and drop it off at your place. Any more of this and he's going to get jealous I found a new backseat."

"Junior's got no worries there, Cletus, but any more of this, and I might as well retire. They keep pulling us to shore like they don't really want us on this boat any longer." She glanced down at her hands, surprised no one had mentioned the ring Berkley had placed there since she'd decided to put it back on after Berkley had gotten back with the NCIS agent.

"They'll have to let us pull out eventually, and once we lose sight of the shoreline, we should be free of all this political intrigue." Berkley kissed her before walking her outside.

The crew buckled her in as the ship started to pick up speed. Once the hatch was shut she took a few deep breaths since now she knew what was coming. Takeoffs from the deck were like a memorable roller-coaster ride in order to get to top speed immediately.

"You okay back there?" Berkley asked as the engines roared to life.

"I'm okay." The last syllable of the word stretched out in her throat as Berkley punched it and took off, banking to the right to get them over open water. "I swear you're like twelve sometimes."

"True, but I think it's best if you don't overthink it. Junior would be upset if you threw up in his office."

"Give me more credit than that, Cletus." She tried to sound miffed but couldn't help laughing.

"So I can have a little fun?"

"Not now. If you flip this thing over, I'm going to have my father court-martial you."

Berkley laughed too as she climbed and leveled off. "Sit back and relax. This won't take long."

"Let's hope that's true when it comes to these meetings."

Wiley studied the area and glanced every so often at the report General Greenwald had provided. The shot wasn't impossible, but it also wasn't a gimme. The intelligence agencies were right in that not many marksmen could've pulled the trigger with such deadly accuracy. Unfortunately for her, she was on that short list, but being in New Orleans gave her a rock-solid alibi.

"Are you ready, or do you need more time?" Don asked.

"Did you arrange for Aubrey and Tanith's transport?" She entered the elevator of the hotel she'd saved for last and handed him back the file of Peter Khalid's investigation so far.

"They're waiting at the White House, and if you don't need to reschedule, we have twenty minutes to get there." Don followed her out and into the government vehicle that had driven them from place to place with an escort in order to skirt traffic.

"I'm ready, and I'll try not to embarrass you," she said. Soldiers became snipers because they lacked diplomacy skills, her father had always said. He'd become the family's diplomat, while she preferred the solitude of the nest and her canvases when she wasn't with her own family. Today, though, merited a change in that philosophy, and she'd give President Michaels whatever she needed to succeed.

Aubrey had told her a meeting with the president rated taking the dress uniform out of mothballs and pinning all the shiny tidbits to it, which made the security check easier at the White House. She heard her code name whispered between the two guys and smiled when the younger one shook his head as if not believing the much-older one. A lot of soldiers knew about the Black Dragon, but they all imagined a Rambo-type guy who walked around with the big hunting knife between his teeth and bulging muscles. That was okay with her since she wasn't a glory hound.

"Major Gremillion," Olivia Michaels said, standing with her hand out. "Thank you for coming, and for allowing me to meet your family." Aubrey and Tanith were both sitting in the Oval Office as if they were there for a friendly visit. "How about one family photo before we talk?"

Wiley was sure Olivia had a million more important things to do, but the small things got people elected to public office. "Thank you, ma'am, and it's an honor to meet you."

"I went with Wiley to vote for you and President Khalid, ma'am," Tanith said, then slapped her hand over her mouth as she glanced up at Wiley. "Sorry, Mom."

"I'm sure President Michaels would still like us if we'd voted for the other guy," she said, and Olivia laughed.

The photographer took a few shots before the room was cleared and Jonas Chapman joined them with two of his most reliable FBI agents. "Major, please tell us your opinion," Olivia said.

"I believe Agent Mosley was correct in her assessment," Wiley said as she pointed to the large aerial view Jonas had brought with him. "The shooter was on the roof of this hotel." She tapped the spot. "During the day it's not a hard shot, but when you take it in the dark, into a crowd, and make such an effective kill shot, that narrows your pool of suspects if you believe this came from someone in uniform."

"Who are your top three guesses?" Jonas asked.

"Beside me, Booker Roman, code name Justice, and Kevin Skinner, code-named Dagger. Since you won't find me on any security tapes the hotel has, I'd start looking for any sighting of Skinner or Roman."

"Do you know them both?" Agent Erin Mosley asked.

"I worked with Booker Roman in South and Central America right before my retirement. He seemed like a decent-enough guy and was a great shot. I know Kevin Skinner only because I was told he was set on breaking my records in both training and in the field. He'd set those goals when he found out the Black Dragon was of the female persuasion and that simply wouldn't do." She sat down and accepted a cup of coffee from Don. "I'm not interested in working with anyone who goes into General Greenwald's service with that motive. It's what solidified my decision to retire."

"Erin, go ahead and check, please," Jonas said. "It can't be that easy, but you never know."

"What can't be that easy?" Wiley asked. "If you can share, I mean."

"If you heard anything about our mission in North Korea, plenty of details were left out of what we shared with the media."

"That's reasonable. I doubt anything I've done has appeared in the news, and if it was, I wasn't given the credit."

Erin nodded, and Jonas waved her on. "While Captain Levine was trying to carry her partner out of that place, Captain Sullivan was dealing with a group aboard her ship working to undermine her success. One of the people who tried to sabotage the mission was Ensign Hattie Skinner." Erin flipped through the file until she found Hattie's mug shot. "She denied everything—still does, but her actions are what landed her at Gitmo."

"Is she Kevin's relative?" Wiley asked.

"I'll have to go to the Pentagon for that information. It's not in her file," Erin said.

"It wouldn't be. Once you commit to General Greenwald, your information is a little more difficult to access, but since Hattie was working against Captain Sullivan, let's assume they're related."

"And if we do?" Olivia asked.

"A family with more than one enlisted member is committed, but in this case misguided. We need to find Kevin Skinner and ask him to turn himself in, either voluntarily or otherwise." Wiley locked eyes with Olivia to see if she understood what she was saying. "If he doesn't go with the voluntary option, then he should be released from his commission before he hurts anyone else."

"We don't know he's the one," Jonas said.

"We don't, but do you want to take a chance of leaving him out there to practice his trade? One he's really good at."

"Major Gremillion, I realize you've given more than your share, but—" Olivia said.

"Ma'am, I don't mean to be rude and interrupt you, but this is no time for any of us to sit on the sidelines. We do everything by the book, because if we don't, we're no better than the people working against us, but we need to start taking care of our business." Wiley glanced at Jonas. "We all have to realize that whoever this is won't be playing by the rules, and they intend to start eliminating the people working hard to wipe out their revolution, or whatever they're calling it. If threatened, I'm going to do my job without hesitation, and I'm pretty good at it."

"Thank you, Major," Jonas said.

"Yes, thank you," Olivia repeated. "Captains Levine and Sullivan are reporting to Defense Secretary Drew Orr's office, and I'd like you to join them if you can get there in time. This damn thing has so many moving parts it's hard to keep track, but I'm confident we have a good team in place."

"Thank you, President Michaels, and until we're done, keep your head down."

Speaker of the House Chase Bonner sat in the waiting area, finally having gotten an appointment with Michaels. That the bitch was actually sitting in the Oval Office was driving him crazy, but he had to stay calm and bide his time. It was an exercise in patience, though, since the fucking country was falling apart after Khalid's death, and she'd done nothing remotely presidential. America needed a strong leader, and in no fucking way was that Olivia Michaels.

"Sir," his assistant Ron Bollinger said softly in his ear. "We need to talk before you go in there."

"Speaker Bonner," a woman said. "Please come with me. President Michaels will see you now."

He stood and held his hand up to silence Ron. "Thank you," he said to the woman, "and whatever it is, I'm sure it'll keep."

Olivia didn't stand when he entered, and Director Jonas Chapman was sitting in one of the chairs across from her desk. "Chase, thanks for stopping by," Olivia said, waving him to a seat. "Sit, and let's talk about the next few weeks."

"The country won't stop just because you wish it, Madam President." He choked on the title, which made her smile widen. "We need to get back to work."

"We'll do that, but Peter Khalid deserves our respect. You might not have given it to him in life, but you might dredge some up now. At least while the cameras are rolling."

He feigned shock. "That's not fair."

"You didn't believe he was born in the United States, but his death certificate will certainly be issued here. Go back to the Hill and start working out your response to your buddy Chandler. Tomorrow, though, we'll start the process of laying to rest one of our greatest patriots. One who gave his life in front of his family because his only crime was being a forward thinker who believed in equality for all people. That he was assassinated in the presence of his children and wife inflicted a wound that will not heal in their lifetimes, and I'll blame and prosecute every single person responsible for that family's pain."

"Don't question my love of country." He curled his fingers into fists. "You may not like me, but you have to work with me."

"Why wouldn't I question your patriotism since you spend most of your days questioning mine? I plan to move the country forward and to find every single person responsible for President Khalid's murder. Like I said, when they are found, they'll face the harshest punishment we can give them under the law. If they come forward before then, they might have a chance for some leniency." Olivia's hands curled into fists as well, and her tone had grown icy. "Think about that as well, but for now, get back to work."

He stood and walked out. Something was different, since he wasn't expecting this level of hostility from Olivia. Her people might have found something. "What?" he asked Ron as they headed out.

"You got a call, and the guy wasn't about to take no to being put off."

"Where did the call come from?" He finally lowered his voice.

"Virginia," Ron said. "He got word about what's happened to his family and wasn't happy with the outcome. Now he wants what you promised him, and he said all of it."

"If I were president, I'd be able to give him whatever he wanted, but I'm not. He's going to have to be patient, since no one but Olivia has the power to grant his wish list."

"His parents and two younger brothers were just picked up for questioning. I don't think patience is what's on his mind, sir. He accepts that his sister might be out of his reach, but the rest of the clan wasn't an option." Ron handed him a slip of paper and pointed to the car. "I got you a burner, so the call can't be traced."

Chase stared at the numbers and suddenly wanted all this crap to be over. "Not yet. Let's see exactly why this happened first."

"Please think about this, sir. Ignoring this one has the potential to open us up for more than jail time."

"Stop worrying about that." He placed the paper in his pocket and got in the backseat. "If anything, we need to speed up the process. This might be the thing that forces everyone's hand, and if it doesn't, there's no paper trail back to us."

CHAPTER TEN

Berkley was briefed but wanted Aidan with her since she guessed what direction all this was headed. Jin Umeko was still in custody but now was within the walls of the Pentagon, and from what she could see, that wasn't changing in the near future, but the attack on the compound where she'd been had finally potentially loosened her tongue.

"Has she said anything at all?" Berkley asked Rooster.

"She asked for you, then sat and waited. Make her understand whatever she says will be recorded and shared. Later on, I don't need someone telling me I violated her rights." Rooster appeared to be a man wanting to hit someone, but the right target hadn't come along yet.

Aidan followed her in and offered Jin her hand. "We met briefly, but hello again, Captain Umeko."

"Please call me Jin, and thank you both for coming." Jin stood and offered them a seat in the very plain room that had to be a drastic change from the compound that had been her home for months. "Your president is dead."

"One of our presidents was killed, but we have a new one," Berkley said. "The people responsible for having me shot down are to blame, and they will be punished. During World War II, one of the Japanese admirals was supposedly quoted as saying, 'I fear all we have done is to awaken a sleeping giant and filled him with a terrible resolve.' Many may see the United States as the aggressor in numerous cases, but for the most part a sleeping giant is what we are. We want democracy and freedom for all people, but when provoked, all the firepower at our disposal will rain down on anyone poised to do us harm."

"Do you think I in some way played a part in what happened here?" Jin asked, her facial expression not changing.

"I don't. I actually think you're as much a victim as I was when my man double-crossed me, and President Khalid was when he was gunned down. If you know something and choose to stay silent, I will think differently about you."

Jin nodded and turned to Aidan. "That is fair. Will you go back to my old home?"

"We haven't received our final orders, but maybe. It all depends on where the man who's leading these people will be found," Aidan said.

"I have told Berkley about my mother, Minseo Umeko, and a little about my father. I am sure your people might know better than me exactly what happened to him, but I have my theory."

"Berkley told me some, but then our day got out of control for all of us, I think," Aidan said.

"My father was General Pak Kwang Lee. He was the security commander for our supreme leader and trusted with many of Kim's secrets."

"He *was*? Do you think he's been replaced?" Aidan asked.

"The mission of the facilities you destroyed was to perfect a nuclear weapon, and my father Kwang Lee's job was to see that nothing happened to them. He placed who he thought was the perfect person to see that job through, and I failed him miserably. I then escaped and lost the supreme leader Lowe Nam Chil, the man with all the secrets. The destruction of the plants was bad enough, but Chil's capture by the United States sealed Lee's fate. By now, some other monster has taken his place."

"Berkley told me you lost your mother, and I'm very sorry," Aidan said. "But what does all this have to do with us?"

"Chil was sent to deal with me and my partner Yong Nam. She has flown with me for years, and I went willingly with him, hoping Yong would be set free. I doubt that happened, but Chil took me to his home before he could sentence me to death. That is where I saw Yong for the last time, and I begged her in my own way to get out. It did not matter where she ran, but she needed to."

"You don't think she did?" Berkley asked.

"I could not say too much since Chil was watching us, of that I am sure. All I knew was that was my last day to live, and I would go willingly since I had tried my best with Yong. I am still not sure why he kept me alive for as long as he did, but my love for Yong has kept me silent all this time."

"He's in a place he'll never escape from, and there's always hope that Yong survived," Berkley said.

"I truly believe what I told you in that I am now alone, but there is a chance to get justice for all those I lost. Beginning with Chil, the loss of his power is the greatest punishment you can inflict on him, but while I was there, I was surprised that some of the guards were not Korean." Jin stopped, as if wanting everyone to understand.

"They were American?" Berkley fought the urge to shake Jin to make her speak faster.

"I believe so, but they all seemed to speak Korean, from the brief encounter I had with them. Whoever they were, they had the run of Chil's home, and that is what I found most rare."

Berkley nodded and glanced back at the two-way mirror. "Jin, before you say anything else, people are listening. You don't have to do this until you speak to someone. You have the right to an attorney."

"All my life, people have been listening, Berkley. I have stayed quiet because I feared more for Yong than for myself, but I believe now I am the only one left who can speak for the dead, and there are so many. My family is gone and so is my friend. Someone should pay for that." Jin slammed her hand down and finally showed some emotion other than her usual calm façade. "I will lead you to Chil's home and to the office in it, but I want to go with you."

"We weren't planning to return on the ground," Aidan said.

"Berkley survived, and with me she will again, but you need me. Whatever secrets you are searching for are all in Chil's fortress. If the person you are looking for is hiding in North Korea, whatever information he possesses was the price he had to pay to live within the supreme leader's borders. Of that I would bet my life on, and if he gave him what he wanted, it will be found in Chil's home."

"Excuse us a moment," Aidan said.

They stepped back out, and Rooster seemed even more agitated. "What the holy fuck?"

"All the intelligence we have is that Chandler has disappeared effectively. Maybe he'll be found in the most remote place ever," Berkley said.

"You trust this woman?" Drew asked, having come in after they started.

"There's really no way to verify her story, but do we take our foot off the throttle now? Either we walk into an elaborate trap, or we walk out with Chandler and the list of who's working for him. To me it's worth the gamble."

"You would, Miss High Adventure," Aidan said. "She's right though. We've been at this for too long with no results. Chandler is in the middle of a literal black hole. We've all seen the satellite images of that pit at night."

"This call will have to come from someone higher than me," Drew said.

"The president needs to understand this might be our best option because it's our only option," Berkley said before going back in. "Jin, you have my vote, and it won't be long before you have an answer. This isn't the prettiest place, but you'll be safe here until we know."

"Only my revenge is important to me now. Thank you for listening."

"It's time for action, gentlemen, and I expect you to make our case with the president. It will be her call, and she needs to know the ramifications of blinking now," Aidan said when they were ready to go.

"Hang tight for a few more days, and everything should be in place one way or another," Drew said. "Your prisoners have been moved and secured, and I want to thank you for a job well done. Jeffery Chandler is now in custody."

"I'd put everyone on high alert then. Men who see themselves as lions will do anything to get their cubs back," Aidan said.

"He's somewhere that doesn't exist," Rooster said.

"Unless you sat in the wizard's chair for eight years. Then you know all the secrets," Berkley said. "Know your enemy, gentleman, because he sure as hell knows all about us."

"Sun Tzu, Captain, is something I know well," Rooster said. "Chandler was the biggest cheerleader for the opening of all these special places no one wants to admit exist, but when a new landlord takes over, we change the locks."

"The locks but not the locations?" Aidan said.

"Some of the locations, and Jeffery is somewhere new that was not in the system when Chandler was in office. The more I think about it, though, the more I realize we should've placed him somewhere more accessible. That big a piece of bait might draw out some bigger fish," Drew said, and Berkley nodded.

"It's good to know yourself as well, sir," Berkley said, and smiled. "Either way, make sure the people at the location are vigilant. The ones who tried to bomb the *Jefferson* and tried to take me won't give up easily."

"And remember, we're ready to go," Aidan said.

"I think that goes for everyone involved," Berkley said, looking at Jin, who sat like she was waiting for a coffee date.

Rachel Chandler stood deep enough in the woods of the compound her people had hit so she wouldn't be seen and tried to let go of her anger.

Her younger brother had been captured because he hadn't followed orders, and her father had blamed her. It would be impossible to find where the feds were holding him, no matter how many of their minions they questioned.

"Why are we here, ma'am?" one of her men asked.

"You failed to grab or kill the woman who's been living here, and you failed to realize how important it was to bring the Korean bitch down." Her phone rang, and she wanted to ignore it since it was her father, but he would only become more demanding. "Keep an eye on the personnel that shows up now."

"Where are you?" Dick asked, and Rachel moved her phone a few inches from her ear.

"The compound where they were keeping Umeko. Do you need something?"

"Why are you wasting time there? You need to concentrate on finding Jeffery."

She leaned against a tree and took the phone completely from her ear to sigh loudly. Dick Chandler still couldn't accept the fact that of all his children, she was the best equipped for battle strategy and leadership. That wasn't the vision of his New World order, though. He wanted his sons to carry out the vision he'd started, while she was supposed to fade into the background once he took over the government.

"This place is too important to abandon, and I want to see who comes back. It might or might not give me a clue as to where Jeffery is, but these bastards have him somewhere that's not on your list of possibilities." The lights in the house came on, and a unit of guards started taking up positions outside. Maybe the Korean bitch was back, and she could finish the job by putting a bullet in her head.

"He's your responsibility and top priority," Dick yelled again. "Don't forget that." During the brief reprieve from his lecturing, Rachel didn't feel the need to fill the silence. "Shit. I need to go, but keep me informed."

"Yes, sir." Something had happened on his end, but she had time enough later to find out. She needed to concentrate on her piece of the puzzle for now. "Come on," she took out the long-range rifle and attached the silencer, "show yourself."

Dick leaned back in the leather office chair he'd taken from the vice president's office when he and George had completed their two terms.

All the preparations and planning he'd put in for all those years under George's unfocused gaze had made him a rich man, if he chose to use the defense money he'd redirected. This wasn't about personal gain though, and eventually the American people would understand the choices he'd made and why.

Relocating his family and most loyal troops to North Korea wasn't ideal, but the ability to work without having to worry about defense or detection had been a godsend. The only problem was these visits the fucker who ran the country insisted on to remind him of his side of the deal they'd made.

General Pom Su Gil had been promoted because of the debacle of Pak Kwang Lee's failure. The man who'd learned his cruelty from Jin Umeko's father was his most frequent visitor and spoke for the supreme leader. At least he claimed to do so. "General, welcome." He stood and bowed slightly when the short man entered with his usual air of arrogance.

"Mr. Chandler, I came to ask what happened." Pom ignored his outstretched hand and sat down. "Do you often make empty promises?"

"I told you I'd fix Lee's mistakes and return Chil once I'm back in power. I do not understand how you think I have failed in that promise."

"According to our contacts in the US, Umeko is still alive. Your people fail to kill her."

"It's not like the government was keeping her in the open, and none of it matters. My contacts in government assure me that Jin Umeko hasn't opened her mouth from the day her plane went down. She thinks her silence will keep Lieutenant Nam alive." He sat and poured two whiskeys. "Is Nam still alive?"

"Nam is breathing, but she probably prays to die more than once a day." Pom accepted the glass and took a sip. "The supreme leader lost Comrade Chil, so a suitable replacement is being trained. Nam has been good for Ji Woo Min's training. Min has broken her, but Nam's will to live has been hard to get past. It is only a matter of time though, when death will be preferable to the pain."

"I'm sure, and when Min succeeds, stay quiet about it. That's the only thing keeping Umeko silent."

"Do not concern yourself with things that are none of your business, Mr. Chandler. Instead, concentrate on all the pretty words you spoke to build your compound here." Gil stood and smoothed his tunic before placing the ridiculous uniform cap on his head. "I suggest you do everything you can to keep your promises, since the Kim family is not known for its patience."

He poured himself a drink and turned on the four televisions in his office. Both CNN and MSNBC were covering the live press conference Olivia Michaels was having with George Butler. Good ole George, who'd ridden his daddy's coattails to office, was dumb as horseshit, but the voters loved him anyway. The moron should be thanking him for giving him a legacy to be proud of.

"What the hell are you up to?" He turned the volume up and threw his glass against the wall as he listened.

"I stand before the American people today to apologize for ever subjecting them to Dick Chandler and for placing this man in power. To stand against America and attack our soldiers on US soil is the act of a coward. Any ally or adversary would do well to heed the president's warning to turn Chandler and any of his followers over to face prosecution," George said.

"Is Chandler responsible for President Khalid's murder?" a reporter asked.

"That is an open investigation, but we're not ruling out any possibilities," Olivia said as she stood shoulder to shoulder with George.

"If Dick Chandler wanted to change what he didn't like about our great country, he should've run. But the track he's on, and anyone who follows him, is treasonous. That will not be tolerated no matter your party or your reasoning. Above everything else, we are all Americans." George looked directly into the camera and pointed his finger at it. *"Chandler, if you're listening, it's time to turn yourself in. You can't and won't win this, and you'll burn in hell for killing Peter Khalid in front of his wife and children."*

"It's time to show these assholes we aren't bluffing," he said into the phone.

"Are you sure, sir? We're two weeks ahead of schedule already, but that might be pushing it."

"Fucking get it done, or have your assistant do it if you don't have the balls." He slammed the phone down and punched the top of his desk. "You'll pay for this betrayal, George."

"Did you say something?" Ruby Chandler asked quietly as she sat across from him. Her black eye was still swollen shut, and the cut on her upper lip had to make talking painful, which was why he'd put it there.

"It's time to light the world on fire and watch it burn."

❖

CIA Director Marcus Newton stood by Walby Edwards and stared at the young man on the other side of the mirror. According to the report, Jeffery Chandler had been an exemplary student at the US Naval Academy, liked by his fellow cadets and instructors despite his last name, and had gotten in on his own merit. Dick had used every excuse to avoid the military service his son had embraced, and it had set the younger man apart as far as the academy's senior officers were concerned.

Marcus had called Walby back in to persuade the kid to talk after Jeffery had only recited his name, rank, and serial number. "He doesn't act like a fanatic," Walby said. They'd spent the last few hours interviewing prisoners they'd captured with Jeffery. "And after the last two, we witnessed the total definition of what fanatics sound like," Walby said.

"This is daddy issues then?" Marcus asked before laughing. "I doubt he'll give us much, but you're free to get creative. Sounds like this morning was the straw that broke President Michaels's patience with all this."

Walby usually worked at Gitmo and the CIA's facility in the Middle East. The man had no family and no problem doing whatever he had to in order to get the job done. "You sure?" Walby asked, his eyes never leaving Jeffery.

"The president needs results, but keep in mind she's not George Butler. Try not to leave any marks, and report to me directly before you report to anyone at the White House."

"Don't worry. The bruises I leave will all be under the skin." Walby took only a small notebook and a pen with him.

"Who are you?" Jeffery asked when he sat down. "Where am I? It's my right to know."

"Where's your father, Jeffery? I'm sorry. May I call you Jeffery?" Walby started writing and never looked up.

"Who are you?"

Walby stood up quickly, and Jeffery did the same, but before he could do anything else Walby had pressed his head against the metal table with one hand and jammed the fingers of the other up and under the edge of his rib cage. Jeffery stopped moving when Walby pulled up with relentless pressure, not caring how much pain he was in. "Where's your father, Jeffery?"

"I don't know," Jeffery screamed before clenching his jaws shut from the pain in his side. Walby knew the maneuver was like having your chest cracked in two. "I don't know—I swear."

"Pay attention, Jeffery." Walby let him go and sat back down, but stayed vigilant for any move on the young man's part. "That was some bold move you made today, and I commend you for being in that first boat. You knew when to bail to save your life, but a lot of your friends weren't so lucky."

"Where are the rest of my men?"

"You're not here to ask questions, Jeffery. I'm going to say that only once, so hopefully you're a quick study. My goal here today is to leave here without facing too much opposition from you."

"Fuck off," Jeffery screamed but shut his mouth when Walby stood up.

"I see you're not going to cooperate, and if you're not, this is how we'll play it. Quite a few of your buddies died today, but plenty of them survived. For every day you deny not knowing the answers to my questions, and I mean all my questions, I'm going to kill one of them. That is, after all, the cost of treason, but I'll be happy to tell them why I'm doing it."

"You can't," Jeffery said, much more subdued now.

"You can't be serious?" He leaned over and flicked Jeffery on the forehead hard enough to make his eyes water. "No matter what, though, I'm not going to touch you again. I'll record every execution and play each one of them for you every day for the rest of your miserable life. Can you live with all that on your head?"

"Yeah, right. The president and Congress won't let you do that." Jeffery rubbed his side and laughed. "This act's pathetic."

"Joanna, go ahead," he said into his cell.

"Yes, sir. Any particular one?" Walby's partner Joanna Barker asked.

"The youngest one, I think. No sense in making him live out his life, which could be years, in a cell no bigger than a bathroom stall. Might as well cut the pain off early."

"Yes, sir."

A few minutes later a stretcher went by with the body on it, and Jeffery stood at the door to watch. "You bastard." He lunged at Walby and ended up pressed against a table again, but this time he yelled in pain when Walby pulled much harder on his ribs.

"Remember the rules, and I'll see you tomorrow."

CHAPTER ELEVEN

"When do you sail?" Mary Beth Sullivan asked as she sat on the bed and watched Aidan dress for dinner.

"In two days, and when we come back I'm going to marry Berkley and make you a grandmother." She smiled when her mom hopped up and hugged her. "I can't admit it to Berkley, but I'm scared. She runs into every situation like she's invincible, and it drives me nuts."

"She's a carbon copy of your father, only much taller and better looking. You can't change them, my love, but you can balance things out by loving them no matter how crazy their choices."

"I do, which is why she drives me nuts." She laughed and closed her eyes when her mom kissed her on the forehead.

"Just remind her often of what she's coming home to, and everything should be fine."

"What do you think they're talking about?" She stared out the door for a second and couldn't wait for the night to be over so it would be just her and Berkley, but she did want to go out to eat with her parents. After they left, they'd be gone for at least a few months, and she wanted to leave them with as little worry as possible.

"You know Triton," Mary Beth said. "He's great at the pep talk. Not that Berkley needs it when it comes to you, but he's reminding her, like my father did when it was your father's turn, about what's the most important thing in her life. I doubt Berkley needs that either, but it'll make your father feel better by beating her over the head with what's most important in his life, and that's you."

Berkley glanced in her direction briefly and winked before returning her attention to Preston.

"What exactly are you two going to do?" Preston asked.

"They haven't finalized the scope of our mission, but according to our latest orders, we're sailing back toward North Korea. Intelligence doesn't know exactly where Chandler is, but it's got to be someplace like that. As far as the rest of the Pentagon is concerned, we're headed in the complete opposite direction, but that was only a diversion in case any of Chandler's moles are feeding him information."

"I've attended a couple of the briefings, and they don't have any clue about a lot of things. Because of that, don't let these yahoos separate you from Aidan. One thing I've learned from my years of experience is that people like Chandler are unhinged, and the more they dig in, the more unhinged they become."

"Until he's brought in though, we're in this, and for once, I'd rather be someplace else. We should've turned in our papers when we got back last year, but I made a promise to President Khalid, and I intend to honor it." Berkley sat on the sofa and scrubbed her face with her hands. "I understand people like Chandler. History is littered with megalomaniacs. But I don't understand the people who follow and believe so blindly."

"That's why I gave you my blessing to marry my daughter. If you'd understood these assholes, we'd have some problems."

"Nah. You gave me a blessing because you love me. You can admit it," she said and laughed. The buzzer stopped Preston from rebutting her. "Yes, can I help you?"

"Berk," a woman said, and the voice sounded familiar. "It's Wiley Gremillion. Can we come up? I hope you don't mind, but my dad gave me the address."

She pressed the release for the door, and the mission came more into focus. The powers that be probably hadn't shared everything with them, and Wiley's appearance meant there would be a ground operation. That was fine if all they had to do was provide air cover, but her luck hadn't been great at work lately.

"You've been a busy little bee, haven't you?" Berkley asked when she opened the door to Wiley, a kid, and a woman holding Wiley's hand.

"I've actually been damn happy and extremely lucky. This is my wife Aubrey and our daughter Tanith," Wiley said, placing her free hand on Tanith's shoulder.

"Congratulations, and this is a good-looking group with you. I'm happy for you," Berkley said, waving them all in and opening her arms when Wiley stepped forward.

"You're ruining my retirement, pal."

"You know me," she said as she embraced her old friend. "If I can't have fun, then I'm going to ruin it for everyone else. Come in, and I'll change our reservations."

"We actually have plans, but I wanted to talk to you before the brass throws anything else at me. You'd left your meeting with Secretary Orr before I got there, so I hope I'm not keeping you from anything."

Berkley introduced them and held her hand out when Aidan and Mary Beth emerged from the bedroom. "This is my fiancée, Aidan Sullivan."

"I'm not the only one who's been busy," Wiley said. "Looks like we've been buzzing in the same hive."

"True, and if you're in New Orleans when all this is over, you can celebrate with us," Aidan said, offering them a seat. Berkley was surprised that Aidan had been so quick to extend the invitation, but it proved they'd come a long way. "How long have you two been together?"

"I met Wiley when we were eight," Aubrey said, taking Wiley's hand back. "She spoiled me for anyone else, and she's stuck with me now."

"With me too," Tanith said, and they all laughed.

"It's a good place to be," Wiley said. "Like I said though, I didn't want to intrude on your evening, but I wanted to talk to you two. I think I've been invited to your party, and I'd like to know what I'm getting into without the bullshit the suits are going to feed me. Sorry for my language," Wiley said to the Sullivans before leading Berkley a little distance away for the talk she obviously wanted to have. "I've got way more to lose than when I started my career, and I'm not willing to piss it all away in some hellhole, so tell me the truth."

"Believe me, we all have plenty to lose. Tomorrow we'll be at the Pentagon again, but basically we're sailing toward North Korea and trying to reach a house where we should find a majority of the pieces we're missing when it comes to Chandler and his little posse of misfits."

"A house? Are you serious?" Wiley stared at her like she was standing there with little green men on her shoulder.

"I'll fill you in completely tomorrow when we meet, but at the end of our mission, something happened," Berkley said and told her about Jin Umeko and all she knew about Chil and his compound. "The admission that she'd seen Americans where none should have been is telling, and with any luck, whatever he had at the compound is still there."

"That makes sense as to why they asked me to come along."

"It does, and if you tell me where you're staying, we'll pick you up so you can get it firsthand in the morning. If you can change your plans, though, I'd love for you all to join us tonight."

"My mother's expecting us at home, so thanks, but we'll pass. I'll see you in the morning."

They couldn't convince Wiley and Aubrey to have dinner with them, so they headed out with the Sullivans. The dinner was a bit subdued, since they all seemed to realize their time together was growing short, but they tried to have fun and talk about the future. Preston paid, and Mary Beth hugged both Berkley and Aidan longer than usual.

"Why do you think they want Wiley Gremillion to come with us?" Aidan asked when they were alone. She smiled as Berkley started taking her clothes off for her.

"Tomorrow should be a truth day for everyone involved, at least it better be, but you have to know Wiley can't shoot anyone from the deck of the *Jefferson*. She's going ashore somewhere to deal with our problems, and I'm guessing she's going to ruin more than one person's day." Berkley unzipped Aidan's skirt and hissed in a breath when she saw the white satin underwear. "Right now, though, I don't care about anything but this. You are so incredibly sexy."

Aidan moaned when Berkley unhooked her bra and slid her hands down until she went under the pretty panties and squeezed her ass. "I love when you touch me—oh, shit," she said when Berkley picked her up and pressed her closer. The move made her center press against Berkley's abdomen, making her wetter than she was already. "Baby, don't make me wait."

Berkley set her down and got her completely naked before getting her own uniform off as fast as she could drop it onto the floor. This was probably the last night they would have all to themselves, and she was desperate for an orgasm. "Go inside—fuck," she said when Berkley flicked her finger over her clit. "Go inside."

The sensation of Berkley's fingers quickly filling her and her thumb massaging her clit made her hang onto Berkley's shoulders for the ride. "Uh…yes, please don't stop," she said right into Berkley's ear, and Berkley followed orders. She pumped her hand until her hips came off the bed, and she reached the peak where she had no choice but to slide quickly down the other side. It was so fast and hard she almost regretted not taking more time, but she had to have Berkley right then.

"I really love when you touch me," she said after her heart rate finally slowed. "But then, I love you period."

"I love you too, but you're not done. Tonight I want to hear you," Berkley said as she held her.

"Don't worry. I'll keep up." She pulled Berkley into a sitting position on the side of the bed and knelt between her legs. "Question is, can you?" She smiled when Berkley's thigh muscles flexed taut as she sucked her clit in and ran her tongue over it. "I want you to come with my mouth on you, baby." If her orgasm was fast, Berkley's was lightning quick, with her hands in her hair as she drove her completely insane.

"We need to practice being quiet," Berkley said when they lay back down, Aidan on top. "There's no way I can go weeks without touching you."

"Ah, there is my rule breaker," she said, kissing Berkley's shoulder. "But you also mentioned that tonight is no time for quiet. We'll have weeks of silence, but it won't start tonight."

"There are rules that are meant to be broken, and you just inspired my rebel side," Berkley said as she put her hand back between her legs.

"Thank God for that," she said as she gave in to her desire for Berkley again.

❖

"I have to say I didn't think you'd hold out this long, Jeffery," Walby said as he sat across from Jeffery Chandler in the interrogation room that was six by nine. He liked small rooms with desperate people. Sometimes confined spaces did more to ratchet up someone's fear than anything he could think of.

Jeffery would be frog-marched here every twelve hours, where he'd watch another of his friends parade by on a stretcher. That, combined with the very little sleep he was getting, was making him almost frantic. Walby could detect the rising tension in the way he couldn't sit still and his eyes darted around the room. Jeffery Chandler was a trapped animal who couldn't find a way out even if he chewed off his own leg.

"There aren't that many guys left back there, and they're all cursing you for playing God. We were happy to tell them you value your father's location more than their lives." Walby tapped on his ice-cold soft-drink can, smiling when the repetitive noise seemed to bother Jeffery even more than his presence did.

"They know that's not true. They'd do the same if they were in here with you. We all believe in the cause," Jeffery said, whipping his head around when someone knocked on the door. "What, today you aren't even going to ask before you murder someone else?"

"There's no murder in war, little man." Walby stood and let two of his men in. "Isn't that why you won't answer my questions and, instead, serve your father? You're at war with us, and you're running around pretending to play war games." The two men stood next to his chair and waited. "Of course, when there was a real war and your daddy got called, he didn't go. First it was school, and then all you little bastards came along to save his ass from the fight, and if that hadn't done it, I'm guessing he would've faked an illness. Thankfully for him the war ended before he ran out of excuses for his lack of backbone."

"My father is a great man," Jeffery screamed. "Fuck you."

"Your father's a fucking coward," one of the men said, grabbing the back of Jeffery's head and pulling it back so far that Walby smiled.

He nodded and stood up. His orders were to stop with the subtleties and get this kid to talk. Walby was now working for Drew Orr, and the defense secretary wanted answers. "I'm going to finish my Coke. That should take twenty minutes, but I could go for a smoke too if you need the extra time." When he reached for his can and stood, Jeffery's look of fear changed his demeanor completely.

"I thought you said you weren't going to hurt me," Jeffery said, almost panting.

"I'm not—I'm leaving. My friends here, though, made no such promise."

"You can't go and not do anything to prevent this. We're in the United States, for fuck's sake."

"You attacked a naval carrier intending to sink it. Seems to me you don't give a shit about the United States, Jeffery. Why the fuck should we give a shit about you?"

"Because you're supposed to stand for something. Isn't that what you said separates you from my father?"

"What exactly are you worried about, Mr. Chandler? I'm sure Daddy trained you on all the procedures he championed when he was in office. Dick rallied for enhanced interrogation and changed the rules, so if you're going to blame anyone, it should be your macho daddy. But I still don't see a problem. If you know what's coming, there's no way for us to win, so this will be more for your bragging rights later. If you ever see the light of day again, you can tell your entire family how you beat the likes of me."

"Fuck off, because I'm not talking. You can't scare me."

"Then we'll consider this a training exercise on how to beat the shit out of all the tests we can throw at you. Before I go, though," Walby tapped his chin with his index finger, "who's your choice today?" Jeffery glared at him and tried his best to break the hold his men had on him. "Let's change it up today and go for the oldest of whoever's left. The big blond kid looks like a good candidate. We'll make sure to tell him you send him your love. He can leave this world with a full heart, since he looks like someone you'd go for in a romantic sense."

"I'm going to have fun killing you," Jeffery screamed.

"Maybe later, pretty boy," Walby said. "For the next hour or so, though, you'll be busy shitting your pants."

CHAPTER TWELVE

Berkley woke up two days later but kept her eyes closed, enjoying the silence and the feel of Aidan pressed up against her. The last forty-eight hours had been jammed with meetings with the US Security Council, preparing the *Jefferson* to sail, and putting the personnel they needed in place. Because it was a big boat and a larger mission, she brought in three new pilots to replace David Morris, and the new team seemed to be working well together. At least they understood the gravity of what they faced and the importance of getting this right.

The rest of the pilots coming would be backup for the main team and to protect the *Jefferson* at all costs. Now all she could hope for was to not have another David Morris in their ranks ready to shoot down or sabotage one of their own to advance Dick Chandler's organization. Her other thought went to someone like Hattie Skinner and her murderous brother. Hattie had worked for Edgar Caldwell, the *Jefferson*'s head mechanic. There was more than one way to bring down fighter jets, and who better than someone charged with keeping them running at their best.

"It's too early for deep thoughts," Aidan said, sounding drowsy.

"I was going through my checklist, until you woke up and gave me something else to think about, since your nipples are rock hard."

"Ha. That's because you keep it cold enough in here to make penguins happy. Stop changing the subject and tell me why you're awake at four thirty in the morning?" Aidan raised up on her elbows and squinted at the clock. "And I'm not giving you anything else to worry about—"

"I didn't say I was worried about anything," she said, putting her hands around Aidan's waist and pulling her back down.

"Please, baby, I know all your moods, and I'm familiar with the worry side of you. It's not your usual state, but you like to run the gamut every so often," Aidan said, stopping to kiss her. "Spill it, Levine."

"The first time we sailed, I thought what they were asking us would be like threading a needle in a hurricane in the dark." The way Aidan was gazing at her made her stop a moment and inhale. "This time, they want us to walk in there and breach a place that probably has more security than where their leader lives." She smoothed her hands down Aidan's back to her ass. "I like planes for a reason."

"I've been thinking about that, and I don't think you should go." Aidan seemed to be the one who was suddenly a bundle of worry.

"If I go and we get what we need, it means our freedom, sweetheart. Don't lose sight of that."

Aidan nodded, then rested her head on Berkley's chest. "I know, but for once I want to be selfish. I want to keep you in one piece. It's someone else's turn to go into the belly of the beast, as it were."

"Hopefully, by the time we get there Kim's dogs will have gotten hungry, and that belly-of-the-beast thing will make total sense. Don't worry about it so you don't drive yourself nuts."

"You drive me crazy," Aidan said, and bit her on the chest.

Before she could flip Aidan over and enjoy the morning, the phone rang. "When we buy a house, can we skip a landline?"

"Sullivan," Aidan said, nodding and listening for a few minutes. "Yes, sir. I'll call Berkley, and we'll be there in less than an hour."

"Don't tell me something else went wrong," she said, sitting up when Aidan did.

"That was Jonas Chapman, FBI Director. According to him, whoever they sent to work with Agent Mosley broke Jeffery Chandler. He started talking about an hour ago." Aidan combed her hair back and walked toward the bathroom. "What exactly do you think he meant by 'broke him'?"

"This is a good time for the 'don't ask and hope they don't tell policy.' I don't agree with enhanced interrogation, but the people in charge must think it's warranted if the situation is bad enough. Chandler wants civil war, and he sent his kids to try to hurt you." She stood in front of Aidan and took her hand. "If he'd done that, I would've taken him and everyone else with him apart myself, and I wouldn't have stopped until every single one of them was dead."

"How the hell do we trust anyone until this is over?" Aidan tugged her to the shower.

"We have a core of loyal people, so we'll have to go with that." The phone rang again, and Aidan groaned. "Yes," Aidan said as she moved back to her side of the bed. "Hold on a minute." She put the phone on speaker and motioned for Berkley to join her. "Go ahead, Drew."

"Jeffery started talking," Drew said.

"Director Chapman just called and told us. He said his second, Agent Mosley, was working with someone on the questioning, and they had a breakthrough."

"What else did he say?" Drew sounded aggravated.

"He wanted us to meet them at the facility as soon as we can get there. He said there were some facts only Berkley could verify."

"I have every faith in Jonas," Drew said, and Berkley could hear the news in the background. "Like me, though, he's invested in getting the people responsible for Peter no matter what needs to be done. The president was one of those guys who you could always count on and had your back. It's why I took this thankless job, and why guys like Jonas have been fanatical about getting a foothold on finding these assholes."

"What does that have to do with this morning?" Berkley asked

"You have to get from Aidan's place to the facility Jonas told you about. Considering what happened on that ship, we can assume Chandler has someone watching you."

"Chapman's using us as bait?" Aidan asked.

"You've never been alone from the beginning, Aidan. Neither Peter nor anyone on the Security Council you've worked with wanted anything to happen to you."

"I feel so much better," Berkley said, and Aidan laughed. "We plan to meet the director and whoever rocked little Jeffery's world, and if someone takes a shot at me, or especially at Aidan, they aren't going to like what will happen next. I've already taken a couple of these bastards out, and I don't mind upping my count."

"That's totally understandable. I just wanted you to know the score. Also, Peter will be placed in the rotunda for a day of visitation later this afternoon. Dress whites, ladies. We'll be escorting Eva Khalid and her daughters, and President Michaels wants you both there as part of the honor guard."

"Thanks for the heads-up, Drew," Aidan said, and leaned against her. "We'll be there this afternoon."

"Who exactly did you have watching us?" she asked, not ready to forgive just yet.

"It turns out Special Agent Erin Mosley has a really good friend, Brenda, who's also an agent. Brenda's team has very discreetly watched over you for the last year, and her reports have included only any suspicious persons watching or remotely interested in you. We didn't tell you so you wouldn't give away that you knew she and her team were there." Drew took a deep breath and blew it out. "The jobs you've chosen are ones you've excelled at, both of you. Eventually things might be different, but you've proved yourself enough that President Khalid and now President Michaels became very powerful guardian angels."

"Thanks for that," Berkley said. "But if it becomes a problem, I expect you to come to me, and I'll resign. You leave Aidan out of it."

"I do that, and Triton will rip my balls off, and Corbin will feed them to me. No one will ever know your name, but your actions will be the basis for change in the policy that no longer makes sense."

"If anything, it'll piss Chandler off," Berkley said, and both Aidan and Drew laughed. "We'll let you know what happens."

Berkley drove, liking the light traffic. If someone was watching or waiting to attack, they'd be easier to spot. "What do you think about what Drew said?" Aidan asked.

"It was interesting, but right now I can't cram one more thing into my head. I promised your father to never disrespect you, and I sure as hell won't let anyone else do it." She sped up and two cars kept up. From the type of sedan they were, it had to be Agent Brenda's people.

"You're right. Let's not think about it since it doesn't seem like a problem."

Berkley took the long way to the address Jonas had provided. The place looked like a typical office building the federal government had thousands of, with a fence around the perimeter and sophisticated surveillance cameras. Considering what it was, only one guard was in the shack outside. The guy opened the gate for them as she drove up. Then as she and Aidan walked to the front door, Berkley noticed the guards with automatic weapons in the windows and on the roof.

"Captain Sullivan and Captain Levine," Jonas said. "Thank you for coming. I think you can verify some of the information since Mr. Chandler sounds like an open book now."

"Director Chapman, I'll be happy to do that, but remember that things always go smoother when everyone is upfront." Berkley squeezed his hand. "You get me?"

"I believe I do, and I gave President Khalid my word to be as covert as we could make it. If something had happened to either of you, he would've dumped a world of hurt on me. He liked you both and became very protective, even if he didn't outwardly show it. Nothing in any report that has ever been written about your surveillance has included anything except possible hostiles watching you."

"And you'll keep it that way, right?" she asked, not letting go of his hand.

"You have my word."

"Director," an older guy said from the end of the hall. "We're ready."

"Berkley Levine." She offered the man her hand.

"Walby Edwards," the guy said, shaking Aidan's hand too. "You two have kept me busy at Gitmo for some months, but right now Mr. Chandler is ready to talk to us."

Berkley and Aidan stepped into the observation room, and from outward appearances Jeffery didn't have a mark on him. If anything, the young man with a buzz cut actually looked despondent.

"What's he said so far?" Aidan said.

"He won't give up his father, no matter how pointed our questions, but he did admit that about ten percent of the military is committed to the New Horizons mission. That number seems high, but we can't take any chances," Erin Mosley said. "The most loyal are with Chandler, wherever he is, but the remainder are currently serving here and abroad."

"So the only reason we're here is to be a target for anyone trying to find this little son of a bitch?" Berkley said, and Aidan gave her a look as if trying to get her to calm down.

"Not quite, Captain," Walby said. "After a session of questioning early this morning, he mentioned North Korea. It was the one slip he made, from what we could tell, and you were on the ground, though not by choice, so I felt it important you hear what he had to say. Since you may be headed back there, I thought you'd want to put it on your radar."

"Are you sure his slip," Berkley said, making air quotes, "wasn't a calculated bit to make you stop roasting his testicles?"

"Funny, Captain, but we're not in a James Bond movie."

"Shame, since 007 always comes out on top," Aidan said, and Berkley smiled since Aidan knew she loved Bond movies.

"Has he given up any locations?" Berkley asked.

"Not yet, but I'm going to leave agent Mosley here with one of my people to continue the interrogation. The next part of what we need isn't here, so I'm headed to Gitmo to talk to Mr. Chil."

"If he was their enforcer, he won't break," Berkley said. "Not easily anyway. On him, you might want to take the testicle-roasting equipment out of moth balls."

"Tempting, but it's amazing what sleep manipulation does for your conversation skills," Erin said. "We're going with the fact that Chandler may be in North Korea, and that any military personnel in the area might be compromised."

"We don't want to send you anywhere that might be loaded with people working against you," Jonas said. "Considering how many military personnel are based in the area, ten percent isn't acceptable."

"If you think about the people in custody from the *Jefferson* and the men working with them, ten percent might be right," Aidan said. "Have you gotten anything about something happening here on US soil?"

"The planes that attacked us on our return from North Korea haven't left my mind. The area where they took off had room for a lot more than the ones that were downed," Berkley said.

"That's been our main goal after what happened to President Khalid," Walby said as he flipped the switch on the wall, and Jeffery immediately raised his hands to his ears. "Our goal is to stop another attack here."

"Can we share the North Korea part with the Security Council? There's time to reposition satellites to maybe see something we missed." Berkley kept her attention on Jeffery, who resembled every young guy who joined the marines, but at the moment he appeared to not like whatever was coming out of the speakers. "Was he enlisted before all this?"

"He was a marine," Erin said. "And the president wants all this on a need-to-know basis. We'll report this breakthrough directly to her."

"Everyone keeps telling me we need to change the game and start playing offense, and if we do it right, we should start drawing some of these people out," Aidan said.

"What do you have in mind?" Jonas said.

"To start a very public process every person who serves fears most. Mr. Chandler is technically not only a traitor, but a deserter as well." Aidan stared at Jonas, and he nodded.

"That might be too tempting for Mr. Chandler to pass up. We'll take care of it."

"You're going to have to move him before you do that," Walby said. "It's time to start treating these people for who they are and what they've done."

"That I totally agree with," Berkley said. They were still shooting in the dark, but she saw the beginning of a glimmer in the distance. "Now it's time to bring our team up to speed."

"Sir, are you sure?" Franklin Porche asked as he sat in his bedroom in the dark. At first he was honored when he heard Mr. Chandler's voice on the other end of the line, but what he'd asked was making him question why he'd gotten involved with all this. "With the security surrounding the event, I doubt we'll get out alive."

"I have every faith in you, Major. With your elite training, this shouldn't be that hard. We need to send a message that nothing is safe and changes are coming. If we want maximum effect, it has to be today."

"Yes, sir. I'll prepare the men."

After the line went dead, he dropped to his knees to pray for guidance. Franklin agreed the country was headed in the wrong direction, but this move was not only suicidal but a huge mistake. They needed the public, or at least a majority of it, on their side, and this action could have the opposite effect.

"Meet me in the park close to the base in twenty minutes. We've gotten our orders," Franklin said to US Army Sergeant Stephen Collins.

"Finally," Stephen said and hung up.

"I'm so glad you're ready to die," he said to the empty room. It fucking sucked that at only twenty-eight, he was about to invite death to claim him. If he did meet his maker today, this would be the only thing that defined his life, since he had no family or children.

They prepared the combined unit of army and marines and were in position three hours later. All they had left to do was wait for the moment that would cause the kind of panic Chandler was after. They were in uniform, and so far no one questioned their presence since they looked like part of the day's security. The mall area in front of the Capitol was starting to fill, and he tried to show no emotion every time Stephen glanced his way with a gleeful expression. This had to be done, but he didn't look forward to killing civilians.

"This is fucking nuts," Stephen said, wiping the sweat from his brow. "You got an exit plan once all this shit goes down?"

"If you did what I told you, all you need to do is blend in. Mr. Chandler said once we make it back to the muster point, he'll take care of extracting us. This will buy us a spot at the main compound."

"Let's hope it's that simple, because once we start there's no turning back, and it ain't going to be so easy blending in no matter how much the crowd scatters. Khalid was an asshole, but all these sheep loved him."

"Heads up," Franklin said into his radio when he heard the sirens. "We're a go."

It took another twenty minutes before they saw the hearse stop at the Capitol. Khalid would lie in state for the next day and a half, until he went home to be buried next to his grandparents who'd raised him. The honor guard of marines lifted the casket out, and Franklin waited until they were inside before he motioned for everyone to follow. If what Chandler had said was true, plenty of potential heavy hitters would be waiting to kiss this dead motherfucker's ass. Those people were their targets and part of Chandler's master plan.

"On my mark," he said, and Stephen moved with him. "Move," he yelled, and chaos broke out as the firing began.

They entered the rotunda and opened fire, having no problem for the first minute since most of the marines who'd carried Khalid in were dead on the ground and the casket had pieces missing from their automatic weapons' fire. Security arrived immediately and returned fire, taking out some of his men, including Stephen.

Franklin continued firing but touched the device at his throat and waited for a response. "Go," he said, his adrenaline pumping as he took cover. It took less than two minutes to strip off his uniform to the shirt, tie, and slacks he wore underneath. All he had left to do was blend in with the evacuating crowd and drive off. The airstrip was two hours away, and his ride to Chandler would be waiting.

The explosives they had set that morning went off, really panicking the crowd, so he started running. This would definitely send a message as well as replace some of the people who would have been a problem to Mr. Chandler going forward. Outside, all he heard were sirens and screams, and he used the pandemonium to get clear, hoping most of his men had done the same.

He encountered no problems running the fifteen blocks to his car and drove slowly until he reached the interstate. The news coverage reported the carnage that had happened and how the entire city was going on lockdown. He had to get out before any footage from the scene was released and he was identified.

His cell rang, and it was a private number, but he couldn't take a chance it was about his escape plans. "Hello."

"Are you clear?" a woman asked.

"Yes. I'm on the interstate en route. You made contact with anyone else?"

"Keep your speed—you don't want to get pulled over. The guard at the gate is waiting for you." The woman sounded calm, though he was anything but.

He didn't know if any of the forty men he'd led into the Capitol were still alive and he was abandoning them on the field of battle. That went against everything he believed in, but hopefully, like all the patriots who'd formed the country initially, he'd be remembered once the new order was in place. Chandler had promised him at least that.

"I'll call my contact if I have any problems." He hung up and glanced in his rearview mirror. The traffic was picking up, probably with people trying to leave the city, but that was good for him. After what had happened, the government would have no choice but to fall into crisis. Their rise would come during the confusion.

"So far, we've confirmed three senators and five staff members dead. Police personnel are not giving any more information."

The news anchor spoke rapidly from notes, as the scene behind him was filled with EMS personnel. The body count was far higher than that, but it'd take time for the story to unfold. Once the American people realized Michaels and her government couldn't keep them safe, it would mean the beginning of the end for everything wrong with the country he loved. That he had played such an integral part made him proud.

"History books will remember the name Porche forever."

"Are you ready?" Robyn Chandler asked his sister Rachel.

"For what exactly?" Rachel was sitting outside a coffee shop waiting for her new assistant, Marva Brian. The young woman didn't have Vander's military experience, but she also wasn't there hoping for an eventual career-enhancing marriage.

"It's time to redeem yourself for your failure at the compound. Dad had another visit from General Gil about that, and they're pissed Umeko is still alive."

As always, Robyn sounded superior and condescending, even though the only reason he had a position of leadership was his last name and that he was born first. She'd like to think of it as winning the genetic lottery, since every one of the Chandlers would be garbage collectors if it was up to someone like Robyn to make their family fortune. Her grandfather and the few men before him had secured their future.

"I'm sure you could've taken a heavily armed FBI safe house all alone, Captain Marvel," she said with as much sarcasm as she could dredge up. "Oh, wait. You've only fired at nonmoving little paper targets." Robyn was willing to blame her for everything, but no matter what a screw-up he thought she was, he also wasn't willing to leave the safety of their father's shadow to prove himself in battle. Robyn and her father were both willing to fan the flames of destruction, but neither of them was willing to enter the fray lest they get burned.

"You know I'm too important to the fight to risk on something like that, so don't disrespect me again." Robyn tried to sound menacing but only came off as comical. "Pay attention. I have your next set of orders. After watching those bitches and hearing from our contact, we know where Jeffery is, and we need to get him back. With the chaos our troops managed, today is a perfect time to break into the facility and release him. Dad wants it done before he might say something, if they're treating him poorly. Our contact also ordered the guard count cut by half, so it shouldn't be that hard."

"DC *is* a shitstorm right now, but you're asking me to send my people into a suicide mission. We've already lost a couple trying to grab Levine, and that'll be nothing compared to assaulting a federal prison especially meant to house people like Jeffery." Marva got in and handed her a cup and a bag. "I don't have that many people available."

"Either do it, or report back here and face insubordination charges," Robyn said, and he seemed almost gleeful to deliver the news. "We could always use your help in the mess-hall kitchen."

"Fuck you, Robyn," she said, and Marva's eyebrows went up. "You can act like a smug bastard all you want, but it doesn't change the numbers on the ground. At least it doesn't unless you want to sacrifice everything and everyone else in place to save Jeffery. Whatever will all these people lined up to fight for us say if you answer yes to that question?"

"The team leader from today just called, and he's clear. If he made it out, the majority of the others could've made it out as well, so find them. Dad has something planned to help you get in and out, so call me when you're ready to go. I expect that call within twenty-four hours. It's time to strike before the situation on the ground there goes back to normal."

When he hung up, she wanted to smash the phone, but she didn't have a lot of options. She'd be a fugitive not only in the US, but anywhere in the world that wasn't a shithole. Any US ally would gladly turn her over if she decided to run. Fuck it, she thought. It might be better to get shot and get it over with than to end up like Jeffery, who was probably drowning in his own vomit by now.

"Problem?" Marva asked, taking a muffin out of the bag and breaking it in half to share with her.

"We need to move and go back to our place here."

Marva started the car without hesitation. "I thought we were going to the base north of the district."

"Change of plans." She took out her book of contacts and found Franklin's number. "We need to pick someone up before we reach the next phase."

"That's easy enough," Marva said, starting back to the house they rented under a dummy corporation.

"Not unless we have plenty of explosives and luck."

CHAPTER THIRTEEN

The next morning Berkley called a meeting on the *Jefferson* with her flight team, glad to see them all together again, especially her flight partner, Harvey "Junior" Whittle. They'd had the rest of the day off after the attack on the Capitol, but she wanted to start planning for their upcoming operation. After their meeting the previous afternoon, she and Aidan knew the president was pissed, and once they had a hard target, they'd get a green light to take it down.

"Junior, you ready to get back to work?" she asked as Whittle gave her a bear hug. He'd ended up with a slight limp after their experience in North Korea, but he'd never considered retiring. Harvey had been hit by part of their plane when Berkley had ejected them, and the impact had badly broken his leg. Berkley had carried him out, and he'd worked hard to return to duty.

"Thanks for all those calls and visits," Harvey said as she slapped him on the back. "You can even kick my ass long distance, Cletus."

"You don't need me to kick your ass, and I'm glad you decided to stay. If I'd had to train someone new, I would've had to rethink the ass-kicking option."

Lake "Killer" Goram and Sonny "Vader" Forche stood right behind Harvey and gave her the same greeting. They'd known each other for years, and Berkley trusted them on her wing. The only missing original team member was David Morris, but he'd been sitting in custody not talking and had tried to kill himself twice.

"We ready to go?" Lake asked.

"I wanted to add one more team member before we leave, but I doubt we'll be doing anything like last time," she said as they headed to the conference room next to her quarters.

"Wouldn't hurt, and we can always train someone on our luxury cruise," Sonny said. "It might not be like last time, but with all this shit going on, we'll need all the backup we can bring with us. I'd rather be overloaded than a plane short."

"Any ideas?" she asked.

"Another year's gone by, so how about we pick someone who impressed Captain Jepson," Sonny said of the Top Gun program director. It was where Berkley had spent the last few years of her life before Aidan had come back to her. "This time, let's screen a little better before whoever it is screws us without buying us flowers and dinner first."

"I vote for that," Harvey said, and they laughed as the alarm sounded.

"All available pilots to the deck—all available pilots, report for duty," someone said excitedly over the ship-wide intercom.

"What the hell?" she asked, but all of them started running.

One of the crew handed her a radio as she sprinted to the deck. She could hear the *Jefferson*'s engines firing up, and they were moving. "Captain Levine," someone on the radio said. "We have black fighter jets spotted en route to the capital. They're about thirty minutes out from entering restricted airspace and have evaded ground defenses, so we need you in the air."

"Command is also scrambling planes from Andrews. We'll inform them you're coming," someone else said.

"Are we clear?" Berkley asked as she and Harvey ran for their plane.

"Two minutes and you're a go."

The planes were on deck, with more coming up, and she and Harvey buckled in as she opened communications with the rest of her pilots. "Two spear formations once we're airborne. One follows me, one behind Killer."

A slew of *yes ma'am* came over the line, and she got ready to be the first off the deck. "Cletus." She heard Aidan's voice.

"Captain, keep the lights on, and give us some room to land later." This time they hadn't had a chance to talk before she had to go, but she had to believe Aidan knew in her heart all she needed to know about her feelings for her.

"Will do, and don't be late."

"A quick trip to take out the trash, and I promise we won't sightsee afterward."

❖

"Are you in place?" Dick Chandler asked Franklin Porche. It was early in the morning in DC and perfect timing for what he had in mind.

"We have enough men for two teams, and we're ready to go, sir."

"Good," Dick said, staring at Robyn. "Keep this line clear, and we'll call when we're ready to move."

"Yes, sir," Franklin said, and his enthusiasm made Dick smile.

"You're clear to go," Dick said to the next caller after Robyn handed him another phone.

"Are you sure you want everyone, sir?" the man asked, and from his tone, Dick could hear he didn't totally agree with his plan. "We've already lost a large number off the West Coast and haven't been able to replace them."

"Everyone, Captain. If we lose anyone else, we have the resources to replace inventory. I need all those planes in the air in ten minutes."

"It's not so much the inventory, sir, but the pilots to fly them," the man said, then paused as if realizing he didn't intend to change his mind. "Yes, sir. We'll be airborne soon."

"Have them hit the targets we talked about, and add one more." Dick read off the coordinates of the building across the street from the prison facility. "Have two planes break off and take this target out, and only this target."

"I'll put two of our best men on that, sir."

"Good. Have them all underway by seven." He hung up and stood, needing to move. "Are you ready?" He took one last call.

"Are you that anxious for me to die?" Rachel asked.

"Get back here with your brother, and we'll talk about your role going forward. You've done everything I've asked of you, and you deserve a spot with me."

"Don't blow smoke, Dad," she said and laughed. "It's so not your talent."

"There's never a reason for disrespect, Rachel. You never have learned that."

"What I've never learned is to be a willing sacrificial lamb, and believe me, there's a difference. Since you don't care a shit about me, all you need to know is who's in place and ready to go. Eventually you'll realize we're not pieces on the board of some game you're playing. I'll call you when we're done. If you don't hear from me, tell Mom she was right."

Rachel disconnected the call first, for once, and handed the phone to Marva. She lowered the window of the truck they were driving and glanced at the time on her phone. It was five to seven, and the sky was a beautiful shade of blue without a cloud in sight. The five minutes she had before hell rained down on them was clicking by faster than the phone showed, and she wanted to do something normal with the few moments she had left. She leaned over and pressed her lips to Marva's.

"Ma'am?" Marva asked, obviously confused, but she didn't move away.

"For once I wanted something that has nothing to do with this war I was drafted into."

Marva gazed at her and moved closer. "I understand, and being with you is making me less scared." Marva placed her hands on Rachel's face and kissed her again.

Rachel's watch beeped three times, and she reluctantly ended the only intimacy she'd experienced in months. "Time to go." The sky was still clear, but she heard the jet engines, so they were close by. Only a few seconds later an explosion rocked the car with an impressive fireball that rose over the pile of rubble a few hundred yards away.

"Go, go, go," she said into her radio, and gunfire followed the order. "Stay behind me," she said to Marva as they exited the truck.

Grenades cut the fence down, and she waited for Franklin's guys to go through first, since they had the most firepower. They hit the front doors with grenade launchers, and she was about to cross the street when the firefight really began. The speed with which their men were being shot down made Rachel realize they'd walked into a trap.

"Get back in," she said to Marva. "They were waiting for us. Abort," she said into the radio, but no one answered. She wasn't close enough to see the front of the building through the thick smoke, but they needed to get a look before retreating. She drove to an elevated parking lot a few blocks away and made her way to the top. "Damn."

Plenty of still bodies with visible wounds littered the ground around the parked cars, but a few men still alive were on their knees waiting to be cuffed. One of them was Franklin Porche, and he knew too much to be good for them. "Ma'am, what do we do?" Marva asked.

"Clear out. It's all we can do for now, and with any luck, we can eventually fight back." She got back on the radio and took a deep breath for what she had to accomplish next. "Eagle One, we need another flyby with machine guns. Clear the area."

"Yes, ma'am."

"Completely clear."

❖

"Okay, Junior, you know what to do," Berkley said as they dropped altitude and flew into the heart of the district.

"Head on a swivel, ma'am," Harvey said, and his voice in her ear made her think her life was getting back to where she was the most comfortable. She just couldn't believe it was over the capital.

"Good. Now tell me what you see."

"Radar shows thirty targets that have broken off into four smaller groups. One seems headed to the Pentagon, two squadrons are on course for the two big targets on the National Mall, and a much-smaller group is somewhere I can't identify. Reports are the last small group has already dropped some stingers and is swinging back in for another run."

"Vader," she said and waited. They had to cut these assholes off before they reached the Capitol, the White House, or the Pentagon. They were the same targets the terrorists had targeted on nine eleven in Washington, DC, and that Chandler had chosen the same list made her ill.

"Go ahead, Cletus."

"Take three with you, and sweep the area that's already been bombed. Try to lead them back over water, but no matter what, don't let them drop another thing."

"Aye, Captain," Vader said.

"Cletus," Killer said, his voice shrill. "The Pentagon's been hit."

"Let's take these bastards out," she said, pissed. "Keep your eyes open for the teams scrambled from Andrews. It's about to get crowded up here, and I'm not in the mood to go parachuting today." She heard a slew of agreements, then swung toward the White House. Ten planes were flying close together about ten miles ahead of her, painted the same black color as the first ones she'd faced as they neared the West Coast after their mission in North Korea. "If it's the same as before, they won't be taken alive."

"Fuck," Harvey said, and she knew why. Nothing but houses stretched below them. It wouldn't matter if they were able to stop an attack on the White House. Taking these guys down here would kill people on the ground when the debris field rained down on them.

"Killer, we need to get these guys off one scent and onto another. If we down them here, the most casualties will be on the ground."

"Got you, Cletus. A good game of chase should do it."

She opened up her guns and started firing as she inverted the plane. She sliced through the wing but not enough to make it inoperable. The pilot of that plane came about and fired back, which made her team repeat the move with their guns. They all turned at once, and the objective now was to not get hit. The miles they were covering at least brought them over open land.

"Cletus," Harvey said, sounding excited. "The lead plane is smoking but trying to lock."

"Keep an eye on the guy to his right." She banked to the left and climbed enough to dive and turn around. With the all-clear, she fired and took out the plane's fuselage. It went down over land, which at least meant this time they would get some answers.

"Cletus, we need to move."

The first plane had been fixated on bringing them down, and this was a lesson she'd always preached about when she was an instructor at Top Gun. When you were willing to sacrifice someone for the glory of the kill, you lost sight of everything but the target. But if your enemy was a cohesive team, then your nearsightedness got you killed. One of her crew shot the guy down, and she had a clear aim at the plane trying to lock on her savior.

"Clear these out so we can go back to hold the last team off," she said to the guy on her wing.

"Captain Levine," a man said over the radio. "Do you copy?"

"Go ahead," she answered as she rejoined the old-fashioned dogfight.

"This is Poncho out of Andrews, ma'am. Our team has neutralized the remaining force. Your man Vader was shot down, but we have reports that he and his partner ejected successfully. Do you need backup?"

"Negative, but we need to set up a perimeter around the city in case they have more fighters hidden away somewhere." She shot down one more, and her team took out the remainder. "Contact Andrews and tell them we need a recovery team out here to go through the wreckage. I don't see any ejectors, but we need to identify the pilots and where the planes came from."

"Yes, ma'am, and our backup should be here shortly, loaded for bear," Commander Bruce "Poncho" Thompson said. "We'll take it from here."

"Contact me once you're on the ground. I have a new assignment for you if you're interested."

"Yes, ma'am."

"Lead us home, Junior."

"You got it."

"This is Cletus," she said, calling the *Jefferson*. "Come in, *Jefferson*."

"Go ahead, Cletus," the radio operator said.

"Have Captain Sullivan check on Vader. If he and his backseat are okay, he's going to need a ride back on board."

"We'll take care of it, Cletus. Just get back here before they start sending us a bill for all this hardware you guys keep destroying," Aidan said.

"Yes, ma'am." They headed back, but she set a course to where Vader had been shot down. The area that had been bombed was out of the way of the high-level targets, but there had to be a reason they'd used resources on it. "What was the other target today?"

"We'll update you when you get back," Aidan said.

"We're coming about, ma'am. See you in a few minutes."

"The attack today, in our professional team's opinion, was a diversionary tactic," Director Jonas Chapman said as the emergency Security Council meeting got underway. "The Capitol incident yesterday put us on high alert, and their fighter jets were meant to ramp up the fear and panic already in the streets."

"Chandler sacrificed a squadron of fighters to free Jeffery?" Marcus Newton asked in a way that made him sound skeptical.

"We'll have to find him to ask him, but we believe so. If that's indeed accurate, it gives us insight into Chandler's mindset."

"Can he be delusional enough to believe he can actually pull off a coup?" George Butler asked. "I mean, Dick could be a real asshole, but I never thought he was freaking crazy."

"Mr. President, he's laid the groundwork," Marcus said. "How he was able to recruit what seem like dedicated and able-bodied soldiers is a mystery, but he's done that in spades."

"The dead men identified at both the Capitol and in the perimeter of the detention facility were active members of both the army and the marines. These guys were in no way mercenaries," Jonas said. "The preliminary reports on the downed planes and pilots are that the hardware is Russian and Iranian, but the pilots are all homegrown ex and active members of the armed forces."

"Has Jeffery Chandler said anything else?" Olivia asked, still upset that these idiots had desecrated Peter's body. It was bad enough that they'd killed him, but what had happened yesterday had added insult to that already sad fact. "Chandler is a threat that must be contained. We need to focus on how in the world he's getting all these guys to commit these acts of terror. No service people, active or retired, should ever think of firing on the capital of the United States for any reason."

"Yes, ma'am," Jonas said, and Marcus nodded. "This has been a joint task force between the FBI and CIA, and not only have we gotten what we think is reliable information, but a way to bring Chandler in."

"You say that, Jonas, but you've cut us out of the loop when it comes to Jeffery Chandler. Remember that Walby Edwards works for me."

"Mr. Edwards, I believe, works for the US government," Drew said. "Worry about doing your job and not about what everyone else is doing. Right now, the CIA needs to find any chatter about Chandler, no matter where it's coming from."

"I am doing my job," Marcus said with what seemed like extreme agitation. "Madam President, we have to proceed cautiously. We can all argue that Chandler's the head of the snake, but he's fortified the body with fanatics," Marcus said, speaking directly to Olivia. "When we move, it has to be when we can ensure we capture the information we need to weed out the rest of his followers, no matter how many there are, and not before."

"I agree, but we have five dead senators, twenty-one dead congressional staff members, five Secret Service members, and twelve MPs. That's something neither I nor the American people will forget anytime soon, since it played out on national television." Olivia placed her hands flat on the table, her voice calm and soft. "The time for action is now, gentlemen. If anyone doubts my resolve for absolute justice, he will be sadly mistaken."

"I'm a hundred percent for that," George said and saluted Olivia.

"Thank you," she said. "I also want heavy security for Peter's funeral. Eva and the girls deserve to lay him to rest with the upmost decorum."

There was a chorus of "yes ma'ams" before they stood to go. The funeral was that morning, and they were all attending. The United States did not negotiate with terrorists, and her leaders did not hide in fear at times of uncertainty. Olivia was steadfast in her decision-making.

"George, I'd like you and Victoria to join Gabriel and me. If anything, it'll make it easier on the security detail," she said.

"We'd love to, and you have a good team here, Madam President. I'll be forever in your debt for letting me sort out my legacy by allowing me to help however I can. Peter and I had some long talks as we went through the transition, but we both agreed on you as his choice for vice president. You've done him and the rest of us proud in the last few days."

"Thank you, and my mom always said you sometimes don't recognize crazy until it hits you in the face with a pie. You couldn't have known Dick was this kind of nut before you chose him, so no thanks necessary."

"I appreciate you all the same. Let's go pay our respects to our friend."

"Gone way too soon."

CHAPTER FOURTEEN

The honor guard stood at attention in the rotunda as Eva and her daughters entered, followed by Olivia's family, George and his wife, and all the living presidents and their families, the foreign dignitaries in attendance bringing up the rear. There would be a procession to the National Cathedral before his burial in Michigan, and eventually he and his grandparents would be moved one more time after his presidential library was completed.

Berkley stood at attention with tears in her eyes as Eva and her girls made their way to the casket and laid their hands on its top. Her emotions were on overload from watching the two little girls trying to be brave for their mother, but their pain was right at the surface. Anyone could see that with no problem. That President Khalid had to be placed in a new casket after the attack was a national disgrace, she thought as Eva was joined by her extended family. The late president had only a few living relatives, and those elderly aunts would be at his burial.

After a call for silence, the Khalids' pastor said a short prayer before they made their way out. The marine unit placed their hands on the casket and slowly started to the caisson waiting outside the Capitol. In two days, the same ceremony would be carried out for the senators who'd been killed in the rotunda, but today was Peter's day.

All the military personnel who lined the stairs of the Capitol saluted as the flag-draped casket was carried down. On the street, the DC police estimated the crowd to consist of over a million people along the route. The same number that had come to watch his inauguration was here now to pay their respects. From Berkley's understanding, the secret-service detail had wanted the Khalids, the president, and the other dignitaries to ride to the cathedral in bulletproof vehicles, but Eva had chosen to walk, and Olivia wouldn't hear of letting her do that alone.

Aidan walked beside her, and Berkley's eyes were restlessly scanning the windows and the crowds along the way. The president had died because he'd shaken up the status quo, and in a nutshell, she and Aidan were some of the biggest examples of that turnover. If President Michaels was a target, the two of them were also high on the list of people Chandler would make an example of, if given the opportunity.

"Believe me." Wiley Gremillion's voice came through her earpiece. "If Skinner's out here, he's going for the money shot."

"Where exactly is that?" she said softly. It was an honor to be walking right behind the president and former first lady, but she wasn't keen on it being the last honor of her life.

"I'm thinking that would be the leader of the free world while you're still close to the seat of government, aka that building behind you. But don't worry. I'm watching."

Wiley was on a roof somewhere that hadn't been disclosed on the chance they had a mole and would be moving as they made their way along. "If you let these guys mess up our pretty uniforms, I'm going to seriously question our friendship."

"Keep your eyes open, and try to appear regal with all that stuff pinned to your chest. Any more shiny bits on that pristine uniform, and I'd be blinded by the reflection."

"Remind me to punch you in the eye later."

"What would the nuns from Sacred Heart say if they could see you now?" Wiley said, making her smile.

The procession was now assembled, and they were all ready to move. She saw Aidan take a deep breath, and she understood the nervous tic, since she was more comfortable in a cockpit than with all these eyes on her. President Khalid deserved to be remembered for his short but effective tenure, though, so she started walking. They'd be walking a mile or so at the beginning and the same distance again at the end to minimize the danger as much as the Secret Service could talk the president and the former first lady into.

"Anything?" Aidan asked softly.

"She didn't tell anyone where, but Wiley scoped the area and chose the second-best nest."

"She left the honors of the best nest to her competition?"

"If he shows up, he's in for a brain enema he won't soon forget," Berkley said softly, and Aidan groaned.

"Don, heads up," Wiley said, having put Don Smith on the other side from where she was. Her handler Don wasn't in charge of a couple of retirees simply because he'd drawn the assignment, but because he'd served General Greenwald as well.

"Got it, but there's two," Don said and hummed. "And then there was one," he said seconds later.

"Get some agents up there," Wiley said after obviously eliminating the shooter that was left.

"Scan for any others," Berkley said, glancing at Aidan momentarily. "If there's a third we have to move all these people to cover."

"Our team is scanning, Captain," Don said. "They're reporting all clear for the next mile, so Wiley and I are moving."

"Trust him, Cletus. We don't want to give these people the satisfaction of any more panic. That's what President Michaels wanted to avoid at all costs," Wiley said.

"I also don't want the honor of attending another presidential funeral, so be sure." Berkley stared ahead to Agent Lainey Willcott and gave her a nod. The sign made Lainey move closer to Olivia, and that prompted the rest of the details to do the same with their charges. Lainey switched her radio to Berkley's channel and nodded back. "Two snipers eliminated, and our team is moving to the next nest. We hold for now."

"Are you willing to gamble with the president's life?" Lainey asked.

Lainey stared at her as if trying to override her need to keep her charge safe, especially now that she'd been promoted to the lead of the president's detail. Shimmy Laurel, the former lead of the president' detail, was still there, but he was now the number-two agent in charge, and he glanced back with the same worry. The helicopters probably transporting Wiley and Don flew wide of them and forward. "I'd never put her in harm's way, Agent Willcott, but you have the final call."

The decision seemed gut-wrenching, but Lainey looked forward and stayed at Olivia's elbow. "Keep up the chatter, but we hold for now," Lainey said, speaking into her sleeve.

"What now?" Aidan asked.

"Two down and hopefully none to go," she answered, the sound of the helicopter rotors in her ear. "Anything, Wiley?"

"I'm a minute from my new position, but all clear. Repeat, all clear," Wiley said.

"Good. Keep talking. Lead Agent Willcott will be listening in," Berkley said as one of Lainey's people moved closer to her and Aidan.

They walked on, the crowds never thinning and surreally quiet. For once the sentiment of the mob was of the mindset of Ronald Reagan's doctor the day the president had been shot. Dr. Benjamin Aaron had told the story after the surgery that saved Reagan's life of how the president had asked him in the emergency room if he was a Republican. Dr. Aaron had responded, "Today, Mr. President, we're all Republicans."

Today, for as far as Berkley could see, they were all Americans, and the number of people there to honor President Khalid had to give Eva and her girls some iota of comfort.

"A block to go, Cletus. Be prepared to move. If they have a plan B, this is where it is," Wiley said, obviously in position. "Don."

"I see them, but no kill shot if you can help it," Don said, and Berkley raised her hand to the agent watching her.

Lainey glanced up and appeared to be cursing under her breath, but she didn't rush the president anywhere. "I'm leading my group in first, after our people sweep the church again like we discussed," Lainey said, and the agent next to her seemed to repeat the order.

"We've spotted two more but are clearing the threat," Wiley said.

"We'll wait to go in with the honor guard once the major players are in their seats," Berkley said.

"Keep us in the loop," Lainey said, taking Olivia's elbow and making her walk faster, following the plan everyone had had to memorize before they left the Capitol. Eva and her girls were led in first, followed by the others, and held in the vestibule until the building was cleared.

They didn't need to wait long before Wiley reported in. "Two more, but only one shooter. Go in, and I'll finish with Director Chapman's team," Wiley said, since the FBI had been listening in the whole time.

It took ten minutes, but everyone inside stood when the honor guard entered and placed the casket at the front of the church. Berkley and Aidan stood, along with the other military personnel present for the service and Olivia's eulogy. Plenty of people believed Olivia had lost the nomination to Peter because she wasn't as gifted a public speaker as he was, but there weren't many dry eyes in the cathedral and outside watching on the large projection screens when she was done.

After the service concluded, Berkley was glad to see the most prominent dignitaries present get into armored limousines, effectively taking them out of the line of fire. It had been reported that the Michaels family would attend the burial service as well, but with the threats they'd dealt with here, she knew Lainey would argue strongly against it. She also knew Olivia would go anyway, and if she didn't change in the coming years, she and Lainey would be constantly butting heads.

"Are you ready?" Aidan asked her. They were having dinner with the Sullivans and her parents, and they'd already had to cancel twice after her parents arrived in town.

"Dad texted, and he's around the block." She pointed to the right and walked through the churchyard to avoid the crowd outside. "You want to change before we go?"

"Maybe they'll let us cut the wait line if they see you in the spiffy uniform," Aidan said, tugging on her sleeve.

"Ha." She glanced down at her beautiful partner. The dress blues made Aidan's blond hair really stand out, and she knew that today, like every day that didn't include a physical, Aidan was wearing underwear that was in no way regulation. "You're the rock star here, Captain Sullivan, and I for one really enjoy serving under you."

"You're a troublemaker is what you are." Aidan slapped her shoulder. "There are your parents, and they're going to wonder why I'm blushing."

"They put up with me for years, so I really doubt they'll have to guess, pretty lady."

Wiley changed into her uniform before heading to the hotel where her family was staying. Aubrey had told her they'd stick close by until she got back, her only plan being to take Tanith to the pool. As the cab made its way through the heavy traffic, she didn't really focus on any one thing. It was an old strategy to blur her surroundings out as a way of forgetting how the world was missing a few more people because of her.

At first, the assignments had been exciting and had meant something. She'd go somewhere and sit in a nest or lie in wait until she was done. When she was, there was one less evil person in the world, but seeing what was going on in DC, she had no choice but to question her choices more than she had already. Just because someone outranked, they didn't necessarily have the greater good in mind. How many orders to send her out had Dick Chandler signed himself, but only to further his own cause?

"Did you want me to wait?" the cab driver asked.

"No, sorry." She handed over the fare and got out. It didn't surprise her that Aubrey was standing in the lobby. It actually made the piece of herself that lived only in the shadows crave the light even more. "Do you know something?"

"I know plenty, but right now I need you to take me upstairs and kiss me before we have to go out. I'm not looking forward to sharing you,

but I'll do it if you promise to come back here and let me ravish you."
She smoothed Wiley's lapel and smiled. "That sounds like a good plan, but did you forget about the kid sharing a room with us?" She took Aubrey's hand and started for the elevator.

"The kid is spending the night with her very doting grandparents since, according to your mother, they don't get to see her often enough to properly spoil her." The way Aubrey squeezed her fingers made her want to stay in, but she didn't want to pass up the opportunity to spend time with both Tanith and Aubrey before she had to leave them. When she sailed with Berkley and Aidan, it wouldn't be her usual weekend gig.

"My mother is in our guest room once a month, so don't believe everything she tells you. When my father finally decides to retire, we'll have to change the locks or enter witness protection to ditch her." The room was high enough to give them a good view of the city, but right now they could've been in a cave for all she cared. She saw only Aubrey, the beautiful girl who had loved her for as long as she knew what love meant. "You are gorgeous. Do you know that?"

"I don't think of myself like that, but I can't help but believe it when you look at me like this. That you see me at all has been the greatest gift of my life." Aubrey unbuttoned her tunic and part of her shirt to stick her hand inside. "Was today hard?"

Leave it to her partner to cut right to it. "I'm glad I was here, but that's all I can tell you, my love."

"I'm not worried about the gory details, baby. I'm worried about you and what's going on here," Aubrey tapped the side of her head, then laid her hand on Wiley's chest over her heart. "The army might still have ahold of you, but you're mine, and I need you to be okay."

"That I am, darlin'." She walked Aubrey backward until her butt hit the dresser across from the bed. "And you're mine." Aubrey didn't say anything when she picked her up and placed her hands momentarily on her knees before sliding them up and under her skirt.

"We're going to be late," Aubrey said, then inhaled when Wiley's fingers went under the elastic of her panties. "But I don't really care right this second." Wiley smiled when Aubrey unbuttoned the rest of her jacket, took it off, and placed it next to her. Her belt went next, and she laughed when her pants pooled at her ankles. "I need you, baby, and I don't care who's waiting on us."

"Do you need me here?" She moved her thumb from Aubrey's wet sex to her clit, finding it hard and pulsing.

"Take them off," Aubrey demanded as she pulled her briefs down enough to put her hand between her legs. They'd had sex probably far too early in their lives, but damn if it wasn't as exciting now as the first time. She stripped Aubrey's panties off and got her fingers wet as she stroked Aubrey's clit. "No. I want to come with you inside me," Aubrey said with her eyes closed and her free hand clutching her shoulder.

"I love you," she whispered as she gave Aubrey what she wanted by thrusting her fingers in and out fast and hard. The urge to stop almost swamped her when Aubrey's fingers sped up, making her want to come way too fast.

"If you stop so will I," Aubrey said, placing her feet behind Wiley's knees. "And I don't really want to stop since I need to come, baby. I really do."

The desperation in Aubrey's voice made her take her fingers out and slam them back in with a steady rhythm, hitting her clit with her thumb every time she went inside. She loved the way Aubrey sounded when she was excited, the way she bit her lip when she didn't want to get too loud, and how she bucked her hips up to meet her. Her lover was the sexiest woman she'd ever met, and right now all she wanted to do was to unleash the orgasm that was so close she could almost taste it.

"Wait," Aubrey said when she dropped to her knees, but she didn't say anything else when she left her fingers in and put her mouth on her. "Uh-huh," Aubrey said, growing louder. "Right there," She grabbed the back of Wiley's head and held her in place. "Don't…harder, baby, harder. Jesus, your mouth is so good."

Wiley sucked harder on her clit and curled her finger slightly upward, sending Aubrey over the edge, and Aubrey held her in place as she went rigid. A moment later she pulled her hair hard as a sign to stop.

"You ready to go?" she asked as she straightened up.

"You're kidding, right?" Aubrey asked, placing her hand at the center of Wiley's chest and pushing hard enough to make her take a step back. She walked backward awkwardly as Aubrey continued pushing her, since her pants were still around her ankles. "I'm not letting you sit through dinner tight as a bow."

She hit the bed and fell into it as Aubrey dropped to her knees. "Besides, for as much as I complain about the military, you look hot in that uniform, baby, and I've been wanting to touch you since I saw you walk up."

She would've made some sarcastic comment, but Aubrey followed her compliment by dragging her tongue up from her center and over her clit in a hard, possessive way. The firm stroke was exactly what she craved, and when Aubrey did it again, she pressed her toes into her shoes. She was so hard and so ready she was about to start begging when Aubrey sped up her movements. The relentlessness of Aubrey's mouth made her frantic to come, but it happened much too fast. "Fuck," she said so softly that she spread her hands on the bed before clutching the blanket in both fists.

When she went limp, Aubrey kissed her sex, then hovered over her and kissed her gently on the lips. "See, you can't tell me you didn't need that."

"I'm always going to need you, my love, and that I can have you makes me deliriously happy." She sat up and reached for her pants to follow Aubrey into the bathroom. "I love you so much," she said, holding Aubrey from behind and watching her in the mirror. "And I'm sorry about all this."

"About what?" Aubrey turned around and slapped her hands away so she could zip her pants for her. "What are you sorry about, love?"

"This isn't my usual assignment of a couple of days and I'm home. It won't be a quick turnaround, and I'm not sure how you and Tanith will handle it."

When she'd walked away from Aubrey years before to keep her safe from the consequences of her choices, she'd tried to shut herself off from the memories and the feelings of happiness as a way to survive the loneliness. If she lost Aubrey, and now Tanith, by leaving, she didn't think she could do the same thing again. This time the darkness would swallow her whole, and she'd find no way out but through a bullet.

"Listen to me, okay," Aubrey said, placing her hands on her face to force her to look at her. "Don't be scared that you doing the right thing will make me leave. You don't like to talk about it, but I bet today, because of the Black Dragon, President Michaels and everyone around her stayed safe." Aubrey completely unbuttoned her shirt and pulled it down enough to see the large dragon tattoo Wiley had on her left upper arm. Along the dragon's body were the names Tanith and Aubrey, put there long before Tanith was even a dream of theirs.

"Tanith, the pagan goddess of war and protection," she said as Aubrey ran her fingertip along the names of her and their daughter. It was something Tanith liked to do whenever she wore something sleeveless to work out in. "And Tanit, her sister, the goddess of justice and vengeance," she said when Aubrey touched the other smaller tattoo on her right arm.

"These are a part of you, just like the honor and code that define your life. Today all those people didn't have to worry about what was out there because you were on post, and you did what you were trained to do.

That makes me proud of you, baby, not disgusted. What happened today was a job for Tanit, it was justice for all the bad these people have done, and I'm glad it was you who carried it out."

"But maybe one day it'll be too much." She was comfortable enough with Aubrey's hands on her to voice her greatest fear.

"The day you don't go when called might be the day I don't understand," Aubrey said and stood on her toes to kiss her. "Or if you walk away again and disappear without an explanation of why. That'll be the only thing that would be too much. You have a family who loves you, Wiley, and we're proud of you," Aubrey said and smiled. "And…"

Wiley tugged her closer when she stopped. "What?"

"I am proud of you, love, and Tanith is too. When it's her turn to go in your place, you'll have laid a solid and honorable path for her to walk."

"I'd rather have her do something else."

"We have to face the truth that she was born with the Gremillion warrior gene, baby. That kid not only loves you, but she idolizes you, and that means she wants more than anything to be just like you." Aubrey kissed her again and took a deep breath as she pulled her shirt back up and started buttoning it. "If I'm right, this next kid will probably be the same way. I don't see either of them wanting to go into a career in the mayor's office. That's highly unlikely when their other mom is like our own private version of Wonder Woman."

"This next kid?" Wiley asked, her eyes widening as she gazed down at Aubrey.

"You did understand that whole process we did at the doctor's office, right? I don't have time to explain the birds and the bees to you right now if you didn't."

They'd talked about another child six months after Aubrey and Tanith moved in because Aubrey wanted to share the experience with her from beginning to end. She told her she'd gotten off easy in the diaper-changing and fussy-nights departments, and if they waited much longer, it'd be too late. They'd gone to the doctor and used the same donor Aubrey had found for Tanith, and Wiley had been reluctant to get too excited since the doctors said it might take a few times before they were successful.

"You're pregnant?" she asked slowly.

"You do good work, stud, and I know you'll be gone a while, but try to come back before I reach the stage where I really crave sex. Flying solo isn't my thing." Aubrey laughed when she lifted her in the air and hugged her as she turned in a circle.

"We're going to have a baby? Really?"

"It's early yet, but at the beginning of next year don't make any plans to go anywhere. You and I have a date with the doctor, so you can hold my hand while I push." Wiley closed her eyes when Aubrey combed her hair back with her fingers and kissed her cheek. "We've had our share of pain, baby, but that won't happen again. I love you, and I don't want you to forget that no matter how long you have to be gone. Tanith and I love you, and baby Gremillion is going to adore you."

"Thank you, and I love you too."

"That's all I need then. I need you to love us and come back to us in one piece."

"I promise."

Chapter Fifteen

Berkley and Aidan met her mom Maggie at the hotel where they were staying, since Preston and Mary Beth were back in their home close to Aidan's condo. "Change of plans," Preston said when they stopped at the entrance. "Give your folks a ride and follow me." Corbin got out and moved to the backseat with her mother.

"Where are we going?" Aidan asked.

"To dinner, only we've been invited to the Gremillions'. It'll give me a chance to debrief you about today's developments with Wiley there. It'll also let you relax a bit before you ship out, at least more than you could in a restaurant."

"I'm all for that," Berkley said as her mom got in.

"Sorry we haven't had a moment free since you guys got here," Berkley said, glancing at her parents in the rearview mirror. "It's been a crap show."

"Don't worry about it, kid. We're here to sightsee, not bother you," Corbin said, and she and Aidan laughed, knowing her father wasn't much on the sights except for the Smithsonian Air and Space Museum.

"We're here because you never remember to call your mother," Maggie said, and Aidan reached for Berkley's hand and pulled on her fingers.

"We're working, Mom, so we're not ignoring you," Berkley said, listening to the GPS to get them to Buckston and Danielle Gremillion's home. "Once we're done, I promise I'll be in your kitchen having coffee every morning."

"And we'll leave our kids with you, so you can babysit every chance I can talk this one into taking me somewhere romantic," Aidan said.

"You've been around my kid too long, Aidan, but I *am* a great babysitter," Maggie said, and Berkley nodded. "I'm cutting you some major slack though, considering we're spending the last of our time with you at the Gremillions' place."

"I don't want to share you either, Mama," Berkley said as she felt her mom's hand on her shoulder. "Lately I've been thinking more and more about home."

"We think about that too, kid, but right now I need you to keep your head in Chandler's very sick game," Corbin said. "I don't daydream as much as your mom and sisters, but I'm looking forward to one more wedding, and to really enjoy myself, I need you back without a scratch on you. Either of you."

They arrived, and she hugged both her parents before they went in. "I love you both, and I really am excited about coming home. I've been away too long, but it took me a while to find a girl."

"I give you a hard time, Berk, but your father and I are so proud of you." Maggie kissed her cheek, and Corbin followed with a tight hug. "You've got more ribbons and medals than your father, and they are so well deserved. Your grandparents and sisters are over-the-moon proud of you too."

"Your mama's right, in that you're a great soldier, kid, but we're also proud of the woman you're going to share your life with. She reminds me a lot of this one," Corbin said, pointing at Maggie. "She'll give you hell for a lifetime, but it's only because she loves you, and you'll never be able to live without her." Corbin's very uncharacteristically sappy comments made her hug him again.

"Thank you so much, Mama and Dad. You two always made me believe I could do the impossible, and I just have to channel that for a few more months."

"You okay?" Aidan asked when they all headed for the door.

"Great, and they love you, so I'd start getting used to her fussing. That not-calling offense goes for you too."

"I know, and I'm taking notes. Eventually we'll have more than one who'll act just like you, and I'll need pointers on how to handle them." Aidan stopped her close to the car and kissed her.

"Get in here before someone calls the cops," Wiley said from the door. "Though I admire you for keeping your hands to yourself on that carrier, Berk. If Aubrey was coming, I don't know if I'd be that disciplined, even if they'd probably make me walk the plank if the powers that be found out."

Berkley chuckled when Aidan blushed, and Aubrey showed up and dragged Wiley away by the ear. "Take a deep breath, and let's get this over with," she told Aidan. "The sooner we get out of here, the sooner I can see what color panties you chose for today," she said softly into Aidan's ear, and her blush deepened.

Everyone exchanged greetings, then congregated in the large den for drinks before Buckston led them to his study, where Drew sat with a glass of whiskey and his tie off. Berkley knew Drew and the Sullivans were friendly, but she'd never asked for the whole story of how they knew him. The only important thing to her was how protective Drew was when it came to Aidan and her career.

"This can't be good if you're making house calls," Berkley said.

"Buckston is still active military, but he's also part of the NSA, so we meet regularly. That he's also the father of the Black Dragon means we meet more often than I'm sure he likes, but I've been here before." Drew stood and poured himself another small bit of liquor. "Today was enlightening, but it brought about some more possible answers that could help us."

Berkley sat next to Aidan, and the others chose their seats around the room, with Wiley perched on the desk. "This is what we have so far," Buckston said, standing next to Wiley.

"Today Wiley eliminated Kevin Skinner before he shot someone in the procession," Drew said, and everyone seemed to be entranced by every word. "We can't be sure who he was aiming at, but our best guess is the president was his target."

"My partner Don Smith took out someone else, and I figured it was Booker Roman, the other suspect we thought could've shot President Khalid," Wiley said.

"It wasn't?" Aidan asked.

"His name is Brendan Sanchez, a young man currently in Carl Greenwald's program," Buckston said. "Carl's group falls under my command, which means we speak often, and I'm probably more interested in this branch of the army than any of my other responsibilities, for personal reasons. Because that's true, I'm familiar with his talent pool, and Carl's correct in that Sanchez was talented and almost done with the training that would've placed him in the field within six months."

"How did he go from promising soldier to wannabe assassin?" Aidan asked.

"We're not sure just yet. Nothing in his background or his evaluations would've clued us in to this," Buckston said.

"There's more," Wiley remarked.

"Of course there is," Aidan said, and Berkley squeezed her fingers. "As you reached the church, we spotted two more people, but only one with a long-range sniper rifle," Wiley said. "That one Don and I wounded but didn't kill."

"Who was it?" Berkley asked, a headache setting in when she thought about the danger Aidan had been in when they'd been out there.

"Rachel Chandler and a woman who identified herself as Marva Brian. It was Rachel with the rifle, and she appeared to know how to use it," Wiley said.

"I don't think I'd ever seen any of Chandler's children before we visited Jeffery in custody," Berkley said. "That Dick has such a cooperative family willing to commit homicide for him is beyond the pale."

"Since Rachel Chandler is an unknown entity when it comes to her talent as a shooter, we don't have any way to know exactly who killed President Khalid," Drew said, glancing at the liquor bottle as if he was contemplating another drink. "Thanks to Wiley, though, I doubt she'll ever pull the trigger again."

Drew handed over the pictures of Rachel and the shot through her shoulder. A few inches closer to her neck, and Rachel Chandler would've been a footnote in history. Berkley studied the wound first but then glanced at her face. "Wait." She tapped on the picture. "We had our doubts, but this is who hit me on the head when those guys grabbed me. I gave a description, but it happened so fast it was hard to capture her likeness. This is definitely her."

"You're right. We had our suspicions but weren't sure she was in the country. Ever since we found Jeffery, we've been trying to figure out how they got in without the border patrol knowing, but thank you for the confirmation," Drew said. "Jeffery is now at Gitmo and being much more cooperative as he settles in. Once she's stable, Rachel will be joining him there, and the only way they're getting out is if we have to turn it back over to Cuba, which isn't happening in our lifetime."

"What now?" Aidan asked.

"Now we give you everything we have, and we deliver the president's order to sail. You leave tonight," Drew said, and the room seemed to have the air sucked out of it.

He placed the reports they'd need on Buckston's desk. "I'll wait for you at the dock, but I want you to enjoy your family dinner. That's an order, so take your time."

"What about Captain Umeko?" Berkley asked.

"It's in the report, but you'll have enough time on the *Jefferson* to get through it. Right now, don't waste a moment you have with your families," Drew said.

"Thank you, Drew, and thank you, Wiley. If you hadn't been there today," Aidan said, and stopped when Wiley nodded.

"Believe me. We'll all need to stick together before all this is over," Wiley said.

"Then let's go eat and enjoy the night as much as we can," Berkley said. "We can lay all this aside for the moment and enjoy the company of the people we do this for. Later on, we'll pick up our swords again and fight the good fight."

❖

"Tell me," Dick Chandler said. He stood on the wide porch of the house he'd built as a replica of the house he'd grown up in. The ranch in Montana that had been in his family for generations had always been his sanctuary—a place where he remembered listening to the stories his grandfather told him over and over again of a time when people were much more civilized. A time when people knew their place and didn't want more than they deserved. They were satisfied with what their leaders and bosses gave them.

"They're loading the last bit of supplies," Dick's contact at the base informed him. "From the activity around the ship, I'd say it's ready to sail. The thing is, though, the crews aren't just loading the *Jefferson*."

"What do you mean?" The troops in his compound were performing the last training exercises for the day, and they appeared unstoppable. They were ready, had been for months, but the nervous tingle of excitement still went up his spine as he thought of the moment the combat would be real instead of training.

"It looks like some destroyers are accompanying the *Jefferson*, and that might be a problem if they know where you are."

"The move to release Jeffery might've failed, but there's no way he told them anything. His training was too complete, and I have every confidence in him. He knows we haven't forgotten him, and we'll rescue him when the time is right." Some of his soldiers seemed to notice his presence and went at each other harder as if to impress him. "Stay on post, and call me if you notice any changes. From all the reports I've gotten, it doesn't matter how many ships they send. They're all headed in the wrong direction."

"Yes, sir."

He saluted the troops and went inside. The failed attack had been his idea, and Rachel had been adamantly set against it. In fact, her displeasure had manifested in her not calling him since he'd put her in harm's way. She'd been right in that he'd allowed his feelings for his son to come before the mission, which he'd sworn never to do or even contemplate. He also would never admit it, and she'd have to accept that as well.

Most important, he had to make Rachel understand her job wasn't finished. He pressed her number, and his anger ignited when it rang more than ten times with no answer. For someone who kept complaining about wanting more respect and responsibility, she was acting like a spoiled child.

"What's wrong?" Robyn asked when he sat and placed the updated reports they got from the Pentagon on his desk.

"Have you spoken to your sister?"

"The day before we attacked. I haven't heard from her since." Robyn crossed his legs and tapped the heel of his boot with his index finger. "Is there a problem?"

"She's not answering," he said, trying her number again.

"Sir, this is Private Marva Brian," the woman said, and whoever she was, she seemed to know him. "I'm with Rachel."

"Put her on."

"She was injured, sir, but she's recovering. A call would've come sooner, but she's in no shape to talk, and we were trying to stabilize her."

Dick hesitated, not quite trusting anything about this, and until he was sure he hung up. "Who's Marva Brian?"

Robyn moved to the computer and searched their system. "She was in the national guard, and Vander recruited her. Once he was killed, I guess Rachel replaced him with Brian. Why are you asking? This is a nobody."

"The nobody answered Rachel's phone and said Rachel's been injured." He pressed the phone's antenna against his chin and considered the best course of action. "I thought we had protocol in place for that."

"We do, so we should've heard from this bitch before now. What happened to Rachel?"

"Brian didn't say. Who do we have left in the area?" He waited for Robyn to look so he could plan their next move, which would be to bring Rachel home. It was time to regroup before he gave the final command that would either destroy him or change history. "Locate someone trustworthy and find Rachel. I want her back here."

"I'll take care of it," Robyn said, saluting.

"Do that, and then get ready. Olivia Michaels is sending who she thinks is her best into battle, and I want them crushed no matter where they sail to."

❖

Erin Mosley sat in the cell with her laptop on her thighs, filling out reports to use her time wisely while waiting. Jonas had ordered Jeffery Chandler moved, so he'd been relocated that morning and was probably already in his cell enjoying Walby's company again and Cuba's hot climate. Depending on how quickly Rachel Chandler decided to cooperate, she'd be joining her little brother for however long they lived.

"Agent Mosley," the guard at the federal prison said. After what had happened at the facility where Jeffery had been kept, this time Jonas had chosen someplace outside the Beltway, so they were in Baltimore. "The director would like you to report in when you can, ma'am."

Erin glanced at Rachel's face, smiling when she saw her breathing change. "Thank you. If he calls back, tell him I won't be long." The relaxed appearance of Rachel's features had changed from the drug-induced sleep of surgery, so Ms. Chandler was probably trying to covertly assess her situation.

Usually injured prisoners and detainees were placed in the infirmary, but this was a special circumstance. Rachel would stay in the cell with two locked doors between her and the guards until she was ready for questioning.

"You can go ahead and open your eyes, Ms. Chandler. This will go smoother if we don't waste each other's time," Erin said, turning on her recorder. Joanna Barker was watching on the closed-circuit system, and she'd give pointers for the next time she sat with Rachel.

"Where am I?" Rachel's voice sounded raspy, but Erin couldn't guess what it usually sounded like since she couldn't find a recording of her in their files.

"You're in the FBI's custody, and when you're fit, you'll be charged with the attempted assassination of the president." Erin spoke louder when Rachel started to say something, not in the mood to be interrupted. "I don't care to listen to your claims of innocence, so save it. I'm here to say that you'll receive health care until you recover, and then your job will be to answer questions."

"Do you plan to beat me like my brother, Jeffery?"

"Please, Ms. Chandler. You're going to claim torture right away, considering you killed President Khalid in front of his daughters? Was that your genius idea, or your father's?"

"The killing needed to happen, and if you were a forward thinker, you'd agree with that fact. Hate me if you want, but we won't be talking about anything. All your little tricks will be a waste of time on both our parts."

"That's what your brother said, and we're having a hard time shutting him up now. His reward for his complete cooperation was a nice room somewhere outside the United States," she said, and smiled when Rachel glared at her. "You know, one of those places where the CIA guys won't be hamstrung by all those pesky rules and laws."

"He doesn't know anything."

"Touching," she said, and laughed. "I would think you'd take your own wise advice. Trying to be the overprotective sister and convince us not to question Jeffery is a waste of time, at least on your part."

"He wouldn't have talked unless you did something to him, so save yourself any embarrassment by telling me he wanted to do the right thing." Rachel winced when she moved, and according to the doctor's report, she'd never use her arm again and would have a lifetime of pain. "Once my father realizes what you've done to us for no reason, he'll stick your head on a pike and display it on the White House fence as a lesson to anyone else disloyal to America."

"I'll be sure to make time to worry about that later. I promise I will, since it'd be a real drag on my day, but right now we'll concentrate on the fact you were trying to kill the president," Erin said, not losing her smile. "Or were you aiming for the little girls mourning their father?"

"I'm so glad you think this is funny."

Erin shook her head. "I'll never find killing innocent women and children humorous. It's an act of uncivilized people who believe in nothing."

"I'm no different from the founding fathers who fought to save us from tyranny, you bitch. I'm a patriot."

"Wow. Did you all practice that line? The first couple of guys we found made it sound so convincing. They were so passionate and believed in your great utopian society until they bit down on their cyanide pill instead of facing the consequences of their actions. You don't exactly scream patriot when you're foaming at the mouth." She stood, and the guard immediately unlocked the doors. "Enjoy our hospitality for a while longer. I'll have a television brought in if you like, so you can watch Jeffery's court-martial. Every state has an opinion about the death penalty, but treason—the federal government still kills you for that shit."

"I demand to see him," Rachel screamed, and Erin rested her hand on the bars that separated them.

"And I'd like to know exactly where your father is, but no one seems to have that information. Right now, sharing it is about the only thing that'll save you and your brother." She started to walk away and hesitated when Rachel screamed again.

"I have rights."

"You sure do, and one of them is to remain silent. As for the rest of all that, you can thank your father, since he was instrumental in changing the rules for enemy combatants. Under the new laws, you have the right to either talk or rot, but sadly not to an attorney." This was the approach Walby and Joanna had instructed her to take. Only time would see if it would work.

"Any last instructions, ma'am?" the guard asked.

"Make sure you monitor the number of painkillers they administer. We don't want Ms. Chandler dying of an overdose before her big family reunion. It would definitely ruin the touching moment."

CHAPTER SIXTEEN

D o you have everything you need?" Maggie asked Berkley as they stood together in an office close to where they planned to board.

"I do, but thanks, Mom." Berkley put her arms around her mother and smiled when her dad placed his hands on her shoulders. "I'll be okay, and hopefully we'll be back sooner than we planned."

"Promise me you'll keep your head down. The damn military doesn't tell us anything, but you don't get spiffy metals because you look handsome in the uniform." Maggie sounded scared, and Berkley could tell she was doing her best to keep her emotions in check.

"You know I won't do anything to mess up my pretty face." Her comment made Corbin laugh and her mother groan. "Find us a house while we're gone, line up the movers, and tell Junior we're coming back for him," she said of their dog. "There's nothing that'll keep me from that last ceremony you have to plan. I love you both."

"We love you too, Cletus, so listen to your mother. Stay safe and come back to us," Corbin said, giving her a bear hug. "I'm so damn proud of you, kid."

"Thanks, and keep in touch with the Sullivans. Preston might not be able to share everything, but at least he's in the know."

"Don't worry about that," Preston said, joining them while holding Aidan's hand. "We're all family now, and family looks after their own."

"Yes, sir, we are," she said, and Aidan nodded. "Take care, and we'll see each other soon."

"You remember everything we talked about, Cletus?" Preston asked.

"Every word, sir, and I won't let you down."

The captains of the destroyers accompanying them entered and greeted everyone. "Attention on deck," the guard outside yelled, and even the retired guys snapped to attention when Olivia Michaels entered the room.

"At ease, everyone, and forgive me for intruding on your family time," Olivia said softly. "I wanted to come and deliver the orders myself, since this is the first time I'll send someone into harm's way on behalf of the American people."

"We'll do you proud, ma'am," Aidan said, and Olivia smiled.

"I trust you and your team will, but I realize this isn't without peril on your part. The percentages my people have shared with me about the potential numbers working against us are beyond disconcerting, and if they're accurate, you'll have more than one person with you who'll be up to no good." The president waved an older gentleman forward and tilted her head slightly in his direction. "This operation will be run from the Situation Room, and I've placed General Carl Greenwald in charge. He and Drew will be providing everything you need."

"Thank you, ma'am, and we look forward to whatever intel you have, General Greenwald," Berkley said.

"You're taking my best with you," Carl said, glancing at Wiley. "And we'll back that up with whatever you need, Captain. Let's get this done so we can do some housecleaning after you finish. I don't know about you, but I'm ready to go back to trusting the man in the foxhole next to me."

"Don't worry, sir. I'll make sure she keeps up," Wiley said, and Berkley laughed.

"You'll have some more backup on board the *Arlington* and the *Anchorage*, but your final orders won't come until we've verified a target," Carl said as Drew stood silently next to him. "I don't have to explain the importance of our mission, and the importance of handling dissenters in the ranks. *Do not* tolerate any acts of insubordination from anyone, and if dire enough, you're to handle them out at sea. Understood?"

"Yes, sir," Aidan and the other captains said together.

"They'll be some consultants on board as well," Drew said, handing folders to each captain. "Should you encounter a problem, these people will handle the questioning. We trust you all implicitly, but it's important to get the answers we need as the situations arise."

"They'll stay out of your way, but let them do their jobs if there's a problem," Carl reaffirmed.

"Thank you, sir, and with all that, we're ready to go," Aidan said.

"Good luck, all of you, and God speed," Olivia said, saluting them when they came to attention again. They were left alone once more with their families, and Aidan and Berkley said their last good-byes after pointing to the private office so Wiley could do the same.

"You ready?" Berkley said as they boarded together and turned to face their folks one last time.

"You're here with me, so I'm ready for anything."

"As far as sentimental goes, I can't top that, my love," she said softly, trying to lighten the mood as she waved to the four people standing on the dock staring at them as if trying to memorize everything about them. "Go fire this thing up before I start crying."

Wiley shut the office door as Aubrey closed the blinds, so they'd have one more moment of privacy. The steady tears falling down Tanith's face were like little daggers to Wiley's heart, and leaving now was making it hard to get air into her lungs because her chest hurt so much. She dropped to her knees, and Tanith ran to her and wrapped her arms around her neck.

"Will you do me a favor?" she asked, holding Tanith close, and felt her nod against her neck. Tanith had a hard time with words when she was upset. "I need you to take extra good care of your mom for me. You did a great job of that until you guys found me, but I need you to pick up my slack while I'm away."

"I promise," Tanith said, her voice barely audible.

"Don't let her pick up anything heavy, and make sure she gets plenty of rest." Tanith pulled back a little with a confused expression, and Wiley almost laughed when she saw her mom grip her father's arm hard enough to make him wince.

"Mama, are you sick?" Tanith asked Aubrey.

"No, sweetie, but you're going to have a little brother or sister soon, and we wanted you to be the first to know once we were sure." Aubrey ran her hand over the top of Tanith's head and smiled.

"That's so cool," Tanith said, and Wiley was glad to see some of her sadness disappear.

"Don't forget your promise, kiddo, and know I'm going to miss you every second I'm gone. I love you."

"Please come back okay," Tanith said, hugging her again. "I love you too, and I'll write to you. You can read all my letters when you come home."

"Thanks." Wiley kissed both of Tanith's cheeks before standing and facing her parents. "This might incentivize you to retire," she told her father, and her mom hugged her.

"You remember your responsibilities while you're out there, and you come back. I'll be praying for you, and I'm going to help Tanith with Aubrey after they go home." Danielle squeezed her and stepped away to allow Buckston a chance to say what he needed to. "I love you."

"I love you both, and I appreciate you watching over my family while I'm gone."

"Remember," Buckston said with his hands framing her face, "in and out. I know how much you love the countryside, but this is no time to linger. You go knowing how much you're loved, and you come back."

"Yes, sir. Believe me that I don't want to miss a minute of this baby with Aubrey and Tanith. Thanks for everything, Dad."

"You bet, and how about we go see the ships before your mom has to leave, Tanith?" he asked, and Tanith seemed reluctant but nodded and followed them out.

"Promise me you'll take care of yourself until I get home," she told Aubrey when they were alone. "I love you so much, and if I had my way, I'd stay."

Aubrey nodded and stepped into her arms. "Whenever you've had to go before, I always had time to prepare myself, so this sucks. I want you to remember something too. You're taking a huge part of my heart with you because you own it, my love. It's that love that gave us Tanith and this baby." Aubrey placed Wiley's hand on her abdomen. "Our kids need you and everything you bring into their lives that I can't give them. I want you to remember that as well."

Wiley took her time kissing Aubrey, trying to make it last for all the days she'd be gone. "You are the love of my life and everything that brings me joy. I love you." She kissed Aubrey again before bending and kissing the spot where her hand had been. "I love you too, little one, so take it easy on your mama until I get back. No making her throw up. She hates it."

"I love you, Wiley. We all do." Aubrey hugged her and held on with what seemed like all her strength. "Don't forget what your father said."

"I won't, and I'll miss you," she said, kissing Aubrey one more time. "Let's go, baby."

The family exchanged their last good-byes dockside, and she showed Tanith the picture in her cap that Tanith had given her of her and Aubrey. It was the first and only thing of a personal nature she'd ever taken with her on a mission.

"I won't be long, love," she said to Aubrey before she climbed the gangplank and stood close to Berkley and Aidan. Her torture would truly begin when her family was out of sight.

Chase Bonner's assistant Ron Bollinger got back into his car and headed for his boss's home. Nothing had come across the Speaker's desk about any type of military action, but enough firepower was leaving Andrews to level any enemy. He was glad he'd listened to the contact they had on base to get there before the *Jefferson* sailed. Olivia Michaels's presence meant this was more than an exercise of any kind, so perhaps they could use this against her.

"Sir, I'll be there in forty-five minutes," he said to Bonner and hung up.

He'd outgrown the role of lackey years ago, but he'd accepted the position with Bonner when Dick had asked him to. Anyone with a pulse and a bit of intelligence knew of Chase Bonner's unquenchable ambition, but he'd proved useful. That the idiot thought he'd be president still amused him, but he wouldn't crush his dreams until the day he outlived his contributions to the mission.

"You need to call a press conference in the morning to question Michaels about initiating actions that might lead to war," he said when he sat down with Chase and explained what had happened that night.

"Not unless we know what it was about. You know that bitch will deny it all, if pressed. The sad fucking thing is, everyone in America will believe her, and I'm not up for looking like an idiot."

Ron almost laughed at how formal Chase appeared in his baby-blue pajamas, robe, and slippers. "That doesn't matter. Right now, the public is on edge about everything, and we need to keep up the pressure."

"Then what?"

"Then it's easier to get answers. We need to know where the ships are sailing," he said slowly, hoping not to have to repeat himself. "If they're heading toward Mr. Chandler, we need to prepare, and possibly move him before it's too late."

"Fine—take care of it," Chase said, crossing his arms over his chest. "And, Ron, don't forget who you work for."

"No, sir. I never forget that."

Aidan ordered them underway but told the bridge to hold to half speed until further notice. She was in her office going through the file General Greenwald had given her, and the first item was the reason for not opening the *Jefferson* up to full throttle. Of anything she'd done during her military career, the coming days would be the most bizarre.

"Come," she said when she heard a knock. "Hey, you need to get back to the deck," she said to Berkley when she stuck her head in. "You're getting a special delivery."

"Did my bath salts and massage oils come in?" Berkley asked. "Good. I needed something to take up my time until you get us there."

She laughed and shook her head. "Not yet, but your North Korean captain should be here in about fifteen minutes."

"She's not exactly mine, Captain, and I thought the defense secretary had changed his mind." Berkley scanned the page she handed over and moved her head from side to side to crack the bones in her neck.

"He wanted to make sure she'd get here as safely and covertly as possible. Until I say otherwise, she'll be assigned to your team. Let me know if you have any problems with that." She stood and closed the door, not wanting anyone to eavesdrop. "I'm putting Wiley with you too, unless you'd rather her be with the guys on the *Arlington*."

"Wiley's a good egg, and she'll be fine with us. We were in high school together but lost touch when she headed for West Point and I went to the Academy." Berkley handed the sheet back and sat in the visitors' chair.

"Wow, that must have been an impressive class," she said and winked.

"Military dads, what can I tell you, but joining Greenwald's unit is like trying to get into the SEALs. That makes Wiley not only a badass, but the top badass. I never got the whole story, but something happened a few years back, and she went covert for years, so this might be a good time to catch up. You saw her when she had to walk away from Aubrey and Tanith, and I'd like to look out for her."

"You're a good egg too, baby, and you took two things off my list of stuff to worry about," she said, locking the folder away. "I can concentrate on just worrying about you."

"That's an easy job—I'm totally low maintenance."

She laughed harder this time and pinched Berkley's cheeks. "Later on, we'll review what happened the last time you were in North Korea before you spin any more tall tales."

"I can guarantee I won't get shot down this time," Berkley said, standing to follow her out.

Aidan realized the truth of why that was, and it didn't make her feel better. "Don't remind me." They walked toward the bridge together and returned a few salutes along the way. "Go welcome our guest, and I'll meet you both in the mess hall after I can speed this baby up."

The ship was cutting through fairly calm seas, but the cloud cover made for a dark night. She ordered them to slow down even more when the radar reported a helicopter approaching. Jin Umeko had been cleared for this mission to act as a guide to get their team close to Lowe Nam Chil's compound, so it was like déjà vu when she stepped onto her deck.

"Wait for the escort to get clear and go to full speed."

"Aye, Captain."

"I'll be in the mess hall, but call if anything comes up." She stood from her chair and motioned for Devin to follow. "You might remember our newest crewmember, but let's get reacquainted."

They were just underway, but the crew was already busy with their assigned task as Aidan moved through the corridors. Two years ago, she would've relished the beginning of another tour, but this time her stomach was in a knot. "Let's hope I'm just being silly."

"Ma'am?" Devin asked.

"Nothing. Just talking to myself."

Jin was sitting with Berkley having coffee, but she stood and saluted when Aidan was in her sight. "Captain Sullivan, thank you for this opportunity." Jin appeared different in the US uniform, but she didn't seem displeased with her lower rank of commander.

"Welcome, and I hope we'll have the opportunity to speak as we make our way. This is Commander Devin Clark, our security officer. He'll get you squared away in a room close to Captain Levine's. Your gear is already in there, but let us know if we forgot anything. It's late, so you can retire if you like." Aidan nodded slightly when Jin did and smiled. "You should get some sleep." Aidan pointed at Berkley. "This one likes to run the deck every morning, and if you're on her team, there's no getting out of it."

"That'll be nice after so many days of being in one place."

"Good night," Berkley said to Jin and stayed with Aidan. "You staying up much longer?"

"For a bit." Aidan poured herself more coffee. "I want to get us farther out to sea before I go to bed. You can head in if you want. I'll tuck you in if you're still awake."

"I will, but not yet." They separated, and Berkley headed outside. She walked the deck until she reached the bow and wasn't surprised to find Wiley there gazing out at the darkness. The lights of the coastline were getting dimmer, but they could easily make out the lights of the *Arlington* and the *Anchorage* as they kept pace. "You have a beautiful family, and I'm sorry you got dragged into this and had to leave them behind."

"Thanks. Leaving was tougher than I thought it'd be. Before, it was hard, but both Tanith and Aubrey's sad faces were hard to walk away from." Wiley leaned against the rail and turned to gaze into the wind.

"Even when they can come with you, it's tough." Berkley looked up at the bridge and thought about Aidan. "As much as it sucks, though, I appreciate you being here."

"I missed the high school reunion and figured this was the next best thing."

❖

"You're wasting your time, amateur," the translator told Walby. From the moment of his capture, Lowe Nam Chil had refused to speak English. But Walby suspected he spoke it fluently.

"The only thing captivity has done for you," Walby said with a smile that he hoped didn't hide his amusement, "is make you finally succeed at staying true to a diet." Lowe did appear much slimmer than the last time Walby had questioned him. "That'll make you really popular when I bunk you with someone who's plenty lonely and waiting for those seventy-two virgins."

Lowe spoke again, his tone harsh and laced with so much venom Walby didn't need the translator to understand his intent. "He says he's killed more people than you've ever met, sir," the translator said.

"That's true," he said, knitting his fingers together and placing them on his knee. "I almost admire a man who can take what he's dished out for so long. I'm sure you never expected the tables to be turned."

"If what you've done is your idea of torture, you have little imagination," the translator said after Lowe laughed at the short statement.

"We have standards, and we abide by them even though we understand people like you won't return the courtesy. It's not that we claim the moral high ground, but it's the decent thing to do."

"It's your hypocritical decency that makes you weak," Lowe said and waited for the translator to finish before slamming his hand down. "The world saw you for the cruel cowards you really are during the Gulf War."

"Like you, I do things for the good of my country, and I sleep fine at night." He glanced at the piece of sky he could see through the high window and exhaled. "Don't think of that as me trying to explain myself."

"Do I look like your priest then?" Lowe laughed, which only made him appear crueler.

"No. I was explaining why I think this job would be better done by someone more familiar with you." Walby stood and headed for the door. Even with the air conditioning, Guantánamo Bay was oppressively hot and uncomfortable, since the cinderblock buildings heated up so much that the units couldn't keep pace.

"You admit defeat so quickly?" The translator delivered the taunt in the same deadpan tone she always used, and he smiled, thinking how it lost the bite Lowe put into every exchange.

"I'm more of a supervisor who understands the importance of rewarding my employees," he said, placing his hand on the knob.

"What does that mean?" It was such a paradox listening to Chil's unhinged personality, followed by the translator's monotone delivery. It was another technique of theirs since he personally knew the woman translating, and she was extremely animated, except when she was with someone like Chil. If they spoke English, the subject went a little nuts hearing that flat delivery of their words.

"You sound like you're so proud of your life's work, and to honor that, I want to introduce you to someone who's familiar with it firsthand." He opened the door to Henry Lee, the youngest member of his team.

Henry was brilliant and driven since he'd come to the States alone at the age of eleven. From the moment of his arrival he'd worked hard and succeeded in school, despite the horrendous foster homes he'd been placed in until he'd aged out, and he started contacting the CIA during his senior year at Harvard. His persistence got him a meeting, and the agent he'd spoken to contacted Walby before Henry had left the building. After their initial meeting and hearing his story, Walby had offered him a job, and today would be Henry's reward for all the shit he'd gone through.

"You probably don't remember Henry, but he remembers you." Walby waited for the translator but noticed how intently Chil was staring at Henry.

"Who is this puppy?" Chil asked, finally relaxing his face and smiling.

"I've waited a lifetime to see you again, you pile of shit," Henry said in English and put his hand up to silence the translator. "You torturing and killing my family has played a loop in my mind for years."

Chil stared at him and cocked his head to the side as if trying to remember something about Henry. "Do you think this will make me talk?" he asked in perfect English that had a bit of a British accent.

"I'm not sure," Walby said as Henry laid out his tools, and Lowe showed fear for the first time. It wasn't much, but it was a crack in his façade he couldn't help but let slip. "It's not about that any longer." Two men came in and bound Lowe to the chair. "Talk or don't, it doesn't interest me now, but helping Henry replace his memories with something much more satisfying does."

"Wait," Chil screamed when Walby took a step out. "What do you want to know?"

"I'm curious as to how loudly you can scream before you pass out from the pain." Walby closed the door and moved to watch from the next room.

"You killed my family for keeping part of the crop they worked hard to grow," Henry said, removing a small knife that was rounded at the tip. "You did it in the village center so they'd be an example to everyone else." He placed the flat of the knife under Lowe's chin, forcing his head back. "Do you remember pulling out their guts slowly? Do you remember how they screamed in pain, or how my parents begged you for the life of my sisters? They were only six and eight years old."

"I was only following orders," Chil said, his breathing quickening when Henry cut the buttons off his shirt one by one.

"If it makes you feel better, so am I," Henry said, slapping Lowe gently on the cheek. "Only they're my orders, decided by me the day you killed my family." He moved the knife to the spot under Lowe's belly button and laughed. "It's like Christmas, so thank you for not talking to my boss. If you'd spilled your guts, I wouldn't have the opportunity to literally do it now."

"I have information you need," Chil said, pushing back from Henry as hard as he could and dragging the chair until it hit the wall. "It's important."

Henry used his cell phone to call him, and Walby figured Chil would pass out from how hard he was breathing. "I doubt he has anything useful, but he claims he does," Henry said.

Walby made them wait a half an hour before he came back and sat across from Chil. "If this is only to delay what you have to know in your dead heart you deserve, I'll make sure Henry takes more time with you than he already planned to. This building will be cleared, and we'll deny anything to anyone who asks about what happened to you. The only useful thing you'll do in this life is feed the fish off the beach outside."

"I want protection," Chil said first, then started talking like a man trying not only to save his life but unburden his soul. They listened, and even Walby was surprised by what Chil knew.

"It's going to be a long couple of days," he said to Henry when they had Chil taken back to his cell. "Let's take a run at the others again and see what we can add."

"Yes, sir, but I am a little disappointed," Henry said.

"Don't let go of your dreams just yet, Henry. Karma has a way of either punishing or rewarding us, and you're due a reward."

Chapter Seventeen

Aidan joined Berkley's team for their daily meeting, wanting to know every part of the plan General Greenwald and his advisors were putting together. They'd been sailing for a week and received updates at least five times a day. Every report seemed to contain something new, but it was making her a little crazy that they were sharing a lot of it with Jin Umeko.

Jin had done a good job of fitting in, running with Berkley's group every morning, eating with them, and giving her opinions on occasion when they allowed her in the strategy sessions. Nothing in all that raised any specific red flags, but the woman had shot Berkley down. In that one instant she could have blown Aidan's world to shit, and it wasn't until Aidan was in Jin's company that she realized she hadn't gotten over it, much less forgiven her for it.

"That's it for today," Berkley said, and everyone saluted before they exited the conference room. They'd already had dinner, but it was too early to turn in. Berkley locked the door before she sat next to her but didn't touch her. "Is there some specific reason you look pissed?"

"Sorry. I'm not mad," she said, taking Berkley's hand because she couldn't resist the urge to feel some part of her. They hadn't had much time alone since they'd sailed, and she missed the closeness of the last year. Granted, they'd been working, but they'd slept together every night and woke up next to each other every morning. "Not with you anyway."

"Ah, so you're a little pissed."

"I keep looking at Jin, and I don't know what to do with myself."

Berkley leaned over and kissed the side of her neck. "Are you trying to make me jealous?"

"I don't have a crush, baby. It's more like I want to punch her in the throat. She shot you down." Admitting it out loud made her sound childish, but talking about it might help.

"It's true, and it is hard to wrap my head around the fact that she's here, but I'm confident she hates these people more than she wants to betray us." Berkley kissed her lips next. "We need her to find the target we're after and to speak for us if we're spotted. I don't know a word of Korean, and I'd like to keep it that way."

"I know that on a deep level, but she could've taken you away from me," she said, caressing Berkley's cheek. "I miss you, Cletus."

"Want me to read you some poetry? I brought a book with me."

She laughed, and Berkley joined her. "Poetry? Really?"

"It's more a book of limericks, and it might give you some ideas if I get through enough pages."

"Think you can stay awake long enough for me to set the night watch and navigation?" She stood and leaned over Berkley so she could kiss her.

"Go ahead, but make it snappy. I miss you too, darlin'."

She smiled when Berkley saluted her before heading for her room. At their current speed, they'd be in position in another week and a half, so she was praying for calm seas. She didn't want to send Berkley into danger any sooner than she had to, but once they arrived, they could at least complete their mission.

The only way to make herself feel better was to enjoy as much time with Berkley as she could, so after another hour of work, she'd do just that. She stepped out and started for the bridge, finding the corridors fairly quiet, but she heard conversation from some of the open doors and saw Devin headed her way.

"Anything to report, Commander?"

"All's quiet, ma'am, and the weather report is clear so far. It would've been easier to start this cruise from the West Coast, but maybe we can sightsee on the way back if we take the same route," he joked as he turned and walked with her.

"I'll see what we can manage, and we can both tick some stuff off our bucket lists." She was chuckling when she noticed a petty officer walking toward them. The man didn't look familiar, and he appeared out of place and strange, with a towel draped over his hands. "Who is that?"

Devin didn't answer right away as he placed his hand on the holster under his arm and slowly started to withdraw it. "Halt, and raise your hands slowly," Devin ordered him.

Aidan glanced at Devin briefly, wondering what the hell he was doing, but then the guy dropped the towel and she saw the pistol in his hand. She'd been so worried and focused on Berkley, she hadn't thought about any real danger to herself. Whoever this guy was, he seemed ready to die as long as he was able to take them with him.

"Drop your weapon," Devin said, raising his. The guy raised his as well, and Aidan held her breath.

The man's arm suddenly jerked up, and he fired, hitting the ceiling and causing the bullet to ricochet but not hit anything. He then arched forward at an odd angle before the gun fell from his hand, making a clanging noise when it hit the metal floor, but the sound was almost drowned out by the guy's moans. Devin was on him before their would-be assassin could pull the knife sticking out of his side free, but Aidan doubted the woman who'd put it there would've allowed it.

"Thank you, Jin," Aidan said as Devin radioed for backup. "I truly appreciate your timing."

"I am glad I was here, but you should thank Captain Levine. She told us all to take turns watching out for you," Jin said softly. "Tonight was my turn, but this was not to prove myself, Captain. I realize what happened before might make you uncomfortable, but I am only here for some sense of justice for everything that was stolen from me."

"Please call me Aidan, and Berkley told me the same thing about why you came with us. Please forgive me for any lingering doubts," she said, and Jin seemed to study her thoughtfully.

"We all have doubts when someone we love is harmed," Jin said for only her to hear, and it was a bizarre conversation to have while her people subdued the guy on the ground and the medics tended to his knife wound. "Like I said before, I am here because I want to help someone I care about, if she is still alive. That I was able to keep you from getting hurt makes me happy." Jin stood back and bowed slightly.

"If he doesn't need surgery, lock him up and meet me in my office," she said to Devin.

"What the hell?" she heard Berkley say as she walked rapidly toward them, and Aidan put her hands up to stop her from getting near the guy.

"Give me an hour, and I'll have everything you need," Devin said.

"Let's try for twenty minutes," Berkley said, holding the gun the guy had used. It wasn't military issue and was too shiny to be practical for everyday use. "This is either a gift from a friend with tacky taste or a showpiece for some wannabe pimp."

At Berkley's comment, the guy struggled against the MPs, and Aidan figured Berkley had decided to insult him instead of punch him in the face. Berkley was at times a rule breaker, but hitting someone who was being held down wasn't her lover's style. She did, though, enjoy being the subject of Berkley's overprotectiveness, and she'd been that way from the very beginning.

❖

Hawaii Nine Years Earlier

After a week of rampant screwups throughout the base, their commanding officers were making everyone run the obstacle courses until they either threw up or passed out from the heat. Aidan refused to let that happen if she could help it, so she was pacing herself as she started her fourth round. She reached the wall and was wiping her hands on the sides of her shorts so the ropes wouldn't slip and blister her palms. It was hard to keep them dry for this part since the heat was unrelenting.

Berkley was almost to the top, her shirt and shorts soaked with sweat, but from the look of her, she could do this for the rest of the day with no problem. If she'd learned anything about her new girlfriend, it was that she possessed plenty of stamina and proved it whenever she had the opportunity. Berkley straddled the top and seemed to be waiting for her, so she started up, only to have the guy behind her reach up, slide his hands under her shorts, and palm her ass hard enough to make her drop down.

She felt instantly dirty, but before she could do anything about it, Berkley flew past her, landed on the guy, and pummeled him with a flurry of punches before he could get to his feet. "You son of a bitch," Berkley yelled when the guy was finally able to stand up. His friends who'd been egging him on stepped back when they heard the sirens.

"You fucking bitch, you're going to pay for that," the guy said, clearly embarrassed by what had happened.

When the MPs showed up, the guy was charging at Berkley and landed a fist to her right eye, opening a gash along her eyebrow. That didn't stop Berkley from hitting him a few more times before the MPs pulled her off the guy.

"Berkley, please," she said when Berkley strained to fight the guy again. "Calm down, and we'll go with you," she said of the men and women who'd lined up to tell the MPs what had happened.

The action of fighting for her honor could've gotten Berkley thrown out of the military, but there'd been enough witnesses to what had happened that a month of weekend obstacle running had put Berkley back in the cockpit. It had been a lonely month, but that Berkley had defended her without hesitating touched the very center of her heart.

❖

USS Jefferson, Present Day

The scar on Berkley's brow the asshole's punch caused had faded some with time, but her overprotectiveness had not. "Make sure you check him for any device he can use to kill himself," Aidan said as they loaded the guy onto a stretcher and sedated him to keep him still.

"Yes, ma'am. We'll scan him before we do anything else," the medic said.

"We'll be in my office," she told Devin, confident Berkley would follow her. "Thanks for looking out for me, and for having your people doing the same," she said to Berkley once they were finally alone. "You've been doing that for a long time," she said, running her finger over Berkley's eyebrow.

"I love you, so of course I'm going to take care of you, and Jin isn't exactly mine, but I owe her one." Aidan closed her eyes when Berkley put her arms around her and held her in a way that made her feel cherished. "Do you know who this guy is?"

"Unfortunately, I don't know every single person on the ship, sweetheart. After our initial sail, the Pentagon supposedly did some background checks and switched out some of our personnel. So much for that." She rested her head against Berkley's chest and, tired, had an urge to go to bed. "Now we need to know who this guy befriended."

"Lately I feel more like Eliot Ness than a naval pilot," Berkley said, kissing the top of her head. "After the hell I had to go through to get into that cockpit, I should be able to concentrate on only that, just like you should focus on nothing but the *Jefferson*."

"We'll get there eventually, but I need you to channel your best gumshoe for now, Ness."

Devin returned thirty minutes later and handed Aidan a list of everyone Petty Officer Dale Whitner had been friendly with since he boarded. "He was assigned to maintenance, and the guys in the pool said he seemed fairly normal," Devin said, handing over an information sheet on Whitner. "He complained a little about the number of women he had to salute around here, but when no one else joined in, he backed down."

"And armed himself, obviously," Berkley said, clearly aggravated.

"I got all the information off the pistol, and I'll pass that along to Command when we're done. We need to question him, but the doc has him sedated so he could sew him up. Captain Umeko knew what she was doing. She didn't hit anything important, so this asshole shouldn't be laid up that long."

"What a shame," Berkley said.

"Okay," Aidan said before Berkley got any angrier. She picked up her phone and requested a line to General Greenwald at Command. Five minutes later, Carl appeared on her screen, and she gave him a rundown of events. "I'm not sure where he came from and why he waited until now, but he was ready to kill me and my security officer if he'd had the opportunity to pull the trigger."

"We expected something, and I think you did too," Carl said, rubbing his chin. "This crap is maddening since we'll never have the mindset to sabotage a mission, but these bastards are willing to die for their cause."

"You're right about that, sir," she said as Devin finished his email with the facts he had to share.

"You need to involve the consultants on board the *Arlington*, and the people Whitner talked to are going to have to understand they're in for some tough questioning. This is no time to go soft."

"Yes, sir, we'll handle it," Aidan said, and Berkley and Devin nodded.

"The command of the ship is yours, Aidan, but you need to acquire a shadow until we're done with all this."

"We'll take care of that as well, sir," Devin said.

"Is there anything new?" Berkley asked.

"You all need to prepare for every foreseeable situation, starting now," Carl said, and Berkley glanced at her briefly. "Tomorrow Jeffery Chandler will become a reality-TV star when his trial begins. The whole thing will be broadcast live, aimed at an audience of one. All the people who are smarter than me keep saying that seeing his little prince in leg irons should send Dick into a frenzy. All of us learned early in our careers that when you engage your enemies in anger or with any kind of crazy behavior, you make mistakes."

"What will they charge him with?" she asked.

"First, desertion, then terrorism for his attack on the *Jefferson*, and treason, which all carry some stiff penalties, but they plan to kill him for that last one." Carl put his glasses on and scanned the email Devin had sent. "And the odds are he'll get the needle, because no one's in a forgiving mood."

"That should poke daddy bear with a sharp stick," Berkley said.

"We need to ramp things up to pinpoint where we need to paint targets," Carl said, rolling a cigar in his fingers. The habit made her think of her father, who liked to do that until he was someplace he could light it. "The folks who like to dissect people's brains think the attack on the building across from the detention facility and the other targets you helped thwart were all diversions to free his little boy."

"Can you share what happened to Rachel Chandler?" Aidan asked.

"She's in a secure facility recovering from Wiley's calling card. From what I understand, they're giving her a few more weeks. Then she's going to work on her tan and heat tolerance for as long as she has left to breathe on this earth. Any legal action against her might take some time since she's not enlisted, but DOJ will probably charge her as an enemy combatant." A door opened behind Carl, and Aidan smiled when she saw her father. "We'll let the government folks worry about that, but our job is to give you everything you need to get this done as quickly as possible."

"We're ahead of schedule, and that should hold if the weather cooperates," Aidan said, and Preston nodded. "If you can rush the fact-finding on Whitner, we'd appreciate it. The information might find the point of recruitment, and that could lead to anyone else on my boat trying to kill us."

"That's priority, and your next update should include the information they've gathered from their interviews with Chil. He started talking a week ago, but Agent Edwards wanted to vet the information he's spilling like his life depends on it. And knowing Walby, this Chil guy is anything but chill and believes his days are numbered," Carl said firmly. "Now excuse me a moment. I have to step out before we lose this link."

"I'll be outside," Devin said, leaving as well.

"Cletus, are you falling down on the job?" Preston asked once they were alone.

"No, sir. She just attracts trouble," Berkley said, and Aidan glared at her. "Don't worry, though. I'm posting Devin as her shadow while I stretch my legs later on. If he lets anything happen to her, I'm throwing him off the boat with a raw-meat life vest."

"Good, and you arm yourself," he said, pointing, Aidan guessed, at her. "Something like this happens again, you shoot and hang the bastard from the bridge as an example to anyone else thinking of taking a pot shot at you."

"That's a little dramatic, Daddy, but we'll be careful. I'm beginning to believe we're not the popular kids on the playground anymore."

"The world's going nuts, kiddo, and it's our job to get it in a straitjacket and beat it with a rubber hose. Take care of yourself, so I don't have to report you to your mothers."

"That'd be worse than a firing squad," Berkley said, and Preston laughed. "Thanks for crashing Greenwald's party line, Pop. It's nice to see a friendly face."

Preston smiled like an idiot at the way she'd addressed him, Aidan guessed, and she knew her father had asked it of her. That was the final thing that made her think he accepted Berkley as part of their family and the most important person in her life. "No problem, and I'll call your folks. They're staying with us a few more weeks, and that's as much advance warning as I'm giving you when it comes to Maggie and Mary Beth."

"My life won't be my own, will it?" Berkley asked, shivering.

"I doubt it," Aidan said as the screen went black.

Chapter Eighteen

The *Jefferson* was close to the South Korean border a week later, and Berkley was in the air leading her pilots through defense drills one small squadron at a time.

The consultants on board had been questioning Whitner all week, but the self-described patriot for justice seemed to almost relish sitting and locking wits with who he said was the enemy. Aidan had told the guys not to use what was considered enhanced interrogation, but the brick wall Whitner had thrown up was making Berkley think about talking to Aidan to change her mind.

The other people Whitner had been friendly with had checked out and had fully cooperated. That didn't convince or lower Berkley's suspicions, considering the number of possible traitors in their midst. She gave the order to come about and head back, wanting to be on deck again before the sun went down.

"You still awake back there, Junior?" she said as she circled toward the *Jefferson* at a low altitude.

"I'm taking in the pretty water and pink sky. Radar's clear, and we've only got two ahead of us before we hit the chow line. It's apple-pie night, and the cooks used the captain's recipe."

She laughed at Harvey's response as she banked left to circle around again. "Cletus," the communications officer said, cutting into their conversation.

"Go ahead."

"We need you to do a visual check at these coordinates." The guy gave Harvey the numbers, and the spot was about twelve miles from the *Jefferson*'s current position.

"Report back when you get there," Aidan said.

"Should take less than two minutes." She dropped altitude again and followed the track Harvey had punched into their system.

"This is it," Harvey said, and all they saw was open water.

"*Jefferson*, what am I looking for?" She dropped altitude again and flew over the spot one more time, practically skimming the water.

"We've got something on radar, and it should be right there and big enough for you to see something," Aidan said. "We wanted a flyby to perhaps give us visual confirmation."

"We're losing light, but there's nothing here."

"Fuck," Harvey said as she turned toward the right and started climbing.

It wasn't until she was coming out of her turn that she saw it. "Fuck is right."

The guided missile had broken the surface and seem to be locked on them. All they could do now was give it a new target, but the only thing around was the *Jefferson* and the destroyers, so it would come down to a long game of chase.

"Missile in the air," Harvey said, reporting the situation to the *Jefferson*. "Repeat, missile fired and locked on us."

"Cletus, what the hell?" Aidan asked.

"A little busy right now, but your radar blip is well armed and under the water, not on it. They fired on us, so I've got a very determined admirer on my ass."

She led them away from the ships, not wanting to take any chances. The missile didn't have any problems keeping up, no matter how much she maneuvered, and the fucking thing was gaining.

"Cletus, you want backup?" Vader asked.

"Shit," Harvey said, his tone truly panicked now. "There's another one in the air, Cletus."

"Negative, Vader. We can't chance any more hardware. Stay clear and keep us in sight." With two missiles locked, it would be impossible to avoid them forever. Only in the movies did the damn things run into each other, which left her with only one viable option.

She was at fourteen thousand feet—high enough to eject. The damn things had split and were coming from opposite directions. "Junior, get ready, and keep your damn head down."

"Yes, ma'am." Harvey sounded eerily calm all of a sudden, which was something to be grateful for. "Whoa, look at that."

The sub had surfaced, and she suddenly had a bad feeling that this situation had more to it than being fired on. "*Jefferson*, they're putting boats in the water, so get to us before these assholes do. I'm a free spirit who won't do well in captivity."

"We'll be right there," Aidan said. "Keep the chatter up, Junior."

"Yes, ma'am. We're on a western path coming closer to you, and—"

Aidan, like everyone else in the bridge, was staring at the radar. "Cletus," she said, and her word was followed by silence. "Junior?" The continued silence that followed was like a hot poker through her heart. Berkley wouldn't answer only if she wasn't in the sky any longer. It had happened before, but Berkley had warned them the moment they'd ejected. Junior's interruption midsentence sped her heart rate and her anxiety.

"Mark Cletus's last location and get boats in the water," she said and didn't see the same urgency in everyone else that she was experiencing. "Now," she yelled. "This is Captain Sullivan," she radioed the *Anchorage*.

"Go ahead, Captain," a man said. "This is Captain Greer."

"I'm launching planes, but if another missile breaks the surface of the water, I need you to blow the submarine they came from to hell."

"Do we know who we're firing on?"

"Start setting your coordinates, Captain. One of our planes has already been shot down, and if they fire on us again, our orders are to sink them. They obviously didn't give a damn as to who they were shooting at, and I'm giving them the same consideration." She cut Greer off and ordered Vader into the sky.

"The boats have deployed, ma'am," one of her men reported.

"Good. I need a clear line to Command." She stood and waited until the guy she'd spoken to nodded. "Report the second you hear anything." The sound of jets flying off the deck made her swallow hard.

"Captain," Carl said, and Aidan kept her eyes on the horizon. "The entire team as well as the FBI director Chapman are present, so go ahead."

"I need to know what submarines are in the area, and I need to know immediately."

"We have two Los Angeles-class submarines nearby," someone not Greenwald said. "Why?"

"A sub just downed Captain Levine without provocation. We have more planes in the air now, and if they're fired on, I'm going to fire back, and keep firing until I see a visible oil slick on the surface."

"This is Neil Perry, Captain. I'm President Michaels's national security advisor. Keep the line open, and don't fire until I get back to you," Neil said. "The subs in the area aren't near enough to have fired those missiles. If the sub belongs to another government, we'll find out, but stand down."

"Our planes are in the air, the rest are lined up, and I've got boats away. Captain Levine and her backseat are in the water, and we're going to look for them. I'm not sending anyone out there without backup or handcuffed if they're attacked."

"Understandable, Captain. We're checking," Greenwald said.

"Vader, I need you to provide cover," she said, muting the line to Command.

"Yes, ma'am. We'll start where she went down and work out from there."

"Don't take any shit from anyone. You understand me?"

"You got it, ma'am."

She sat with a ramrod-straight back, resenting that she had to be here instead of out looking for Cletus. This was like the type of nightmare you had that only progressed to something more horrible instead of the relief of waking. Berkley was probably treading water, pissed that she'd been sucker-punched again, but that wasn't going to stop her from worrying.

"Ma'am," Vader said.

"Go ahead, Vader," she said and linked him to the command communication.

"We have a sub on the surface, and Cletus was right. They appear to be putting boats in the water and heading in the direction she went down," Vader said.

"Commander, provide a description," Greenwald said.

"It appears to be a Russian Akula-class sub, sir," Killer said.

"Vader, continue the search, and we'll keep our thumb on these guys."

"Eyes open, everyone," Killer said.

"The Russians deny anything in the area," Neil said, but the video feed coming from Vader's plane was damning.

"From what I'm looking at, I say Commander Gorham is correct. That's a Russian Akula-class sub, and if it fires another thing I'm going to send it to the bottom," Aidan said, and she meant every word. "Send their people the feed. It's hard to deny something that's right there."

"Captain, I'm asking you to hold your fire," Neil said as he held another phone to his ear. "We don't need to escalate this situation any more than we have to."

"Did you miss the part where the damn thing fired and hit Captain Levine?" Carl said, saving Aidan the breath of having to form the words.

"They're diving, ma'am," Vader said, and Killer confirmed. "Are we free to fire if fired upon?"

"Try to make radio contact with the idiots," Aidan ordered.

"This is the USS *Jefferson*," her communications officer said. "Please return to the surface and open your hatches. If you do not comply, you will be fired on."

"Mr. Perry?" Aidan said, giving the suit one more chance before she defied a direct order. She was willing to put her career on the line if it meant keeping her crew safe. "Mr. Perry, we don't have a lot of time if they intend to fire, and as you can see, they're not interested in dialogue."

"The Russians confirm it is an Akula-class, but it's not theirs," Neil said, and Aidan cut him off.

"Fire at will," she told her pilots.

"Aye, ma'am," Vader said.

"Get Washington and Greer in on this conversation," Aidan said of the destroyer captains.

"We're listening, and we're taking evasive action in case they get tired of shooting straight up at all the cool planes. We got your back, *Jefferson*, and the *Anchorage* will cover the boats we've deployed as well. They've disappeared from radar, which means a rapid descent."

"Thanks, Captain Washington," Aidan said to the *Arlington's* captain. "If they dove and left some of their crew topside, they're not going whale hunting."

"I don't know. Cletus is a pretty big fish in our book, but we were thinking the same thing. If they fire on us, their ass will be in a tight spot, and they better pray they can hold their breath for a really long time."

"Ma'am, they're back on radar and changing course. They're closing on us," her head radio operator reported. "They're fourteen miles out."

"You down that thing before it does any more damage," Carl said forcefully.

"Let's see if we can't send them running home to mama," Gary said. "Starboard guns." He painted a target on their radar, and his operator filled in the coordinates. The spot hit close enough for the sub to veer away from them and toward the *Anchorage*. "Heads up, Captain Greer."

"I can get my own dates, thank you," Kevin Greer said, and Aidan smiled. Berkley had mentioned that dangerous situations didn't mean you had to lose your sense of humor, and these guys were definitely friends of hers. "Port guns," Kevin said and hesitated until the sub had reached the target area he'd put on radar.

The near miss changed the sub's course again, only now it was headed for the small rescue boats they had in the area. Before the damn thing could target them directly, Kevin and Gary shot again within seconds of each other, and the rogue vessel stopped moving. The two captains had aimed to the front and back, and the charges stopped the sub cold.

"They're going deeper," she said and watched the descent on radar.

"They're trying to get out of range," Gary said. "*Anchorage* and *Jefferson*, what's the ETA on the rescue boats?"

Aidan had her people radio the crewman leading their team. "We were about to call, ma'am. We have Captain Levine and Lieutenant Whittle's life-vest beacons on our radar."

"They're in the water?" The steadiness of her voice surprised her.

"They seem to be, ma'am. We're still quite a few miles out, but they're holding steady."

"Radio when you spot them."

"Yes, ma'am."

How many close calls with death would they get before fate finally caught up with them? The question made her not want to reach the point where it would need a definite answer. "Command, we need more information on how someone acquired an Akula-class sub if it didn't belong to the Russians. Those are still in service, and if I'm not mistaken, you can't order one on Amazon."

"We're on it, and we're redirecting our subs to join the party and stick close to you," Carl said. "They're better equipped to find and monitor this thing."

"Thank you, General. We'll stay on the line until we're clear."

"Good. Our communications people will keep tabs with your second. Go see to your people."

"Vader and Killer, monitor and patrol until I get all these boats back on board."

"Yes, ma'am, and we put Poncho's group with the rescue teams, so we're covered."

"Roger that." She sat back down and slowed their speed to keep their group relatively together, accepting a cup of coffee from Devin. "This shit's getting old."

"While all this was going on, we might've had a breakthrough," Devin said, sitting next to her.

"Good news?" she asked, and he nodded. "Hell. I might not know how to take it," she said and enjoyed laughing for the first time in what felt like days.

❖

Berkley had been maneuvering as best she could, trying to lead the bastard shooting at her away from the ships, when the third missile made her eject sooner than she'd have liked. They were lucky not to get riddled with pieces of the plane after it was destroyed just past them. As they floated down, they saw what appeared to be rafts being placed in the water. These fuckers were incredibly motivated. She had to give them that.

"Junior," she yelled, and he raised his hand. "Release before you hit the water," she said, trying everything she could to avoid capture.

"Just tell me when," Harvey yelled back.

They needed for the parachutes to float away from them, if the wind was cooperative. She turned into it, looking to make sure Harvey did the same and glad when he did. This would bring them closer to their potential captors, but when she was about thirty feet from the water she released, and the parachute caught the wind and kept going.

"Either I'm your lucky charm or a hex," Harvey said when he swam close to her.

She activated the beacon on her vest and laughed. "As long as I walk away from all these dramatic war landings, I'm okay with that. Don't worry. I'm keeping you, Junior."

"Good. Now tell me who the hell shot us down."

"Good question, and I only glimpsed this thing, but it didn't appear to be one of ours. It's a bonus if it wasn't."

They both had to kick hard to navigate the swells that were picking up with the late-afternoon winds. "What kind of bonus?" Junior asked.

"Not everyone in the armed forces is trying to kill us. That has to count for something." She was especially glad she'd put Preston's compass in a waterproof bag. "You okay?"

"My ducking has gotten loads better, so I'm fine. Thanks for keeping us in one piece."

"No problem. We both need to be healthy for the upcoming events, and really, there's no better way to enjoy the last of the sunset than from water level. All we're missing is a mai tai and hula girls."

He gazed at her and laughed. "If we had drinks and girls, that might change my mind, but I'd much rather enjoy the deck view of that scene. That I'm still breathing and can move all my extremities is nice too. As for the other thing, will you take me with you? We haven't practiced any bombing runs, and it makes me believe that's not what we're doing."

"No more North Korean tours for you, Junior, so pick someplace different. Trust me. You'll be much more comfortable on the boat."

"I can't watch your ass if I'm not with you." He swam closer and spoke with conviction.

"I catch you watching my ass, and I'm going to chum the water with you," she said, and he shoved some water at her.

"I'm being serious. Wherever you go, I'm supposed to go so we can take care of each other. I might not be your best friend, but I *am* your friend, and I want you to be okay." He stopped and lowered his head slightly. "You don't have to tell me, but I know you have plenty to live for."

"Thanks, man, and—" She didn't quite know how to finish.

"This is a weird time to talk about it, but I'd never be an asshole and mess things up for you. I only wanted you to know that I'll always have your back, and hers too. We're a team, right?" Harvey smiled and held his hand out to her.

"I'm glad you said that, and later on, once we're done with all this crap, I'll need you to stand up for me. I really was going to ask but was waiting on my retirement papers before I popped the question."

"I'll be proud to do that, and I'm happy for you. You think you could do something about all this water?" Harvey moved his arms back and forth to stay afloat. "I know we're navy men, but being a wet navy man for hours is going to suck, and Captain Sullivan isn't going to be thrilled either."

"Be more specific." She glanced all around them to make sure no hostiles were headed in their direction. "If we catch a ride with the wrong people, it won't bode well for any future kids you want to have."

"Why?" he asked, moving next to her.

"I can't be sure, but hooking those electrodes to your family treasures might fry all your swimmers. They were putting boats in, but I doubt it was to find us and apologize for blowing us the hell out of the sky. At least they didn't appear to be as fast as the ones our rescue teams put in."

"Shit. That's just great."

"Breathe. We have time." She moved until their arms were touching. "Here." She yanked the locator beacon off his lifejacket and gave it to him. "Put this in an inside pocket of your flight suit and try to hang on to it. If the boat that picks us up aren't our guys, take your jacket off." She repeated the removal and placed it in her pocket. "I don't want them to notice we took these out."

"I'll follow your lead." Harvey hung on to the strap of her jacket as the sun started to set.

"Do that, and stick to me."

"Don't worry. They'll have to pry me off you."

Berkley grabbed his jacket and pulled him until they were shoulder to shoulder. "Okay. We've got maybe ten minutes before the sun has completely gone down, and when it does, this is going to be like a deprivation chamber since there's no moon. If we float apart I'll never find you."

"At least I'll have another story to tell my parents. My father was sitting with his mouth open the whole time I told them about our last adventure."

"Any more of this and he's not going to let you come out and play with me," she said, and they laughed. "I don't know about you, but I'm tired of ejecting out of planes. I don't want that to become our thing. If we do it again, I'm afraid all they'll let us do is clean the windshields."

"Three missiles was overkill, so I'm cutting us some slack."

The sound of engines was easy to identify in the silence, and she tensed when the last of the light disappeared. She couldn't see who it was until they were right on top of them. She felt Harvey tighten his hold, and she'd been right. It was so dark she really couldn't make out his features even this close.

"Yell so we can find you," a man called.

They were getting closer, and she whispered in Harvey's ear. "Unbuckle your lifejacket but hold on to it until I tell you to let go." She hung on to him until he was done, then repeated the process. "I don't think this is the cavalry."

"Okay," Harvey said, and she was glad to hear his voice was calm and even.

"Where are you?" A spotlight started to sweep around the vessels, but the large swells were working in their favor.

"When it comes around, go under," she said softly as a vessel cut its engine. Whoever this was obviously had the ability to track their locators.

"Why don't they know who we are?" Harvey asked, going under with her when the sweep light grew brighter.

"They shot us down," she said when they came back up. "Start kicking and stay low." They swam together, diving when the light came around their way.

"Are you hurt?" Their would-be rescuers tried again, and from the sound of it they were paddling. "All you have to do is—"

The man didn't finish, and his last word was followed by a splash. Berkley turned to see if they'd been spotted, and the guy was swimming behind them. She couldn't see anything as the spotlight went out and the engine started.

"Come on, Junior." She started swimming, not wanting to get caught in the prop. "Swim."

It sounded like more than one boat was there now, which wasn't good in total darkness if you were the one in the water. "What in the hell is happening?" Harvey asked.

"I don't know, but I don't want to get ripped to shreds by a fast prop, so get ready to dive if anyone gets close. The Kodiaks on the *Jefferson* have smaller engines, which means we'd survive a hit, but I like my butt cheeks just the way they are." One of the boats sounded close, so she dove, letting the lifejackets do their job and bringing them back to the surface when it sounded like a danger had passed.

"Cletus." It sounded like a woman this time. "Speak up before we chop your fingers off."

"Wiley?" The voice didn't sound familiar at first, but Wiley's sense of humor was a lot like hers.

"Yeah," Wiley said, and her acknowledgment was followed by a lot more spotlights. "Keep talking so we can get you up before the sharks around here rip your feet off, since I was nice enough to provide them a midnight snack that's bleeding profusely in the water."

"Over here," she said, and one of the beams of light landed right on them.

"You know," Wiley said, offering her a hand up as the guy next to her took Harvey's. "Just because you're in the navy doesn't mean you should ditch your plane for a swim. That really pisses off the taxpayers. Don't those things cost like a gazillion dollars?"

"Okay, smartass," she said, sitting down and accepting a blanket from the heavily armed man with Wiley. "They were testing my reflexes by shooting three missiles at me. That last one did the trick."

"Let's head back then and cull our catch. It's been a successful night of fishing aside from finding you guys." The guy at the controls followed Wiley's orders and gunned the engine.

"Anything you'll want to gut and mount on your wall?" she asked Wiley, who kept her gun at the ready.

"I have a feeling these are more like guppies used for bait, but I'm an eternal optimist."

"That's easy to see, judging by your sunny disposition and your wardrobe enhancements," she said, laughing at the three guns Wiley had strapped to her aside from her sniper rifle. "Thank you for clearing my dance card though. I doubt those guys wanted to offer us a ride to be kind."

"I was just being all I could be. The army frowns when you don't live up to the motto."

"Good to know, soldier," she said, saluting Wiley and making them both laugh. "*Semper Fortis.*"

❖

"Eagle's nest, this is *Vengeance*," Captain August Shields called in as he dove to get out of range of the shots the destroyers were sending his way.

"Go ahead," Robyn Chandler said, and August wanted to sigh. He believed in Dick Chandler and in their mission, but Dick's children except for Rachel were weak links. "I repeat, go ahead."

"On a regular patrol we spotted three vessels sailing toward the coastline off South Korea. They had planes in the air, and we brought down one of their jets but had to dive to avoid fire."

"Were there survivors?"

"I deployed a team, but we had to leave them topside. They have radios and enough fuel to reach land, so keep the line open, and send transport if you hear from them."

"August," Dick said, sounding upbeat. "Any idea who you brought down?"

"No, sir. When we surfaced, we saw it was the *Jefferson* and two destroyers and took action when we saw a lone plane. From the maneuvers they were doing, and their flyovers, I believe the ship or all of them picked us up on a radar." August studied the sweep of the radar, relieved when it was empty.

"Impossible," Dick said and laughed. "You're in the most expensive and advanced piece of equipment we have, and we chose the Akula class because of its stealth capabilities. And are you sure it was the *Jefferson*? According to the Pentagon, that ship is not supposed to be anywhere near here."

"They've found a way around it, since they fired on us, and I believe they missed on purpose as a way to drive us. It was most definitely the *Jefferson*, since they tried to raise us on radio and threatened to fire on us." The sub wasn't fully crewed, but the guys he did have were able to do a decent job of following the course he'd set. They would go back to patrolling the coastline and avoiding the naval ships in the area. "From radar, we're the only ones down here, but if we hang around, they'll send whatever subs they have in the area to hunt us. We'll resume our patrols and inform you of any enemy approaching."

"If you're close to the *Jefferson*, I want you to punch a hole in her hull."

"Sir, if we were capable, I'd have done that by now. If they can spot us on radar, they'll sink us before we're close enough to make a killing shot." He took his fingers off the radio and took a deep breath for patience. "We'll need the *Vengeance* if they intend to bring the fight to you."

"I don't agree, but okay." Dick said the words rapidly, and then August heard a strangled scream, followed by cursing. Whatever was wrong, Dick had disconnected, and for that he was grateful.

"Set a course for the same loop we had before, and take our speed down. I don't want to surface if I don't have to, and avoid those ships at all costs," he said to his second.

"What about the men topside?" the young man asked. "We're already shorthanded, sir."

"They should be able to make it back, and once we hear from them, we'll pick them up. All they have to do now is avoid the show of force Michaels has in the area, and they'll be fine." He turned and left after that, since he detested liars, and the more he dealt with Dick, the more he saw his inability to tell the truth. But he was committed. He couldn't turn back and had to keep the crew from turning on him.

"The only smart play I've made today was sending out the grunts. Eventually the others will see we've lived to fight another day, but I need the more experienced sailors on board."

CHAPTER NINETEEN

Every major news outlet carried the beginning of Jeffery's treason-and-desertion trial, and the reporters seemed frenzied, since this was the first time they'd been granted access to the base on Guantánamo.

Army Colonel Herman Garner stared out the window of his office, missing the quiet that usually prevailed over his base. After the beginning of the Gulf War, the army had almost completely taken command here from the navy, and now they mostly held the men, and some women, who'd tried to bring harm to America through acts of terror. He didn't particularly love his new assignment as base commander, but he didn't totally detest it either. The place was hot, but he'd been fucking hot the entire time he'd served in Iraq, so when his orders came through, the addition of a beach had softened the blow.

"Don't let any of these guys wander from the group," he told his assistant. "If any of them try, have them either locked on the boat that got them here or put them in a cell. This isn't some excuse for an exposé of how we run this place."

"Yes, sir, and I've already briefed the entire base regarding that order," Lieutenant Michelle Singleton said as she stood in front of Herman's desk. "The only one we allowed access to Jeffery was the JAG attorney representing him, and his team."

"Good. Keep it that way. We don't need to fan the flames the Chandlers have started more than we have to. I always thought that boy was off a few crayons of a full box when he was vice president, and this proves it."

"The Pentagon sent a statement for you to review and deliver, so whenever you're ready, we'll begin." Michelle handed over a page and waited for him to read it. "Secretary Orr's people want you to read it as it's written, sir."

"They're trying to get a reaction out of someone, and I don't think it's Jeffery," he said, holding the sheet up and scanning it. "Did you read this?"

"Yes, sir, and I have an opinion about it, but I'm sure you're not interested."

"Actually, we have some time, and I would like very much to hear your thoughts." He pointed to a chair and told his secretary to hold his calls. "What's on your mind?"

"I know you said you worked with Mr. Chandler and weren't impressed, but I've read a little about what he's after," Michelle said, and Herman nodded. "With someone like that in charge, we can start to rebuild the respect we've lost around the world under the current administration."

"You mean the United States as a whole or the armed forces?" He leaned back in his chair, glancing out the window. "Some of that erosion of respect and trust came because of Chandler *being* in power. Surely you can see that."

"Respectfully, sir, I disagree with you." Michelle leaned forward a bit as if trying to intimidate him. "Mr. Chandler worked hard to take the shackles off us when it comes to dealing with these scumbags we take care of and feed."

"That's true. It has made some cases easier, but should they be? Everyone is for throwing the rules out when it comes to dealing with really bad people, but when it's decided you're the bad person, then it's not so good."

"Deciding between good and evil isn't hard."

He dropped his feet and faced her. "I'm glad you think so, Lieutenant. You should hold on to that unwavering belief in the coming months." He stood and started to button his jacket.

"What do you mean?"

"That you didn't make this very hard for us. You should've paid attention to what goes on here, and what it'd be like if you were on the other side of the bars."

"Are you trying to scare me, sir?"

"Me?" he said, laughing briefly. "No, but people like Walby Edwards should terrify the shit out of you. I know he does me."

Michelle stared at him, and he could almost see the sense of self-preservation kicking in. She lifted her hand slightly, as if reaching for her side arm, but he wasn't concerned. When he smiled, she made her move, but her eyes rolled back in her head as the MP Michelle had missed standing in the corner pressed a Taser into her back. The young man allowed her to drop to the ground before he let up on the trigger.

"Where should we put her, sir?"

"Walby wants her strapped to a backboard in the darkest interview room we have. Pick one with no windows and turn on the metronome. He'll deal with her later."

"Yes, sir."

Herman folded the statement down the middle and walked out to the podium they'd set up. "Welcome, everyone." That greeting calmed the crowd but started the cameras going. "We'll allow you into the court proceedings in a few minutes, but please stay quiet and courteous as the government presents their case."

"Will you be taking questions later?" a reporter asked.

"Not today," he said, holding his hands up when a few others shouted questions. "We're here to try to convict a traitor to the United State government. Jeffery Chandler is charged with very serious offenses, and he'll have to answer for those. We just want to show we have nothing to hide because we have a free and democratic system in place, which is vastly different from what Jeffery Chandler and his family would like to replace it with."

"Are you still searching for Dick Chandler?" another reporter shouted over the crowd.

"The best thing Mr. Chandler can do is turn himself in, but considering the cowardly actions he's exhibited throughout his entire life, starting with the lengths he went through to not serve his country, in my opinion he'll only be brought in kicking and screaming. We, though, will never stop looking."

The doors to their courtroom opened, so he stepped down and headed toward the detention center. Walby was filling out paperwork with headphones on, but he lowered them when he spotted him. He enjoyed talking to Walby and respected him for the job he did.

"Are you finished reviewing everything?" he asked, seeing a few devices along with Walby's folder on Michelle.

"Good call, and an even better call of waiting until now to move in."

Herman had noticed Michelle's rising rhetoric, but she'd tried to keep it under control. Jeffery's arrival seemed to have broken through all her restraints, and she'd become Jeffery's link to the outside world.

"She's sent a few messages, but they've all been to people in the States. This is the connection, though." Walby pointed to a graph he'd been working on, which listed all the numbers they'd collected from the people in custody. She'd used one of them more predominantly than the others.

"Who do you think it is?" Herman asked.

"Could be a major link between some of our unknown big fish." Walby took the page back and added some more numbers from Michelle's phone and computer. "I bet a root canal with no meds it's a burner phone, but we have to start somewhere."

"What about Michelle Singleton?"

"Give it a day," Walby said and smiled. "The tick-tick of the metronome is simple in design, but it has a way of crawling into the center of your brain and lodging there like a virus your body wants to dispel. We'll only do that, once you engage your mouth."

"That's one more experience I'll put on my list of things to avoid."

The rescue boats were loaded on board, and Berkley searched the faces of those waiting for them, smiling when she spotted the one person she knew would be there. "Are you both okay?" Aidan asked.

"Cletus got us out in time, ma'am, so I just have water in my boots," Harvey said, saluting Aidan.

"You head to a hot shower, and we'll debrief you after that," Aidan said as a crewmember started to put the equipment away.

"Commander," Wiley said to Devin. "If you'd like, I'll talk to you first. I had to eliminate one of the men from the sub when he pointed a weapon in Captain Levine's direction. The ones who surrendered peacefully are on the *Arlington* talking to the consultants."

"Thank you, ma'am. If you'll follow me." Wiley gave her a short wave and tilted her head in Aidan's direction.

"If you'd like my statement, Captain," she said, and Aidan nodded before following her to her quarters. No one was around, so Aidan closed and locked the door, then gazed at her as she stripped out of her wet things. Once she was naked, Aidan removed her uniform and pressed to her so they were skin to skin.

"My god, I was scared out of my mind when Harvey stopped so abruptly, and then neither of you answered." Aidan shook her head, but that didn't stop the tears. "I can't lose you, my love."

"I'm so sorry for scaring you," she said, placing her fingers under Aidan's chin and lifting her head. "That was the worst part." The list of things to be done had to wait a few minutes as she kissed Aidan until she raised her legs and wrapped them around her waist. They both needed to reconnect, if only to dispel all the fear and turmoil her episode had created. "I have to touch you," she said as Aidan pumped her hips into her.

"Please, baby, I need you inside me."

It was all she needed to hear to lay Aidan down and put her hand between her legs. Aidan was hard and so wet, her fingers went in fast until her thumb was pressed against her clit. "No matter what, I'm always going to fight to come back to you." She pulled out and tugged Aidan's clit between her fingers. "You're mine, and I love that you are." Aidan raised her hips, and she fingered Aidan's clit again. "I love you, and I need you to come for me."

Aidan threw her head back and clamped her jaws shut, obviously trying to stay quiet, but Berkley challenged her resolve by thrusting fast and deep until Aidan squeezed her shoulders so hard she was sure she'd have bruises.

"Fuck," Aidan said in a ragged whisper as her hips bucked under her. "I'm...coming...fuck." She pulled Berkley down to cover her when she was done and shed the rest of her tears. "You're mine too, so please don't ever leave me alone. The thought of life without you will break something inside me that I'll never be able to piece back together."

"Don't think about that, darlin'." She rolled over and put her arms around Aidan to comfort her, knowing the best thing was to let her cry. "You're never going to be alone, no matter what. My sisters, nieces, and family won't ever allow it."

"No. You promised me a home and a family, baby. Don't you dare renege on that...you swore."

"Beautiful, you know I'd never go anywhere away from you voluntarily." She held onto Aidan tighter and kissed the top of her head.

"Thank you for letting me freak out on you," Aidan said after a long silence.

"That's my job, along with a long list your father keeps adding to," she said, glad to see the smile back on Aidan's face.

"The first night I spent with you, I knew deep down my dad was going to love you. You two don't look anything alike, but in here..." Aidan placed her hand on Berkley's chest before kissing the same spot. "In here, you're both the same, and you love me as fiercely as he has my mom from the day they met."

"We're also going to be like them in all the happy years they've shared and all the ones yet to come." They kissed one more time before she slapped Aidan's butt to get her up. "How about we tend to our cluster, and then we can head back here, and you can take your time worshipping me?"

"So cocky," Aidan said, pressing her lips to her chin.

"Believe me, I'm in pain here, but I don't want anyone coming to look for us if we're too long."

They showered quickly before they moved to Aidan's office and called for Devin and Wiley. The *Arlington*'s brig was full, but as with all the others they captured, none of them were talking. Captain Washington had gladly left the consultants with his prisoners, so his crew would be free to perform their duties.

"They've been photographed and fingerprinted, and all that information has been forwarded to Command," Devin said. "None of them had anything that would've identified them, and Greenwald said it might take some time to sort out."

"How close are we to our go point?" Wiley asked.

"Two days, and one day from the two subs being close enough to us to make a difference if we see our friends again," Aidan said. "We're almost there, and I'm hoping they've got more for us than this speculation they've provided so far."

"Captain?" A man's voice came over Aidan's intercom.

"Go ahead," Aidan answered.

"Command is requesting a conversation with you, Captain Levine, Major Gremillion, and Major Sterling."

"Let them know we'll need about thirty minutes to get Major Sterling on board from the *Arlington*," Aidan said, and everyone with her appeared more alert. The *Arlington* was not only housing the regular crew and their prisoners, but also a SEAL team that would accompany their people when they went in. The team's commanding officer was Major Baylor Sterling, an old Academy buddy of Berkley whom she had fond memories of. They'd gone in different directions, but she still spoke to him occasionally, and she was glad to have him guarding her back.

"Will do, ma'am."

"Gary," Aidan said, patching through to the *Arlington*. "Can you send Major Sterling over, please?"

"Only if you say *red rover* first," Gary said, and Aidan snorted. "He's on his way. We got the same call, and it sounded like we're getting ready to send some of our crew inland."

"Thanks, and I think you're right."

Baylor arrived ten minutes later, wearing a hoodie, shorts, and flip-flops, making Berkley a little envious of his casual attire. He shook hands with Aidan and bumped fists with her and Wiley. "Remind me never to piss you off, BD," he said to Wiley, shortening her code name to initials. "That was a wicked shot earlier."

"Thanks, and we appreciate the backup. Ready for a hike?" Wiley asked.

"The big dogs were born ready," Baylor said, and Berkley laughed.

"You ready, Cletus? We're not going to have to carry you in and out on a litter, are we?" Baylor joked. "All that sitting you do hasn't made you soft, I hope."

"Hey, if you're offering." She joked back. "My backseat wants to join the party—will that be a problem?"

"Not to be harsh, but is the limp going to slow him down?" Baylor asked, all business now. "I understand why he's asking, I do, but the faster we get in and out, the less likely we'll get an up-close view of the million-man army."

"I totally agree with you, and while Harvey appears to be a big nerd, the guy's a beast."

"I hear ya, since I know what you two went through to get out. Let Junior know to wear comfortable shoes and sunscreen. We'll make it work."

"Thanks, Baylor," she said, and the big guy nodded. "Once we're done with this call, we'll have your guys join us so they can meet Jin Umeko. If we run into any problems, she'll be our translator."

"As long as she doesn't tell anyone we come across, 'Hey, kill all these damn American infidels,' we'll be cool." He slapped her on the back.

"Captain," the communications guy said. "We're ready to go in the conference room."

"Thank you." Aidan moved everyone next door and locked them in while Devin stood guard outside. "We're all present, Command."

"Good evening, everyone, especially you, Cletus," Carl said, and Berkley raised her hand more for Preston's benefit. "In two nights' time, we'll bring our team in with the Apache helicopters on board. After all the interrogations our guys have completed, we're confident of a few things."

The national security adviser, Neil Perry, went first. "After some very pointed questions, the Russians admitted to the sale of four Akula-class subs in exchange for not only money, but some highly sensitive information. They wouldn't admit from whom, but the important thing here is there are potentially three more besides the one that fired on Cletus."

"Have you narrowed the source and content of the breach?" Aidan asked.

"The information had to do with troop movements in Iraq, and some have been linked to attacks that resulted in heavy casualties for us. Unfortunately, the likely source was Jerry Teague and Adam Morris. There's no recourse there, but it makes you want to dig them up and kill them all over again," Neil said. "The stolen money from the Pentagon budget financed the monetary portion of the sale."

"What else?" Captain Kevin Greer asked from the *Anchorage*.

"You'll probably find a trove of information at your target location," Carl said. "There's a chance the scumbag who last occupied it wasn't truthful when he gave up the combination to the wall safe and the passwords to his computer, but don't leave anything behind. It sounds like Chandler cut some deal with the Kim family for his own reasons, and asylum was his part of the deal. After we found out about the sub deal, he could be there or somewhere in Russia."

"Anything else? Not that everything you've shared wasn't plenty," Aidan said.

"We may have found one of the sources of recruitment, and they're under surveillance. The FBI is casting a wide net while still keeping the person contained. Once they move to pick them up, we can compare the information they'll get with warrants to the information you extract." Carl looked directly into the video camera and stayed quiet for a moment. "We need this, ladies and gentlemen. All this chaos Chandler's after has a potential to fracture our nation, and the president wants to avoid that at all costs."

"We'll be quick but thorough, sir, and we'll have the Black Dragon keeping an eye on us," Baylor said. "It'll take death to keep us from completing our mission, and I don't know about these yahoos, but I plan on going out at ninety with a pretty girl and a bottle of Jack."

"Good to know you have goals, Major," Carl said, and everyone laughed. "Pack your guys up, and enjoy Captain Sullivan's hospitality until you're back from your hike. We'll talk again before you go. Each of you has a trusted security officer manning the computers until we're a go. We'll be sending any updates as they come in."

"Yes, sir," Aidan said, tapping her fingers lightly on the table.

"For each captain, the protocol for any necessary action until otherwise noted will be echo, Charlie, whiskey," Neil said.

"Understood," Aidan, Gary, and Kevin replied.

"We'll have some space for you guys by the time you make it back, Major," Aidan said. "Sounds like the fun isn't far off, so everyone get some sleep, and we'll notify you of any new developments."

"Thank you, ma'am. We'll do our best to stay out of your way."

"We'll be honored to have you aboard," Aidan said, and Baylor saluted.

"We're big fans of your dad, so we'll look forward to working with you. We're also looking forward to showing Cletus and her group what real running looks like in the morning."

"In your dreams, Jughead," Berkley said, and Baylor lunged at her, stopping short.

"I miss you, Cletus. You were the only one at the Academy and beyond not intimidated by my greatness."

"As you can see, Captain," Berkley said to Aidan, "he's still a big wallflower with self-esteem issues."

"I can see where you learned it, Cletus," Aidan said, and the way Baylor laughed guaranteed they'd be friends.

CHAPTER TWENTY

S ir, none of our contacts have heard from her after the failed attack on the holding facility," Ron Bollinger said as he glanced around the mall he was in. He always chose open public spaces when talking to Dick, on the off chance someone detected that communication. The location would never be anywhere near the capital or his home.

"There has to be some sign of her," Dick said, clearly aggravated. "She couldn't have simply disappeared."

"The base north of us recorded the radio contact they picked up when she ordered the pilot to come about and clear the yard. That can only mean some of the potential prisoners the MPs were about to round up were acceptable casualties in order to keep our secrets. But I can't confirm if she was standing right next to them when the pilot complied."

"Can you make contact with Marva Brian? I don't know who this is, and I can't chance being compromised. She's called me more than once to talk about Rachel."

"I'll take care of it, and I'm hoping the call she made was legit. Losing Rachel isn't good for morale, and for you personally. You must love her a great deal."

"Get it done and get back to me," Dick said, not giving away any feelings, as usual.

"Certainly, sir." He took a sip of his now luke-warm latte and watched the guy in the bistro across from him read the paper while drinking some kind of juice. The tingle of fear at the base of his spine made him wonder if the guy was covertly watching him, making him hold his breath when the guy looked directly at him and waved. "Shit," he muttered, forcing himself to keep his seat.

A second later a woman walked by him and waved back. When she stopped in front of the man and kissed him, Ron's heart seemed to start beating again. "I need a fucking drink," he said softly as he clutched the phone and did his best to relax. He didn't want to call attention to himself, and to distract himself, he figured it was time for a new burner phone.

Before he could stand, it rang, and he recognized the personal number of Chase Bonner, Speaker of the House. He considered ignoring it, but Chase could be childish when ignored. "Yes, sir?"

"Where are you? Our follow-up press conference you insisted on is in twenty minutes." Chase might've wanted the ultimate power of the presidency, but he was at times afraid of his own shadow. "I need you here."

"I'm sorry, sir, but I told you I had to attend to a matter this morning I couldn't reschedule. Marjorie from my office has everything you need, and if you follow the script, you'll do fine."

"If you're finished, get over here. I'm not counting on Marjorie. I'm counting on you."

Ron hung up before Chase got any whinier and threw the phone away after removing the SIM card and snapping it in half. That he threw into the next trash can and made his way to the electronic store to replace it. The guy behind the counter was kind of old for the location, but he understood the economy was bad. "Thanks, Pops," he said as he took his bag and change from the hundred dollars he paid with. Cash guaranteed that no paper trail would lead to him.

"No problem, and thanks for shopping with us."

He tossed the box with everything else outside and headed for his car. If he hurried, he could make the press conference, but he was in the mood for something else. "Hey, are you free?" he asked, handing over the money for his parking. "Good. I'm on my way."

"Did you get that?" the agent in the booth in the parking lot asked.

"Loud and clear," Jonas answered from the van outside. "Wrap it up and head to the address we identified last week in Georgetown. Our boy is looking to let off some steam."

"We're on it, Director."

The back door of the van opened, and Charles, the agent who'd sold Bollinger his phone, climbed in. "I think the loving couple freaked him out—good call, Boss. If you want, we'll take it from here."

"Thanks, Charles, but don't lose him. We didn't get anything on that last call, and it was important enough to change his phone after he was done. Make sure the guys get the old phone and do the analysis here," Jonas said, thinking he'd like nothing better than to pick this guy up and beat the answers out of him. "If he's setting a trap to check to see if he's being watched, I don't want the location services to give us away."

"We'll take care of it, and we'll be in touch if there's anything else," Charles said, changing his shirt from the polo the electronics store had issued him. "Don't worry. We want this as bad as you do, and we won't cut any corners."

Jonas nodded and put his finger up when his cell phone rang. "Chapman."

"Sir, we found something." He recognized Erin's voice. She'd been traveling to Baltimore to oversee Rachel Chandler's interrogation, but she'd continued working the overall case while she was out of the office. "You want to come here, or should I come in?"

"I'll send a plane," he said, bracing his feet on the ground when the van started moving. "We'll meet when you get back."

"Something important?" Charles asked.

"Might be," he said before he leaned over and tapped the driver on the shoulder. "Stop at the corner and let me out."

He hailed a cab and had the driver drop him a block from FBI headquarters "Erin called and found something," he said softly into the phone.

"Keep us posted unless you want to come here. We're not far from deploying, so I can't leave," Carl Greenwald said.

"I'll review whatever it is, but we're closing in on Speaker Bonner's assistant. We've got him under surveillance. That should warrant me reporting in, if nothing else."

"Get here as soon as Erin touches down then, and if whatever she has is enough, I may drive the paddy wagon myself."

Jonas changed his mind and retrieved his car, waving off his driver. Hopefully Erin had found the needle in the gigantic haystack of information they had. "If you found the key that lets us through the back door," he said of Erin as he drove out of the parking lot, "you can have my job."

"We have one more briefing before we hit our target site," Aidan said as she sat with Berkley and Jin for breakfast.

"I am ready to go," Jin said as she held a cup of tea with two hands.

"Are you afraid of anything?" Aidan asked, and Berkley glanced between them.

Jin didn't answer right away, and she was about to take the question back when Jin shook her head. "As you know, my family is dead, so that part of my life holds no hope or fear, but Yong—that is something unfinished. Whatever I find when it comes to her is the only thing I truly fear. If it is bad, it is my fault, and I will never be able to make it up to her."

"Think of it this way," Berkley said softly, and her soft tone made Jin lean in toward her. "If she's still alive, there's hope. All you need to do is accept what happened and help her put the pieces back together. You obviously care about her, and because you do, Yong will eventually be fine. She's a lucky woman."

The way Jin stared at Berkley made Aidan's heart ache for this somewhat broken woman. "I think it is you, Aidan, who are a lucky woman," Jin said, glancing at her before turning back to Berkley. "Thank you, Berkley. Hopefully you are right, and I will find something I can live for."

Jin left them alone and Wiley took her place. "You okay, Berk?" Wiley put her plate down and started pouring sugar into her coffee. "You survived that strike, but ejecting out of that thing can't be pleasant."

"Unfortunately, it's become a habit since these guys painted a bull's-eye on me, but I'll be ready to go."

Wiley pointed her fork at her and shook her head. "I'm not worried about that, buddy. We can walk at a snail's pace, and the outcome will, still be the same. I only want to know if we need to."

"You make me feel better," Aidan said. "Just make sure she doesn't wander off."

"And miss Cletus getting her wings clipped—no way," Wiley said and laughed. "She'll be okay, Captain. Once I saw Baylor and the other SEALs, I felt better myself. Whatever's in this place you're giving us a ride to must be the mother lode because of the company we're keeping."

"We didn't think so until Jin reported seeing Americans when Chil held her captive, or who she thought were Americans making themselves at home," Berkley said quietly. "When something's that out of place, it's memorable."

"I'm not an intelligence officer, but for Chandler to succeed, he needs backing from men who love nothing better than to turn our country into a twisted version of their world. Think about it," Aidan said as she took a bite of Berkley's toast like she didn't realize what she was doing.

"Turning the US into a more totalitarian government would not only give Chandler power forever, but it'd also change the world."

"So he blew up his house and ran into the arms of the Kim family?" Wiley asked.

"Or the arms of Putin, or a few others like him I can think of," Aidan said, shrugging. "Of course, I could be wrong."

"I doubt it." Berkley smiled. "You're not an intelligence officer, but you're highly intelligent."

"What she said," Wiley added, pointing at Berkley again. "All this stuff that's happened isn't even a scenario they cover during battle-strategy classes at West Point, and up to now, all I've done is read about it in the paper with a sense of disbelief. I was happy in my little cocoon in New Orleans, but you guys have been neck deep in this since it started."

"We're sorry to take you away from that," Aidan said. "You really do have a beautiful family."

"Thanks," Wiley said, running her finger along the top of her cup as if she couldn't sit still. How she managed the stillness of the nest baffled Berkley. "It was a change for sure."

"You don't have to tell me," Berkley said, and Wiley lowered her head. "How did you end up with a kid who looks and acts just like you?"

Wiley laughed, her head still down. "The thrill General Greenwald's team promised was hard to turn down, and when I made the cut right before graduation, I took the offer without talking it over with Aubrey first."

"Uh-oh," Aidan said, and Wiley nodded. "Let's go to my office to finish this. It's no one's business, and I don't want anyone listening in."

They walked together, and Berkley was surprised Wiley went so willingly. Talking about herself was never her forte during the years they'd known each other. "I can understand the allure. It's the same thing with me and jets," she said when Aidan closed the door.

"I figured a year with Carl and I'd be set, but that turned into a few years of me going out when called and home to Aubrey when I was on leave." Wiley sounded almost disgusted with herself. "I was at the point then where I'd had enough and was trying to either transfer or muster out and settle in New Orleans with Aubrey. It was that last job, though—it had legs that followed us home. We'd just landed, and I had the phone in my hand to call Aubrey when I watched most of my unit die right in front of me. One guy had just been welcomed by his whole family, and they were all gone just like that. I didn't want that to happen to me, and my only thought was to keep Aubrey safe."

"And you left for her sake?" Aidan asked, her voice the very definition of compassion. "God, that must've been so hard."

"I did, and I couldn't even really tell her why. For years I buried myself in death and missions, trying to forget the pain of walking out I'd caused until I realized I couldn't erase her from my heart through the Black Dragon."

"Damn, Wiley, I had no idea. Why didn't you call me?" Berkley asked.

"I was like a wounded dog who didn't want comfort from anyone, and if serving was bad, retirement was its own death sentence of loneliness. It stayed that way until Aubrey reached out and said it was past time for me to fulfill my obligations." She told them where she'd found Aubrey and Tanith, and what she'd done to free them from the trouble they were in. "The danger's still there, but I couldn't walk away again without bleeding to death from the pain."

"I'm glad for that, Wiley. You've given enough to deserve every bit of happiness you have now," Berkley said.

"We're going to have a baby," Wiley said, and her face took on an expression of wonder.

"Really?" Berkley stood up and pulled Wiley into a hug. "Congratulations, buddy. What the hell are you doing here then?"

"I'm here to watch over you so you can experience the same things I have now, and also because Aubrey insisted I not turn the assignment down. She said, if ever I was needed, it was this go-round. By telling you, I'm hoping you'll walk faster once we're on the ground. I'm not interested in anything but getting home to my girls."

Aidan laughed and hugged Wiley as well. "Congratulations, and we do want the same things. Aubrey seems like a wonderful and understanding woman."

"You two are probably a lot alike. I always knew Cletus would pick someone good and that it'd be for life," Wiley said as she released her. "I'm glad she found you."

"Wiley Gremillion, sappy?" Berkley asked, slapping her hands together. "Write that down, baby, because I doubt it'll ever happen again."

Wiley stared at Aidan before taking her hand. "Are you sure about this one? If you go through with the wedding, put me on speed dial. I have a pellet gun at home that'll help keep her in line."

"It's a deal," Aidan said before her intercom buzzed. "Yes?"

"Captain, Command is requesting an earlier link. Would you like it in your office?"

"Patch it through."

Carl, Neil, and Preston appeared on the screen right after that, and they all appeared serious. "Good, you're all together," Carl said, skipping his usual greeting. "There have been some new developments."

"What now?" Aidan asked, almost sorry she had when each man spoke in turn.

❖

Erin Mosley stood in the White House Situation Room and took a deep breath to settle herself before she started through her presentation. She'd been working on it for the last couple of days and had backup for everything she'd found. At Quantico her instructors had always preached that any case without proof was merely speculation.

"Agent Mosley, whenever you're ready," Olivia Michaels said. Erin knew Olivia had postponed the announcement of her vice president because of this meeting, and she wanted to make sure it was worth the wait.

"Thank you, ma'am." Someone dimmed the lights for her when she put up her first exhibit. "Six months ago, President Khalid asked for and received Army General Homer Lapry's resignation."

"Good call on his part," Carl said. "The man's an idiot, but that didn't take away from his arrogance."

"Yes, sir," Erin said. "Lapry didn't agree with the president's changes to the troops, which were in his purview to make, and by all accounts, Lapry left voluntarily but has complained bitterly ever since about being pushed out." She moved from Lapry's official picture to copies of plane tickets and video of Lapry going through customs in South Korea. "Two weeks before the president's assassination, Lapry traveled to South Korea on vacation."

"That's what he listed on his entry documentation?" Drew asked.

"Yes, sir, but he hired a car to take him to a small fishing village on the West Coast, as verified by the agents I had check. He sat in his small hotel room for a day until he hired a charter boat for a fishing trip." She put up a map of North and South Korea. "After a little over four hours of fishing, the same car service drove him back to the airport in Seoul, and he returned to the United States."

"What did you find so strange about this trip?" Pentagon Security Chief Rooster asked. "I mean aside from traveling an eternity for basically a four-hour fishing trip."

"The South's security forces have brought the charter captain in for questioning, and after hours of interrogation, he admitted his business is merely a taxi service at times."

"A taxi service for who?" Olivia asked, narrowing her eyes.

"He waits at certain coordinates, and North Korean forces pick up his passengers, with an agreed-upon arrangement to bring them back. It's a way to bypass any sign you've been in the rogue state," Erin said, and she could see the ramifications of what this meant appear on everyone's face. "According to the captain, Homer Lapry was one of the people requiring that unique service."

"What was he doing in North Korea?" Carl asked.

"That I can't verify yet, but it might be where Chandler is," she said.

"The charter guy make many of these trips?" Olivia asked, and Erin nodded as Jonas stood up.

"We might've connected this to our ongoing investigation in DC," Jonas said, and more than one person shook their head as if not understanding. "We've had Speaker Bonner's assistant under surveillance for the last week, after one of our agents put together a pattern Ron Bollinger has that raised a red flag," Jonas said.

"Which is?" Marcus Newton asked. "The CIA could've helped with that." He sounded irritated.

"If there's a case to be made, we want it done by the book. Your guys can help as we expand our South Korean investigation," he said, but Marcus still appeared peeved.

"I don't like being left out of the loop. It's like you're trying to hide what you're doing."

"Excuse me," Jonas said with heat.

"Back to the pattern," Olivia said, sounding like a scolding mother.

"Ron Bollinger sits in a crowded mall, has lengthy conversations in hushed tones, and changes his phone every couple of days. He tosses the old one into a mall trashcan and the SIM card into another one. Yesterday we forced a quicker change, and he's using a phone we modified."

"Seriously?" Carl asked. "Can you do that?"

"We got a blind warrant that'll stand up in any court, which covers us if Bollinger ends up in a regular legal channel. From what we've been able to find, some of his most frequent calls are to Homer Lapry and Speaker Bonner."

"Bonner makes sense, since that's his boss," Marcus said in a tone that sounded like he was leaving "fucking idiot" off the end of his statement.

"It does, but it's also possible that Bollinger is the courier between Chandler and Bonner," Jonas said, and Olivia appeared shocked. "We've investigated the military, security intelligence personnel, but not one elected official."

"And we should have," Olivia said.

"Yes, ma'am, and if we can prove that this is accurate, the attempt your former lead agent made on your life makes total sense. If you were out of the way, the next in line at the seat of power would've been Chase Bonner," Erin said. "If he's really working with Chandler, what better way to pave an easy path to victory for Chandler?"

Olivia chuckled a little and Drew joined her. "Obviously Dick doesn't know Bonner as well as he thinks he does," Olivia said.

"What do you mean?" Erin asked, wondering if some big piece of her puzzle was missing.

"It would've taken another well-planned assassination to get Bonner to give up the Oval Office if he'd actually been sworn in." Olivia gazed at her and winked. "You're a good agent, but I'm familiar with politics and its ravenous power-hungry people."

"True, but back to Lapry," Drew said. "How's he fit into all this?"

"When Captains Sullivan and Levine first uncovered this conspiracy quite by accident, they thought it had worked because only the lower ranks were involved. Captain Levine had used the term worker bees, but recruitment had to have started high enough to make the worker bees not fear serious repercussions if they'd been discovered."

"Enter General Lapry," Carl said.

"Precisely." Erin nodded. "Anyone serving in your command might have feelings about this last election that mirrored Chandler's, and up to now you've had to bear it until the next election. If it was a military general who told them it was their duty to work against the government, you'd probably snag quite a few recruits."

"That's true," Carl said, "but Lapry is a certifiable idiot. He was promoted more from politicking than by merit."

"It's the authority of his rank, sir, not so much the man," Jonas said. "Once he secured a few, they probably found like-minded people to swell their ranks."

"So now what?" Olivia asked.

"We wait and listen, and once we have the evidence, we'll remove Chandler's eyes and ears within the capital. While we wait on that, we'll continue to work on Rachel Chandler," Jonas said.

"Any progress there?" Rooster asked.

"She has very colorful language, but none of it is relevant to this case," Erin said.

"I bet," Drew said with a smile. "The government's case against Jeffery is almost done, so maybe it's time to move Rachel to a more permanent home."

"Get it done," Olivia said. "If there's nothing else, we're due on the Hill, and you should all know I've chosen Drew as my vice president. Once he's sworn in, he'll take charge of the day-to-day operations of this investigation. Commander Palmer will replace Drew as defense secretary at the Pentagon, but I'm sure he won't mind if you still call him Rooster. Congratulations, gentlemen."

The group gathered stood and clapped, obviously approving of the choices. "As for the rest of you, you'll remain in your posts since we have a good team in place. You all were loyal to Peter, and I hope you'll stay on and work with me to finally finish this."

"We'll follow you to hell and back, Madam President," Carl said, saluting at attention. "To hell and back."

CHAPTER TWENTY-ONE

"Wow" was all Berkley could think to say when Carl was done. "If Lapry was one of his recruiters, was there someone similar in the navy?"

"Rodney James would be my guess, but he got caught with his hand in the cookie jar. Once Drew's sworn in, I'm sure we'll have more flexibility when it comes to interrogations that'll actually get us somewhere."

"Does all this change our timeline?" Aidan asked.

"Tomorrow at dusk you've been invited to dine with the South Korean and British captains as if you're there for typical war games," Carl said and pointed to Preston.

"The Apache that'll deliver you to their ship will be accompanied by a few more, which will continue inland and deliver our team to the drop-off spot," Preston said, and Berkley smiled at the large cigar in his jacket pocket. "You have however long it takes to get what we're after, then make it back to the extraction point. That's the only time you'll break radio silence, as agreed."

"Thank you, sir," Berkley said. "Will you be updating the team tonight?"

"We'll leave that up to you, Cletus, but this is strictly need-to-know. All of us must work from a compromised position in that someone is plotting against you. There's no reason to give Chandler any more advantages," Preston said. "Be careful out there, kid, and Godspeed."

"Thanks again, sir," Berkley said, giving him a casual salute. "We won't be long."

"See that you aren't, and watch out for each other," Carl said. "Buckston shared some good news with me, Wiley, so try to stay on Karen Tarver's good side. If only to keep her off my ass."

"Yes, sir," Wiley said and laughed.

"Who's Karen Tarver?" Aidan asked once the link dropped.

"My mother-in-law, and up till recently not my biggest fan. Aubrey's dad was a SEAL, who was gone a lot, and Karen didn't care for it. When I started dating her daughter, she didn't want the same kind of life for her, and I figured it had more to do with that than anything about me personally. She wanted someone more stable for her little girl."

"If she likes you now, let's not do anything to fuck that up," Berkley said, and Wiley nodded.

"Let's go round up our need-to-knows, so we can take it easy for the rest of today. Tomorrow will be hard enough," Berkley said.

They had an extensive strategy session with Baylor, and Jin joined them at his request. They all listened intently as Jin described again the layout of the main house as she remembered it, considering the short amount of time she was there. The two most important spots were the office and the master bedroom. If Chil hadn't lied, the team going in would be quick once everything was unlocked and ready to take.

"Do you think Chil was being truthful?" Baylor asked Jin, cocking his head to the side as he seemed to study her diagram closely. "In my experience, nothing worth anything is that easy to walk off with."

"My father also had many state secrets. The vaults where they are kept, according to him, would open with a certain combination, but it would also send an alert to his security forces," Jin said, glancing between Berkley and Baylor. "He might have given you a combination, but it will turn out to be a trap." The question now was who to believe right before they found themselves in the middle of a hostile situation.

"So he's lying?" Baylor asked.

"It is not completely a lie if the door opens, Major, but it is a half-truth if the key unlocks the means to your death."

"Okay," Baylor said, stretching the word. "How do we open the vaults without the death option? I don't know about you, but I'd like to skip that part no matter how many shiny objects are on the inside of the safe."

"If the setup is like my father's, it is a fifteen-digit code," Jin said.

"That's a lot of possibilities," Aidan said, whistling. "*How* do we open it?"

"Kim knows Chil is never going to return, so the nice house probably now belongs to the new enforcer, or some general," Jin said, placing her hands in her lap. "That person should be our first target."

"Seems to me, we'll be in the same boat with a different captain, but the same results," Baylor said. "It won't matter if we capture the new landlord, if he or she won't give up the combination easily."

"You are in their land, Major, so you are allowed to play by their rules," Jin said, as if that explained everything.

"I can be dense sometimes," Berkley said with a tight smile, "but what does that mean?"

"Major." Jin locked eyes with Baylor.

"Please call me Baylor. It's easier."

"Thank you." Jin bowed her head slightly. "Baylor, if you had the choice between seeing your penis in my hand when I am across the room from you or opening a safe, which would you choose?"

"That's hard to answer in a room full of women," Baylor said and blushed a scarlet red, as if he hadn't expected the question.

"We're guessing you'd squeeze your legs together and cry softly while I rifled through your valuables," Wiley said for him, not being able to stifle her chuckle.

"The problem is, I don't think we're allowed to do that," Baylor said, moving his head like he was cracking the bones in his neck. "But God knows I've wanted to on occasion."

"I can and will. If it is the only way we can succeed, your government can punish me if that is their wish when we return. But I ask you not to try to stop me," Jin said.

Baylor slapped his hands on his thighs and nodded. "Good enough for me, and I'm no snitch. You can come home with a necklace of Johnsons if that's what it takes to get what we need, and I'll swear on a stack that I didn't see a thing."

Jin hesitated before asking Wiley, "Is this a good thing?"

"It's a good thing," Wiley said and laughed. "Let's go eat so we enjoy that relaxing the captain mentioned."

The team ate together and thanked Aidan for her apple pies when Berkley explained why she baked them. The dessert was an American icon and reminded them of who they fought for and what was waiting when they came back. Berkley enjoyed herself but couldn't stop the thought of the danger from within. They had to fear the terrain they were going into, but perhaps the one trying to kill them wouldn't be the guy who'd inherited Chil's house.

"Devin, can you set the watches and navigation for the night?" Aidan asked when they were done. It was still early, but they had only the one night left.

"You got it, ma'am, and thanks for inviting me tomorrow. I promise to keep an eye on you," Devin said, glancing at Berkley.

"You'd better, and remember what will happen to *you* if something happens to *her*," Berkley said.

"Your graphic explanation is scarred into my brain," Devin said and smiled. "I'll forget my own name before that slips my mind. However, tomorrow night she'll be more apt to get hit on than attacked. No offense, ma'am," he said to Aidan.

"None taken." Aidan laughed at the somewhat awkward compliment.

"If that happens, it should be an entertaining time for you," Berkley said, knowing Aidan could handle a situation like that with no problem.

"Here's hoping," Devin said with his fingers crossed, and Aidan laughed harder.

Berkley met with her pilots on the deck and placed both Vader and Killer in charge of the flight crew since, as far as everyone on board the *Jefferson* knew, she was joining Aidan for the dinner she'd been invited to. Preston was right. The fewer the people who knew the whole plan, the less likely they'd be double-crossed by someone alerting the North Koreans of their arrival.

She walked back to her quarters and entered Aidan's room through the conference room. Aidan wasn't in her office, so she headed back to the private part of the space. When she entered, Aidan was sitting on the side of the bed in white silk bikinis with a matching bra. She'd let her shoulder-length hair down from the usual ponytail she kept it in while they were at sea, and Berkley stood and stared. Aidan was incredibly beautiful.

"The first time I saw you, the thing that popped into my head," she said, and Aidan stood up and started unbuttoning her shirt, "was wow."

"I thought it was that I was so short." Aidan undid the belt next and unzipped her pants. "You teased me, remember? Relentlessly if *I* recall that night accurately."

"I did, but every one of us has that primal part of our brain that says, 'That's one fucking hot girl.' The thing is, though, if you don't want to sound like a Neanderthal, you only admit to *wow*." Her pants dropped to her ankles and her shirt behind her.

"You know what I think?" Aidan snapped her fingers, then pointed down. She kicked her shoes to the side and took her pants completely off, but didn't say anything. "Aren't you curious?"

"What?" She yanked her undershirt off but left her underwear on.

"I happen to love that caveman part of your head that craves touching me, that thrum in you that wants to be inside me more than anything." Aidan pulled her sports bra up and sucked her left nipple so hard she almost came.

"Do you?" she asked, wanting to regain whatever control she'd ever had. Aidan responded by sucking on her other nipple until she stopped moving. She knew of only one way to slow the assault, so she turned Aidan around and pressed against her back. "Are you wet for me, baby? Have you been sitting here thinking about my hands on you?"

She cupped Aidan's breasts and squeezed. "Tell me," she whispered in Aidan's ear. "Tell me, or I'm not going to fuck you on this ship, even though that would definitely be against all the rules. And Triton's kid doesn't like breaking the rules."

"Yes," Aidan said, leaning back farther against her and taking hold of her wrist. She flattened her hand as Aidan moved it down her abdomen until it was at the elastic of the panties. "You've made me wet from that first day too. The best thing in my life is that I'm yours and you want me."

She moved past the top of the underwear and kept going until her index and middle fingers were between Aidan's legs. Her fingers were instantly slick with Aidan's wetness, which made it easy to run them over the rock-hard clit before squeezing it between her fingers. "Tell me what you want."

"What do you want?" Aidan asked as she reached up and put her hands on the back of her neck.

"I want to touch you until you come—until you can feel me everywhere."

"Shit," Aidan said when she pressed her fingers closer together and thrust her hips forward into Aidan. "Baby." She smiled when Aidan pulled her hair hard enough for it to hurt. "No teasing tonight."

She kissed the side of Aidan's neck and started pumping her fingers over Aidan's clit, her touch growing firmer with each pass. Nothing was better in life than watching and feeling Aidan move against her. Aidan's hips bucked in time with her touch and sped up as a signal for her to do the same. Aidan's clit was so hard, and she was so wet, Berkley was turned on even more.

"Don't let me go," Aidan said as she moved her hand up and wrapped her fingers around her forearm hard enough to leave an imprint of each one. "Damn," Aidan said, and her movements grew jerky.

When she slumped against her right after her body had gone rigid, Berkley scooped her up and cradled her. The tears on Aidan's face made her stop, but Aidan shook her head. "I'm just happy, honey."

She moved to the bed and sat down, still cradling Aidan in her arms. "Are you sure that's all it is?"

"I only cry when I'm upset or you undo me," Aidan said, bringing their heads together so they could kiss. "All my life, no matter how long it is, it'll be you who reaches so deep inside me. I don't want anyone else."

"I'm glad, and I feel the same." She sat back against the plain headboard and smiled when Aidan straddled her lap. "You know what I've been thinking about?"

Aidan's gentle fingertips caressing her face paused. "What? You can tell me anything."

"That I can't wait to tell everyone I run across for nine months that you're having a baby when we finally get pregnant. Our baby," she said, and Aidan's eyes filled with tears again. "I'm not sure how Wiley keeps all that inside without bursting."

"She told us because of just that—she couldn't keep it in anymore, and she does seem deliriously happy. We need to stay in touch with her when we're settled." Aidan leaned in and kissed her, coating her abdomen with her wetness. "Are you really going to be happy with the life we talked about?"

"I want it all." She put her hand back between Aidan's legs, loving this position. It gave her lover the control to go as fast or slow as she wanted. "But mainly I want you in our bed with me every night so I can feel every bit of you against me. I don't want anyone ordering me to stay away from you."

"I want...fuck...to touch you," Aidan said as Berkley's fingers slipped back inside. Her hips came forward as if searching for her thumb on that one spot she craved her the most.

"We've got time, but you look so delicious, I have to have you again." She moved her hand as much as she could as Aidan kissed her again. "I want your mouth on me, but first I want you to come for me again." She palmed Aidan's ass, bringing her closer. "Do you think you can do that for me, baby?"

"God, yes," Aidan said and started moving her hips, picking up speed as she steadied herself with her hands on Berkley's shoulders.

Berkley's clit was so hard she thought she might have permanent damage if she didn't have some relief soon, but she could watch Aidan with her head thrown back, pumping her hips, her bottom lip caught between her teeth for hours. This was one of the positions they'd tried on their first night together, only then Aidan had been shyer about it.

"Shit," Aidan said softly. "I'm coming." She tightened her grip on her shoulders, and Berkley opened her mouth to her, swallowing every one of her moans.

"You're so gorgeous like this," she said when Aidan straightened up.

"You want an even more beautiful view of me?" Aidan asked after another long kiss.

"I can't imagine you can do better than this," she said, raising her hands when Aidan moved down the bed, spread her sex, and sucked her in. "But I could be fucking wrong."

CHAPTER TWENTY-TWO

The helicopters were loaded, and the first one away was the group joining Aidan for the dinner aboard the South Korean ship. Berkley watched her go, her lips still feeling the lingering passion of Aidan's kiss.

Their parting was the same as always, with Aidan kissing her but not wanting to have the conversation about the folder in her desk with all the information she'd need if something happened to her in the field. It was morbid, true, but she wouldn't have anything hovering in the corners of her mind if something went wrong. Her father had always taught her to cover all the bases no matter what, and taking care of Aidan was a major priority for her.

"You remember how to use that, right?" Wiley joked, pointing to her gun.

Camouflage wasn't her usual wear, and she frankly felt ridiculous, but Baylor and Wiley had insisted. The weapon matched her outfit, and she would help carry out whatever they found at this place in the empty pack at her feet. "I'll try not to wound you," she joked back. At least this time they weren't going to literally crash this party.

"You do, and Aubrey will take you out with the Mini Cruiser she just got. She says I have enough scars already," Wiley said in her ear, not to be overheard. "Did you really carry him out of here?" They both glanced at Harvey as he sat next to them with his eyes closed.

"He did a lot of the work, and we stole a horse."

"A horse? Hell, man, they might make a movie about you once we're done saving the world." Wiley winked when she raised her middle finger in her direction.

The helicopters swung to the right now that it was totally dark and headed to the closest town near where Jin remembered Chil's compound being. Jin sat on her other side wearing the exact same clothes and equipment and, as if sensing her staring, opened her eyes.

"Are you nervous that I am here?" Jin asked, looking at her like she really wanted to know the answer to her question.

"No," she answered honestly with no hesitation.

"Are you sure?"

"I believed your story about your mother and your grandparents, so yes, I'm positive. Pain like that is hard to fake, or it would be for me."

"Good—I am not your enemy," Jin said, placing a hand momentarily on her knee. "One day perhaps you will call me friend."

"Thanks, but I don't need any more time for that, my friend. Once this is over, you won't be alone," she said before placing the headphones back on for the rest of their ride.

It took forty minutes to reach the deserted spot devoid of light and people before the pilot spoke. "Captain, we'll pick you up here unless you send new coordinates. Major Sterling's team will deploy first and lead you in. Good luck, ma'am."

"Thanks, and safe flying. Hopefully we'll see you tomorrow night, if not sooner," she said before they were cleared to rappel down.

Baylor's guys had spread out and secured the area, so they could start walking. If Jin's memory was right, they had a four-mile hike to the location. That gave them plenty of time to formulate a plan they could execute in the early morning. With Chil gone, hopefully the place was somewhat empty, but life was never that easy.

"Hold." She heard Baylor's voice in her earpiece for the first time in an hour. They all took cover as a truck drove by on the road fifty feet from them. They had hiked through the bush to avoid any traffic, even if the roads didn't seem very well-traveled. "Must be changing the watch."

Berkley saw the truck through her night-vision goggles, and the passengers in the back did seem to be military. "If that's the number, it should be manageable." About fifteen guys were riding out from the direction they were headed.

"Yeah, if that's all of them. A big if," Wiley said.

"You're such a downer sometimes."

Baylor gave the go-ahead signal.

Low Nam Chil was probably still pissed he'd been taken away from all this, Berkley thought when they got their first look at the compound and its sprawling main house. It sat on a lake, had extensive gardens, and was lit up brighter than Times Square. The back of the house seemed to overlook the lake, and many of the rooms featured large windows to take advantage of the beauty around them. Guards were posted at the corners of the house, but that's all that was visible from the grove of trees they were standing in on the other side of the small lake.

"What do you think?" she asked Baylor as his guys protected their perimeter.

"Someone's got to be in there considering all those lights, but it's not heavily fortified," he said as Wiley nodded. "Looks can be fucking deceiving, though, so we have to get closer. Could be the guards are scarce back here, but it's Fort Knox in the front. If we take out two guys and the rest see them, they could go batshit, you know."

"We need to find out," Wiley said.

"Tito," Baylor said, and a young guy instantly appeared. "Take two guys and go around that way." He pointed to the left. "It'll keep you in the trees."

"Yes, sir."

It took twenty minutes, but Tito radioed about the seven guys guarding the front. With a closer view he also reported a shirtless Korean man sitting at the desk in what appeared to be the office. That was the only person they saw, so it was time to gamble.

"Hold, and we'll be right there," Baylor said. They walked until they had people on both sides of the back of the house. "Okay, guys, you know the drill."

"Yes, sir, shock and awe," Tito said, and his two guys followed him to the front.

"Goose, take the west side on the front, and KO, you got the guy scratching himself on the opposite side of us. In and out, guys. This is no time to ration bullets."

"Yes, sir."

"Wiley, can you make that shot?" Baylor asked, staring at the guy in the office. His eyes were on the monitor on the desk, and his hand had dropped to his lap. "Remember, we only want to scare him some."

"I'll take it as soon as you're done outside. No sense raising the alarm because of broken glass," Wiley said and set up. "Once it's done, I'll head up top and keep an eye out."

"Okay. We're a go on my mark," Baylor said.

Berkley, Harvey, and Jin waited, and everything seemed to happen at once when the two backyard guards faced each other and Baylor said, "Go." The night was suddenly filled with the puffs that weapons with silencers make, and the only real noise was the scream from the guy in the office. "Let's hit it, Captain."

They followed Baylor and his men inside. They had to get to the semi-naked guy in the office before he called for reinforcements. "This way," Jin said, leading them down a hallway in the middle of the house and shooting the two men outside the locked door. It appeared as if they'd been trying to get inside the office to see what the screaming was about.

"Move aside," Baylor said, kicking in the door after putting a bullet through the heavy-duty lock. "Make sure there's no one else in the master bedroom," he said to the guys at the back of the hallway.

"Do you know him?" Berkley asked Jin when she turned the guy over onto his back. Wiley had put a bullet in the same location she'd shot Rachel Chandler.

Jin shook her head as she studied the guy's face. "I have never seen him before." The man gazed up at Jin and said something hard sounding in Korean, and Jin kicked him in the ribs before answering him. "He said we are all going to die."

"What did you say?" Berkley noticed the guy's jockey shorts around his knees. That oddity made her glance at the screen, where the film showed an orgy scene.

"That it shouldn't take him long to swallow his own penis when I cut it off. Pornography is frowned on here." Jin kicked him again, and the man moved into a semblance of the fetal position. She said something else, and the man shook his head violently.

"Tell him he made this easy on us," she said as Baylor removed his knife from its sheath and pressed it to the guy's scrotum. Jin translated, and he appeared to be going into shock, so Berkley elevated his feet. "What's your name?"

The man only shook his head back and forth rapidly, and she glanced at Baylor, who pressed down with enough pressure to draw blood.

"What's your name, asshole?" Baylor asked, exhaling a long breath as if out of patience. "And," he interrupted Jin, "you damn well understand me. Tell me your name, or I'm going to cut clean through and feed this tiny thing to the first dog I run across. I hear your head guy loves that kind of thing."

"Ji Woo Min, and you are illegally in my home. My men kill you."

"Only if they rise from the dead," she said, and just then Wiley radioed in.

"Another group's headed toward the house."

They all waited and listened to Wiley breathing.

"Shit," Wiley said, and Berkley wanted to shake her to make her talk.

"Shit what?"

"Another fifteen guys are on their way, and more than half appear to be American. What are they doing here, and can I shoot them?" Wiley asked. "You don't have a lot of time, guys. I need an answer. They're moving double-time, which means your wounded butthead in there probably called for backup."

"Wiley, are they armed?" Baylor asked.

"Loaded for bear."

"Start working, and my guys will do cleanup. Tito, once it's clear, head to the buildings they came from and gather what you can. Wiley, you stay put," Baylor said. The outside filled with screams when Baylor's orders were carried out. "Who else did you call?" Baylor placed his knife back on the spot where Min didn't want it. One of the other guys with them started documenting what was in the room and Min himself, in case their body cams that allowed Command to watch missed anything.

"You are dead," Min said, spitting in Baylor's direction. "I tell you nothing."

"Then you really want to die a eunuch." Baylor made a small slice, and it seemed to break something in the small man, who tried his best to slide away from Baylor. More screaming came from outside, and Berkley turned and glanced that way, but the back was clear.

"Wiley?" she asked.

"This place is full of hostiles. We're under fire so pick up the pace in there."

Berkley started a perimeter check in the room and found the vault behind a gilded full-length mirror. "Open it, or I'll personally carve your eyes out. I've had enough of your country and your sucky hospitality."

Baylor jerked Min up by the hair and dragged him to the combination. "You were right, Jin. That's a long-ass combination. Open it, motherfucker, or I'll stick your dick in your head when my friend finishes ripping your eyes out."

"That will kill me," Min said, as if they didn't understand the purpose of torture.

"You say that like it's a bad thing, but think," Baylor said with a genuine smile. "We're going to make you an international star when we show the media how you like to spend your time. Bestiality porn—really?"

"No," Min said and started struggling again.

"Yes, so at least smile for the camera. We can always blow the door, but shit like what you were doing is damn entertaining. If I think so, I'm sure plenty of others will too," Baylor said, and one of his guys started wiring the vault. "Think about the rest of your family when all this comes out. Doesn't your leader have a thing about punishing the whole bunch when really there's only one pervert in the barrel?"

Min lunged toward the safe and punched in the combination, surprising them all, from what Berkley could tell, when the door swung open a sliver. Harvey opened it the rest of the way, and they stared at the piles of external hard drives inside. Harvey unshouldered his pack and started clearing the shelves.

"If they're encrypted it'll take months to crack them," she said, and Jin nodded as Harvey finished and took Jin's pack to transport the rest of the files. "We need to take Min with us."

"You're right. We have the lock, so we might as well bring the key with us. I'll finish in here, and you guys start back to the trees," Baylor said, pointing to Min as one of his men started packing the desktop computer.

"We have to sweep the rest of the house, and it'll go faster if we help out," Berkley said to Harvey.

They left Baylor and his men, but Jin went with them as they cautiously walked the long hallway, checking each room. The only room with movement seemed to be the one they'd passed, which appeared to be the master bedroom. Everything else was quiet and empty as they headed for the last three doors, and she nodded when Harvey went first. She aimed her pistol against any bad surprises and took a deep breath. "Go ahead."

Harvey turned the knob and stumbled backward, falling on his ass and knocking her off balance when six large masked men ran out fast enough that Berkley couldn't get a shot off. The jolt of the Taser leads hitting her leg caused her to drop next to Harvey, and Jin fell immediately on top of her.

The thought that went through her mind was Aidan whispering how much she loved her right before they parted. She prayed more than anything she'd hear those words again.

"Fuck," she whispered when the guy who'd Tasered her raised his mask and she saw his blond hair and blue eyes. He was an American with a cruel smile, and he laughed as he squeezed the trigger again. She tensed and then there was nothing.

"Cletus, Baylor, take cover," Wiley said as she spotted four trucks headed their way. "Backup is closing in, and we need to go." She lined up her shot and took out the driver of the first vehicle, causing it to veer off the road, dumping out the soldiers in the back like they'd been shot from a cannon. "Let me know when you're out."

"Roger that," Baylor said, picking up the packs and pushing Min toward one of his men. "Cletus, time to boogie." There was only silence. "Stop fucking around and respond."

"What's wrong?" Wiley asked as she reloaded. "Cletus?"

"We'll check it out, but start moving toward the woods. We're going to have to call for a ride much closer than where we decided on," Baylor responded, and it sounded like he was running. "Fuck," he said, his voice rising suddenly.

"What?" Wiley asked as she saw the SEAL team headed for the back of the house. It was time to retreat while it was still their decision to do so.

"One of our guns is on the ground, and she's gone. Her, Jin, and Junior." Wiley saw the front door open, and a group headed out. They were trained well enough to move and laid down cover fire that prevented her from getting off a shot without risking a bullet to the head. "We have to pull out."

Wiley saw Baylor and his guys run out of the back with two people over their shoulders, and she followed, thinking it was Berkley or one of the missing. Helicopters with spotlights appeared a few seconds later, but she ran along with the group as the SEALs aimed for the lights and the back rotors of each craft. Three of them had gone down before they reached the thickest part of the woods, and Baylor stopped to radio the *Jefferson*.

"Zookeeper, this is Tiger One, over."

"Go ahead, Tiger One."

"We need a vet and a muzzle now. Sending coordinates, and we need a tracking party."

"Got it, and where do we need to send the bloodhounds?"

"To our target location. They poached three of my cubs. We need to evac some, and we'll follow our lost sheep. I'm not leaving them behind."

"Tiger One, we received your location, and we'll be there." The communications guy cut off the line after that, which didn't surprise Wiley. Short spurts on the radio were harder to pinpoint and decipher.

"We need a vehicle, and we need to go now," she said after Baylor's radio guy put the equipment away. "If we speed, we should catch these assholes."

"Wiley, you need to bring these guys back, and whoever this poor girl is," Baylor said, placing the emaciated and bruised young woman on the ground gently. Her eyes were open, but she seemed incoherent.

"Send a couple of your guys, but I'm not going back without Cletus. You can forget arguing with me, so save your breath." Min started laughing when she finished, and Baylor seemed to have had enough. He cocked his fist and punched Min in the mouth so hard he knocked two teeth to the ground.

"We've got some company," one of his men said, and they heard voices getting closer.

"Tito, grab the asshole and I'll get the girl." They double-timed it through the woods, following Goose's lead, since he had the handheld GPS.

It took an hour to put some distance between them and the North Korean forces, so it was unlikely they'd catch up with Berkley and the others on the road. "Let's hope they bring more than one ride. If not, they're going to make a detour," Wiley said, sweeping the area with her scope. "How the hell did this happen?"

"When all hell broke loose outside, she went to clear the rest of the house, and I didn't think it'd turn into this cluster fuck. We have to find her before Captain Sullivan rips my balls off and chokes me with them. Shit. I didn't think anyone else was there. They should've come out when we broke in. This dumbass made enough noise for the whole countryside to hear him."

"Sounds like they were waiting for the right time to carve away some of our people," Tito said.

"I agree, but I don't understand where they'd be taking them. Think about it. They waited, true, but this guy just has men piled in a room on the chance a bunch of people come by to steal all his important shit?" Wiley asked as they stayed under cover.

"They were waiting on us, and if you saw Americans, then we all know who they were working for," Baylor said. "We really need to find them."

A helicopter was close, but not one of theirs. She found a spot where she could brace her weapon and took a shot. The helicopter veered to the left in an awkward pitch, finally inverting before crashing. It caused such a fireball that it lit the countryside momentarily before flames consumed the rest. "We need to clear this area and give our birds a safe landing spot."

"What we need is to put some more distance between us and them," Baylor said. "Let's go before our ride gets any closer." They started running again while trying to make their way without breaking a leg in the uneven terrain in the dark.

Three more miles put them at a meadow ringed by trees, but the woods were thinner and quieter here. Every one of Baylor's guys was in great shape, but they were all breathing hard by the time they could sit and call in their new coordinates.

Wiley wiped her brow and figured they had only one more option if they were ever going to find the three people they'd lost.

"Baylor," she said, staring at Min for a second before turning her attention to Baylor. "We agreed to find them, but we need a hint as to where to start, and he can give us that."

"Tito," Baylor said, and Tito took out his knife as Goose held Min down.

❖

Berkley's face was all Aidan could think about as she waited for the final drinks of the evening to be served, and the vision was making this dinner grow unbearable. Usually she didn't mind the meet-and-greet before the pretend games that had no real consequences except bragging rights, but the game her people were playing had real potential for disaster.

Devin nodded at one of the porters and glanced her way before he walked out of the room. He'd been gone only ten minutes when he reappeared and waved in her direction. "Ma'am, we need to get back now."

She nodded but took a few minutes to thank their host before almost sprinting back to the deck. "What's going on?" Their ride was circling to land, but she already knew whatever came next wouldn't be good in any way.

"The team made it to the target and got what they were after with a few added bonuses," Devin said into her ear. They were standing on an ally ship but saw no reason to take chances.

"Get to the *but* part of that equation, Devin, because your expression is a neon sign that there is one." She started for the helicopter as soon as it touched down and held the headphones but didn't put them on. "Tell me," she said, leaning close to him.

"It was like they were waiting for them," Devin said, and she inhaled deeply. Damn you, Berkley. I'm going to be pissed if something happened to you, she thought. "They breached the compound and got the information we wanted, but somehow a team was able to get away with Berkley, Harvey, and Jin. We can't be sure if they targeted them specifically or if they were after any American who showed up."

"They were taken? Where exactly?" Her skin felt like it was on fire, and she closed her eyes momentarily to try to focus since her vision had dimmed. No way in hell could they be this unlucky again.

"We don't know, but Baylor and Wiley are staying on the ground. We just sent our birds to pick up the bonuses they walked away with." Devin tried to control his tone, and she appreciated that he wasn't screaming in her ear.

"Okay." She put on her headphones and glanced out to see how close they were to the *Jefferson*. "Save the rest until we land." She had about five minutes to get her shit together and put all her upset over Berkley at the back of her mind. It was like slowly dying from a gaping hole in her chest, but she had a job to do and people who were waiting for orders.

Once they were back, they headed to the bridge, and she held her finger up when Devin started to speak. "Okay, what bonuses?"

"Baylor and Wiley are sending back a woman they couldn't identify and Ji Woo Min."

"Who is?" she asked as she closed the door firmly behind them.

"Considering where he was, he might be the new Chil. They said when you see the girl, they're not off on that one. We're preparing a room in sick bay, and the doc said they'd probably quarantine her just in case. Whoever she is, according to the guys, she's in bad shape."

"Ma'am," one of the men said after knocking. "The helicopter is five minutes out."

She went down and waited, ordering Devin to get the consultants ready, but it was something he'd obviously done since the small group of guys in civilian clothes was heading toward her. From what the crew of the *Arlington* said, these guys had barely left the brig, taking turns talking to their one prisoner, who she heard had clammed up for what he said was his own mental health. After a few days of questioning, Dale Whitner, according to the consultants, was an empty shell with a real chance of breaking from reality.

"Whoever this guy is, I need him to tell you everything he knows about where they took our people. We don't have time on our side," she told the tall guy who seemed to be the most outgoing. "Do you understand me?"

"Perfectly, and you got it, ma'am."

The helicopter landed, and only one SEAL got out, with a guy whose naked chest was smeared with blood. Aidan was about to ask why when she noticed he was holding his left hand tightly against him, and a few of his fingers were gone. "What happened?"

"He tripped a few times, ma'am, and landed on one of our knives," the man who brought him back said.

If she thought about getting upset, the woman Devin had told her about changed her mind. She was so skinny Aidan doubted she could stand by herself. That was the first noticeable thing about her, but the bruises, scars, and healing cuts covering her abdomen and back were hard to miss. "Rush her down to the doctor and find her something to wear," Aidan said. "Then get the translator to see who she is."

"Ma'am, I need to talk to you," the SEAL said.

"What's your name?" she asked.

"Robert Jones, ma'am, but everyone calls me Bubba. If you don't mind, the faster we talk, the sooner I can get back to my brothers."

"Come on." She decided on her office since it was closer, and Devin walked by her side.

"Wiley wanted me to tell you we had a talk with that guy Min while we were waiting for our ride, and he told us he had an idea where they were taking Cletus and the other two," Bubba said, accepting some coffee from Devin and guzzling it like it was a beer. "Baylor and Wiley were pissed we were ambushed, and they wanted to know where to start looking since they ain't about to leave Cletus out there to rot."

"Did they find out anything useful?" she asked, exchanging some of the blinding pain in her heart for hope.

"According to him, Chandler the dick is here," Bubba said, then shook his head. "Sorry about the language, ma'am."

"I totally agree with the description, but did he narrow down a location?" This wasn't going to be like finding a large militia in Washington DC—North Korea was vast. If they had to start guessing, they'd never make it in time.

"All he knew was off the coast of someplace called Monggumpó," Bubba said, pouring himself some more coffee when she waved him toward the urn. "I don't know if I'm pronouncing it right, but it's not that far north from South Korea on the West Coast. It's where the guys are headed, but I'd keep talking to the total perv we found with the girl if I were you. Once you review the footage we got, you'll see what his biggest weakness is aside from weird porn."

"Believe me, we're sending backup with you, but before you go, I need you to repeat what you told us." She put in a call for Carl and whoever else was at Command. A few of her commanding officers and her father, plus Drew, who was now vice president, Rooster, and Carl were in the Situation Room.

Bubba repeated his story, and they put up a map of North Korea. There was a place called Monggumpó, and it was where Bubba had said. "We need an hour to reposition the satellite to see what we can pick up. We'll probably have to wait until the sun rises to spot anything, but we'll start as soon as we can get this thing aimed in that direction," Carl said.

"We need to prepare to keep looking in case this guy was lying," she said, not willing to accept that Berkley, Harvey, and Jin were expendable.

"Trust me, ma'am," Bubba said. "That guy was too uncomfortable to lie, and Baylor kept reminding him how many more parts he had."

"There's that, and the evolving investigation into General Lapry," Drew said.

"Congratulations, sir," Aidan said, and Devin nodded.

"Thank you. We'll have time enough for that later," Drew said and pointed to the map. "Retired Homer Lapry visited South Korea just recently but was able to cross the border by sea into the north. If that's true, the spot he left from puts him damn close to this place." He told them what they had so far, and the town they were looking for, which gave credibility to what the FBI had reported.

"The SEAL team and Wiley stayed behind and are following. Is that going to be a problem?" she asked and stood when President Michaels walked in.

"Thank you. Everyone, please sit," Olivia said, taking the chair at the head of the table. "Neil filled me in, and I heard your question, Aidan. If the intel is correct and Chandler is there, we need to finish this. We all know that if he had us in this position, he would deliver the killing blow. Let's try our best to make sure our people are clear first."

"We're sending an elite team located in South Korea as backup, ma'am," Carl said, and he rubbed his chin when Neil entered. "You're right that we need to finish this, but we have to try to do it without too many repercussions."

"You know the North's regime and what they'll try to get away with if they can get involved in this fight. We need to avoid giving them an excuse to drop a bomb in the center of Seoul," Neil said. "But if they're harboring someone responsible for killing the president, we need to act."

"What's the ETA on the backup?" Olivia asked.

"They'll be there by morning, and with any luck, the SEALs will be in position to have put eyes on our missing," Carl said.

"Thank you all, and we'll be ready for anything," Aidan said, looking at her father. He looked concerned, and she appreciated having his steady presence even if he was thousands of miles away.

"Have your pilots ready, Captain," Carl said. "If we get the opportunity to finish New Horizons with what our guys do best, we intend to let them clear the field."

"Yes, sir." It was a good thing they were all for finding Berkley and the others, and for killing the people so set on doing them harm.

All she needed now was for Berkley to hang on so they could actually save her.

CHAPTER TWENTY-THREE

The pothole in the road jarred Berkley awake, and she immediately shut her eyes when a wave of nausea hit her hard enough that she took some deep breaths to keep from throwing up. From what she could tell, Harvey was tied to her back, and she couldn't imagine where Jin was. With luck she was on her way back to the *Jefferson*.

She kept her eyes closed and listened, surprised when she understood every word the guards were saying as they rode to God knows where. The guy talking about his girl back home had what sounded like a Tennessee accent, and it was surreal to find it here. If they were indeed Americans, this was bad on so many levels.

"Harvey," she whispered, but got no response. She took a few more deep breaths and opened her eyes again, but could move only her left one. The attack at the house had involved guns, but they'd been aimed at the SEALs behind them. A blow to the head had swollen her eye shut. "Harvey."

"He has not woken up yet," Jin said softly as she lay right in front of her. "We have been going for a long time, stopping only for petrol."

"Where do you think they're taking us?" She leaned forward to hear Jin better and felt Harvey come with her.

"I do not know. It is still dark so I have not been able to see anything outside the flap. All I know is they are determined to take us somewhere and that they are not Korean."

"That I got, since I didn't think I'd understand anything, but from the little I heard, they're not saying much."

"I said to your people they were Americans when Chil brought me there. I think they did not believe me."

She heard the moan from behind her and cursed that her hands were tied behind her. "Harvey?"

"What the hell happened?" Harvey still sounded a little out of it, which probably meant he had a matching knot on his head.

"They cut us from the herd and are going to mount our heads on pikes the first chance they get, so stay quiet and let me think." The truck stopped, and she heard plenty of doors slamming as all the engines went quiet. "Close your eyes and play dead. We might've arrived."

"This fucking place is getting on my nerves," a man standing close by said and got a grunt in response, as if someone agreed with him. "Get the guys a couple of trucks down to cut that shit up and clear the road."

"How're the idiots doing?" another less-than-intelligent-sounding guy asked. "Matty knocked that big bitch pretty good."

"Hold on." The truck bounced some, meaning the first guy was climbing up. "For fuck's sake. Where'd these morons learn to tie knots?" Berkley kept her eyes closed as he sawed close to her and Harvey's hands. "Their fucking fingers are blue."

"Hey, you said tight, so they wouldn't get away," the genius said.

"Where they gonna go, Einstein? There's fifty of us and miles of jungle. They couldn't walk out of here with a map and a car."

Berkley let her hands fall limply to her sides, even though she desperately wanted to shake them as the circulation started again, making her hands feel like they were covered in fire ants. "Put a guy outside here until we get going. If they wake up and run, have him put a bullet in each kneecap. It won't kill them since we don't want to fuck with what I'm sure the general has planned for later."

"I almost feel sorry for the poor motherfuckers."

"You're going to be even sorrier if those guys come looking for us. I'd bet my ass that was a SEAL team or some other elite force. If Lapry and his buddy hadn't given us the heads-up to be waiting, those guys would be sunning themselves by now, and we'd be rotting in that sick fucker's house," the head guy said, sounding farther away now.

"You think they'll find us out here?"

The first guy laughed. "What? They gonna use their dicks as propellers and fly after us? Stop thinking and clear the road. We need to get moving. I'll feel better once we're in the middle of our five full brigades, but we're still a couple of hours out."

The only sound after that were chainsaws, or Berkley guessed that's what it was, and chopping noises. They'd probably stopped because a tree or maybe more was blocking the road. The sun was up, which meant Jin was right. They'd been riding for at least five hours and had two to go.

There was a slim chance Baylor and his team would find them before she ended up with some bad disfigurement or dead, and even if they did, five full battalions consisted of at least twenty thousand men. That was impossible odds, even with the element of surprise on Baylor and his team's part, so they stayed quiet for the eternity it took to clear the road. The truck rumbled back to life, and the only good news was that their hands were now free.

"Look in the pockets by your knees," Berkley said softly, "and move slowly in case they're watching us from the front."

She did the same and took out the transponder that was usually in the life vests they wore on the plane. With a small press of the top, it turned on, and it represented the only chance she had left that someone would find them. Jumping and running would just lead to a quick death or crippling injury, and that would only save them from the torture that was coming.

"That was damn genius," Harvey said, and Jin agreed.

"It is if someone checks, but hopefully not too quickly. Maybe they're taking us to their unfearless leader, and our guys can finally put a bullet through that big mouth of his." She sent a silent prayer that the *Jefferson*'s crew found what they looked for only when one of their planes went down.

"We will at least be remembered for trying," Jin said.

"Don't make martyrs out of us yet. I've got a lot left to do, plenty to enjoy, and I'm taking you with me even if I have to drag you along kicking and screaming," Berkley said, willing it to be true.

❖

"General Lapry," Jonas Chapman, FBI director, said as Homer and his wife walked toward the Capital Grille in DC.

"What do you want?" Homer Lapry asked with as much indignation as Jonas had ever heard.

"I'd love for you to find yourself in front of a firing squad for betraying your country, but for now, get in." Jonas held the door open as two of his men came up behind them. "You can walk over here and get in, or I'll handcuff you and throw you in myself. Ma'am, the vehicle behind this one is for you," Jonas said to Homer's wife.

"Do you know who I am?" Homer asked but shut his mouth when the agent to his right grabbed an arm and yanked it up behind his back while his partner placed a cuff on it. A series of pictures by media-outlet photographers followed as they practically dragged him to the SUV and laid him on the backseat. "Why are you doing this?"

"Please, Homer, if you start with stupid questions, there's no sense in delaying your trip to Gitmo. The news needs another lead story since they're tired of reporting that Jeffery Chandler was found guilty and received the death penalty. That happened in record time, and we didn't have as much on him as we do on you. Dick can't save you from the neck-deep shit you're in." Jonas snapped his seat belt on and ordered his driver to the private airstrip outside the city.

"You can't do this."

"You played, Homer, and now it's time to pay. Don't be sad, though. You'll have plenty of company," Jonas said as they got on the interstate. "You're going to burn, but the president wants to make sure it's a big blaze before we're done."

"That stupid, fucking bitch."

"There's only one stupid bitch I see here, and that's you, errand boy. You got to kiss the ring in North Korea, but Dick is going to leave you flapping in the breeze all by your lonesome."

"I thought you said I wasn't going alone?" Homer seemed to be taunting him as if he were indeed untouchable.

"A plane left an hour ago for a secure CIA facility with Speaker Chase Bonner and his entire family on it. Unlike you, he went quietly and kept his mouth shut," Jonas said as they reached the plane surrounded by agents he trusted. "We don't need you to talk, though."

"Oh yeah. Why is that?" Homer's laugh sounded like it genuinely came from his belly.

"We'll let the tapes, and your wife, do the talking for you. We'll give your wife the opportunity to tell us what she knows once we introduce her to the young, beautiful mistress you keep in that great condo downtown. See, both those special women in your life will understand it's going to be a long conversation or life in prison. That's how I asked Walby Edwards and his CIA interrogators to handle it anyway. I'm praying a novena you want to keep quiet and burn for your part in President Khalid's murder. If I get an early Christmas wish from President Michaels, I'll be part of your firing squad."

"Wait a minute—I have a right to talk," Homer said, all his bravado disappearing like frost under bright sunlight.

"You have a right to silence, and I suggest you use it," Jonas said, once again amazed at how right Walby could be. General Homer Lapry was one of the great cowards in their history, who had picked a bully's side and would fold once the hero woke up to the fight.

"You'd like that, so you can watch me burn."

"I'm only interested in saving two people in your family," Jonas said. "Your wife and daughter, but even that is up for negotiation, depending on how it goes. If your daughter is anything like Rachel Chandler, then it won't go so good for her."

"What about my sons?"

"Kindling for our bonfire, Homer, but we'll need to find them in North Korea first. When Captain Sullivan starts her bombing runs, they'll probably never see it coming. We're going to wipe you from the history books except for a small blip on traitors. When people think of a turncoat in the future, I think you might surpass Benedict Arnold," Jonas said, and the driver laughed. "Start praying, Homer. Your time is up."

"Wait—just wait." When the agents opened the SUV door and started to pull Homer out, he sounded like a cornered animal.

"That's just it. We're done waiting."

"Zookeeper, this is Tiger One," Baylor said.

It had taken some time, but they'd been able to get the truck Wiley had sent into the ditch on the side of the road righted, and they'd been able to follow the line of trucks back far enough to not be seen. The cab had fit only him and Wiley, and five of his guys lay in the back out of sight. The rest he'd ordered to take cover wherever they could and hang by the radio.

The farther they went, the thicker the tree canopy became, reminding him of a rain forest. Even if they'd been able to follow by helicopter, they would've lost them hours ago in the dark.

"Tiger One, go ahead." He recognized Aidan's voice.

"Ma'am, we have them in sight, but we have a problem." The tree they'd climbed gave him a great view of the two massive ones that had fallen and blocked the road. "The party they got invited to is crowded."

"Can you keep with it?"

"We plan on it, but we'll keep sending coordinates," he said, trying to see any sign of Cletus, Junior, or Jin. "According to our maps and the GPS, a few more hours and we'll be swimming."

"Make sure to check in so we can figure out where the party is," Aidan said. "We started on the party favors you sent back."

"Anything interesting yet?" The trees blocking their way started to resemble firewood since these guys were really going after them, so they didn't have a lot of time left.

"Not yet, but I've got the guys working overtime." Aidan stopped talking and addressed someone else. "How many in your party?"

"The compound had about twenty, but I'm looking at double that now. They're well-armed and organized, and too many to chance the health of our people with them." A group of the soldiers gathered around a guy who walked from the front of the caravan and seemed to listen intently. It didn't take long, and the ten men started toward their truck. They were almost to the ridge, and on the other side was their ride out of here.

They'd covered the truck as best they could, but Baylor looked into his binoculars and saw a lot of walking in their future, especially when they heard the gunfire. Whoever these guys were, they didn't care about any consequences since they'd shot up a North Korean government vehicle. He wasn't worried about his men, since they were on the other side in attack positions in case he gave the order.

"What the hell?" the guy who'd sent the trigger-happy soldiers yelled. "Get back to your rides, you morons." His men hesitated but followed the order, and he stayed behind to look inside the truck before scanning the area. "Move out."

The front truck started rolling, and it took the large number of what appeared to be American-trained soldiers all dressed in black with it. Their only problem was their ride was sitting with three flat tires and no spare. Wiley covered him as he climbed down, and the heat of the day, even though it was still early morning, was making the sweat soak his undershirt.

"We're fucked," Wiley said as they were enveloped in silence.

"That we are, but where can they go out of here?" he said as his guys quickly moved across the road and joined them.

"You'd be surprised. I spent a lot of years in South America in hellholes like this. Sometimes people can disappear into the bush, but that many guys and trucks might take some time." Wiley shouldered her weapon and leaned against a tree. "We need to call the *Jefferson* back."

Baylor got his radio guy to connect to the ship again. "Go ahead, Tiger One."

"Zookeeper, this is Nest Leader," Wiley said as Baylor stood close by.

"Go ahead." Aidan was back.

Wiley gave her a rundown of what had happened and their dilemma. "We need a ride out of here since our only chance is to backtrack and find another vehicle. I really don't see that happening, since this is like a thick sauna filled with plants on steroids. There's no people or vehicles to be found."

"You don't have any way to follow?"

"Black Dragon is only my nickname, ma'am. Believe me. I wish it wasn't and I could flap my wings and go."

Aidan was silent, then loudly she said, "Shit."

"What?" Wiley asked.

"Sit on that location. I'll send a cab to pick you up. Once you're clear, we need to formulate a new plan from new information we have."

"Something good?"

"It's a step in the right direction, but hopefully not for everyone."

"What do you think she meant?" Baylor asked, sharing a granola bar with Wiley.

"I don't really know Captain Sullivan well," Wiley said, taking a bite and chewing slowly, "but Cletus and I go way back. That's someone you shouldn't take for granted. A lot of guys we went to high school with did just that and ended up bleeding on their shoes when they missed the right hook to their nose. I can't imagine all that much has changed about her personality and ability to handle fools well."

"Oh, I know Cletus, and my nose remembers her too."

"Let's pray she pulls some magic out of her cap on this one, and Captain Sullivan's reaction might be that she just now found Cletus's rabbit."

Aidan held the radio as if it were a talking snake ready to deliver another piece of bad news. It was time for karma to change the direction of their luck. She pinched the bridge of her nose as she thought about what Baylor had told her and what Wiley was asking her for. A ride out was a ride away from Berkley and the others. The fear of Berkley getting beyond her reach was as real now as the sky was blue.

"Ma'am," one of the younger guys on the bridge said as she was about to tell Wiley sarcasm was unnecessary.

"Yes," she said, holding the receiver away from her mouth.

"Three transponder signals just came on radar. We thought it was a mistake, but they're ours."

"Shit," she said loudly and got Wiley off the radio until she could compare the radar to where Baylor and Wiley were right now. "Where's the rest of Baylor's team?"

"They landed somewhere remote and are awaiting orders, ma'am," Devin said. "And we're on our way for Baylor and the others."

"Wait on that," she said, radioing Wiley again. "Do you remember how we found our lost sheep before?" she asked in case someone was trying to listen in.

"Recently?" Wiley asked.

"Yes," she said, trying to avoid spelling it out. "Send our ride, but tell them we'll be headed in the opposite direction. If we can hopscotch a few times, we can keep up."

"Ma'am." A young man interrupted again. "Command says it's important."

Like an action-packed reality show, Washington could now watch covert missions from the Situation Room, so they were well aware of what she was facing. "Hold on for your ride, and I'll get back to you shortly," she told Wiley. "Yes, sir," she said to General Carl Greenwald.

"We'll cut to it, Captain," Carl said as a satellite image of what appeared to be a training facility or military grounds appeared on her screen in the small bridge office. "We were able to narrow the location after some questioning of new detainees. You have people in the field, but that's not enough, so we're sending more backup. If this turns out to be our hard target, we need Vader and Killer to lead a raid to make it a fair fight."

"Do you have exact coordinates? Like you said, I have people in the field and don't want to take them out with friendly fire." She split the screen with Command and the three moving blips that hadn't been there before. Maybe Berkley was okay. "Also, I have a new development." She shared the split screen with them and sat back in her chair. The exhaustion that tension could bring was at times overwhelming, but she couldn't sleep now, no matter how tired she was.

"Is that Cletus and her group?" Preston asked. Her father had to be going through the same torment she was feeling. She could see it etched on his face. The worst part of it for him, aside from Berkley being missing, was most likely seeing the Levines every night and not being able to tell them about the situation.

"It has to be," she said as the transponders continued to move closer to the coast. "You know Cletus. She's like half Eagle Scout and half MacGyver." The dots represented life and her love, but they were far from being free of all this. "If it's Chandler, what's he going to do when he figures out it's her?" she asked her father, but the others in the room simply stared at her.

"We need to get her before that," Preston said gently. "We all know Cletus represents everything he detests in what he sees as the new America, but he doesn't know what she's capable of. Cletus won't ever give up, and he'll never break her. He's going to try, though, because he needs to make her admit she doesn't belong."

"Aidan, we've got to do this without leaving any fingerprints," Carl said. "We need to use the troops you've got close by, but not give Chandler the fight he wants."

"What exactly are you asking me?"

"Our best strategy is you," Carl said, then explained what he meant. "We'll wait to hear from Baylor and Wiley before we move, but you need to prepare to finish this once the president gives us a go."

"If Cletus, Junior, and Jin can be rescued, trust Baylor and Wiley to do it," Drew said. "Those two are the best people for the job, and Baylor's guys are the tops in the business."

"Thank you, Mr. Vice President, but know I won't give up on them. We leave no one behind."

"Of that I have no doubt, and I'll tell the president the same thing."

"We'll be ready to go, sir, and we can get the job done with everyone who started it—everyone."

CHAPTER TWENTY-FOUR

The truck stopped, and all the engines cut off. Jin stared at her and shook her head. This was clearly different from the other stops. "If we get separated, be ready to move at the first opportunity. We're all walking out of here together, or we're not going at all."

"At the other stops, not all the people got out," Jin said, leaning in so Berkley could hear her. "I think we are at the place they want us."

"Cletus," Harvey said, putting his hand on her back. "Do you have any kind of plan?"

"Let's see what we're up against, and you can take notes for the story of our dramatic escape later. It'll be so good our grandkids will get tired of listening to it," she said as someone lowered the back of the truck, grabbed Jin by the shoulders, and dragged her out.

She heard something drop to the ground and figured it was Jin when more than one man laughed. She didn't have time to guess as she and Junior came out together, and she saw Jin on her knees spitting out a mouthful of blood. The clearing they were in was full of equipment and vehicles, and all of them seemed to be American-made.

That small glimpse was all she got as a man in front of her brought the butt of his gun down, pulling the blow at the last minute but enough to knock her head back. The pain seemed to reach the center of her skull, and she closed her eyes but refused to go down. Harvey copied her and stayed on his feet when the man repeated the action.

"Finally, men." A redheaded man stood before her, and all she could think of was that the black uniform clashed with his hair. "We finally got someone who can take a punch and not whine about it." He punched her in the mouth, and she didn't make a sound, which made the men around them laugh again.

"Lapry," someone else yelled. "Is this what you were ordered to do?" The newcomer scattered the crowd, and Berkley tried to guess why. Whoever he was obviously outranked them, but he didn't carry himself like a soldier since he seemed to be out of place in the uniform. "Bring the prisoners. The general wants to talk to them when he returns, and they'll actually have to be able to do that."

"Where is he?" the guy named Lapry asked.

"Are you keeping his schedule now?" The small, pudgy man looked familiar to Berkley, but she couldn't place him.

"It's just a question, Robyn."

"It sounds like disrespect, and you should think before you do it again. You're not in as much favor as you think, and instead of acting macho out here, you should go watch the news. You aren't going to like it."

This had to be Homer Lapry's kid, but Carl hadn't given them any information about the rest of the family. She watched Lapry stalk away, the anger making each step stiff and savage. Her attention refocused when she heard a gun cock and saw Robyn holding the same kind of shiny pistol Dale Whitner had tried to kill Aidan with.

"Try anything, and I'll put a bullet in your head," Robyn said and pointed to his right. "Start walking."

The camp was full of men in the same black uniforms they'd seen so far, and Berkley was a bit disheartened when she realized that five full battalions might be exactly right. You didn't easily escape from that many people. Their walk ended in the center square that held a cage, and they were locked inside it like rabid dogs.

"Sit, and forget about leaving. I don't know who you are, but you don't belong here, and my father won't allow you to return."

This had to be Robyn Chandler, and it made sense that the men took orders from him. She looked at Harvey and Jin and shook her head, then pointed to her ears, then all around them. They might've been in an open cage slightly larger than those used by Al Qaeda, but their captors had to be listening in.

"Remember the horizon always promises blue skies, even if you have to sail through stormy seas to get there," she said, repeating something her father had told her.

It had been Corbin's advice when she finally admitted what had happened with Aidan and the pain she was in because of it. He had explained that for everything that was hard enough to break you, all you had to do was keep your eyes and mind on that one thing you had to look forward to that would make you happy. Those wise words would hopefully serve her well in the coming days.

Robyn reappeared, with three other men carrying fire hoses. "Huddle up," Harvey said, and they all faced each other as the men turned the powerful streams of water on them.

"It will cool us off, so we should thank them," Jin said, and they all couldn't help but laugh since their heads were so close together.

Berkley kept her head down and hung onto Harvey and Jin, thinking this was only a warm-up for things to come. Once Dick Chandler returned and figured out exactly who his men had managed to capture, the real torture would begin. He'd do his best to break her and Jin to prove women didn't belong in a man's world.

"Remember, too, the joy," Jin said as the water stopped. They looked at each other, and she figured Jin had reached the same conclusion. "If you do, it will steal away their satisfaction."

She nodded and closed her eyes, thinking of Aidan. That was her joy, and nothing Chandler could come up with could take it away from her.

❖

The chance to get first crack at Berkley Levine was too good to pass up, so Robyn had started with the cage his father had confiscated during the Gulf War and the fire hoses. That had been the first part of his training, and the pounding of the water's pressure had made him raise his hands in surrender after ten minutes. The trio he had locked up had stood in one place for an hour and not said a word. The Lapry brothers didn't realize who they'd managed to stumble across, but he'd recognized the tall aviator right off.

"Think before you do anything else," his mother Ruby said when she joined him on the porch. "If you deprive the master of his chance to prove himself, you'll be in that cage next."

He stopped staring at Berkley and glanced at his mother. The latest black eye from a few weeks ago was starting to fade, but the bruised and split lip were new. Ruby had never learned to back down and give his father the total control he craved in all things, and Dick had never learned to leave the bruises where no one would see them. It was one of the main reasons Ruby had very seldom appeared in public when his father was in office. In Robyn's opinion, his parents had a sick, codependent relationship that would be severed only in death.

"I couldn't help myself," he said, kissing his mom's forehead. "This all started when he was elected with George and saw an opening to get everything he's ever wanted. He couldn't resist finding an excuse to get it. That tall bitch is one of the main reasons we're stuck here. He keeps preaching about how he's doing all this for us, but I know better, and I know there's no going back to the life we had before."

"Who is it?" Ruby asked, turning from him to stare at the tall woman in the cage.

"There's no name on the uniform, but I bet my life that it's Commander Berkley Kaplan Levine."

"It's true he uses people like her as an excuse, but don't kid yourself. Your father is the type of man who'll do anything to get what he wants." Ruby touched her lip before placing her hands on the porch rail and gazing out at the yard. "Her being here, though, signals the end of all this. Before that comes to pass, let me tell you what I'll never be able to admit to Jeffery and Rachel."

"What is it, Mom?" The sadness his mom carried like a heavy boulder on her shoulders was at times contagious.

"I'm sorry I wasn't strong enough to keep you away from all this," Ruby said as the tears rolled down her cheeks and fell on their hands. It was like she cried so much she didn't bother to wipe them away anymore. "He told me we had to sacrifice to get what we wanted, but I didn't think he meant my children."

"You think there's no way to win?"

"The people who love your father are here." She waved her hand in a semicircle. "They love him because he's given them permission to be cruel to those who aren't like them—the people they think are lesser than."

"I get that, but exactly what do you mean?" They should've had this conversation months ago.

"There was a reason your father was one of the most hated men ever to serve in higher office. These men love him, but they don't make up the whole of America. He could kill everyone in Congress, the White House, and in the Pentagon, and the people will still hate him. With all this, they'll hate him even more."

"But we have so many more than this helping us." He'd resigned himself to not being able to return to a normal life, but he hadn't considered death. "We captured someone important in our fight, which means we're making headway."

"You're going to have to kill a million Berkley Levines, and it still won't make a difference," Ruby said, placing her hands on his cheeks.

"If you want to gain favor, tell him what I said, and with any luck he'll finally put me out of my misery. I didn't share that with you to make you feel less about your dad, but to be honest with you."

"You always talked to Jeffery more, so thanks. I didn't realize you cared as much about me—like I wasn't the son you wanted." Dick had always told him there wasn't any room in his life for children. That had been Ruby's job. But his mother had never doted on him like she had his siblings.

"I'm sorry you think that, and I spent more time with Jeffery because he wasn't as independent as you and Rachel were when he was a boy. You, though, flew from our nest and soared, doing what you loved, and I was proud that you never looked back. I'm still proud of you, but try to regain some of that freedom you enjoyed for so long. You might need it."

She went back inside, but he signaled for the men to turn the hoses back on before he did. He loved his mother, but she was wrong about their chances. For once in his life he wouldn't be overlooked, and every win wouldn't take so much effort since he was his father's heir—the only one now that Jeffery and Rachel were gone.

"What?" Dick said when he answered his call. He had been summoned to the capital of North Korea to meet with Pom Su Gil, and his presence hadn't been voluntary.

"Mark and Tyler Lapry brought back three prisoners from Min's house," he said, smiling even though Dick couldn't see him.

"Anyone of value?"

Dick had obviously missed the news coverage of Jeffery's trial. Without consideration from the president or any government agency, Jeffery was a dead man. "One of the women is Berkley Levine."

"Call Gil's office and tell them I had to go back, and have Waspit pick me up. I should be at the helipad in an hour. Don't let anything happen to Levine. I'm going to enjoy taking pieces of her until I reach her heart." Dick was talking fast and more animatedly than he had in months.

"We can do it together," he said, but Dick had already hung up. "Stop," he yelled, to get the water turned off. "Stand guard and keep everyone away from them. The general's on his way back."

Dick was definitely on his way, and their short conversation had opened his eyes to one thing; perhaps his mother was right. This was all about his father and what he wanted. He didn't give a shit about anything but that. "Fuck me. What do I do about it now?"

❖

Wiley was set up three hundred yards from what appeared to be the perimeter of a massive compound full of guys dressed in black. None of them were Korean, and judging by just the equipment visible from where she was, these fools could start a war and put up a good fight for a while anyway. She sat in a tree under a leaf canopy, temporarily using only a powerful scope. But she couldn't help but swing back to the three people in the cage.

The area below her was clear except for Baylor and his full team, who were making their way slowly toward the compound. She was there to see that there were no casualties on their end. "These assholes look like the type to booby-trap around the perimeter as an added layer of security, so slow down and be vigilant," she said into her radio.

"Do you have eyes on our targets?" Baylor asked.

"Yes." She watched the fire hoses aimed at her friends. "For someone who said he hated Al Qaeda, Dick sure lifted a lot of pages from their playbook."

"Why?" someone who sounded like Tito asked.

"They're being held in a small cage, and they're getting high-pressure-water treatment like they're at a spa." The low whirl of a helicopter stopped her description.

"Report when you see something," Baylor said.

"Affirmative." She watched the water being cut off again and Berkley and the others sit down. It took twenty minutes for the aircraft to circle twice before landing close to where the motor pool was.

The first man out surprised her because the man was definitely North Korean, down to the uniform, and from the way he pointed and men ran to do things for him, he was an important figure. He was followed by someone she recognized, and he was wearing the black of his troops, but his outfit made him appear ridiculous instead of regal, which she figured he was aiming for.

"I have eyes on our hard target," she said as Dick and his friend rode from the landing spot to the wide yard as if the distance was too much for them.

"Are you sure?" Baylor asked.

"He hasn't changed much except for his wardrobe. It's like he went for an SS paratrooper look," she said as a Korean man's face transformed to one of glee at the sight of Jin. "Someone should've given them the good news that those guys lost, and our target has company who seems very happy to see his old air-force buddy who's native to this place."

"Can you ID him?" Baylor asked.

"Negative. He's a mystery to us." The man slammed his hands on the bars and put his face close to say something to Jin, but she barely looked at him. Whatever he was threatening, Dick was doing the same to Cletus and Junior, but they too appeared oblivious to the attention.

"As much as I don't want to, we have to ignore that for now and concentrate on why we're here," Tito said. "We can't do anything until it gets dark."

"He's right, so hold your positions and report if anything changes, eye in the sky," Baylor said to Wiley.

"We have to wait for dark, but this shit isn't going to be fun to watch," she said as the cage was opened and Berkley was pulled out, along with Jin. "The fun's about to begin—for Dickie anyway."

"Fuck," Baylor and Tito said.

"Exactly."

CHAPTER TWENTY-FIVE

D ad," Robyn said as Dick walked around Berkley with a bounce in his step. Nothing in his life lately had brought this much anticipation. That was huge since his ultimate plan was to take over the government—permanently. "You might want to wait until I've had a chance to talk to you."

He ignored Robyn and stopped in front of Levine, who seemed to be staring into a deep abyss as if he weren't there. Gil had already put his fists on Umeko, but she hadn't made a sound. That wouldn't do when it came to Levine. "Do you know who I am?" he asked her, but she stayed quiet. "I asked you a question. Do you know who I am?" She finally made eye contact, and her expression left him thinking she found him lacking. That earned her a slap across the face hard enough to make her head snap to the left.

"Who is this?" Gil asked, leaving Umeko alone.

"If I'm right, she led the team who destroyed your facilities last year." He had to hold Gil back when he lunged at Berkley.

"You must ready the helicopter, so I can take this prisoner back. Supreme Leader Kim will want to deal with her himself."

"Not yet. If she lives after what I need to do, then you can have her, but not before," he said, not liking the set of Gil's mouth. "You can take *her* if it makes you happy," he said about Jin.

"I'll be taking her and Umeko as soon as your pilot is ready," Gil said as he turned and pushed Umeko back into the cage. "Before you speak, remember where you are, and who I am."

"Dad." Robyn tried to interrupt again, but Dick wasn't about to back down like some powerless punk. "It's really important."

"Lapry," he said to Tyler. "Get in touch with Waspit and tell him to get the helicopter ready again, but no one leaves here until I give the order. Understand?"

"Yes, sir." Tyler Lapry stood at attention and saluted.

"What?" he asked Robyn, curling his hands into fists and straining not to hit his son. If his stupid wife had been worth anything, his children would've been so much better than this.

"The military tribunal found Jeffery guilty, and they decided the death penalty was warranted." Robyn spoke quickly and took a step away from him. "I thought we could trade him and Rachel for her."

"Rachel?" he asked, grabbing Robyn by the shirt and pulling him forward. "I thought Rachel was recovering and staying low?"

"She never contacted me, and I thought she was pouting because she screwed up Jeffery's recovery. Now it seems she was shot and has been charged with trying to kill the president."

"The president's already dead," he said like Robyn was simple-minded, which he really believed most of the time.

"She tried to kill President Michaels," Robyn said in the same condescending tone. "She's being charged as an enemy combatant. That'll give the government an easier time killing her after a short hearing."

"They have Rachel too?" he asked, glancing back toward Gil, who was pointing at Tyler and then the cage. For once Robyn was right. The only bargaining chips he had were locked inside, and Berkley Levine might be the exception to the government's rule of not dealing with terrorists, especially now that the weak-willed Michaels was in charge. "Get them something to eat, and tell everyone they're dead if they think of touching them."

"What about General Gil?" Robyn asked, and he seemed to know like he did that Gil was going to be a problem. "If he leaves without what he wants, he'll come back with an army."

"He doesn't understand what my sons mean to me." Robyn smiled at that, but in the months after starting this quest he'd realized the next leader would have to be Jeffery, with Rachel at his back. The men would never follow Robyn because they didn't respect him, and for that he couldn't blame them. "If he can't grasp that important fact, then we'll handle it."

"You and me?"

He nodded and placed his hand on the pistol on his hip. The shiny, nickel-chrome guns were status symbols he'd ordered by the thousands after one of the generals in Desert Storm told him Patton had worn one in World War II. Patton had been one of his heroes from the time he was a small boy because he was a man's man who didn't take shit from anyone, and he'd fought for the America he wanted to bring back.

"Come on," he said, and walked back to Gil, who'd started screaming at Tyler, but Tyler seemed unfazed. "Stop," he said in a loud voice.

"Tell your man to bring the prisoners," Gil said, and poked him in the chest with two fingers. "If you disagree, your welcome in our country will be sacrificed." Gil poked him again, so angry his spittle was hitting Dick in the face.

He wiped his cheek and shook his head. "They're not going anywhere, and you're going to just accept it."

"Are you insane?" Gil asked, laughing as if Dick were telling jokes. "I informed General Lee he was a fool for telling the supreme leader to allow you to come here. He paid for that mistake with his life and cried like a woman when the dogs started with his feet." He went to the spot where Jin Umeko was standing in the cage listening. "Kim wanted to shoot him, but I convinced him to use the dogs because he put you in charge of protecting the nuclear facilities, even though he knew it was a mistake before you even began."

"You thought my father was a fool?" Jin asked him and laughed.

"He had his boot on my neck for years, and he fooled leader Kim just as long. Now he is dead, and when you're gone, any trace of him will disappear as well."

"Your victory will be short-lived, which makes me realize why General Lee kept you down for so long. A man who is staring at death but is blind to it is truly an idiot," Jin said, then turned her back on him.

"Look at me," Gil said, rattling the door. "Open this door."

"Lapry, you heard him," Dick said.

Tyler opened the cage and pushed Gil in. "I hope that's what you had in mind," Tyler said.

"Yes, it was," he said, and Tyler opened the door again. "Take her out," he said of Berkley, and she walked out before Tyler could touch her. "What's your name?"

She stared at him out of the one unswollen eye this time but kept her mouth closed. The disrespect infuriated him, and he slapped her. He put some heat into it, but her head hadn't moved, and she hadn't made a sound. When she smiled slightly, he lost control.

"Remember, when you tell me what your name is, I'll stop," he said as his fist connected with her side where her kidney was. He hit her ten more times, but she stayed quiet. "You're not going to outlast me." When she went back into the cell Gil tried to lunge out, but the young guard hit him with the butt of his rifle and kept at it until Gil fell to his knees and covered his head.

"You'll break eventually," he said, shaking the bars, but Berkley only gave him a hard stare that showed her defiance.

"You will pay for this," Gil said, his bravado and bravery back now that there were bars between them. "Your actions here will mean not only your death, but the death of all these fools. That I promise you."

"If you call death, General Gil, then it should be your own." Dick removed his pistol, aimed, and fired before he gave it too much thought. Overthinking every step was why he hadn't gotten farther along than this.

Gil's head exploded at the close range and splattered across Berkley and the man with her, but neither of them flinched or made a move to wipe the gore from their face. "You'll break eventually," he repeated.

"Do you say this to convince her, or you?" Umeko asked, and he raised the pistol again, but Berkley stepped in front of her and finally showed some emotion when she laughed.

"You will." He tightened his finger on the trigger, but she only laughed harder. He walked away before his temper stole his last chance to get Jeffery back. "You will, because I want Michaels to have to piece you back together whenever I decide to let you go."

The sun setting brought an end to the drills the men in black did with the fervor of new gung-ho recruits, and most of them went to what appeared to be their mess hall. Wiley watched all the movements, her own finger tightening on the trigger when Chandler aimed his weapon at Berkley.

It took three more hours before the compound's watch was set and the unnatural quiet settled over the area. "The good thing about an underdeveloped country is the lack of good lighting," Baylor said, and she hummed her agreement. "Everyone in position?"

Every man with them scattered around the perimeter checked in, and the backup team that had arrived from South Korea was positioned a quarter mile away in case any other troops were arriving to join the party. Their orders for tonight were simple. All they had to do was paint their targets for precision bombing and, if they could, release and retrieve their people.

Aidan had given the order, and Wiley had admired how steady her voice was when she added the last part. If this had been Aubrey, she would've fucked the rest and done everything to get her back, and that's exactly what she planned to do. "Everyone get ready for when these guys start their circuit again," she said. "I'll eliminate any problems that get past you from up here."

"Remember, don't destroy the house at the west side of the square. We need the information that's inside it," Baylor added. "Tito, you know what to do."

"Yes, sir. As soon as BD opens the door, I'll guide them out."

"We're a go," Wiley said as the guards started their walk again to cover their area. This had probably become rote by now because there wasn't, up until now, any danger in the dark.

She lined up her first shot, and the head of the guy who stood guard next to the cage snapped back as the rest of his body followed. Berkley and her group had stood together at the back opposite the door to stay away from the dead guy they left in there with them, but Wiley needed them to one side or the other, so her next shot was to the ground to the right.

Thankfully they understood and moved to the left to give her a clean shot to the lock. She peered through the scope and exhaled before pulling back gently on the trigger, hoping Tito was ready. A bullet through metal in this unnatural quiet would be like firing without the silencer, and when it hit, she knew she was right, since she heard it even from this distance.

The noise faded, but more than one light went on, and men started to open doors and look outside. Thankfully, the rescuees didn't waste time and had followed Tito to cover before the spotlights came on. Hopefully now all that was left was to disappear into the dark and wait for their ride.

"Find them," Chandler yelled when the spotlight stopped on the cage that now held only one victim. "Radio the unit and tell them to close in."

That last command stopped Wiley from climbing down as she continued to watch. The chaos this should've caused wasn't materializing, and the only explanation was mind-boggling. "Baylor," she said.

"Go ahead."

"Everyone, stop where you are and go to evasive maneuvers." Before they left the ship they'd had one last meeting with Berkley, Aidan, Baylor, and herself. The term "evasive maneuvers" indicated that the people who should've been on their side were compromised. If the group of elite soldiers they'd sent from South Korea was compromised, they were sandwiched. To get out meant either going through Chandler's men or through a team as well trained as Baylor's.

"What evasive maneuvers?" the backup team's leader asked.

"We need to go to the east and loop back around," Baylor said. "It's more distance, but it's a bigger opening, and we need to get out as cleanly as possible since we've got baggage."

"Roger that. We'll be ready for you."

Wiley watched as the young guy who'd beaten the Korean soldier with his rifle stood in front of the porch in the yard and talked to someone inside. A few minutes later a group joined him, and they headed east. Obviously, they'd been sabotaged from the moment Command called in their saviors, but where along the line had Chandler started giving the orders?

She switched radio channels before hitting the ground and meeting Baylor at the spot where they'd decided. "What the fuck?" Baylor asked when he lowered his weapon after he saw it was her.

"The team at our backs is working for the other side," she said, radioing the others. "Shoot anyone who points a gun at you," she said after explaining what was happening. "We need to get moving and make it to the other side of the line we brought with us, or find cover until the guys redecorate this place."

"I'd rather not be here when the wrecking crew comes through, so we'll use the dark to slip by," Baylor said. A few of the men made it back to them, but they stayed put until she saw Berkley, Harvey, and Jin. "When I get my hands on that marine unit, I'm going to make a lei out of their ears."

"I'll be happy to help you with that," Berkley said softly as she put her hands on their shoulders and squeezed. "You're both getting a bottle of something good for Christmas this year."

"What about me?" Tito asked indignantly.

"I won't forget any of you, believe me." Berkley winced as she spoke, and Wiley knew it had to be from the beating Chandler had delivered, but she seemed to be able to move on her own, which was a huge bonus. "What's the plan?"

"Command sent a local team, but they found out Chandler offered dental, so they changed employers."

"If we give these fuckers the night and all day, they're going to find us," Tito said, and Goose nodded, along with some of the others.

"We're moving, and Wiley's order stands. I don't care whose uniform they're wearing. They point anything at you, and you don't hesitate," Baylor said.

"Come on, since the east diversion is only going to last so long," Wiley said, making Tito move ahead as if to clear their path.

"Did you paint the area?" Berkley asked, and Baylor nodded. "We need a mile, then call it in."

"How's a half a mile?" Baylor asked as they heard the sound of helicopters in the air. They'd be easy to spot when they turned their searchlights on. "Hold your fire and take cover," he ordered, not wanting to give away their position.

Tito raised his fingers to his ears, so Baylor and Wiley switched back to the previous secure channel. "I say, Tiger One, report."

"Sorry. We're stuck behind a building on the east side of the square and can't move without blowing our way out. Any way you could draw these motherfucking scumbags off?" Baylor asked, sounding like he enjoyed saying every word.

"We're on it," the guy said almost excitedly. "Don't move."

One helicopter peeled off, and their group moved forward and away from the light in a tight circle. Their marine buddies obviously wanted to cover their asses, and Goose held up a fist when Wiley saw the two men on the slight ridge thirty yards away. She held her fist up as well, and everyone dropped.

She crawled slowly to the left as Baylor went to the right. They had to move far enough to stand and make the shot. Her target was sweeping the area with binoculars while his buddy held his rifle to his shoulder as if ready to fire. That's who had to go first, and Baylor obviously agreed when the man suddenly slumped over to his side. Before the other guy could figure out what had happened, he was dead.

They moved forward cautiously, and Baylor's men took possession of the dead men's radios and pointed forward. A few minutes later one of the guys said, "All clear, sir."

"Tito, climb and tell me what you see," Baylor said when they reached a tree with low branches.

They stood still behind something as they waited, and Goose checked the GPS. "It appears clear, but it's as black as the inside of my ass, so we go slow," Tito reported.

"We got another half mile, sir," Goose said.

"Cletus, you're okay to go?" Baylor asked.

"You saw me on the deck every morning," Berkley said and laughed. "I don't like to do it for fun, but to train in case I have to run for my life. I think this qualifies."

"Let's hit it," Wiley said, and they made their way quietly into the unknown. "No matter what, you three are with me," she told Berkley.

They stopped at Baylor's order as his team cleared the next section, and Berkley put her arm around Wiley's shoulders. "Thank God you got there before they ripped all my fingernails out."

"Chandler could have done a lot worse than that, buddy," Wiley said, confused.

"True, but the fingernail thing would've ruined my love life."

"Captain," the *Jefferson*'s lead radar man said. "The targets are visible, so we're a go on your mark."

"Thank you," Aidan said, knowing Command was listening in. She picked up the receiver and took a breath. "Tiger One, this is Zookeeper." It was like throwing a penny into a wishing well, waiting for Baylor to respond since the team had gone silent.

"This is Badger One, ma'am," the marine leader responded. "We're trying to find them but have been unsuccessful."

"You lost them?" she asked, suspicious of that response.

"Black Dragon ordered evasive maneuvers, and they're pinned somewhere in the target area. Hold your fire until we're clear."

"Confirmed, and we'll hold until otherwise noted."

"Ma'am, bogeys coming from the north," another radar operator said.

"Vader, you're clear for takeoff." The flight crew had been on standby, since she was confident Baylor and Wiley wouldn't waste time getting clear of the area. "If the bogies are black and they don't respond, you're clear to fire."

"Yes, Captain"

"Killer," she radioed next.

"Ma'am."

"Evasive maneuvers," she said, changing the channel, and Devin intercepted the crewman who moved closer to see what she'd done. "Devin, have him cuffed and gagged for now. I don't have time for a trip to the brig. Call the CIA guys, and they'll deal with him."

"Wait a minute." The crewman put his hands out in front of him.

"Either place your hands behind your head," she said with her service weapon in her hand, "or I'll shoot you where you stand. Treasonous behavior during wartime gives me that right. I'm also tired of you assholes, so option two would be preferable."

"You can't win," he said as he dropped to his knees and placed his hands behind his head. Devin removed the earwig the guy wore and handed it over. "Give me a ping if we're still a go," someone said, and she placed a pistol against his forehead while Devin cuffed him. "Repeat, are we a go?"

"Man his station and tell me what channels he's on," she said, and the guy who'd been sitting next to the man on his knees turned his head in that direction. "Don't make the mistake of joining your friend here."

"Here you go, ma'am.," Another young guy gave her a tear sheet.

"Send a ping over this channel, then cuff that bastard as well and get them the hell off my bridge," she said of the man who'd hesitated.

"Captain, one of the targets just went off-line," the radar leader said.

"Killer, your team is clear, and we'll send coordinates since the target beacons are being cleared. Make sure they're all eliminated."

"With pleasure, Captain"

"Tiger One," she said, holding her breath a moment longer than usual before exhaling.

"Yes, ma'am," he said, and that was all.

The answer, though, was enough.

The group stopped again, and the heat even at night was enough to make them sweat like they were in a sauna. Berkley wiped her face and sat as she rolled her tongue around her mouth. She was thirsty, but she could wait until they reached a safe rendezvous point. Everything seemed to hurt from her hair down, but she pushed not to fall behind.

"Here," Wiley said, handing over a canteen. "How are your ribs?"

"My ribs are okay, but my kidneys will be pumping blood for a while along with my urine." She took a sip of water, and it hurt to swallow. "Can you believe I was standing that close to that bastard, and you couldn't get a shot off?"

"Believe me, I wanted to before he went off on you, but it would've brought all those assholes down on us and you three." Wiley drank after her and handed it back. "Don't worry, though. The captain has plans of her own, and they include him not getting away."

"She holding up okay?" Making Aidan go through all this again was causing her to hurt more than any blow she'd taken.

"You know the most important thing I've learned after Aubrey came into my life?"

"What's that?" she asked, stifling a moan when she straightened her legs.

"They're strong women on their own, which means they can stand on their own and hold us up as well."

"So she's okay?"

"She's dying inside, but she's doing her job, and because she is, we're walking out of here with you. You're as lucky as I am in this life. Aidan wouldn't accept any scenario that didn't include all of us getting out of that place, and she told Command exactly that."

"The second that door opened I knew I'd put her through hell again, and that was worse than a bullet to the head." She took one more swallow and handed the canteen back. "My other question is, how's retirement?"

"You need a hobby to keep you sane. At least I did, but the kid and wife part are great."

"You fish or something?"

"I paint and dabble in some stuff. Don't worry. I'll help you adjust." Wiley gave her a hand up and smiled when she slapped her gently on the cheek.

"Dabble?" she asked, curious about that one word.

"Time to go, Cletus," Wiley said and chuckled.

Baylor's men had cleared the next section, and the ones behind them had given the all-clear, which got them walking again. She motioned for Harvey and Jin to follow her, and she took Baylor's back. She placed her hand on his shoulder, which caused him to lift a fist for an all-stop.

"Listen," she said when Baylor turned around and gazed at her in question. The sound of jet engines was faint, but they were there. "How far away are we?"

Goose stepped closer and checked their position. "Two clicks and change, ma'am."

"It's our guys," she said, and Baylor nodded. "Let's keep going and get ready."

"Ready for what?" Goose asked.

"Captain Sullivan is about to rain hell down, and we can get out of here in the chaos. The only problem we'll have is if they have any jets that will bomb the shit out of their perimeter to stop our retreat. I've already had a bad day, and I don't want to add to that by having any type of artillery dropped on me."

"Let's go," Wiley said, and they started again. "We need to find another spot to catch our ride out of here, Baylor. The area we agreed on is compromised."

"This thick cover goes on forever," Baylor said as he continued walking.

The first explosion sounded like it had gone off right next to them. She couldn't feel the heat of the fireball that rose in the distance, but it lit up the area for miles. "We need to find a space big enough for a helicopter to land. We need two, but they don't have to land together."

Baylor got their long-range radio out and handed it over. "Code name Zookeeper."

"Zookeeper, this is Wayward," she said, thinking Cletus wasn't a good idea.

"Go ahead, Wayward." The sound of Aidan's voice made her smile. "You're running way late."

"True, but I took candy from strangers. You can fuss later. We need a ride home." She pointed in the direction they'd been walking and got the team moving. There was only so much good luck in one lifetime, and she'd used more than her share. Another set of explosions rocked the area, and they picked up the pace.

"Where?" Aidan asked.

"We'll send coordinates as soon as I see a spot with enough clearance to land." A string of helicopters was closing on their position, which made everyone drop and take cover when Baylor put up his fist, then flattened his hand. She cut the connection to Aidan and the *Jefferson*, not wanting to give away their position if that was possible.

"Wiley," Baylor said as she lay next to Berkley. "Do you have eyes on them?"

"I don't think they're for us," Wiley said, looking through her scope. "No markings and flying too high for a search team."

"It's Chandler, and none of our ships are close enough to pick them up on radar." Berkley saw her hope of retirement flying away with the birds overhead. If it was Chandler and he'd escaped, they'd have to start this all over again. "Give me the radio back."

"What are you thinking?" Baylor asked.

"That I'm done letting this guy win," she said, and he handed it back. "Zookeeper, I need to talk to your attack dogs."

"Go ahead," Aidan said, and the click meant she'd made the connection.

"Vader," she said, and it took a minute for him to respond.

"Good to hear your voice, my friend, but we're ass deep in bogies."

"Head in the game then. Killer, you finish your run?"

"Go ahead," Killer said as a few more explosions went off.

"Can you spare a few birds for an errand?" It was still too dark to see anything, but she could hear them now, and it sounded as if Wiley was right. There were at least fifteen of them, and they were hauling ass.

"Always ready to do a favor for a friend," Killer said.

"Mark these coordinates," she said, and Goose read them off. "Anything on radar?"

"Negative. Are they flying super low?" Killer asked.

"They're in loose wing formation, and they're headed to the coast. We can't let that happen," she said, hoping Aidan was listening in. "Our snake head is on the line here."

"Poncho, peel off and check it out," Killer said.

"No problem," Poncho said. "Are you sure they're headed to the coast?"

"It's the only location that makes sense. They're headed west, but don't let them land without an escort." She waited for his answer, but another thought came to her. "Did the entire compound get destroyed?"

"We marked everything except the house we figured was Chandler's," Baylor said. "Unless the fire of the explosions took it out, it's still standing."

"You want to split up, or do we all go?" Wiley asked, stopping when she and Baylor guessed what her next statement would be.

"We stay together," Harvey said as he drank some water. "The only thing we'll need is some guns in case anyone's left on the ground. Don't you think?"

"I will go," Jin said.

"We're going back then," Baylor said, and Berkley hoped this wasn't another colossal mistake.

"God damn it," Dick Chandler said as they flew with the last remaining troops he had that were available to board. If anyone was on the ground, he was counting on them to get out on their own. There couldn't have been too many, since the cowardly attack had come late enough that the destruction of the barracks took his forces in their sleep. The only readily available survivors were the marines who were hunting the escaped hostages and the Lapry brothers' unit who'd been guarding Ji Woo Min's house.

"These fuckers are going to pay," Robyn said as he held a small towel to his forehead. His son had shown so much valor by spending the attack hiding in a shelter under the house.

"The subs are waiting, sir. We can evacuate you and Robyn, and regroup once you're underway. We might have to move our base of operations, but we have plenty of options to choose from," Mark Lapry said as he piloted the helicopter. "We still have enough men serving to keep up the pressure."

"Did you destroy all the equipment?" he asked Robyn, ignoring Mark for now. The bag at Robyn's feet contained the backups from all the computers, but the actual units had to be destroyed, and that was his son's main job.

Robyn stared at him as if he couldn't believe he'd asked him that. "Of course. Did you make sure Mom boarded another helicopter?"

"She'll be on the next flight," he said and thought Robyn would strike him. "She didn't want to come at all, but I'll have her taken out forcibly if I have to." Actually, he was tired of Ruby and all her damn whining all day about her children, like he didn't understand how devastating it was to lose Jeffery and Rachel.

"I'm sure you've been forceful enough lately," Robyn said, and Dick's hand twitched from not slapping him.

"Once you're married, you'll realize that whoever your wife is can't always come first, and she needs to learn how to be a good partner by whatever means are necessary." He blew out a breath and stared at Robyn until he looked away. "If you don't want to be that kind of man, go back to Olivia Michaels's America and pray I don't crush you."

CHAPTER TWENTY-SIX

The group led by Baylor took the same route back, and Wiley stopped at the men they'd killed and gathered their weapons and clips. "They won't need them anymore," Berkley said as she handed a rifle to Jin.

"What do you go back for?" Jin asked as she cradled the weapon with the barrel pointed toward the ground.

"For the answers none of our prisoners have wanted to share with us," she said, and waved Baylor on. The way back didn't seem as far, and the fires still burning led their way closer. "There's a chance Chandler left evidence behind as he made his getaway. If it's still there we'll carry it out."

"You are very interesting person, Berkley," Jin said, and bowed her head slightly as if showing her respect.

"My mother did her best to raise us that way, and my father expected us to do the right thing even when it wasn't the easiest option. I think we have that in common, only, from what you've told me, your mother taught you those lessons."

They took cover at the edge of the clearing, and Wiley climbed to reach the best nest available. "Anything moving?" she asked Wiley by radio.

"Seems quiet, but I'd advise not just walking in like lost tourists."

"I've got a better idea." She radioed Vader and requested another run, but with new coordinates Baylor's men would paint. They'd be done by the time the team reloaded and refueled the planes.

It took an hour, but the new targets would be on the western-most point of the compound, which would keep them safe from flying debris, but close enough to see any stragglers. Vader's group gave warning before they started, and they watched as the bombs fell while their jets streaked by.

"I like seeing those from the safety of my seat on the plane," Harvey said, and she laughed.

"True, brother, but let's go. Wiley, we're moving in. Do you see any problems?"

"Nothing yet, but I'll be watching."

Baylor was waiting at the back of the big house, and that's how they all got in as well. The house was relatively untouched, considering the damage to everything else, and all Berkley noticed was the broken windows and items that had fallen over from the power of the blasts.

"Baylor, we need to clear this place," she said.

"How about you let us do that this time," he said, and Tito, KO, and Goose nodded.

"Thanks. I'm over my quota of being taken hostage for the month."

The SEALs were methodical in their approach and, after a brief breakout of gunfire, finally shouted for her to come toward the front of the house. The master bedroom held three dead soldiers wearing black uniforms and an older lady who sat on the bed crying. "Ma'am," she said gently, standing a few feet away. "I need your name, ma'am."

"Ruby Chandler, and I'll give you whatever you want, if you help me get my children back." Ruby fell to her knees and grabbed her hand. "Please, you have to help me. My husband, the bastard, left me here to die."

"Releasing your children isn't within my power, ma'am, but I can advocate on their behalf, if you help me now." She assisted Ruby to her feet and studied her face. The fading yellowish bruise around her eye appeared tender, but her lip was swollen, pulling on the stitches holding it together. "Are you all right, ma'am?"

"I could ask you the same thing, Berkley. That's your name, isn't it?" Ruby tried to smile but winced in obvious pain. "My husband has spent the last day screaming about you, so don't think I know you because I'm part of all this."

"I understand he doesn't like me very much, and I'm sure he has his reasons now," she said to Ruby before turning her attention to Baylor. "We have to move before the Korean forces show up, but I need all the files and computer records before that happens." She found Ruby staring at her when she turned back around, and she nodded. "If you have any idea of where to start looking, it'll go a long way in helping your children live."

Ruby led them to the office, unlocked the filing cabinets, and typed in all the passwords to the computers, and Berkley took the time to change them for later. It was almost too easy, but she didn't want to stop to analyze the situation since they could review the information in a more secure location. "Call for a ride, and make sure the captain sends some incentive to leave them alone. If the area's clear, we'll have them land here. I'm all walked out for the night."

Baylor called in the request, and she sat with Ruby again. "Does this place have a basement or vault?"

"The vault is behind the picture in the dining room…and yes, there is a basement." Ruby hesitated after the basement admission, and she quickly picked up her weapon and motioned to Tito.

It didn't take long before the firefight broke out when the men hiding in the basement came out shooting blindly. "Goose," Baylor said, and the big guy threw a shock grenade toward the opening that was across from the office. The gunfire stopped momentarily, followed by another shock grenade from Tito. The SEALs kept firing until Baylor called for a cease fire, and the silence returned. A smoke haze hung in the air now that smelled of gunpowder and what seemed to be sulfur.

"How the hell did we miss that?" Baylor said loudly.

"It looked like a closet, Boss," Goose said, and Baylor went down and noticed the false door that was now in the open position.

He came out a few minutes after going in, wiping his face and pointing over his shoulder. "All clear, Cletus. Damn good call."

Ruby had gotten up from the office chair, but Berkley lay motionless in front of the desk, still clutching her rifle. "Tito," Baylor yelled as he watched Ruby raise the shiny gun and aim it at him. Her head exploded before he could raise his own weapon, and he saw a wounded New Horizons soldier take the shot. The guy fell flat after Goose put a bullet in him. "Cletus, if you fucking die on me after all this shit, I'm going to revive you just so I can kill you myself."

He rolled Berkley over and saw four shots to her chest, starting in the middle and working downward. The only bloody spot was on the lower left side and at the side of her head. "Is she still breathing?" Goose asked as Baylor felt her pulse.

As if almost wishing it to happen, Goose's words made Berkley take a deep breath and moan. "That fucking bitch shot me."

Baylor opened her tunic and saw three bullets flattened on her flak jacket, though the fourth had penetrated right underneath, accounting for all the blood. "Jesus H. Christ, my future children thank you," Baylor said.

"What?" Berkley asked, still sounding hoarse from getting the wind knocked out of her. "What are you talking about?"

"I told Wiley I had to find you or the captain would rip my nuts off and choke me with them, so thanks. My family jewels and future beautiful children are safe for now." He pressed the bandage to her side and smiled as he bent down so he could whisper in her ear. "And you're a lucky bastard. Aidan's great, and forgive me if I'm wrong. The way you look at her, though, makes me think I'm not."

"Thanks, buddy. After all this excitement, I'm going to retire and feel lucky all the time."

❖

Aidan stood on the deck after the planes circled to give the helicopters room to land. The SEALs jumped down and gathered at the last one to touch down to help Baylor and Wiley carry the stretcher out. She took another deep breath to calm herself, already knowing Berkley had been hurt.

"Hey, Sailor," Berkley said when she saw her and saluted. "The Chandler family are some really mean people."

"Hey," she said, laughing as she moved with the group that carried Berkley to the medical unit. "I'll make sure to put that observation in the report." The doctor was waiting, but Berkley was alert and talking, which was like a tranquilizer to Aidan's system.

"Everyone wait out here until we're finished with our assessment," the doctor said.

"Thank you, Baylor," she said when the big man came out with her and shook her hand. "You got everyone home safe, and I owe you a debt."

"When we were at the Academy together, Cletus kicked my ass in pretty much everything," Baylor said, sitting with her since she didn't want to leave until the doctor had a report. "It would've pissed me off, but she was so damn likable, you know. She made me laugh even when she was teasing me mercilessly, but she helped me pass calculus. Without that, I probably would've ended up swabbing a deck somewhere."

"Sounds like you two had some fun."

"We did, and when I graduated from SEAL training, she came, since my parents died early. If not, I wouldn't have had anyone there to share that accomplishment with," he said, wiping his eyes with what seemed like embarrassment. "She's always been a good friend, and today was my way of repaying her for always having my back. Because of all that, you don't have to thank me. Believe me, when she took that big breath, I almost went weak in the knees I was so happy. She's got a great retirement ahead, and that bitch almost stole it from her."

"We've run into a few bitches lately, so you have to narrow it down," Aidan said, making Baylor laugh.

"Ruby Chandler shot Cletus. The bitch had been beaten up by someone, I'm guessing Dick, and then gave us all the information he left behind without a problem. She even unlocked the computers for us but freaked out when Cletus asked about a basement."

"What happened to her? Ruby Chandler, I mean."

"When she was done with Cletus she tried to shoot me. Then a New Horizons soldier gave her a piece of his mind by leaving pieces of hers all over the wall."

"Captain." The doctor came out before she could comment about what he'd said. "Captain Levine has some bruised ribs and kidneys, and the gunshot was a through-and-through. She should be laid up for at least six weeks but make a full recovery. We've sedated her, and I'll clean and close the wounds, but I don't foresee any problems."

"Thank you, Doctor. We'll leave you to your job, but could you call me when she's awake?"

"Yes, ma'am. Give her about three hours, and she should be coherent by them."

"Devin will send someone down to keep watch. I don't want to take any chances."

"Captain." One of the medics held up the radio receiver. "Call from Killer."

"Go ahead." She pinched her brow, knowing she'd have to leave since the mission wasn't done yet.

"The helicopters did head to the coast, and they've landed at a pier that has six subs a few hundred yards offshore."

"Are they boarding?"

"Not yet, ma'am, from what we can tell, but we might've missed something in our flybys."

"Keep them in sight, and I'll call Command. I'd like to sink their escape route, but they keep preaching about not leaving any fingerprints. If they fire on you, though, go ahead and do just that." She gazed at the doctor again, and Baylor kept his seat. "I'll be on the bridge. Please call me when she's awake."

"Go ahead, Captain. I've got this," Baylor said. "She won't wake up alone."

"Thank you," she said before making her way up. Devin was waiting outside and gave her a preliminary report on what casualties New Horizons had taken and what forces they estimated were left.

"They had five full battalions, ma'am, and from our room with a view, I don't think that Lapry guy was exaggerating," Harvey said as he walked with them. "Is Cletus okay? I wanted to talk to the commander while it was still all fresh."

"She'll be laid up for a while, but she'll be fine," she said with a smile. "Are you sure he said five?"

"Yes, ma'am, and Cletus and Jin both heard the same thing. I can't figure out why have them all here. It was like a big militia, but they were in the wrong country."

"It'll really be interesting to find out what he promised Kim to be able to operate so freely in his country with this many men and that kind of firepower."

"We locked up the files, hard drives, and everything else they brought back from Chandler's. It was a good call on Cletus's part," Devin said. "The other thing I don't get, though, is why be that helpful, then turn around and shoot Cletus?"

"Because Mrs. Chandler had her ambush party in the basement," she said, and Harvey nodded. "If Cletus and the guys had been curious and started searching the files, letting their guard down, they would've been easier to kill. If you're dead, you take Chandler's secrets with you."

"Cletus was the one who got shot, but she's also the one who warned us about that," Harvey said. "It was bad enough that we had to stand there and watch that bastard whale on her. It doesn't seem fair that she gets the bullet too."

"She'll recover from all that, but right now we've got a job to finish, and I plan to whale on Chandler for a change."

"Sounds good. It's a shame it couldn't be Cletus dropping a bomb on that asshole," Harvey said.

"Don't count her out on that, but I'm sure she'll enjoy hearing about it just as much."

❖

"Those are American jets, sir," the marine team leader said, and Tyler Lapry grunted his agreement.

"We go with our doomsday plan, gentleman, and we finally take the fight home. We have enough troops left to train the recruits back home, and after we replenish some of our equipment, we'll be a go."

"I don't know about that, sir," Mark Lapry said. "We suffered heavy losses of our best people, and we don't have that many stateside for the wave you had planned." Mark was talking but staring at the sky, his eyes widening. The reaction made Dick look in that direction, seeing the jets circle back around.

"Is this your resignation speech? I took you and your brother in and gave you leadership ranks on faith, and on your father's word." The men started making the ferry trips to the subs, one submerging once it was full.

Dick was leaving on the *Vengeance* with the most experienced captain in the fleet, August Shields, who stood on the deck with binoculars to his eyes. The jets were coming back, only flying lower, and he hesitated before getting into the ferry. No way had he come this far only to have Preston Sullivan's little blond bitch of a kid blow him up.

"Sir, it's time to be realistic," Tyler said, and Mark moved closer to his brother. "With the men we had, and people like my father back home, we had a good shot. Problem is, I've tried my father, and he's not answering. He'd never ignore me, which means we have a problem. Robyn made me watch the news, and they're reporting that he's been taken into custody. What are you planning to do about that? I'm not leaving him somewhere to die a slow death waiting for you."

"You don't think I've sacrificed for the cause? You realize my son's facing death, and my daughter is headed for the same fate." The only way to reestablish his authority was through a show of strength—his grandfather had taught him that early. He slapped Tyler, the sound making the men around them stop talking and stare. Tyler took a step toward him, stopping when Robyn and two others aimed their guns at his head.

"My apologies, sir," Tyler said, grabbing Mark by the bicep and stepping back. "We're with you all the way."

"Come on," he said to Robyn, ready to do what he could. August came to attention and saluted when he boarded, and they submerged after the crew and the men with them were aboard. "Are you ready?"

August gave the command to start moving before he faced him and answered. "With the entire fleet we have a shot, but you have to accept losses. We've had a catastrophic day, so I wanted to give you all the possibilities before you make a decision."

"What kind of losses?" He sat and watched all the men working to get them underway.

"At least two vessels, maybe four, if they found a way to locate us on radar," August said softly as if he didn't want to be overheard.

"But we can sink it?" he asked as Robyn stood on his right.

"Yes, sir, but we need at least two vehicles to complete the rest of what you have planned."

"Then the losses are acceptable, Captain. Proceed."

CHAPTER TWENTY-SEVEN

"A re we sure each sub belongs to New Horizons?" Secretary of Defense Rooster asked as General Carl Greenwald sat on his right listening intently.

"From what we think, Chandler and some of his men were able to get away by helicopter to the coast. Our team on the ground saw the evacuation vehicles, and the subs you can see here," Aidan said, showing the video the jets had captured.

"And Ruby Chandler?" National Security Advisor Neil Perry asked.

"We talked to all the individuals present, and they all said the same thing from their position in the room," she said, feeling they were wasting time. "Ruby Chandler shot Captain Levine, one of New Horizons soldiers shot her, and one of the SEALs shot him. The important thing to concentrate on is that Ruby Chandler aimed to kill. That's a dead subject."

"Ma'am," Vader said, interrupting her. "All six subs have submerged."

"We've lost our window," Aidan said, aggravated. "If he intends to fire on us, we have to warn every ship here for the war games."

"We'll take care of that," Rooster said, pointing to someone out of Aidan's view. "Our subs are also patrolling the area, and they have a green light to fire. It might be better if they're taken out under the water and not under the watchful eyes of the North Koreans."

"Regardless of whether they fire on you or not, Chandler is now back in the wind. That's disappointing, considering all you've accomplished," Neil said, and Preston appeared ready to slap him. "What can we do to finally bring him in?"

"We can start with the files our team recovered," she said. "Considering the losses he took, he should be surrendering, but he's boarded a heavily armed sub. We know they have sophisticated firepower on board, since they shot Cletus down. He's planned something other than giving up, which makes it imperative to find and sink him."

"All of you need to be on high alert," Carl said, having brought in Captains Washington and Greer from the other ships. "Chandler isn't our only problem. The North Korean regime has contacted the White House about the bombing and are demanding the people responsible."

"Sir, we'll be vigilant, but we'll also use any plane or ship that fires on us for target practice."

"Ma'am," the radio operator screamed. "Incoming torpedoes."

She put the receiver down and ordered countermeasures. "Vader, Killer, or whoever's closer."

"Go ahead, ma'am."

"Lay down a line of fire on our port side."

"Aye, Captain," Vader said.

"We're clear of fishing boats," Killer said.

Aidan watched through her binoculars, knowing their proximity to the North Korean border and where they had reported the subs. Chandler was now a cornered animal, and the closest target for him to lash out at was the US Navy ships that had brought about the beginning of his end. Until now she hadn't given Chandler the credit she probably should have because his goals had been so bizarre, but he was obviously set on burning the world around him to the ground.

That might not have resulted in the change he wanted, but it was necessary to his plan. If he didn't destroy what existed, nothing new would rise from the ashes. In his mind, she guessed, he saw himself as the phoenix and the rest of them as the heap he had to create to fuel his rise.

"Captain Sullivan." A voice she didn't recognize came over the radio on the intercom so everyone could hear. "This is the USS *Seawolf*, and we're coming around your starboard side. Please hold your fire."

"We'll hold for now, but advise if you need any backup."

"Thank you, ma'am."

"More missiles in the water, ma'am," her radar leader said.

"How many and where?" The urge to deploy countermeasures was hard to ignore, but she had to have faith not everyone was out to sink them.

"Two off our starboard," the man said, never taking his eyes off the screen. "They had to have come from the *Seawolf*."

The impact came half a mile from them before they went through the same exercise three more times. They did have to deploy their countermeasures when the *Seawolf* and the *Saratoga* didn't hit their targets before they were able to get torpedoes away. Their subs destroyed four enemy vessels, but another twelve hours of searching didn't find the other two. That required Washington to contact the Russians again for failing to disclose the sale of two more subs. If they'd hidden that sale, what else had they kept to themselves?

"Our sub captains were supposed to keep our ships from getting hit, but they completely destroyed Chandler's vessels," Rooster said of their naval subs. "That'll prevent us from doing a body count. If Chandler's on the two boats that got through our net, we can't prove it."

"I doubt he's headed to another rogue state," Aidan said as she sat for the first time in hours. "His drive to stay alive and away from the front lines might prove me wrong though."

"You have full security clearance, as do Cletus, Wiley, and Baylor. We're adding Commander Clark to that list in the interest of time and getting this done," he said of Devin. "Start searching through the capture documents and raise anchor. The president wants all of you out of range of the North Koreans and the information you gathered stateside."

"We'll start on that, and Cletus can join us when she wakes up."

"Send her our best, as well as our thanks. Those documents are our best bet to finish this with a red bow on top and have confidence it's done."

"Will do, sir, and we'll see you soon. We're coming home."

❖

"All four have been lost, sir," August said as he slowly placed the radio receiver down. "We aren't alone down here, so we've got to make tracks if we'd like to stay alive."

"We're giving them a good fight if they brought in subs as well," Dick said, not too concerned with the news. He'd tried to sink the *Jefferson*, or any of the others, but it had been a long shot. They'd expected him to make that play, but his next move would balance out all his losses.

"They're anticipating our strategy, sir, which means we should consider surrender before anyone else gets killed."

He stared at August for over a minute, but the captain didn't look away. "If you ever question me again, or speak of surrender, you'll be relieved of duty when I put a bullet in your head." The men around them seemed to try to ignore them as they concentrated on the consoles, but he could tell they were listening. "I'm down here with you, and I have no desire to die or surrender. Set a course for these coordinates, and let's be done with all this the quickest way possible."

August studied the paper he handed over and took a deep breath. "Are you sure?"

"Dead sure, and we're prepared to win," he said, but August appeared skeptical. "Are you?"

"Yes, sir," August said, his voice tight. They had some time before they reached their final destination, and he didn't trust August's sense of survival over what he wanted.

"Take turns watching him," he said to the Lapry brothers and Robyn. "If he makes a move to contact anyone that's not on the other sub, shoot to kill."

"Yes, sir," Tyler said quickly. "What about our parents?"

"Once we're done, your parents will be my first priority."

"Then we meant what we said. We're with you until the end," Mark said.

"It won't be long before we're done."

Berkley opened her eyes and took as deep a breath as she could without pain. The light in the room was dim, but the nurse hovering over her seemed to be writing something in her chart with no problem.

"Welcome back, Captain," the young woman said, smiling. "All your vitals are normal, but now that you're awake, you can tell me how you feel."

"Like I got beat up and shot."

"That's because you have the worst luck in North Korea," Aidan said from the door. "We need to find you a better place to hike in."

"You know me," she said, turning her head and looking at Aidan and feeling like it'd been months since she'd seen her. "I love meeting new people."

"I do know you, and you should know me by now. I get upset when you're this late, and don't get me started on you getting shot. That wasn't in the plan we reviewed before you left." The nurse laughed and excused herself to go get the doctor. "Honey, look at you," Aidan said, touching over the eye that was still swollen shut.

"I'm sure I look like hell, but how else will I get you to coddle me?" she asked and held her hand up. "We almost made it out, and I'm really sorry I put you through that again."

"You kept your promises, honey. You're here and you're breathing. That's all I care about, and I'll remind you of this when I have a GPS tracker installed on your ass." Aidan kissed her fingers, then pressed them to Berkley's lips.

"Will you use your rank to spring me out of here?"

"Before you answer that, Captain, how about Cletus gives me a night. Then she can return to her quarters," he said. "Forget about active duty for at least six weeks. You get in that plane and I'll kill you, if the captain doesn't beat me to it." He examined her and changed her bandages, saying everything looked great.

"Now that we know you'll live, I've got some folks out here that want to talk to you," Aidan said.

"Do you usually have this effect on people? You introduce yourself, make small talk, and it ends in gunfire?" Wiley asked as she entered with Baylor, Harvey, and Jin. "You look like shit, Cletus."

"And she's being kind," Baylor said.

"It was my turn since Harvey ended up in here the last time," she said and smiled sympathetically when she saw Jin's face. The asshole in the North Korean uniform had done a number on her. "You feel okay?" she asked Jin.

"Your doctor gave me stitches and said I would be okay. I must thank you all for not leaving me behind."

"You're one of us now, and we take care of our own," Baylor said, placing his hands on Jin's shoulders.

"I need to thank you anyway," she said, glancing between Baylor and Wiley. "I owe you two and the rest of your team, Baylor. You guys kept up and got us out of there before Dick really got ahold of us."

"You owe us a beer and we'll be even," Wiley said, and pointed to the door. "Come on, you guys. Cletus needs all the beauty sleep she can get. Besides, we have homework," Wiley said to Baylor.

"Yeah, but don't try to stretch this out to avoid work." Baylor pointed to the bed and shook his finger.

"Did we get some good stuff?"

"Let's hope you can remember the new passwords," Wiley said.

"I got it all up here." She pressed a finger to the side of her head and motioned for Harvey to stay. "You got out without any injuries this time?"

"I'm okay, but I wasn't much help," he said, lowering his head. "I should've done more."

"You never left her side and avoided getting shot in the head," Aidan said. "You're a badass, Junior. Accept it." Aidan hugged him and kissed him on the cheek. "If you weren't a badass, Corbin wouldn't have named you after our dog."

"Thanks, ma'am, and I'll come back later." He waved on his way out, and she smiled at the sweet guy.

"What happened after I got my egghead scrambled?"

She listened as Aidan told her about the subs and their new orders. The hum of the engines was comforting, and she fought off a yawn. "We'll finish this conversation later," Aidan said, sitting next to the bed. "Go to sleep and get some rest."

They had so much to do that Berkley thought about fighting sleep, but her body betrayed her, and she gave in to it. Aidan saw her eyes flutter shut and enjoyed simply watching Berkley drift off. It was something she did whenever she managed to wake before her morning-person lover, who was usually full of energy.

"Excuse me, Captain," Jin said softly after she entered the room. "I want to make sure she was fine after all she did to keep me alive." Jin told her about Berkley standing in front of her when Chandler raised his gun and aimed it at her head. "I told her she was an interesting person, but she has also got a courageous and good heart."

"You're right, and she did that because you're her friend. I realize you're sad, but that should bring you some comfort." That Berkley had done that didn't surprise her, but it also made her nuts. "I almost forgot in all the excitement, but we rescued someone from the house. She won't speak to any of us, and I thought you could talk to her and at least get a name. If she sees someone from North Korea, it might relax her a bit."

"I will help however you need me to."

Jin followed her out and across their medical unit to the room where the small battered woman had lain in bed, never saying a word no matter how much their translator tried to communicate with her. "She was found locked in a room in Min's house and was in bad shape when she got here. The doctor has checked her wounds and said they'd heal fairly quickly, but I'm thinking the mental anguish will take some time," Aidan said before she opened the door.

When she cracked the door, Jin stood frozen in place, and the woman on the bed turned her head and stared, crying. "Jin," the woman said in a small whisper that sounded weak and pleading, almost like she didn't believe she was seeing Jin.

"Yong," Jin said, and her feet finally came to life as she practically ran to the bed and put her arms around the woman. They spoke in Korean for a moment, and Aidan didn't need a translator to realize that Jin not only knew this woman, but she truly seemed to care for her. "She is still alive," Jin said to Aidan, and showed more emotion with her tears than

Aidan had ever witnessed from her. "She is my Yong Nam. She flew with me and was my friend. I thought she was dead."

"I don't think it would've been much longer before that was true," she said, smiling at Yong to put her at ease as she clutched Jin's hand. "Does she speak English?"

"I taught her some, but I have more practice now," Jin said, turning her eyes back to Yong like something of her old life was still alive and there in front of her.

"Thank you," Yong said with a heavy accent as she bowed her head.

Aidan nodded and smiled. "You can fill me in later," she told Jin. "Why don't you sit with Yong and talk to her? I think she really needs a friend to start putting what happened to her in the past."

"I asked Berkley if she was not disgusted when I told her what Yong means to me, and she said no. I hope you are the same," Jin said, taking Yong's hand and lifting it to her cheek.

"I'd be the last person on this ship that would be disgusted by what I see," she said and widened her smile. "Love is love, Jin, and when you find it, do everything you can to never let it go."

"Thank you, Aidan, and seeing Yong again made that very true for me."

"I'm glad, because it's the most beautiful thing in the world," she said, glancing back at the room Berkley was in. "I should know."

CHAPTER TWENTY-EIGHT

The tired almost drugged sensation clouding Berkley's head didn't disappear until the next morning, and the doctor gave in to her wish to leave. The nurse who'd checked on her every half hour volunteered to come to her quarters and change the bandages, giving her the green light to return to her room.

For the next three days she and the team went through the files and hard drives until they uncovered the first important cache of information that could help them find every single person in Chandler's army. Berkley did a search to see if anyone else on board their ship and the others traveling with them was on Chandler's list.

"What did you find?" Rooster asked during their daily briefing.

"Two more names, not including Dale Whitner and our radio operator. For a ship this big, that's not a lot, but if they'd killed Aidan, it was plenty. We sent the other captains their potential problems, and they're taking care of them," Berkley said, trying to stretch without hurting herself. "But more important—we found the master list buried in their computer files. It appears that Robyn Chandler kept the roster, and he was pretty good at updating the numbers. If this is right, the ten percent estimate is fairly accurate."

"Encrypt that and send it to us," Rooster said, tapping his finger on the desk. "Any name in particular pop out at you?"

"A few Secret Service agents," Berkley said, highlighting those to make it easier for Rooster to find. "You might want to check who they're assigned to. Right now the most shocking are the Speaker and his staff, but FBI Director Chapman had already found them."

"It'll be a huge pain in the ass, but we'll round up all these people and bring them in. By the time we're done we might need to lease the rest of Cuba to detain them all," Carl said.

"One name sticks out to me, considering how Chandler got out," Aidan said, motioning for Berkley to move the mouse to the next suspect. "Captain Cruise Liskow. He's currently on the eastern seaboard commanding a sub with nuclear warheads on board."

Rooster and Carl both leaned forward and stared at Preston. "Keep searching, but we'll have to chance a dump of all these files into the Pentagon's system. I'll have my second send you the encryption codes so we can limit access to anyone not having clearance," Rooster said, putting his hand on the top of his head and running it over his buzz cut.

"What are you thinking?" Berkley asked, not liking the change in demeanor.

"I want to be sure Liskow or anyone in his position can't drop a nuke in a heavily populated area. We have safeguards against that kind of thing, but I'm not taking any chances," Rooster said and stood up. "Radio in if you find anything else, but we're headed upstairs with this."

"How fast can Chandler make it back?" she asked Aidan after the monitor went black.

"Faster than us since they won't have to contend with surface conditions," Aidan said, making notes and calculations. "If we go top speed, we'll be half a day behind him."

Berkley shook her head and twirled her pen through her fingers. "That'll be a half a day too late. There has to be someone left on that list who can contact Chandler. If we can do that and feed him the right misinformation, it might slow him down."

"If he plans to destroy some place like New York, I doubt he'll stop to take a call from an old friend," Aidan said.

Baylor stared at Berkley, and his eyes widened when he obviously figured out what was on her mind. "Fuck," he said, then clamped his jaws shut. "Sorry, ma'am, but Cletus is right. He's not interested in New York." Baylor got up and put a map of the eastern coast on the screen and pointed to Washington DC. "You park a sub here," his finger slid to the Atlantic, "and he takes the capital. If he does that, it leaves a huge vacuum of power he can readily step into."

"He's not that crazy, is he?" Aidan asked.

"We saw him in that uniform with all the shiny stars, even though he's never served a day in his life," Wiley said. "He's that crazy, and my kid is in DC with my wife and parents." No one in the room gave any kind of shocked reaction to that statement.

"What do you suggest as far as slowing him down?" Aidan asked Berkley.

"We keep looking for a contact person, and we contact the sub captains who took out the other four. They missed these two, and we have like ten days for them to rectify that situation," Berkley said. "I can think of only two for sure he'd stop to talk to."

"Jeffery and Rachel," Aidan said, and Berkley snapped her fingers, then pointed at her. "He's never going to believe that all of a sudden they were granted radio privileges. They're both rotting in Gitmo, and Jeffery's facing the death penalty."

"He'll believe it if we plan it right," Baylor said.

"How do you figure?" Berkley asked as she scratched her side where the stitches were.

Aidan grabbed her hand and shook her head. Her wound was starting that itchy stage, and it was driving her insane, but at least she was able to see a bit out of her swollen eye. The bruise was black and tender, and her eye was so bloodshot she thought it'd never clear, but her vision was back. Without perfect eyesight, her time in the cockpit really was over, and that's what had worried her the most. Too much was at stake for her career to end.

"There's no way the jailbird Chandlers know everyone working for daddy dearest, so we get a SEAL team to break them out. All we need to do is tell the army guys not to be so vigilant," Taylor said.

"And how do we keep the escapees from really flying the coop?" Aidan asked.

"With a little help from a good dentist, we can get it done. They can put trackers in your teeth now," Baylor said.

"That's a lot of moving parts, James Bond," Berkley said, and Baylor shot her the finger.

"We agree that we need them out there," Wiley said, "and with a little teamwork, we can figure it out."

"We need them out of their cells, not off the island," Berkley said, glancing at Aidan, and she nodded as if open to whatever she had in mind. "We'll need to talk to Director Chapman."

"That's easy enough," Aidan said.

"There's easy, and then there's luck. We need plenty of luck for this to work."

Rachel stood and faced the wall as the guards unlocked the door. The game of wits with the interrogators was the only thing she had to look forward to every day, but no matter how long the game lasted, she had no intention of telling them anything. The pain in her arm was about to drive her insane, but fantasies of finding and killing whoever put the bullet through her shoulder kept her grounded.

"Good morning, Ms. Chandler," the young woman said. The pressed chinos and golf shirt the woman had on looked cooler than her orange jumpsuit, but what caught her attention was how familiar the newcomer was to her. She just couldn't place her. "You might not remember me, but we met right after you were brought in."

"You're an FBI agent?" The young agent had been with her for days after her capture but had never pushed her to answer anything. Whoever had assigned her either had too much faith in the agent, or thought Rachel didn't have much information to offer on her father's organization. "I forget your name."

"Special Agent Erin Mosley," Erin said, not making eye contact with her. It was something she'd noticed about this woman the first time they'd met. Granted, she'd been drugged stupid at the time, but Special Agent Mosley had always appeared to be busy with something else when she was with her.

"May I call you Erin?" She'd asked the fucking chief interrogator Walby Edwards the same thing, and it made her wonder what Erin's answer would be.

"No, Ms. Chandler, you may not," Erin said, glancing up from her papers. "We are not friends, we won't ever be friends, and I'd appreciate the same courtesy and respect I'm showing you."

"You have me locked in a cage twenty hours a day in this pit," she said, placing the hand of her paralyzed arm on her lap. It wouldn't move on its own, but leaving it hanging made the pain worse.

"I don't have you locked in here, Ms. Chandler. Any astute person would realize you put yourself in here by trying to kill the president." Erin returned to her paperwork as if she hadn't just called her stupid.

"You can't prove that," she said, her anger flaring.

"You were shot on a building while holding a high-powered rifle pointed at the president. A chimpanzee could win this case since it's a slam-dunk compared to your brother's, and he was found trying to sink the USS *Jefferson*. Neither of you are what I'd call the Al Capone of crime. After all, it took the IRS to finally bring him in."

"Then why are you here, Erin?" she asked in the same condescending tone Erin was using.

"To give you an update since you don't have access to news or a phone." The papers scattered on the table were too far away for her to see what they were, and she refused to embarrass herself by craning her neck. "We found your father's secret little hideaway." Erin placed a picture of the North Korean base in front of her. "Four days ago," the television in the room came on and a video started, "our jets were able to level it, along with everyone in it."

The explosions made her wince, and all she could think of was her mother and her brother. "You murdered all those innocent people?" The anger raging inside was a constant companion, but she couldn't stop the tears at the thought of being truly alone in the world.

"They weren't exactly innocent, Miss Chandler," Erin said, fast-forwarding to the next bombing run. "That was a lot of military hardware for innocent people to have."

"You fucking bitch." She screamed the curse and tried to stand, but Erin squeezed her bad shoulder, making her drop back down.

"Agent Mosley." Someone came to the door and held up a note. "You have an urgent call, ma'am."

"Here." Erin handed over the remote. "Entertain yourself."

The door closed, and she didn't have to start the feed again. The damn thing was playing on a loop in her head. How could their contacts in the Pentagon and in Washington not have warned her father so they could get out? They'd shared enough money with them and promised enough power to prevent this exact scenario. Surely she could still do something to find out if her family had survived.

Erin came back twenty minutes later, and the papers she'd left behind had been tempting, but Rachel was smart enough to know they were always watching. "Now that you realize no one's coming to rescue you, would you like to answer some questions?"

"Go fuck yourself, Erin," she said, getting up again and fighting back the pain to grab this bitch with her good hand.

Erin made the same move but followed with a hold on her hair. The grip allowed her to smash Rachel's face into the table. The impact made her light-headed, and when she tried to stand, Erin did it again until Rachel saw blood on the Formica surface. "Guard," Erin said, not really yelling. "Take her to sick bay." A man grabbed her and moved her away from Erin, who'd already returned to her paperwork like nothing had happened.

"Fuck you," Rachel said, then spit a mouthful of blood at the bitch. It landed close but missed its intended target. Everything went dark when she tried to lunge again and the guard knocked her in the back of the head. It was the only thing that wiped away the images of death.

"It went pretty much like you said it would," Erin said to Walby as they watched the monitor hidden discreetly in the exam area. "I have to say that felt pretty good, since every so often I just want to smack the hell out of one of these people." They'd placed the camera for only this consultation, and then they'd monitor every moment of Rachel Chandler's life until the danger to national security was over.

"People often think they'd act differently in situations that call for something outside their norm, but that's seldom the case," Walby said as the nurse came in with the doctor. The man checked Rachel's head and ordered an X-ray of the shoulder and a bandage for the gashes close to her hairline and face. He then deemed it necessary to keep her overnight to monitor her for a concussion. "When you're raised like Rachel, you're pretty hardwired."

"So she lashes out. Then what?"

"Her emotions are predictably unstable, but she's not without charm." Walby tapped on the screen over Rachel's face. "Look where her eyes are glued."

The radio in the exam room was there for calls from the field, but it could do so much more, and Erin could almost see every one of Rachel's thoughts, as if they were in a cartoon bubble over her head. "There's only one thing between her and that little bit of the outside world."

"Exactly," Walby said as a doctor left and the young nurse started cleaning Rachel's wounds. "We might have to offer Captain Levine a job after she retires from the navy."

"Let's see if she's on the money first," Erin said as Rachel placed her hand on the nurse's forearm and seemed to be speaking softly to her. "But she might know what she's talking about."

"One day when you're bored, read the files on these ladies. Cletus and Aidan are impressive, but you add Wiley, and you'll understand why this will work. They're all master strategists."

"I hope more than anyone she's right, because if not, this will be like trying to find a needle in the Atlantic Ocean," Erin said, watching.

"A very dangerous needle with deadly intentions."

Berkley stood outside on the deck looking up at the moonless sky. "Nothing like a nighttime sky in the middle of the ocean," she said to Wiley. They'd reviewed all the files again in the last week but didn't find anything else to help them find Chandler.

"I'd love to bring Tanith out here and show her this," Wiley said, taking something from her pocket. "She'd enjoy all the stars you can see from this vantage point."

She took the picture Wiley handed over and turned it toward what little light was coming from the bridge above them. "She's a cute kid, and Aubrey's beautiful. They're going to be fine. You know General Gremillion won't let anything happen to them."

"I think our plan is sound," Wiley said, sounding as tired as she felt. "We have time, but if we run out, how many Taniths and Aubreys are out there with no idea there's a maniac ready to kill them? It makes you wonder what happened to this guy to make him think this way."

"I'm with you, buddy. I thought this would've worked by now, but we can't give up. You have to have a little faith." She handed the picture back and pointed to the door. "Let's get some sleep, and we can read the maniac's manifesto again tomorrow."

She made it to her quarters without running into anyone of consequence, giving her the chance to put her pajamas on. It'd been a week since she'd been shot, and she was moving easier, but she wasn't at full steam yet. Her dedicated nurse was still coming by to change her bandages, and she found her nice and engaging as they talked about nothing of consequence. They had a lot of noise in their lives as they sped home, but this was the best part of her day.

"Anything yet?" she asked Aidan when she walked next door.

"Cruise Liskow still hasn't responded to Command and has removed all the locater devices on board," Aidan said, finishing with her own pajamas.

She would've rather done without them, but Aidan was taking the doctor's orders seriously, and she'd said that being naked was too tempting. "Did they give you his last known location?"

"Yes, and they have every available sub in that area searching, but so far no luck. Our little convoy has the best radar guys looking for the two that got away from us, but they're batting zero as well." Aidan walked over to her and put her hands around her neck. "I should've ordered the guys to blow every single one of them when we had them in sight. If something happens, it'll be my fault."

"Hey, no way," she said and kissed Aidan's forehead. "I'm glad you didn't. He should see it coming and know who's responsible. This is something that will happen."

"How can you be so sure?" Aidan gazed up at her like someone who really wanted absolution.

"Because from the day I met you I've never questioned your commitment to country and to seeing a job through."

Aidan smiled, but she didn't seem happy. "You would know since I was such an idiot."

"Sweetheart, I'm with you because I believe with my whole heart you know exactly what commitment is, and that your commitment to me is the one thing that'll be the solid foundation I can count on. We're going to win, and then we're going to enjoy the life we build together."

"I love you, and I'm so glad you're here."

"I love you too, and I'm going cross-eyed reading all that crazy shit Chandler wrote and kept in those files, but it's got to be there."

"What?"

"Every leader, and he considers himself that, has that last doomsday plan. The Hail Mary pass that'll turn even the hopeless cause around so he can claim victory." She moved them over to the bed and lay down to press up against Aidan's back. "He had to realize somewhere deep that all this was a hopeless cause, because the greatest country in the world won't be so easily taken. There's always that underbelly of misfits in any situation, though, and he's tapped into it more successfully than anyone in history."

"Which means he loses, but he leaves his mark on history?" Aidan took her hand and held it to her chest.

"Maybe," she said, and thought of Liskow. "This sub captain, Liskow, he needs the launch codes before he can fire, right?"

"Yes. We don't have any on board, but that's the usual procedure."

"Is there a way to override the system?" This was starting to make sense.

"I'm not sure, but it can't be easy. No one wants to give that kind of power to one guy, as a preventative." Aidan turned to face her. "What are you thinking?"

"Liskow isn't going to join Chandler in this attack—he's giving him the means *to* attack."

"What does that mean?" Aidan rubbed her back when she sat up with a grunt.

"Chandler has the capacity to fire, but Liskow has the hardware he needs to do that."

"Liskow was recruited to hand over his warheads?"

"Makes sense, doesn't it?" She got up and headed back to the conference room.

"What are you looking for?"

"The one spot where our needles will surface."

CHAPTER TWENTY-NINE

S he's taking the bait, sir, but it didn't lead to where we thought," Walby told Rooster, Carl, Preston, Jonas, and the ships headed back from Korea. Aidan called it in after they'd quickly changed, and Berkley explained her thoughts.

"Who'd she contact?" Rooster asked about Rachel Chandler.

Walby explained how he and Erin had watched and listened as Rachel slowly charmed the nurse, or thought she had, since the young woman wearing a wire actually was part of Walby's team. She'd gone along with Rachel's plan to stay in the infirmary and helped her get messages out. But none of those short conversations had been to her father or their missing sub captain.

"It was a grunt at Gromwell Enterprises," Walby said, and Rooster slammed his hand down as if he'd had enough.

"The defense contractors?" Aidan asked.

"That's it, but the guy she spoke to is nobody," Walby said.

"A nobody who hasn't contacted anyone above him," Jonas said. "We've had him under surveillance, and he works, then goes home. No strange phone calls or emails."

"Remember Erica Gibson," Berkley said. "Simplicity is the ultimate sophistication," she said, and Wiley nodded.

"Is that a Sun Tzu?" Carl asked.

"Actually, Leonardo da Vinci said it, sir, but that's what Gibson and her buddy Hattie Skinner did to get David Morris's messages to his father Adam in the Pentagon," Berkley said.

"Morse code?" Jonas asked. "Seriously?"

"You need to search his home and his office for anything that can transmit that's not a phone or computer," Aidan said. "But we might not need the messages."

"We look for any holdings Gromwell has on the East Coast," Rooster said. "The CEO, Tom Bristol, wasn't on Chandler's list."

"Chandler held some back as security, even from his own people," Walby said. "It's a common practice in situations like this. He needs a back door for certain things and can't risk exposing them. If Bristol is taken down, it locks the door that's vital to some part of his plan."

"Gromwell has two facilities in the East, but neither is on the coast," Erin said.

"It's there," Aidan said. "You just have to find it."

"It can't be a manufacturing facility," Preston said. "Not everyone on their payroll will be in favor of whatever their plan is, and that would've been too much exposure."

"This time we search from the top down," Jonas said. "Tom Bristol, Gromwell's CEO, did business with Butler's administration, and they still have viable government contracts."

"I'm on it, sir," Erin said, and Walby agreed to help her.

"If Aidan's calculations are accurate, we've got maybe three days," Berkley said. "Work fast." After the conference call was over, they looked at each other, and she opened the computer again and searched for specific US sites.

"I'll be back early with the rest of the guys," Wiley said as she waved over her shoulder before leaving.

"I don't remember any one place in any of those files, but Chandler reminds me a lot of Hitler."

"How so?" Aidan stood and took her hair out of its short ponytail.

"He writes everything down. The Germans were notoriously good record keepers, and those records helped convict some folks after the war." She stood up and put her arms around Aidan, so she could kiss her. "Do you think there's anything in the *Art of War* about having an orgasm as a way to clear and reboot your brain?"

Aidan laughed but didn't stop her wandering hands. "I believe so, and if it didn't make the cut, someone should add it."

They stripped, and Aidan insisted on straddling her hips and doing all the work, as she called it, as a way of not straining her wound. She felt the sensation of her fingers going in and out of Aidan, and it did make her forget anything but that. She had a long list of reasons why she loved Aidan, but seeing her move against her and knowing she was this wet for her made her let go and enjoy the moment.

Unfortunately, the moment was like a nanosecond, and it made Aidan laugh. "Sorry about that, but it seems like forever since you touched me, and I had zero control."

"I'd say I was disappointed, but you look so gorgeous I don't think I will."

"Let's see how disciplined you are, Cletus." Aidan laid her back and kissed down her body. "Try not to lift your hips," she ordered her. "I don't want to have to explain to Nurse Flirty why you popped something."

"Come on, baby. She's just being nice."

"For a naval aviator you're completely blind and clueless sometimes." Aidan kissed her clit softly, which made her want to forget about the whole hip thing. "That's good for me though."

She would've commented, but having Aidan suck her in hard and fast made her close her eyes and concentrate on not screaming or moaning too loud. Embarrassingly, she came even faster than Aidan had, and she had to laugh as well. "You'd think we were sixteen and clueless."

"You, clueless?" Aidan moved next to her and kissed her on the lips.

"No way. I just think we needed to let a little steam out of the pot."

"Now that I feel boneless, let's get some sleep, and we'll start over early." Aidan kissed her again and moved so her butt was pressed against her groin. "I told you pajamas were a bad idea," she said as she slid her hand from Aidan's hip to between her breasts.

"I should listen to you more often," Aidan said, moving closer.

They slept for six uninterrupted hours, and Berkley sat with a cup of coffee staring unfocused at the papers spread all over the table. Aidan had left to check on their status and the weather ahead, giving her some quiet time alone. She finally shook her head and went back to the laptop and the files Robyn Chandler had so meticulously put together. Most of it consisted of Chandler's delusional writings and his visions of what his government would be.

The list of names and who was missing from it had to be where they'd find the answer. Her gut told her that was a fact.

"Good morning, Captain," Erin said after Berkley had requested a link to her. "What can I do for you?"

"Call me Cletus or Berkley, please," she said as she combed back the hair that had fallen on her forehead. "Did you or your people separate the list between enlisted and civilian personnel?"

"We did about ninety percent of it, but FBI Director Chapman didn't grant access to the bureau at large, which is why we haven't finished."

"Anything interesting on the civilian side so far?"

"Interesting how? I find the whole thing really weird, but maybe it's just me," Erin said as she raised a diet-Coke can.

"You're right about that, but someone in your position, in mine, or someone who works for or runs Gromwell makes sense," she said, and Erin nodded.

"You want the person who doesn't make sense."

"I need that misfit list, but culled from the whole group. What you need to do is tell whoever's doing the work to speed it up."

"I think I could provide some incentive," Erin said, typing something into her laptop.

"If they live in DC, the only incentive they should concentrate on is not being caught in a major nuclear fallout. That'd be a real downer for any future plans with the bureau or otherwise."

"We received this transmission, sir." A crewman handed a handwritten note to Dick. "We deciphered it after checking a lesser-used channel. It was coming through in a constant stream of Morse code."

I know you won't let us down and won't forget us. We are your future, even though we are at an end. We've left you all you need on the seashore. Our greatest ally is waiting for your orders and to fulfill your destiny.

The note was somehow from Rachel and cryptic enough not to give away anything. She and Jeffery were still alive, and waiting for him, but more important, whatever he needed to finish the job was located in the one spot that had been his sanctuary. It was a mystery how she'd managed to send the message, but it did show him that of all his children, Rachel was the most cunning and most like him.

"Do you want me to send a reply?"

"No. We can't risk that," he said, folding the sheet and placing it in his breast pocket. "In a few days, everyone will know my reply, Rachel," Dick said, waving the man away. "And I mean everyone."

"Are you kidding?" FBI Director Jonas Chapman asked Erin when she told him what they'd found. Rachel was still being monitored by Walby, which freed her up to return to Washington.

"I'd have stayed back at Gitmo if I had any doubts. We would've found this eventually, but Cletus thinks differently than most, and her comment about simplicity made me confident this is the main misfit we should be looking at." She placed her finger on the top of the page she handed him and tapped the name. "If I'm wrong, neither of us will be alive for you to reprimand me."

"Let's go, and you can explain the use of the word misfit along the way."

"It was Berkley's word, not mine, but it fits. Did Director Newton's agents have any more insight on this?"

"He's pissed that we've shut him out," Jonas said shaking his head. "His word not mine, so he's supposedly following some leads that came from the CIA's operations in South Korea. I have no idea what they are, since he's punishing me for keeping him out of the loop."

The Situation Room was full when they arrived, and President Michaels gave them the floor after they were securely locked in. "Go ahead, Agent Mosley," Jonas said.

"Good afternoon, Madam President, and everyone," she said, glancing at the screen and noticing Cletus smiling at her. "Captain Levine and I discussed different strategies, which led our agents to one name on the list that made the most sense when it came to narrowing our search for a location."

"Is it someone at Gromwell?" Olivia asked.

"In a roundabout way, yes, it is," Erin said, placing the picture Graham Boyd used for his real estate business's advertising on the screen. He was an older man with red/orange hair that in no way was natural, and a blue tie with a knot popular in the sixties. "Captain Levine asked me to find the one person who didn't fit on Chandler's roster, the one who would in no way seem to contribute to the war Chandler wants."

"And it's this guy?" Rooster asked. "If it's for the most strangely dressed, he's our man," he said, and everyone laughed after obviously noticing the two-toned shirt collar that came down into long points well past his collarbone.

"Until three years ago, Mr. Boyd was a real-estate agent who was barely scraping by, which might've had something to do with his choice of clothing, but now he's a multimillion-dollar seller. That streak started with the sale of this house," Erin changed the picture to a large, beautiful beach home, "to Jacklyn Whitestone."

"It's a regular beach house. Big but regular in the scheme of these things," Vice-President Drew Orr said, sounding confused.

"I'm sure Agent Mosley isn't leading us down a path of wasted time, sir," Aidan said.

"This was the first beach house Mrs. Whitestone purchased on Cape Hatteras, North Carolina. Since that time, she had Mr. Boyd persuade six of her neighbors—three on each side—to sell. Once those sales went through, Mrs. Whitestone closed the beach along that stretch and made it private."

"Is Whitestone by chance a friend of Dick Chandler?" Rooster asked as Erin clicked through all the pictures.

"I doubt she knows him or anyone else, since she's ninety-six and living in a home that specializes in Alzheimer's patients. She's been there for seven years after her health deteriorated following the death of her *second* husband, and she hasn't spoken for five of those seven years."

Berkley seemed to understand as she leaned in. "Who was her first husband?"

"Tom Bristol, Sr," Erin said, putting up an old picture of two young men. "Best friend and past business associate of Richard D. Chandler. Tom Bristol, Jr, as we all know, is the current CEO of Gromwell and also a good friend of Dick."

"We need satellite photos of that area," Rooster said.

"We do, but I found this article in the local paper. The neighbors beyond the private beach complained, then sued over this issue." Erin's last photo was a grainy newspaper clipping of the offshore boat pier Mrs. Whitestone commissioned after the sales were final. The massive structure looked extremely out of place.

"How far are you, Aidan?" Drew asked.

"We're crossing the Georgia coast now, which is near enough for our planes."

"Baylor, we need your men on the ground, and once we verify that Jacqueline Whitestone doesn't own a thousand-foot yacht, we clear this stretch of beach," Olivia said. "If her purchases somehow include Russian subs to attract an American one with its nuclear weapons, don't hesitate to do what you do best, Cletus. That's about the only theory that makes that huge pier and boathouse plausible."

"Yes, ma'am." Berkley stood up and saluted, as did everyone in the conference room with her.

"Are you up to it? I realize you're hurt."

"Madam President, finishing this job for you will be my honor," Berkley said, and no one contradicted her. "Chandler is about to learn a woman's place is not the kitchen, the bedroom, or under his heel."

CHAPTER THIRTY

Baylor had his guys swim up to the beach at one of the houses not owned by Whitestone after they'd jumped from the helicopter that'd brought them three hundred yards offshore. If anyone was home, they were asleep since the house was dark, luckily making the beach dark as well. Whoever was using the main house at the center, they were important or valued their privacy enough to need a lot of guards, who were scattered throughout the six properties. The sliver of a moon provided a bit too much light for Baylor and what his guys had to do, but the cloud cover was helping.

"Do you think anyone's inside?" Tito asked as they lay in the dunes. There were more men in North Korea, but these guys appeared to not want to take chances, and their positioning meant they had some military background.

"We need to find out, but there's way too many pit bulls in the yard," he said as he glanced at the house that was abandoned because of beach erosion. The place was leaning into the Atlantic, had no windows, and its stilts stood in at least two feet of water. Whoever owned it had abandoned it years before.

Wiley had come along as their guardian angel and made her way up there, but she'd been quieter than usual after Cletus found a file that had a black dragon with its wings spread on the outside. None of them had read it, but Cletus told Baylor to give Wiley the opportunity to put a bullet in Chandler's head if it came to that, since she deserved that right more than anyone out there.

"Do you want to thin the herd?" Tito asked.

"See if you and KO can grab one of these muscle necks, and let's find out who we're dealing with. The front is your best bet. The majority seem to be back here, like they're waiting on something." They all flattened themselves to the ground when the sweeping spotlights started. "Fuck, it might be showtime. Eyes open, guys. This might be the opening act."

"Everyone hold," Tito said so they would pass the message along.

"Do you see any opening to move closer?" Baylor asked as he made another sweep with the night-vision binoculars. "We need to get in there and see who's in the house before we call in Captain America and she blows this place to shit."

They were on radio silence, but the activity was definitely picking up, so they would have to start communicating. "The fence line has a break fifty yards from here," Tito said. "Right over there."

"When the sweep light moves to the left again, we go." The strong beams paused on the water, and Baylor stopped to determine exactly what they were trying to see. He didn't have time to notice anything, since the lights went out—all of them. The place suddenly appeared as if it'd been sucked into a black hole.

The strange pier-boathouse facility offshore was large and extremely out of place, but the sudden sound of something breaking the water reached the shore. "Son of a bitch," Tito said softly, but the phrase was appropriate. It wasn't every day you saw a Los Angeles-class fast-attack nuclear sub surface off the North Carolina border in a vacation spot.

"Do you have a clear view?" Baylor asked Wiley, taking the chance to use the radio.

"The hatch opened, and a few people climbed out. They're on a crew boat headed to the beach."

"We need to get closer and take a look in the house at the center," he said, not really worried about Wiley and what she'd read in that file. She wasn't prone to emotional, murderous outbursts that would compromise her fellow team members.

"Get ready to move," Wiley said, and Baylor heard the boat motor, the sound seeming to hold the guards' attention. "Go."

Half the team slipped through the cut in the fence, and the other half raced to the front. Wiley watched them go and made sure no bad surprises would cost them a man. It was tempting to look back at the boat to see who was coming ashore and start picking them off one by one, but she stayed focused on Baylor and the guys.

The file Cletus had found contained information about the people responsible for driving her away from Aubrey in order to keep her safe. Their determination to kill her had cost her so many years with Aubrey and all those years with their daughter. Granted, she and Tanith had a special bond that grew stronger every day, but what would it have been like to be there the day she was born, the day she took her first step, taught her to ride a bike? It was an endless list, and nothing she could do would turn back the clock, thanks to one man.

Dick Chandler had cut a deal with the Columbian cartel, and it had cost her not only the time with her family, but it'd also forfeited the lives of every one of the team members she'd worked with during that last mission that had changed her life. Worst, Chandler had used the murder of all those innocent people to prove his point about women in combat. In his pea-sized brain, she was too good at her job, and she had to die for it.

Karma was a bitch, as the old saying went, and now all she wanted was to pay him back with a bullet to the center of his forehead.

At least she now had the targets she needed to eliminate any threat to her future. She wanted her family to have a happy life, never having to look over their shoulder in fear of something or someone she hadn't eliminated because she'd had no clue where to begin looking. After all this was done, she'd work on her list with or without permission from General Greenwald or the military.

Tonight, though, Berkley had promised that one shot, if the opportunity presented itself, and she was grateful her old friend understood what losing your love meant and how much it hurt.

"Everyone stop moving," Baylor said, and Wiley aimed right at Baylor. No guards stood around him or his companions, so she waited. "Shit, there's like a million trip wires out here. One wrong move and they can serve us all on a chopped salad."

"They rigged land mines with all the civilians around?" Wiley asked.

"These guys must be here all the time to keep everyone not affiliated with them clear, because all this shit's been here a while." Baylor backed away through the same hole in the fence. "We're going to have to get some of the neighbors out of here. If we blow this spot and they've added their own hardware, some of the other houses will be collateral damage."

"We evacuate the wrong people, and we lose this asshole again," Wiley said. "Let's call the boss."

"We hold for now." Baylor moved back to the dunes with his men. The boat had hit the beach, where a group of men jumped ashore, and Wiley took her eyes off her team to see who they were. "US Navy uniforms," Baylor said. "This must be our missing Captain Liskow."

"Hold your position. If we see the removal of warheads or Chandler's vessels, we'll have to up our timeline for the ultimate home makeover," Wiley said, since she saw no sign of Chandler now.

"Cover us," Baylor said as he belly-crawled to the edge of the dunes. "We need some men back out by that pier to put a leash on all these assholes."

"Make sure you're clear. If you get blown up, I'll never be able to eat another chopped salad again."

"Do you eat a lot of it?" Baylor asked and laughed.

"No, but I'll never get to develop a taste for it if you become chum, so get your ass out fast. Fireworks are always more enjoyable from a distance."

"Trust me. I want to finish my popcorn so I can sit back and enjoy the show."

One guard started walking to the beach and raised his hand to radio in but fell when Wiley took him out. It appeared to be Tito who dragged him into the water with them. The men who'd gotten off the boat started up to the largest house in the center, and the guards returned to their patrols.

"Zookeeper." She made a call, knowing it'd take Baylor some time to get back to the pier in the high surf.

"Go ahead," Aidan said.

"We have eyes on our missing sub, but we're in a holding pattern. Stand by until we see the missing party members from the land of vodka and caviar." She noticed the lights in the neighbor's house come on and a man walk out the back door. "Hold, Zookeeper."

The man wore fatigue pants and boots, and when she noticed the rifle in his right hand, she realized the area contained more than land mines. "Goose," she said and aimed at the overweight Rambo in the tight black T-shirt and camouflage pants. "Hold your position. You have an armed neighbor coming up to you. The next house on the beach has to be part of this group."

The guy placed his rifle against his shoulder but didn't aim at Goose and the guys around him. He seated the weapon and aimed toward the abandoned house where Wiley was positioned. She didn't wait and shot through his scope, sending the bullet right through his head and out the back of it.

"Cleanup on aisle five. Clear the deck," she said, and Goose and his guys scooted as fast as they could on their abdomens. They dragged the guy back inside and closed the door behind them.

"You were right," Goose said. "This place is full of bunks on the first floor and enough New Horizon's uniforms to clothe another battalion. He had motion sensors in the dunes and in that house you're in. I wonder why that guy didn't call his buddies?"

"He's probably seen one too many action movies and thought he'd play the hero. Guess he didn't learn the lesson about there being no *I* in the word team. Bring backup and clear the second floor."

A horn-type sound went off from somewhere offshore, and she moved to take a look. "Wiley, we have two more vessels," Baylor said softly.

"Clear out. You need to beat Cletus here."

"Call in the big dog," Baylor said. "We're swimming back."

"Zookeeper, we're a go. Make it fast, and follow the guideposts the guys laid out for you."

"Make sure you stay clear of the work area," Aidan said.

"Yes, ma'am, and tell our friend not to spare any hardware."

The nurse had put a tight bandage on Berkley's wound for more mobility and to help with the pain. She wasn't cleared for duty, but Aidan wasn't going to keep her out of the cockpit. They'd spoken before the SEALs and Wiley had left, and Berkley had nodded when Aidan told her it was time to finish what they'd started together. Aidan wanted her to have a part in this since Berkley had gladly followed her on the mission that had kicked off this crazy year. It was only fair for her to be there at its conclusion.

"The targets are in sight and painted. Don't hesitate, and don't forget your way home," Aidan said as a deck crew locked them into the jet.

"Let's do this for President Michaels and President Khalid," she said as the jet powered on. The bombs the crew had put under her wings had Peter and Eva's names on them as a way to honor the late president and his wife.

She took a breath before she punched it forward and got them airborne, wanting to remember every minute of this night. This wasn't about revenge but about justice. Finishing this would hopefully make her father and her future father-in-law proud of the job she and Aidan had done during their tenure of service.

"Let's give the neighbors something to talk about, people," Berkley said as she leveled off.

They headed toward the coast with Vader, Killer, and Poncho right behind her. "Black Dragon, you and the team clear?"

"We'll be out," Wiley said.

"Tiger One?" Berkley said.

"We're out and close to the beach. Don't hesitate," Baylor said, and Berkley figured she'd be there in five minutes.

"See you in a bit."

"Roger that," Wiley said, and the gunfire started from the house Goose had entered. "Goose?" She radioed him but kept her attention on the closest guards. They were looking in that direction as well. "Try to get one of their radios."

The first guy to pick up the small walkie-talkie as three of his friends started to run toward the house was the one she started with. They had to keep someone from warning Chandler. She thought about how long this asshole had in a way held them hostage, and Cletus was right. It had been way too long, so letting him get away wasn't in her plans.

She took aim and killed the guards now sprinting toward the house that would've made the seventh in the stretch of beach Chandler controlled. The mistake on the investigators' part could've cost them dearly, but they'd have time enough later to discuss every aspect of this mission.

In the rush to help his comrades, one of Chandler's men ran through the yard and stepped on a land mine. That noise almost made Wiley miss the sound of the boat out in the water.

"Wiley," Baylor said.

"Are you clear of the water?" The boat had turned back to the subs when the land mine went off. Wiley adjusted the scope and aimed for the large motor. She wanted to stop them while they were closer to the shore than their getaway vehicle.

"Yes," Baylor said, and Wiley pulled the trigger. The engine stopped dead about fifty yards from the beach.

Another couple of men pushed the first boat she'd seen from the beach and started the engine, as if going out to rescue whoever was in the disabled one. That wasn't going to happen, and she shot through that engine as well. If it was Chandler, he was going to have to crawl to the shore and beg for his life in order to see the morning.

"We're going in to give Goose a hand," Baylor said.

She kept staring at the first boat she'd shot at but couldn't really make out the faces of those aboard. Chandler's death had to be a certainty, so she kept trying to focus. Two people on the first boat started paddling, trying to reach the subs, and she was about to pull the trigger again when she heard the sound of a jet, so she waited.

"Let's see if your rowing skills can beat Cletus to that sub."

"Junior, do we have our targets in sight?" Berkley said as she flew five thousand feet over the water. When the clouds cleared she could see how rough the water was, which would slow the *Jefferson*'s trip back to port.

"We'll be in range in twenty miles. We're locked into the beacons Baylor's team painted," Junior said. "And the sky is clear. No bogeys around to slow us from our plans."

"The subs gave us a problem last time," she said, turning more toward the coast. "Keep your eyes open for anything they shoot at us."

"You got it." Junior started their countdown, and she hoped that Baylor's guys really were clear of the water. "Ready," Junior said and waited a beat, "fire."

The night sky lit up when their first target was hit. Another blast, from Vader, followed, while Killer and Poncho had their backs in case they had unexpected company. She just needed to circle and fire again, and she smiled because the next shot would cut off Chandler's escape route. "You ready, Junior?"

"Three, two, one—fire," Junior said, and she fired the next missile. "Shit."

"We can't have missed," she said, starting to climb.

"You didn't, but the last sub had a chance to fire back," Junior said, talking fast. "Ten o'clock, they got a missile away."

"Cletus, you down another plane, you're going to get fired, or they'll dock your pay until you're two thousand years old," Vader said. "You need to dive, then come back up."

"If you fire on me, make sure you hit the missile," she said when she dove as low as she could and still recover.

She pulled back on the throttle and went straight up. The sense of self-control she usually felt in the cockpit was gone. If her men missed, she doubted she would have time to recover and eject. The explosions made her bank to the left to avoid the flying shrapnel.

"Thanks, guys," she said as she tried to exhale all her tension.

"The beer's on you, Cletus," Vader said.

"No problem. I could use one myself." She flew back over the area, and saw that the pier, along with all three subs, was still on fire. "Wiley, everything okay?"

"Great. Just waiting for my ship to come in."

"I'm in position," Tito said.

It didn't take long for the boat Wiley figured held Chandler to finally make it to the beach. The first two men off held automatic weapons and started firing as soon as their feet hit the sand. Wiley guessed Tito had killed the first one when he went down, and she had a clear shot at the second guy. Quiet returned, since Baylor had gotten most of the guards under control.

"You want me to check the boat?" Tito asked.

"No. Put a line of bullets across the hull, but aim low."

Tito followed orders again, and two grenades came flying out when he finished firing. They landed short of Tito's position, but Wiley didn't want to take a chance their aim would get better. She reloaded and aimed toward the boat where she figured someone would be crouched. This wasn't how she wanted to put a bullet into Chandler, but she'd take what she could get. In reality not many people in her career needed killing, but Chandler was the exception to every rule she could think of.

A yell broke the night, and it sounded like a man who made it. "Stop," the man screamed, and two hands came over the edge. "Don't shoot."

The top of a head appeared, and she recognized the white, wispy hair and jowly face. "Tito, get ready, and Baylor, move to the beach."

"Stand up with your hands behind your head," Tito said. "Move, or I'll finish the job."

Dick Chandler stood up, and another man from the second boat jumped into the water and ran over to help Dick down. Whoever the guy in the navy uniform was, he defined devoted convert from the way he stood in front of Chandler. The naval officer had a side arm, but he didn't make any move to grab it, so Wiley waited.

Chandler might have deserved a bullet to the head, but she refused to kill an unarmed man. "You shot my son—get him some help," Chandler said. Tito stood in the dunes with his weapon pointed at them, and Baylor walked down and moved across the beach. "Do you know who I am?" Dick said as if Baylor should fall at his feet and plead forgiveness for trying to stop him.

When Baylor reached the halfway mark between the dunes and the boat, Chandler yanked his protector's gun free and aimed at Baylor. It was Wiley's cue, and she pulled the trigger. If the revolution depended on Dick Chandler for its survival, the revolution was over.

"Zookeeper, this is Black Dragon," she said, taking pride in the code name. "The snake's head has been severed. We'll need backup, an explosives team for a field of land mines, and cleanup for all those damn subs. Some of the personnel has been terminated, but we'll need some bodies on the ground to help with the rest."

"Thank you. We're right off your position, and Captains Washington and Greer will be sending people in as well," Aidan said.

"Ma'am, you might want to block the road out to the mainland," Wiley said as she climbed down to the water. A lot of the homes now had their lights on, except for a couple that appeared empty. "The number of houses they own or at least have access to goes beyond the six previously mentioned. The team finished clearing out one, but we'll have to check the others."

"I'll get in touch with Command and let them take care of that."

"We'll hold our position then," Wiley said as Baylor walked toward her.

"Is the captain sending backup?" he asked as he removed his helmet and wiped his forehead.

"On their way, but we need to get into the main house. It's occupied, and I want to know who's inside. Believe me when I tell you about the dangers that can follow you home. It's a bitch."

"We've got it surrounded, and the guys are watching for anyone trying to leave by car," Baylor said as he moved to the dunes. "Who else do you think is in there?" He pointed to the boat.

"According to Dick, his son is wounded, but there was more than that," she said, glancing through her scope again but seeing nothing. In the distance they saw the multitude of helicopters headed their way, as well as boats. "Zookeeper, can you have one of our birds sit on the boat beached onshore as well as the other craft dead in the water? We need to see who's left on it before we approach."

"We've got you covered," someone who sounded a lot like Cletus said, and the Apache sat on the boat with their spotlight a few minutes later. When someone raised a weapon and aimed at it, Wiley shot through their hand. That's what prompted the rest of the men to stand and take the position of surrender.

Berkley was the first one out of the helicopter, followed by Aidan, and Wiley and Baylor left the dunes to meet them. Wiley smiled when Berkley shook her hand and slapped her on the back once they were close enough. "Thank you," Berkley said as she glanced at Chandler's body. "I'd drag his ass out to sea, but I don't want to poison the fish."

"Who's in the house?" Aidan pointed to the sprawling structure with a huge outdoor deck that faced the beach.

"I don't know, ma'am. We found land-mine trips on the northern section of that house." He pointed three houses over. "We were waiting for morning before we head up to the big house. Someone has to be up there since it was lit up like now, but the lights went out when the first sub surfaced," Baylor said.

"Where were the guards most concentrated?" Berkley asked.

"Here and the place next door," Wiley said, indicating the house on the left, which was smaller but no less impressive.

"The mines can't be on the main path then," Berkley said, walking to the naval officer who'd been in the boat with Chandler. His name tag said Liskow, so she motioned him forward with the help of Tito and his weapon. "Let's go for a walk up to the house," she said. "You'll be twenty feet in front of us, and if you make any stupid moves, my friend here's going to shoot you through both kneecaps. I'd kill you, but I wouldn't want to mess up your court-martial for you."

"Tell me the status of my men," Liskow said, turning his head to where the sub had been.

"You left them out there to die because you were planning to give a traitorous asshole a nuclear weapon. Hopefully some survived and are in the water, but every soul lost is on you." Berkley was pissed that this bastard had the gall to act like he cared about the people in his command. "Were they at least on the same page when it came to your love of Chandler?"

"I wasn't here for Chandler," Liskow said, taking a step toward her, and Berkley hit him so hard the blow knocked him backward on his ass.

"What, you ran out of gas and ended up next to two enemy subs? Did you show up here because your communications were down? Did you run across a reef that knocked off all your locator devices?" Berkley hit him again, and no one stepped up to stop her. "Get up and get moving, dumb ass. You're no different than Chandler and every other guy who followed him in betraying their country."

Liskow held his hands over his head as if expecting her to hit him again, but eventually he got up and started toward the house, trudging slowly up the sandy slope. When he reached the deck, the back door opened suddenly, and Liskow took off, making it through the opening before Tito or Wiley could get off a shot.

Berkley turned and tackled Aidan toward the dunes. "What are you—" Aidan stopped talking when Wiley fell right next to them and a barrage of gunfire erupted from the house.

"Keep your head down," Baylor said as his team fanned out.

KO threw three grenades in succession at the house, ripping holes in the outer wall, which showered them with bits of wood and glass. She pressed herself over Aidan and put her hands over her lover's face.

"Cletus, are you hurt?" Aidan asked when she winced hard enough that Aidan obviously noticed.

"I think I got a big splinter in my hip, but you keep your head down, or else your father will kick my ass." Aidan laughed, and Berkley raised her head when the shooting stopped.

"Stay here," Baylor said as his guys moved forward and fired as they went through the hole they'd made.

"What were you saying about finding new places to take a walk?" she asked Aidan as they moved to better cover in the dunes.

"I'm beginning to see you're a magnet for trouble," Aidan said and winked. "Now pay attention before both of us get shot. If that doesn't scare you, then remember when I had the flu and what a great patient I was." That made Berkley shiver, and Aidan hit her on the arm.

The silence stretched out, and Wiley went to the top of the dunes and set up as best she could. "Man, I hate sand unless I'm on vacation with a girlie drink and a beautiful woman," Wiley said.

"Don't we all, but save it for later. See anything?" she asked.

"Tito's by the entrance, but I don't see the others."

Berkley moved next to Wiley and peered toward the house as she radioed Baylor. "You okay?" Behind them more soldiers appeared on the beach as the boats arrived, and Wiley warned them about the explosive booby traps along the shore.

"Give us five more minutes," Baylor said. "We're clearing the rooms one by one." Baylor had just finished when some more shots were fired, and he didn't say anything for ten more minutes. "I'm sending Tito out to walk you all in, and you're not going to believe this," he said finally. Whatever it was, it didn't sound good.

They stood and followed Wiley, navigating around the holes in the deck that the grenades had ripped open. "I don't know who these guys are, but they put up a good fight," Tito said as he pointed to the dead guy next to an equally dead Liskow. "Baylor recognized this guy," he said to another man on the other side of the room with a missing arm. "He's a SEAL."

"Where are the stairs?" she asked, and Tito called over another guy to stand post to watch the beach side. They went up the stairs and into the room where Baylor was standing in the entrance.

When they reached the door and Berkley looked inside, her mouth dropped open like she was trying to find the words to explain what she was seeing. A few dead men were scattered around the room, and a woman who appeared vaguely familiar had a bullet wound in the center of her chest and a gun in her slack hand. Whoever she was, she hadn't died without a fight. "Who is that? I feel like I should know her."

"Isn't that the woman who works for Marcus Newton, the CIA director? A Joanna something," Aidan said as she stared at the dead woman.

"I guess we can ask him," she said when she noticed Newton wounded in the bathroom.

"He tried to shoot Goose when he broke the door down. If he tries to claim otherwise, I'm going to shoot him in the other leg," Baylor said.

"Now North Korea and the team waiting on us, as well as all our setbacks in the last year make sense," she said, and Aidan nodded.

"You think you've done a good thing tonight?" Newton yelled as he kept both hands on his leg. "This was our last chance to regain our standing in the world. Me and Chandler would've been unstoppable."

"Next time," she told Goose, "aim for the head."

"Yes, ma'am," Goose said with a smile.

"Baylor, I hate to ask, but does this place have a basement?" she asked, putting a hand on her healing wound. The dive into the dunes had ramped up the pain again.

"We've opened every door, but once we get all these people out of here, we'll start on the walls and closets."

"Let's head back and send in a report," Aidan said.

Newton started to sweat from what Berkley surmised was his wound, since the house was cool. "Tell that fraud Michaels there's plenty more like me," he shouted. "We won't stop until we take back what's ours."

"What's that?" Berkley asked, leaning close to him and looking him in the eye. "Are you going all the way back to before the Civil War, or do you have a specific date in mind?"

"You can make fun of me, but once Washington burns, they'll come running to us."

"Washington burns, huh?" She glanced back at Aidan, shaking her head in disbelief. "You did happen to notice what went down here tonight, right?"

"Captain Liskow can't be stopped," he said, his breathing becoming more rapid when she leaned on his leg.

"Liskow is dead in the kitchen, and his sub is on the bottom out there," she said, smiling. "This bitch made the shot."

"And this bitch took Chandler out," Wiley said, pointing to her own chest.

"No, you're lying. Our plan was perfect."

The medic that had arrived injected Newton with a sedative before he could continue.

"Make sure you check for anything he could use to end our misery before he stands trial," Berkley said.

"Yes, ma'am."

"We need to round up every single person who was working here, and we need to expand our search of the houses along the strip. Make sure Robyn Chandler gets back to the *Jefferson* under heavy guard," Aidan said. "No one gets away."

"We'll take charge of getting that done, Captain," Baylor said, then pointed at Berkley. "Take her with you, and have someone check to see why she's bleeding again."

"Cletus wants to keep the ship's nurse busy," Aidan said and laughed.

"Very funny. Get going, and we'll be back as soon as we contact Command," she said and placed her hand on Baylor's and Wiley's shoulders. "Great job, guys."

They walked outside, finding it now lit up with floodlights, and the closest helicopter started as they approached. It was over for the most part, but this time they weren't repeating the end of the last mission. They were staying aboard the *Jefferson* until Aidan docked it. It was her ship, her command, and Aidan had done enough to earn the right to see it through.

"You ready?" she asked, running for their ride with her head down.

"For what?" Aidan asked.

"We did what we promised, baby, so we're done. I hope you're ready for the picket fence and everything that comes with it," she said, glancing toward the beach houses as they lifted off. They'd put in so many hours to get here, and the conclusion was going to take some time to sink in. But the nightmare was definitely over, for them at least. "We have some sailing to do before then, and I want to see your parking skills."

"You're a romantic at heart, Cletus, and I love you for it," Aidan said right into her ear.

"Only with you, and that's because I love you more than life," she said softly, knowing she had a lifetime to say it over and over again.

CHAPTER THIRTY-ONE

The *Jefferson* sailed on after Rooster sent troops down to take over the cleanup job, and they'd been asked to anchor right off the coast close to the capital. Aidan looked out at the media crews that had been allowed on her ship and shook her head. This was way out of her norm, but President Michaels wanted the American people to know their lives would return to normal now that Chandler was dead and the folks who'd followed him were either dead or jailed. At least they'd invited her parents as well as Berkley's, and she was looking forward to celebrating with them later.

"*Jefferson*, this is *Air Force One*. Permission to land, ma'am," Berkley said, and she sounded happy. It'd been a week since that night on the beach, and Rooster had slowed their return until they could put all this together.

"Permission granted, Cletus."

Berkley came around and buzzed the bridge before she circled and landed on the deck. Once the engines were cut and the cockpit was open, Aidan had Devin call everyone to attention. The first person out of the plane was Berkley, and she helped the president down the stairs.

Olivia gave her speech from the podium below the bridge, and as with her eulogy for Peter, it was one of her most heartfelt. "In closing," Olivia said as they bobbed gently in the water, everyone appearing happy with the cloudless sky and their surroundings, "I'd like to thank every person who made this mission a success. We're all in your debt for giving us back our peace of mind and bringing to justice those working for Dick Chandler and his family."

Everyone stood and applauded, and she joined them. Hell, Dick Chandler was dead, Marcus Newton was keeping Rachel and Jeffery

Chandler company, and the feds were working through the complete list Chandler had amassed. Most of those people who'd been arrested were scattered around various federal facilities, the most dangerous going to Gitmo.

"Thank you for everything, ma'am," Aidan said as Berkley walked over to join her and President Michaels, "and for having faith in us to finish the job."

"Please, Aidan, it's me who should be thanking you and Cletus," Olivia said, taking their hands. "I know you plan to retire, but if you want, you both have a job with me." The White House photographer took a picture of the three of them first, then with their parents, promising to deliver framed copies.

"Thank you, ma'am," Berkley said, but shook her head. "We're not Washington material, but we'd love for you to join us for a visit if you get a chance to visit New Orleans."

"I'm coming sooner rather than later, I hope. After all, Preston promised me a good party, so don't worry. I wouldn't miss it."

EPILOGUE

A re you nervous?" Corbin asked Berkley a year later. After the ceremony on the *Jefferson*, she and Aidan had spent a month in Washington testifying before Congress about the details of their mission and giving detailed accounts of the agents Chandler had working for him within the government. They'd also testified against Marcus Newton, who, Jonas Chapman and the FBI had discovered before the beginning of Newton's trial, had helped Chandler steal millions from the Pentagon and set up in North Korea.

Now Newton had joined Rachel and Jeffery Chandler on death row, and all three had declined the right to appeal. That would hasten the end of their part in all this, so soon the major players in this strange assault on their democracy would be history. Once that was done and they'd answered all the questions everyone had, they'd reached a mutual agreement and returned to sea. It had been a year of enjoying Aidan's commission as the captain of the *Jefferson* and Berkley's time as her flight leader.

"I'll be retired Monday, and I'm ready for the rest of my life. That's going to be smooth sailing because of the girl," she told Corbin as she finished buttoning the jacket of her dress uniform. Aidan's retirement had gone through the Monday before, and she'd asked Berkley to delay hers, so she could wear the uniform today. Aidan loved seeing her in her dress whites.

"The girl is happy, and I'm counting on you to keep it that way," Preston said, trying to sound menacing.

"I'm going to try my best, sir," she said, turning away from the mirror and holding her hands out. "How do I look?"

"Like I should get to my kid since this will be my last chance to talk to her for the rest of the night. When she sees you, I'll be cast aside,"

Preston said as he opened his arms and hugged her. "Thank you for loving her."

"It's the easiest thing I've ever done in my life, Pop."

She took some pictures with her parents and family before heading to the canopy her grandfather had built. Religion hadn't really been a huge part of her or Aidan's lives, but they wanted to make her grandparents happy. And to her grandparents' credit, they'd transformed the yard of their lake house into a beautiful wedding venue now surrounded by the Secret Service, since Olivia Michaels and Drew Orr and their families were in the congregation keeping their promises to attend.

The music started, and her sisters, at Aidan's insistence, served as her attendants and her six nieces as flower girls in the type of ceremony Aidan had wanted. Berkley would've been happy with a barbecue and beer, but their mothers, her sisters, and her grandmother, Bubbe, had quickly overruled her with a lot of questions about her sanity for suggesting such a thing. Her own father, Preston, and Papa had laughed and taken her outside for marriage lessons.

Now she had to admit this was beautiful and a great way to start her lifetime commitment to Aidan. On her side she'd asked Baylor and Harvey to stand up for her, and Wiley, who'd arrived with Aubrey and their two girls, had agreed to serve as her best woman. The rest of their most trusted team were standing with her as well, but they'd teased her about their readiness to celebrate.

The two guests whose presence she was the happiest about were Jin Umeko and Yong Nam. Granted, Yong had a distance to go before she put the ordeal after Jin joined the Americans behind her, but with Jin's help, they had a chance at a life together somewhere they didn't have to fear the consequences of their relationship. For now, they were living in New Orleans and working as translators for an international company. She and Aidan, as well as Wiley and Aubrey, were doing their best to make them feel at home.

She stood with the rabbi, gazing at the house, and sucked in a breath when Aidan stepped out in a white sheath dress that looked spectacular on her. "Breathe and unlock your knees, or we'll have to pick you up off the ground. You do that, and Baylor will run off with the bride," Wiley said.

Preston appeared like the proud father he was, but she couldn't take her eyes off Aidan. Here was the woman who'd grabbed her attention so many years before, and no matter how long she lived, she'd never lose that. She watched Preston kiss Aidan and accepted another hug from him before she took Aidan's hand. "You are so beautiful," she whispered as they faced the rabbi.

The ceremony seemed to fly by, then she faced Aidan and held a ring to her finger. "The day we met, I was happily flying through blue skies until someone shot me down and stole my heart. I didn't know the true meaning of happiness then. You taught me that, and loving you is God's blessing that will guarantee many more days of blue skies. When the storms come, and we have to sail through stormy seas, I'll never fear because I'll have you by my side, holding and loving me. No matter what comes, I'm happy that the adventure of my life will revolve around you." Aidan squeezed her fingers, and Berkley's eyes misted. Whatever pain she had gone through when they parted was almost worth it, because now she couldn't imagine her life without Aidan in it. "I promise before God and our families to love you, honor you, and protect you for all the days of my life," she said as she slipped the ring on Aidan's finger.

"The day we met, I wondered what it would be like to be at the center of your attention, and you surpassed what I found to be my very limited imagination. I love you because you're courageous, my knight in dress whites who has made my life fun, and the one who taught me that breaking a few rules isn't such a bad thing," Aiden said, making Berkley widen her smile. "You make me laugh and help me see the beauty in the world, and you love my parents, which, in Triton's opinion, makes you close to perfect." When Aidan said that, she and everyone else laughed. "From that first day, I knew there'd never be anyone else who could measure up, and I'm so lucky you're mine."

Aidan held her hand in both of hers and placed the gold band on the tip of her ring finger. "I promise before God and our families to love you, honor you, and protect you all the days of my life." The ring slipped into place, and Aidan kissed it.

She stared into Aidan's eyes for the rest of the ceremony until it was time to stomp on the traditional glass, which she did enthusiastically, since it signaled she could finally kiss her girl. That was the part she'd always remember, but getting to dance with her wasn't bad either.

"We don't dance enough," Aidan said as a few strands of her hair fell out of the twist it was in.

"Easily remedied," she said, backing up to admire Aidan. "Have I mentioned how gorgeous you are?"

"Several times, and you're sweet. I hope you didn't mind that I skipped the uniform. It wasn't what I had in mind for when I got married. You, though, look good enough to eat."

"Behave, and you're kidding, right?" She put her hands on Aidan's hips and tugged her closer. "This is our day, and you're absolutely beautiful out of the uniform. Granted, you were really sexy in it, which makes me think I'm so lucky I never got tossed out on my ass for ogling you for all those years."

"Enjoy it while you can, Cletus."

"What's that supposed to mean?" She lowered her head to whisper in Aidan's ear. "You can wear anything you want from now on, as long as I get to take it off you every night, most afternoons, or whenever I'm lucky enough to get you alone. That seems unlikely now that your parents live next door to us, but I'm setting up visiting hours pretty soon."

"Triton *is* kind of a downer when it comes to your amorous streaks," Aidan said and laughed.

"Never mind about the son of Poseidon and his talent for bad timing. Tell me what you meant by enjoying it while I can. Then we can get back to talking about me getting you naked."

"I'm counting on that, but this dress unfortunately won't be an option in about three months."

Aidan didn't say anything else and left the comment hanging. "Three months?" she asked, her feet stopping, and they stood motionless in the center of the dance floor. "It worked?"

They'd started trying two months prior, but the doctors had warned them to be patient since sometimes it took more than a few tries. "You work fast, baby. If anything, our first date should confirm that for you."

"What happened on your first date?" Preston asked, his eyes narrowed as he and Mary Beth danced closer to them.

"Chinese food," they said together, but Berkley tightened her hold on Aidan and lifted her off the ground.

"This is the best day of my life so far," she said loudly, causing people to raise their glasses in their direction.

"Hang on, baby. There's so many more to come."

The End

About the Author

Ali Vali is the author of the long-running Cain Casey "Devil" series, the Genesis Clan "Forces" series, and the "Call" series including Lambda Literary Award finalist *Calling the Dead* and the latest release, *Answering the Call.* Ali also has a short story in the new anthology *Escape to Pleasure.*

Originally from Cuba, Ali has retained much of her family's traditions and language and uses them frequently in her stories. Having her father read her stories and poetry before bed every night as a child infused her with a love of reading, which she carries till today. Ali currently lives outside New Orleans, Louisiana, and she has discovered that living in Louisiana provides plenty of material to draw from in creating her novels and short stories.

Books Available from Bold Strokes Books

A Bird of Sorrow by Shea Godfrey. As Darrius and her lover, Princess Jessa, gather their strength for the coming war, a mysterious spell will reveal the truth of an ancient love. (978-1-63555-009-2)

All the Worlds Between Us by Morgan Lee Miller. High school senior Quinn Hughes discovers that a broken friendship is actually a door propped open for an unexpected romance. (978-1-63555-457-1)

An Intimate Deception by CJ Birch. Flynn County Sheriff Elle Ashley has spent her adult life atoning for her wild youth, but when she finds her ex, Jessie, murdered two weeks before the small town's biggest social event, she comes face-to-face with her past and all her well-kept secrets. (978-1-63555-417-5)

Cash and the Sorority Girl by Ashley Bartlett. Cash Braddock doesn't want to deal with morality, drugs, or people. Unfortunately, she's going to have to. (978-1-63555-310-9)

Counting for Thunder by Phillip Irwin Cooper. A struggling actor returns to the Deep South to manage a family crisis, finds love, and ultimately his own voice as his mother is regaining hers for possibly the last time. (978-1-63555-450-2)

Falling by Kris Bryant. Falling in love isn't part of the plan, but will Shaylie Beck put her heart first and stick around, or tell the damaging truth? (978-1-63555-373-4)

Secrets in a Small Town by Nicole Stiling. Deputy Chief Mackenzie Blake has one mission: find the person harassing Savannah Castillo and her daughter before they cause real harm. (978-1-63555-436-6)

Stormy Seas by Ali Vali. The high-octane follow-up to the best-selling action-romance, *Blue Skies*. (978-1-63555-299-7)

The Road to Madison by Elle Spencer. Can two women who fell in love as girls overcome the hurt caused by the father who tore them apart? (978-1-63555-421-2)

Dangerous Curves by Larkin Rose. When love waits at the finish line, dangerous curves are a risk worth taking. (978-1-63555-353-6)

Love to the Rescue by Radclyffe. Can two people who share a past really be strangers? (978-1-62639-973-0)

Love's Portrait by Anna Larner. When museum curator Molly Goode and benefactor Georgina Wright uncover a portrait's secret, public and private truths are exposed, and their deepening love hangs in the balance. (978-1-63555-057-3)

Model Behavior by MJ Williamz. Can one woman's instability shatter a new couple's dreams of happiness? (978-1-63555-379-6)

Pretending in Paradise by M. Ullrich. When travelwisdom.com assigns PR specialist Caroline Beckett and travel blogger Emma Morgan to cover a hot new couples retreat, they're forced to fake a relationship to secure a reservation. (978-1-63555-399-4)

Recipe for Love by Aurora Rey. Hannah Little doesn't have much use for fancy chefs or fancy restaurants, but when New York City chef Drew Davis comes to town, their attraction just might be a recipe for love. (978-1-63555-367-3)

Survivor's Guilt and Other Stories by Greg Herren. Award-winning author Greg Herren's short stories are finally pulled together into a single collection, including the Macavity Award nominated title story and the first-ever Chanse MacLeod short story. (978-1-63555-413-7)

The House by Eden Darry. After a vicious assault, Sadie, Fin, and their family retreat to a house they think is the perfect place to start over, until they realize not all is as it seems. (978-1-63555-395-6)

Uninvited by Jane C. Esther. When Aerin McLeary's body becomes host for an alien intent on invading Earth, she must work with researcher Olivia Ando to uncover the truth and save humankind. (978-1-63555-282-9)

Comrade Cowgirl by Yolanda Wallace. When cattle rancher Laramie Bowman accepts a lucrative job offer far from home, will her heart end up getting lost in translation? (978-1-63555-375-8)

Double Vision by Ellie Hart. When her cell phone rings, Giselle Cutler answers it—and finds herself speaking to a dead woman. (978-1-63555-385-7)

Inheritors of Chaos by Barbara Ann Wright. As factions splinter and reunite, will anyone survive the final showdown between gods and mortals on an alien world? (978-1-63555-294-2)

Love on Lavender Lane by Karis Walsh. Accompanied by the buzz of honeybees and the scent of lavender, Paige and Kassidy must find a way to compromise on their approach to business if they want to save Lavender Lane Farm—and find a way to make room for love along the way. (978-1-63555-286-7)

Spinning Tales by Brey Willows. When the fairy tale begins to unravel and villains are on the loose, will Maggie and Kody be able to spin a new tale? (978-1-63555-314-7)

The Do-Over by Georgia Beers. Bella Hunt has made a good life for herself and put the past behind her. But when the bane of her high school existence shows up for Bella's class on conflict resolution, the last thing they expect is to fall in love. (978-1-63555-393-2)

What Happens When by Samantha Boyette. For Molly Kennan, senior year is already an epic disaster, and falling for mysterious waitress Zia is about to make life a whole lot worse. (978-1-63555-408-3)

Wooing the Farmer by Jenny Frame. When fiercely independent modern socialite Penelope Huntingdon-Stewart and traditional country farmer Sam McQuade meet, trusting their hearts is harder than it looks. (978-1-63555-381-9)

A Chapter on Love by Laney Webber. When Jannika and Lee reunite, their instant connection feels like a gift, but neither is ready for a second chance at love. Will they finally get on the same page when it comes to love? (978-1-63555-366-6)

Drawing Down the Mist by Sheri Lewis Wohl. Everyone thinks Grand Duchess Maria Romanova died in 1918. They were almost right. (978-1-63555-341-3)

Listen by Kris Bryant. Lily Croft is inexplicably drawn to Hope D'Marco but will she have the courage to confront the consequences of her past and present colliding? (978-1-63555-318-5)

Perfect Partners by Maggie Cummings. Elite police dog trainer Sara Wright has no intention of falling in love with a coworker, until Isabel Marquez arrives at Homeland Security's Northeast Regional Training facility and Sara's good intentions start to falter. (978-1-63555-363-5)

Shut Up and Kiss Me by Julie Cannon. What better way to spend two weeks of hell in paradise than in the company of a hot, sexy woman? (978-1-63555-343-7)

Spencer's Cove by Missouri Vaun. When Foster Owen and Abigail Spencer meet they uncover a story of lives adrift, loves lost, and true love found. (978-1-63555-171-6)

Without Pretense by TJ Thomas. After living for decades hiding from the truth, can Ava learn to trust Bianca with her secrets and her heart? (978-1-63555-173-0)

Unexpected Lightning by Cass Sellars. Lightning strikes once more when Sydney and Parker fight a dangerous stranger who threatens the peace they both desperately want. (978-1-163555-276-8)

Emily's Art and Soul by Joy Argento. When Emily meets Andi Marino she thinks she's found a new best friend but Emily doesn't know that Andi is fast falling in love with her. Caught up in exploring her sexuality, will Emily see the only woman she needs is right in front of her? (978-1-63555-355-0)

Escape to Pleasure: Lesbian Travel Erotica edited by Sandy Lowe and Victoria Villasenor. Join these award-winning authors as they explore the sensual side of erotic lesbian travel. (978-1-63555-339-0)

Music City Dreamers by Robyn Nyx. Music can bring lovers together. In Music City, it can tear them apart. (978-1-63555-207-2)

Ordinary is Perfect by D. Jackson Leigh. Atlanta marketing superstar Autumn Swan's life derails when she inherits a country home, a child, and a very interesting neighbor. (978-1-63555-280-5)

Royal Court by Jenny Frame. When royal dresser Holly Weaver's passionate personality begins to melt Royal Marine Captain Quincy's icy heart, will Holly be ready for what she exposes beneath? (978-1-63555-290-4)

Strings Attached by Holly Stratimore. Success. Riches. Music. Passion. It's a life most can only dream of, but stardom comes at a cost. (978-1-63555-347-5)

The Ashford Place by Jean Copeland. When Isabelle Ashford inherits an old house in small-town Connecticut, family secrets, a shocking discovery, and an unexpected romance complicate her plan for a fast profit and a temporary stay. (978-1-63555-316-1)

Treason by Gun Brooke. Zoem Malderyn's existence is a deadly threat to everyone on Gemocon and Commander Neenja KahSandra must find a way to save the woman she loves from having to commit the ultimate sacrifice. (978-1-63555-244-7)